"I'm expecting great things from Joanne Kennedy! Bring on the hunky cowboys."

—Linda Lael Miller, *New York Times* bestselling author of *McKettrick's Choice*

Praise for *Cowboy Fever*

"A delightful read full of heart and passion. After twenty years as a writer it is hard for me to step into someone else's story so completely that I forget about the world and just enjoy reading, but *Cowboy Fever* was a book that took me away. I look forward to more."

—Jodi Thomas, *New York Times* and *USA Today* bestselling author of *Somewhere Along the Way*

"I loved this book. You'd best not pick it up unless you've got intentions of finishing it because you aren't going to put it down. The characters stay with you long after you finish the last page. HOT, HOT, HOT... with more twists and turns than a buckin' bull at a world-class rodeo, lots of sizzlin' sex, and characters so real, you'll swear they live down the road!"

—Carolyn Brown, bestselling author of *Love Drunk Cowboy*

Praise for *One Fine Cowboy*

"A stubborn city girl meets a stubborn rancher in this novel about how opposites... attract. Kennedy has written an entertaining and humorous romance."

—*Booklist*, starred review

"A refreshing and fun story from the first page to the last. Beautifully done!"

—Fresh Fiction

"Joanne Kennedy is quickly making a name for herself as an author of highly entertaining cowboy romances."

—Suite101

"Joanne Kennedy sure can write cowboy romance! With strong and believable characters... a plot that will touch your heart and keep you turning the pages. The romance was beautiful, the story and plot twists were amazing, and the pace of the story was great. I loved this book so much that I didn't want it to end."

—My Overstuffed Bookshelf

"Absorbing... an intriguing story of people and relationships on many levels."

—A Curious Statistical Anomaly

Praise for *Cowboy Trouble*

"There's plenty of wacky humor and audacious wit in this mystery-laced escapade that provides a fresh take on the traditional contemporary Western."

—*Library Journal*

"Contemporary western fans will enjoy this one!"

—*RT Book Reviews*

"A sure fire winner in my book and a true can't miss... That cowboy charm alone won me over."

—Book Junkie

"Ms. Kennedy's debut novel is a winner. Her characters are refreshing and different... A little romance, a little mystery, good looking guys, and wide open spaces are a perfect combination."

—Night Owl Romance, Reviewer Top Pick

"A fun and delicious romantic romp... if you love cowboys, you won't want to miss this one! Romance, Mystery, and Spurs! YUM!!"

—Wendy's Minding Spot

"Filled to the brim with everything—intrigue, murder, humor, love, quirky characters... It has renewed my love for the modern day cowboy love story!"

—The Romance Dish

COWBOY
Fever

JOANNE KENNEDY

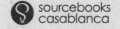
sourcebooks
casablanca

Published by Sourcebooks Casablanca, an imprint of Sourcebooks, Inc.
P.O. Box 4410, Naperville, Illinois 60567-4410
(630) 961-3900
FAX: (630) 961-2168
www.sourcebooks.com

Printed and bound in the United States of America
QW 10 9 8 7 6 5 4 3 2 1

To the Macomber family:
Laura, Wally,
and especially Leighanne

Chapter 1

KEEPING ONE HAND ON THE WHEEL AND BOTH EYES ON THE highway, Jodi Brand rummaged in her purse and pulled out her trusty can of Aqua Net. She'd sworn off blue eye shadow and tossed her rodeo queen tiara without so much as a twinge of regret, but she needed a twelve-step program to kick her hair spray habit.

Aqua Net is to rodeo queens what duct tape is to handymen—a cure-all for everything from shellacking your hair into place to shining your boots. It repairs runs in panty hose, fixes slipping zippers, kills bugs, and pastes your cowboy hat to your forehead so it'll stick at a gallop.

Popping the lid, she glanced down at the label, then back at the road. She could risk a collision by squeezing her eyes shut while she sprayed, or court blindness by spritzing her 'do with her eyes open. Simply letting her hair tousle in the breeze from the open window was out of the question, since she'd just passed the "Welcome to Wyoming" sign. The minute she crossed the border into her home state, her queen persona took over like a perky little demon returning to possess her, telling her to make sure her hair was perfect and ordering her to smile, smile, *smile*.

What she really needed was Rodeo Queen Rehab—a quiet residential facility where counselors would help her emerge from under the shadow of her rakishly tilted cowboy hat.

But rehab was for sissies—sissies and Easterners. Westerners like Jodi believed in personal responsibility, and while she might not want to dress up like a Wild West Dolly Parton anymore, she was proud to be Wyoming born and bred.

So why wasn't she glad to see that "Welcome" sign?

She loved Wyoming. She really did. But coming home meant facing the high expectations of a hometown that had sent her East like an emissary to an alien planet. They'd expected her to bring civilization back to Purvis, or at least some new fashion and makeup ideas. The fact that she'd gone back to being plain old Jodi Brand was bound to be a disappointment.

She turned off the highway and headed for the center of town, a three-block stretch of old-fashioned storefronts and cracked sidewalks presided over by a single traffic light. Pulling into a space in front of the Rexall, she squared her shoulders, gave her hair a quick spritz, and stepped out of the truck. Her cowboy boots gave her courage, making her walk feel like a bona fide swagger as she strode through the drugstore's swinging door and stepped up to the counter like an outlaw bellying up to the bar.

"Jodi Brand." Darla Black widened her eyes and brought one hand to her ample chest in a theatrical gesture of horror. "My God, honey, what's *wrong*? You look *terrible*."

When Darla wasn't stationed behind the pharmacy counter, she starred in nearly every production at the Purvis Little Theater, and her combination of dramatic delivery and downtown scuttlebutt made her the queen of the coffee klatches. It was like having Gypsy Rose

Lee, Dolly Levi, and Auntie Mame all rolled into one convenient pharmacist.

"Why, I'm fine, Mrs. Black. Just dandy." Jodi cocked her head and widened her smile—or was she baring her teeth? She wasn't sure. "But thank you so much for asking."

Darla reached over the counter and placed a soothing hand on Jodi's arm. "You can tell me, honey. Is it one of those, you know, *transmitted* things?" She leaned over the counter and lowered her voice to a whisper. "It's not cancer, is it?"

"Cancer?" Jodi peered over the pharmacist's shoulder, scrutinizing herself in the security mirror. Behind her, six or eight customers peered over the shelves to watch the show, like prairie dogs poking up from their holes to scan the plains for ferrets. Their expressions ranged from shock to dismay to pity.

Dang. She didn't look *that* bad. In normal surroundings, she passed easily for pretty—but in her hometown, expectations ran high.

"So pale," Darla said. "And your hair—honey, you look just wrung out and hung to dry. What happened?"

"Nothing." Jodi straightened her shoulders. "I'm just not a rodeo queen anymore. I'm a certified equestrian therapist with a degree in special education."

"Well, it looks like all that hard work and studying has just worn you right out."

"I'm not worn out." Jodi swallowed her aggravation. Coming home was even harder than she'd expected. "I'm just not wearing makeup. I used to have to pretty up all the time. Eye shadow. Blush. Sparkle powder." Tossing her head, she felt her hair flare out and fall neatly back into place.

God bless Aqua Net.

"But now I've got more important things to do," she said. "I'm back to help my mom with the boutique, and I'm starting a therapy riding clinic."

Darla shook her head in wonder. "I never thought you'd come back. We figured once you'd seen the world, you'd be gone for good."

"But I promised. You remember my speech?"

"Who could forget?" said a deep voice behind her.

Jodi knew that voice. She stood motionless, enjoying the moment—the delicious anticipation of finally seeing Teague Treadwell again. She pictured the hard jaw softened by a five-o'clock shadow, the dark eyes glinting under a battered Stetson, the long, lanky line of him leaning casually against the counter like a dark, dangerous version of James Dean in a cowboy hat—cool and tough and drop-dead sexy. God, she'd missed cowboys—real cowboys—and Teague Treadwell was as real as they came.

She turned with a bright smile, then took a quick step back. The man behind her was Teague Treadwell—but he looked about as real as a New York model in a Boot Barn catalog. He stood like a cowboy, relaxed and lounging, resting one elbow on the high counter like he might rest it on the worn leather saddle of his trusty quarter horse, but his clothes were straight out of Lou Taubert's dress-up section. Clean, creased Wranglers broke tidily over what appeared to be Tony Lama boots, and his white shirt was pinned at the collar with a string tie that sported an expensive chunk of polished turquoise mounted in silver. He held his hat in his hand, a gray felt Stetson with a brand-new sheen unmarred by sun or rain, and his clean-shaven jaw was more *GQ* than *Western Horseman*.

And then there was the jacket. On any other man, she'd have appreciated the way it classed up the outfit and spanned his broad shoulders, but the cut of it hid at least half of a butt she'd been looking forward to seeing in full.

"You took that scholarship and that modeling contract and hightailed it for the city so fast it made our heads spin. I can't believe you came back," he said.

"I promised." Jodi set her jaw.

"I know." He stepped closer—a little too close. "But you don't always keep your promises."

She lifted her chin. In her outgoing rodeo queen speech, she'd sworn to use her scholarship to get herself an education and come back to Purvis in all her big-haired, blue-eyed glory to make the town a better place.

And she'd kept that promise—well, except for the big hair and the glory. A few modeling sessions had exhausted her desire for glamour, and college had been a revelation as she shed her queen trappings and luxuriated in the freedom of comfort-cut jeans and baggy T-shirts. At school, it was her brains that mattered, not her beauty. And nobody expected her to be a role model.

What a relief that was. Being a role model meant swallowing your swear words, acting like a lady, and staying away from men like Teague Treadwell.

She looked Teague up and down, keeping her expression neutral, squelching any outward sign of her appreciation of those snug-fitting jeans or the well-muscled body that wore them. Dragging her gaze upward to his face, she bit her lower lip.

"Teague," she said. "You've changed."

He grinned. "I sure have. You too, Queenie."

The nickname and the teasing note in his voice raised her hackles. "I'm the same as I ever was. But you look like one of those dandies you used to beat up behind the chutes."

"I could still beat 'em up," he said, his smile dimming slightly.

"I'm not so sure," she said.

"Why not? Do I look too civilized?"

She started to nod, then noticed his eyes had narrowed. "Civilized" was probably an insult in Teague's mind. He hadn't taken well to her transformation from rough and ready tomboy to quintessential cowgirl when she'd entered her first rodeo queen contest. He'd said she looked fake when she dolled herself up.

Well, of course she did. Rodeo crowns, with their accompanying scholarships and prizes, weren't handed out for looking like a ranch hand. But he'd also accused her of looking down on what he called "us ordinary mortals."

She hadn't, though. She'd never been like that. She'd turned down his offers for dates because... well, because she was scared of him. Teague Treadwell was trouble, and rodeo queens didn't mess with trouble. A hell-raising bronc rider like Teague could be a friend, maybe even a fling if you kept it quiet—but a date? A boyfriend?

Never.

She cocked her head and scanned him from the top of his gelled hair to the toes of his polished boots. The clothes weren't the only change that had come over him while she was gone. The hard glint in his eyes had softened too, and the firm, stubborn set to his mouth had given way to a smile that was pleasant instead of predatory. She was surprised to find she wasn't the least bit afraid of him.

It was a little disappointing.

"You're just… older," she said. She could have said a lot more. She could have said he *did* look civilized, more civilized than she'd ever expected he could be. He also looked handsome, sophisticated, and, well… successful.

"You look older too," he said.

"Teague Treadwell, that's a terrible thing to say to a lady," Darla scolded. "You tell Miss Brand she looks just lovely."

"Darla, you just got done telling her she looks like she's got cancer," Teague said. "At least I didn't say that."

"Well, *I* am not a gentleman," Darla said.

"Neither am I."

Darla sniffed and turned away. Normally, she was eager to talk to anyone and everyone on the chance they might drop a choice crumb of gossip, but evidently, Teague was not a favorite. Jodi suspected he had plenty of stories to tell—but evidently he kept them to himself.

She tilted her head and smiled up at him. She'd always felt like a mismatched doll beside Teague—a Barbie next to a G.I. Joe. She still felt mismatched, but the tables had turned. She almost wished she'd decked herself out in her queen clothes. Standing beside his duded-up, suede-jacketed self, she felt like a drab little partridge pecking around a prize rooster.

Well, at least a partridge could make her own way, scratching for sustenance. All roosters ever did was preen and crow.

"So if you're not a gentleman, what are you?" she asked.

"Busy." His smile faded. "Sorry. I've—I've got to go."

He strode out of the store, leaving Jodi staring after him while Darla clucked her tongue at his rudeness. Maybe he hadn't changed that much after all. Maybe, underneath the fancy clothes, he was still just as rough around the edges as ever.

She wished he'd take off that dang jacket so she could see for sure.

—⁓—

Teague stepped out of the store and ran a hand through his gelled hair. He could never get used to the texture it took on when he styled it, stiff and spiky as a dog's wet hide. But though he might not be a gentleman on the inside, he had to pretend to be one on the outside—and that meant taking off his ever-present Stetson when he stepped into Darla's store. Without the gel he had terminal hat-hair, despite his hefty investment in a froufrou haircut he'd learned to style like some sissy singing star. He'd duded himself up too, in clothes that fit his new, respectable life as well as the custom boots fit his feet—but they didn't fit who he was inside. He might look like a well-trained show pony, but he was roughstock through and through. And no matter how much he doffed his hat and minded his manners, everybody knew it. In a town like Purvis, nobody ever forgot who you really were.

He glanced back at the drugstore. Jodi was still in there, talking to Darla.

He couldn't get over how she looked. The real Jodi was back—not the one who'd left town all those years ago, polished and shellacked under her glittery wide-brimmed hat, but the Jodi he remembered from childhood—his best friend and neighbor, the girl who raced horses and practiced roping with him until the day she shed her tomboy ways and started chasing after a crown and a satin sash instead of a championship and a prize saddle.

It should have felt good to see the shock on her face when she recognized the man in the classy clothes, and it should have felt even better to cut her dead and walk away. But for some reason, revenge was not sweet.

Maybe because she looked so sweet herself—so vulnerable, stripped of her glossy rodeo queen trappings. So different from the image he'd held in his mind all these years. He'd sworn to himself that if Jodi ever came back, she'd discover he was more than a match for her—and now she was back to being the girl next door, and he felt like a fake.

The door to the drugstore swung open and he realized he was loitering on the sidewalk, leaning against the wall like he had all those years ago when his afternoons had been his own. The only difference was that now he didn't have a cigarette hanging from his lips. He hadn't just gotten richer; he'd gotten smarter.

"Hey," Jodi said, stepping out of the store in a cool cloud of air conditioning.

"Hey." He shifted, resting his shoulder against the plate glass window, and the years melted away. Darla was wrong. Jodi didn't look sick. She looked delicate—fragile. She always had, until she slapped on all that glossy pageant-style makeup. He'd always loved the way her pale blue eyes and smooth, pale skin contrasted with the hell-for-leather cowgirl underneath. And he'd loved her little imperfections—the too-tilted nose spattered with faint freckles, the slight fullness to her lower lip. And her hair—it looked touchable today, unlike the sticky, starched mass she'd perfected in her pageant days. He thrust his hands in his pockets, resisting the urge to reach up and stroke it.

"So you're busy," she said. "Busy doing what?"

He felt himself flushing. "Just busy."

"With what? Got a girlfriend?"

"Not really."

He shifted uneasily. He didn't want a girlfriend, that was for sure—unless Jodi was applying for the job, and that was about as likely as Marilyn Monroe slapping on a Stetson and coming down from heaven to be his cowgirl consort.

But he'd spent some time with Courtney Skelton lately, and she seemed to think they were some kind of couple, even though he'd barely been polite once he figured out she had something more than friendship in mind.

"No girlfriend," he said. "Don't let anybody tell you different."

Jodi smiled. "Breaking hearts again?"

"Hardly." He cleared his throat. "Sorry if I seemed rude before," he said. "I just didn't want to talk in front of Darla."

That was a lie. He hadn't wanted to talk at all. Not until he figured out what was going on with Jodi, and how he felt about her. It was like they'd switched places. Now she was the one in torn jeans and T-shirt, and he was the one in the monkey suit.

"So," he said, dredging up a grin. "Is it cancer?"

"No." She laughed. Her looks had seemed so important to her all those years ago, and now she'd just been told she looked like death—and she was laughing.

What had happened to Jodi Brand?

And what was he going to do about it?

Chapter 2

JODI SCANNED TEAGUE'S OUTFIT AGAIN, HER EYES narrowing. She probably figured he'd stolen it, or robbed a bank and wasted the whole haul on clothes. He was sure she'd never expected to see her trailer trash neighbor in classy threads like these.

"So what are you doing these days?" she asked. "You haven't broken any broncs today, I'll bet."

"Nope." He stepped away from the window and hitched up his belt. "Been to Lackaduck. Had a meeting with the rodeo committee."

"Oh."

Lackaduck wasn't much of a town, but every July they hosted a huge outdoor rodeo that rivaled Cheyenne and Calgary. He was itching to tell her he'd signed a contract to provide broncs for next year's event, but he needed to fit it into the conversation casually, so it wouldn't seem like he was bragging.

"How's your brother?" she asked.

"The same." Teague felt a growl of frustration growing in his gut. She was always more interested in Troy than him. Sometimes he thought she'd only hung around with him to be near Troy. He knew it was Troy who had inspired her to go off to school and make all those promises about making Purvis a better place. It was probably Troy that made her want to come back, too.

Troy. Not him.

Never him.

"The same?" She frowned. "The same as what?"

"The same as always," he said. "He doesn't change much, you know?"

Jodi smiled. "That's one of the best things about him."

Reluctantly, he let a smile tweak his own lips. "Yeah, that's true."

He tried to figure out how to turn the conversation back to his trip to Lackaduck. He couldn't let her walk away without showing her he wasn't the trailer trash he used to be.

"I'm raising roughstock," he finally said. "Just signed a contract to provide some broncs for Lackaduck Days next year." He tried to toss off the news casually, but he knew there was a prideful note in his tone, along with something else—something almost defensive. All in all, he wasn't liking himself too much today.

And that was the problem. When Jodi turned rodeo queen, he'd hated himself for his poverty, his discount store clothes, and his screwed-up family. When she'd left, he'd worked his way up to the opposite—a smooth, suave rancher.

But now Jodi was back, and looking at her clean, unadorned face and practical clothes, he almost wished he was his old Walmart self again.

But there was no going back now.

"Bought a stud up in Miles City a while back," he said."Bucked like a sonofabitch and won a lot of money. Got me started."

He stopped himself. Talking about money was low class. You never heard the big contractors talk about what they paid for stock. Besides, a horse like

Red Rocket didn't need to be bragged on. You just looked at that big lug and knew he played hell with the cowboys.

"He's part Percheron. I put him to some thorough-bred mares and got prime foals—stocky and tough. The ones that have hit the circuit so far take after their dad and spin like the devil." He leaned back against the window, trying to force the tension out of his stance so she wouldn't see how much this mattered to him. "Want to see him sometime?"

"Sure," she said, but he could tell she wasn't really listening. "Maybe." She bit her lower lip. "Does he like kids?"

"Kids?" Teague tried to picture Rocket trotting around the ring with a three-year-old on his back, but the closest he could get was an image of Rocket stomping the kid into the ground. "No. He's, um, not that kind of horse."

"Oh." She sounded disappointed, as if she would have been more impressed if he'd picked up a birthday party pony from a petting zoo. "I was hoping you might have some horses that liked kids."

What the hell? When she was a kid herself, Jodi had been willing to saddle up anything with four legs and a tail. They'd never cared if a horse liked kids or not. He gave her a nervous sideways glance. She was staring at the ground, biting her lower lip. She looked troubled, and suddenly reality knocked him down and ran him over, cutting him up like a runaway combine.

Anything could have happened in the time Jodi had been gone. She'd left right after her dad passed away more than five years before, and she hadn't come back—not even for a visit. She could be engaged by now. Even married. After all, look how much he'd changed during that time. He'd gone from town black sheep to respectable businessman—or at least he'd tried.

"So. You got kids now?" He gazed down the street, squinting like he was watching something or somebody. Like this was just a casual conversation, and her answer didn't matter to him.

"Not yet." She gave him a saucy smile, as though her answer was a joke.

Not yet? What did that mean?

Maybe she'd come back to Purvis to have a baby. That would explain why she looked a little pale. It would explain why she wasn't wearing makeup, too. Stuff was probably toxic—bad for the baby.

He glanced down at her stomach. She didn't look pregnant. In fact, she still had the same slim, sweet, slightly hippy figure he remembered, along with breasts that swelled just enough to be tempting, but not enough to brand her a bimbo. Looking at that body, he wondered if any man could have knocked her up and walked away.

If it had been him, he would have stayed. Would have stayed and…

He clenched his jaw. He would have stayed and screwed up. He had no idea how to be a father, and no intention of ever trying. His own dad had been a nonstop lesson in what *not* to do, and he wasn't going to pass that legacy along to anyone. No kid was ever going to call him "dad." That was a name that brought nothing but bad memories.

Besides, he and Jodi had a past with a capital "P." It wasn't likely he'd ever get the chance to make up for all the mistakes he'd made. She seemed friendly enough, but he sensed a wariness, the kind of caution you used when you were trying to corral a bad-tempered bull.

He swallowed, trying to dislodge the ache of disappointment that was lodged in his throat like a swollen toad. This wasn't how he'd pictured his reunion with Jodi Brand. It wasn't what he'd expected.

He didn't want to admit he'd been expecting anything at all—but looking at her after all these years, he had to confess she'd been the reason for everything. He'd pictured her return a thousand times—how surprised she'd be at his success.

Not that it would change anything. After the way he'd treated her the last time they met, there was no way she'd ever trust him again.

Jodi watched Teague go. What the hell was wrong with him?

First he'd grinned and teased her like he used to, giving her the sense that nothing had changed. Then he'd suddenly cut her dead and walked away. When she'd caught up with him outside the drugstore, he'd bragged to her about his business like he was trying to impress her, and then he'd given her a long, languid look that lingered on her breasts and made her body heat up and smolder like a slow fire.

Then he'd turned and run away.

It wasn't quite the reunion she'd expected. She knew Teague had it bad for her all those years ago, and truth be told, she'd felt the same about him—but dating the town's baddest bad boy could have scuttled her hopes for the crown and all that went with it. Once she'd really committed to winning, she'd made the tough decision to let their childhood friendship lapse, and Teague had been more than willing to cooperate. She'd moved on into a different world, and so had Teague.

She had no idea what his had been like, and he sure as hell didn't understand hers. He seemed to think she *wanted* to be rodeo royalty, when really, she'd just been gunning for a ticket out of town.

She headed over to the parking lot and climbed into her pickup. Pulling down the visor, she scrutinized her face. Without makeup, she did look a little washed out. She was blonde as blonde could be. Her eyelashes just about vanished without a coat of dark mascara, and her eyebrows were all but invisible. Her hair looked good, though—long and wavy, with a glossy golden sheen.

She didn't look like she had cancer. Darla Black was just looking for scandal. Fishing, like she always did.

Well, the gossip queen just might catch something. Teague Treadwell might not look like the cowboy Jodi had left behind, but she was pretty sure the man that had haunted her through all the years she'd been away was hiding under all those expensive clothes. If she wasn't careful, she'd break down and give in to the impulse to strip off all those layers of phony sophistication and find the real Teague underneath.

She'd start with that dang jacket.

Chapter 3

THEY'D PAVED THE ROAD THROUGH PURVIS SINCE JODI left—recently, by the look of it. The blacktop had a tarry sheen, and the yellow painted line stood out sharply from the asphalt. But the minute Jodi hit the county line, the smooth surface ended at a jagged drop-off, dumping the pickup down onto a dirt road speckled with gravel and jolting the chassis so hard it was a miracle the tires didn't flatten on the spot. The old Ford sounded like it was falling apart at the best of times, and now she'd evidently jiggled a few more parts loose. There was a new rattle somewhere near the console, and an ominous clang sounded from the muffler area.

She really needed to trade the thing in. Get herself something new. An F-250 Super Duty, maybe—her dream truck. Something tough enough to take the punishment Wyoming dished out on a daily basis.

Trying to ignore the sounds of impending automotive doom, she bounced along and admired the scenery. Most people wouldn't have found much to look at in the high plains landscape—just long stretches of flatland speckled with stones and sagebrush that eased into a few languid hills rolling toward the horizon. But for Jodi, seeing all that open space was like breathing fresh air for the first time in ten years. She'd tried to appreciate the green, canopied forests of the East, but she'd felt claustrophobic, like a prisoner forbidden to see the sky.

As she neared the ranch, she felt her heartbeat skip and thrill with nerves and dread. She'd spent less than a month there after her father's death, and coming back was bound to stir up her grief all over again. She doubted her mom had kept the place up; Peggy Brand had hated ranching from day one, and after her husband's accident, she'd hated it even more. The place was liable to be as much of a wreck as her family, Jodi knew—but like her family, it was *her* wreck. Her father had left it to her and only her, knowing she loved it like he did. He'd been sure she'd someday build a future for herself out of the bare patch of arid acreage they'd called home. He knew she was a girl who kept her promises.

But Teague didn't know that. She remembered what he'd said in the drugstore. *You don't always keep your promises.* He was wrong. She tilted her chin defiantly, as if he stood right in front of her. She did keep her promises. She'd dare him to come up with one she'd broken. What the hell could he be…

Oh.

She thought back to the summer she'd turned fourteen.

Dang. He was right. She had broken a promise that year—but at fourteen, kissing Teague Treadwell just because she'd lost a horse race had seemed like a dangerous idea.

Matter of fact, it still did.

But hey, she'd actually kept that promise. It had just taken a while, that's all. She'd kissed Teague, and then some, on her last day in Purvis. She'd done one hell of a job of saying good-bye.

She'd been smarter when she was fourteen.

She glanced out the passenger side window at a battered trailer crouched in a grove of cottonwoods just off the road. *Chez* Treadwell was still standing, but it was obvious that Teague had moved out and moved on. Once white, it had rusted so thoroughly it seemed almost a part of the landscape. One end of the roof was curled up as if some cosmic can opener had cranked it back, and someone had put a couple of old tires on top to hold it down.

On a whim, she turned into the overgrown drive. Not much grew on the arid Wyoming plains, but what few plants could work their roots into the rocky soil had sprouted in the driveway, almost obliterating the dirt two-track. Wincing as weeds raked the truck's undercarriage, she slid to a stop and shut down the engine, then climbed out and whisked through the weeds that had taken over the scrubby front yard.

She climbed the rickety steps to the front door, remembering how Teague's father had called the front stoop his "office." He'd spent every evening there, drinking beer from a grubby cooler and surveying his ramshackle domain. He'd talk big about heading out to check on his cattle—all three of them—or wax eloquent on his plans to delve into one of the half-dozen rusting vehicles that moldered in the yard, some up on concrete blocks, others tilting as drunkenly as their owner on half-inflated tires.

Passing the ghost of Mr. Treadwell, she cupped her hands around her eyes and peered into the door's smudged window. She wouldn't have been surprised to see a ghost, but when an actual human face swam into view on the other side of the glass, she screamed and stumbled backward down the steps, her heart thumping so fast it made her dizzy.

"Jodi!" The door swung open to reveal a plump, pretty woman with short black hair standing up in sleep-inspired spikes. "You're back!"

"Cissy." Jodi put one hand to her chest and sucked in a deep, deep breath, trying to return her heartbeat to a normal rate. "You surprised me."

Cissy didn't seem to notice her distress. "Come on in!" She waved her hand impatiently, but then her smile faded as she leaned out of the door and glanced right and left. "How did you find me? Who told you I was here?"

"Nobody. I-I just…" Jodi ducked her head and examined the toes of her shoes.

"You didn't know, did you?" Cissy grinned. "You were looking for Teague."

"No, I found Teague," Jodi said. "Saw him at the drugstore. I was just—I don't know."

"You were just taking a stroll down Memory Lane," Cissy teased.

"I guess." Jodi climbed the steps and gave her old friend a hug. Cissy had been a member of her Rodeo Queen Court—first runner up. Jodi would never have guessed she'd end up living in the Treadwell trailer, of all places. "I didn't think anyone was living here," she said.

"That's kind of the idea." Cissy surveyed the weed-choked yard. "I finally left Cal. Didn't think I could afford a place of my own, but Teague said if I could make this livable I could stay here. And long as I park the car out back and take the long way home, I figure Cal won't find me."

"You and Cal…?"

"Worst decision I ever made." She waved her hand airily, but Jodi saw the telltale sheen of tears in her friend's eyes. "Turns out his success on the football field didn't translate to real life, and when things started to go wrong, he wasn't exactly equipped to handle disappointment. I know he was frustrated when he didn't hang onto his golden boy status, but when he started smacking me around…"

Cal had been the blond God of the Gridiron. Everyone had been surprised when he chose Cissy to be his goddess, but he liked to be worshipped, and Cissy had been thrilled to oblige. Evidently, things hadn't worked out.

"Anyway, he's in jail for now, but he'll be out next Tuesday. So it would be best if you didn't tell anybody where I am."

"I won't. Course not." Jodi paused, but the silence was so awkward she rushed to fill it. "Wow, Cissy, I'm sorry."

"Yeah, me too. Should've realized it wouldn't work," Cissy said. "I knew he was trouble before I married him, but for some weird reason, that only made me more determined to have him. And dang, my folks loved him. They'd have disowned me if I'd turned him down." She looked down at her hands a moment, and when she met Jodi's eyes again, she'd blinked back the tears and changed back into her old cheerful self. "So how 'bout you? Married?"

"Nope."

"Good for you." Cissy stepped back into the trailer's dim interior. "You always were the smart one. I'm living proof how the wrong man can mess up your life." She waved a hand to indicate the trailer. "Come on in. I've been working nights, so I was kind of napping, watching a soap."

The outside of the trailer might have looked abandoned, but the front room was spotless and homey, with evidence everywhere of Cissy's crafting addiction. Pink crocheted pillows in the shape of poodle dogs perched on the sofa, and a tangle of spider plants dangled in macrame holders in one corner. Flickering images from a small television lit one corner. Cissy grabbed a remote from a coffee table covered with crafting magazines and flicked it off.

"You must have some fond memories of this place," she said with a wicked grin.

Jodi smiled back. "You're fishing."

"Can't blame a girl for trying. Darla Black's still the gossip queen, but I'm a close second. And a tidbit about you and Teague Treadwell just might put me out in front."

Jodi laughed and stepped in for a hug. "You're shameless."

"Not completely." Cissy gave Jodi a squeeze, then stepped away and motioned her into the kitchen. "Old friends are exempt. I wouldn't spread stories about you—even if they were true."

"Well, we didn't spend much time here," Jodi said. "Teague kept his home life to himself."

"Understandable," Cissy said. "I think his dad was a lot like Cal. Worse, probably."

"Yeah." Jodi nodded. Teague had tried to keep his father's penchant for violence a secret, but everybody knew Treadwell Senior used his family for a punching bag. "He was."

"So you saw him, huh?" Cissy plopped down on the sofa. "Are you two going to start up again?"

"We never started in the first place," Jodi said.

Cissy gave her a disbelieving sideways glance.

"Oh, well, just barely," Jodi grumbled. "It wasn't anything, really."

That was a lie. What had happened between her and Teague on her last night in Purvis *had* been something.

It had been *really* something—to her, anyway. To Teague? Not so much.

But that night, she'd walked into this trailer with her eyes wide open, knowing exactly what would happen if she ended up alone with him. In those days, Teague was a walking testosterone factory, with sex simmering in his eyes whenever he looked at her—or any other girl. An answering flame flickered inside her for years, tormenting her with dreams and fantasies through her whole high school career. Hard as she'd tried to stay away from him, he'd been like a demon possessing her. She'd convinced herself she needed an exorcism—some sort of official parting ceremony that would finally free her of the hold he had on her.

"You said you were going to say good-bye to him." Cissy grinned. "You um, did it, right?"

Jodi nodded, then shrugged one shoulder and pasted on a smile. Nobody needed to know just how badly that night had gone.

"You said good-bye to more than just him, didn't you?" Cissy giggled. "You said you didn't want to pack your virginity off to college." She held up her hands like she was defending herself. "Don't worry, I never told anyone. Like I said, I don't tell stories on friends. And besides, it was just a fling, right?"

"Right." Jodi wished that had really been the case. Instead, she'd gone all girlie, ascribing way too much meaning to what had happened between them.

God, she'd been an idiot. After she'd come down from the dizzying heights he'd lifted her to, she'd been desperate to make it last. Warmed and dazzled by their newfound intimacy, she'd told him she wanted to stay. She'd offered to ditch school, give up everything to stay in Purvis with him. She'd assumed the magic of their lovemaking was as much of a revelation to him as it was to her, but all he'd done was stare at her with flat, expressionless eyes. Then he'd turned toward the wall and told her to go away. Told her to go live her perfect life and get out of his.

The humiliation of that moment still stung six years later. Jodi Brand, rodeo queen and town sweetheart, had been used and thrown away like a pathetic teenaged slut. She'd never felt more naked, more helpless, than when she'd put on her clothes with trembling hands and walked out of the trailer on legs that would barely hold her.

Shaking off the memory, she picked up a place mat Cissy had fashioned from jute cord and beads and pretended fascination with the handiwork while she blinked back tears. There was no reason to cry about it now, she told herself. She'd gotten over it. Some people might even say she'd done his bidding: gone on and lived a perfect life. A year of modeling, four years of college— she'd done just fine.

But how could you have a perfect life without

perfect sex? The memory of that night had haunted her all through school. Every man she met was mentally compared to Teague Treadwell, and every man she met came up short.

She wanted a re-ride worse than a bronc rider who'd drawn a dud, but this time she wouldn't stick around after the dismount. She'd learned her lesson.

"We have to do lunch," Cissy said. "I'm working for the sheriff now. Dispatcher and receptionist. Like I said, it's mostly nights, so I'm free in the afternoons. Give me a call, 'kay?"

"I will," Jodi said, stepping in for a hug. "Thanks, Ciss."

"It's great to have you back."

"It's great to be back." Jodi wasn't sure she meant it. Already the past was dimming the shiny, bright face of her future.

———

Jodi watched the trailer disappear in her rearview mirror as she spun the wheel and eased out onto the road. When she steered into the last curve before the Brand Ranch, she braced herself for the pain of seeing what had become of her old home. She'd leased out the barn and the pasture, but the house had stood empty once her mom had moved into the apartment above her shop in town.

She blinked back tears as the ranch appeared up ahead. Dang, it looked just the same. If déjà vu was a disease, she had one hell of a terminal case. She could feel the shadow of the past falling over her, chilling the summer air. She'd mourned her father a long time, but seeing the house made her realize she hadn't finished yet and probably never would.

She crossed the driveway, loving the way the hard-packed dirt felt under her feet. How many times had she walked that path, heading out in the morning to feed and water the horses, coming home from school in the afternoon to tack up and take off, leaving all the pressure of grades and high school social stress behind? This land had seen a lot more good times than bad. She needed to keep that in mind.

The hollow sound of her boots on the wheelchair ramp brought the past rushing back as she approached the front door. Shoving her hand in her pocket, she fished for the key ring she'd carried with her all the years she'd been gone. She'd kept it in her pocket or her purse, always with her, so that when times got tough, she could touch it like a talisman, reminding herself of who she was and where she really belonged.

Sliding the house key home, she turned the knob, stepping through the door and back in time.

The kitchen looked just as it had the day she'd walked away. She'd expected dust, dirt, maybe even damage from mice or water leaks—but the place looked tidy, even lived in. Just like always, two chairs stood at the table, along with an empty space for her dad's wheelchair. Just like always, the oven waited to welcome a pot of stew or a sheet of cookies. And despite the slightly musty scent of the air and the eerie silence, the room felt like home—just like always.

She wandered through the living room, touching familiar surfaces—the end table, the back of her father's recliner, the bookshelf—and felt a rush of gratitude that her mother hadn't taken the furniture when she'd moved to town. Peggy Brand had wanted a new life after her husband passed away, but she'd had the decency to leave the old one for Jodi.

Jodi paused at the door to her parents' old bedroom, then turned away. She should probably move to the big master bedroom now that the house was hers, but she wasn't ready to face it yet. She knew the same tray would sit on the dresser, waiting to welcome her father's keys and the other gear he kept in his pockets—a scrap of paper, a Leatherman, a handful of change mixed in with a few bent nails. No, she wasn't ready to open that door. There were layers to her grief, and every reminder of her father uncovered a new one.

She turned toward her old bedroom across the hall. A haze of tears blurred her vision as she opened the door, but she could still see something wasn't right. The bed was mussed, the covers heaped high in the center, the spread thrown back.

Backing out of the room, she swallowed a hot bolt of panic and pulled the door shut. She felt like a high plains Goldilocks, catching the Bear family in the act.

Somebody was sleeping in her bed.

Chapter 4

TEAGUE WAS IN A LOUSY MOOD. HE HADN'T REALIZED how much he was looking forward to Jodi Brand's return until it actually happened—and now, looking around his new and improved homestead, he felt like his sense of purpose had drifted away in her wake like a cloud of prairie dust on a summer breeze. She'd seen how he'd prospered—and she hadn't cared. Not one bit.

He'd meant it when he'd told her to get on with her life all those years ago. He'd known he wouldn't fit in with her plans. But after she left, he couldn't stop thinking about her. And somewhere along the way, he'd come up with a crazy plan to get her back.

He should have known it wouldn't work.

Sighing, he stepped into the barn and found a handy target to pin his bad mood on. The stalls were empty, the barn quiet. Troy must not have brought the horses in like he was supposed to. The mares were still out in the pasture, and Rocket was pacing in the paddock, neighing and stamping for his dinner.

Standing in the middle of the alleyway, Teague took in the silence surrounding him. There was the hum of insects, and the occasional rustle of a summer breeze, but the whole place was way too quiet.

His anger turned to dread. Where was his brother?

"Troy?" he called, stepping into the barn. "Troy? Where are you, buddy?"

A shrill whinny from Rocket was his only answer. His panic rising, Teague ran for the house. Mounting the porch steps in two long strides, he swung open the front door.

"Troy? Hey, Troy!"

No answer.

He cased the house, poking his head into every room. Troy wasn't in his bedroom playing Mario on his computer. He wasn't in the family room watching cartoons. He wasn't in the kitchen, raiding the pantry for snacks.

He wasn't home.

Teague slouched down on one of the two recliners in the family room and took off his hat, running his fingers through his hair. Maybe Troy had gone into town. He was supposed to ask before he took his bike out, and he was supposed to do his chores first, but he'd been rebellious lately, questioning the rules Teague had set down to keep him safe, pushing for more independence.

Teague glanced out the window. The door to the shed where Troy kept his bike was wide open, and his helmet was missing from its peg on the wall. He'd gone off somewhere, and probably forgotten the time.

That, or he'd had an accident. Teague's stomach clenched as he headed for the phone. He had Sheriff Marty Woodell on speed-dial—not because he needed law enforcement that often, but because, well, because sometimes he needed to talk to the sheriff.

"Mead County Sheriff," Woodell droned into the phone.

"You seen Troy?" Teague asked.

"Nope. And hello to you too. Just 'cause you were raised by wolves doesn't mean you can't have manners."

"Sorry. I'm just worried about him," Teague said.

The fact that the "raised by wolves" comment made him smile just showed how far he'd come. His parents had cared more about getting drunk and howling at the moon than raising their kids. Matter of fact, the sheriff had been more of a parent to him than either his mom or his dad. His dad's idea of parenting was to open an occasional can of hundred-proof whoop-ass and pour it out on his kids whenever he felt the urge.

But the old man was gone—the old lady, too. Now there was just him and Troy. And Troy was missing.

"I came home and Troy's not here," he told the sheriff.

"Well, where were you?"

"Out. Around town."

"Then that's probably where your brother is too."

"Yeah, well, he didn't call or anything. So I'm a little worried."

"You call and tell him where you went?"

Teague heaved a hard sigh of exasperation. "Look, I know I'm overprotective. But I can't help worrying."

"You're like a broody hen," Woodell said. "You ever think about settling down and having kids? Maybe you need something to take care of."

"Yeah, right," Teague said. That was the last thing he needed. Troy was enough to take care of.

He sat down at the little desk between the kitchen and dining room where he paid the bills. Taking out a pen, he started doodling on a utility bill envelope, drawing intricate loops and circles that looked like tooling on a fancy boot. "No kids for me."

"You sure?" Teague could hear a smile in the sheriff's voice. "Jodi Brand's back in town."

"I saw her," Teague said. He sat back and looked at what he'd drawn. It looked like a heart. He scratched it out. "What does that have to do with anything?"

"Always thought you two would end up together."

"I burned that bridge a long time ago." Teague started doodling again, drawing a star this time.

"Bridges can be fixed."

"What are you, my mom?" Teague regretted the words the minute they shot out of his mouth. "Sorry. You more or less are my mom."

Woodell laughed. "Somebody had to look after you. Your folks sure as hell couldn't do it."

"Or wouldn't."

"Well, you were a handful."

"Only way I could get your attention."

It was true. Sometimes, when he was a kid, Teague had started trouble just so the sheriff would try to talk him straight. Back then he hadn't wanted to admit it to himself, but it felt good that somebody cared.

It wasn't enough, though. Finally, Woodell had thrown up his hands and let the system have at it with Teague. He'd ended up spending eighteen months at Green River in the reformatory. It hadn't helped. He'd sulked through the group therapy sessions, clammed up on the counselors, and gone home with all his anger and attitude intact.

The only thing that had saved him was Troy. When Teague Sr. died in a car wreck and their mother followed him soon after, he'd had to step up and take care of his brother. He'd been doing it ever since.

Doing a dang good job of it, too.

So of course he worried when his brother disappeared.

He drew a crescent moon to cradle the star while the sheriff went on about how great Jodi looked and how good it was to have her back in town. Teague sighed and gazed out the window. He really didn't want to hear it.

Chapter 5

J<small>ODI</small> <small>SLAPPED HER HAND OVER HER MOUTH AND BACKED</small> out of the bedroom doorway, slamming the door shut and stifling a scream. Who the hell was in her bed? Taking a deep breath and steeling herself, she eased open the door. The lump in the bed shifted and let out a couple of bearlike grunts, and what was going to be a scream turned into a giggle.

"Troy?" She opened the door and stepped into the room. "Troy! What are you doing in my house?"

A tousled head peeked out from under the covers. She caught sight of Troy's familiar features, marked with the unmistakable stamp of Down syndrome, but he couldn't seem to make out who she was. He squinted, twisting up his face; she giggled again and a broad grin creased his cheeks.

"Jodi?" He flung back the covers and swung his short legs over the edge of the four-poster. "*Jodi!*"

She grinned and nodded.

"What are you doing home? I been taking care of it for you. I been helping you."

"You been sleeping," she teased.

"Yes. I mean, no." Troy's eyes widened. "I was hiding. I didn't know it was you. I thought maybe Teague was looking for me." He glanced out the window. "Oh, man, he's gonna kill me. I was 'sposed to be home. I was 'sposed to take care of the horses." His mouth worked as the realization worked him into a panic. "Oh, he's gonna be mad. So mad," he moaned.

"It's okay, Troy." Jodi took his hand and led him from the room. "Let's toss your bike in the truck and I'll give you a ride home." She paused and nodded at the tidy counters in the kitchen. "Did you keep my house clean for me? Was that you?"

"Uh-huh." He threw his arms around her in a bear hug and she thought of Goldilocks again. Troy would be baby bear despite his age. He was almost thirty, but he barely came up to her shoulder. He was sweet as a bear cub and just as affectionate. His simple, unsophisticated sense of right and wrong had always warmed her heart, and his all-out, unabashed affection made her feel at home for the first time since she'd rolled into town. "I kep' it nice for you," he said. "I knew you'd come back. You said. You promised."

Well, at least someone counted on her to keep her promises.

"But how did you get in?" she asked.

Sheepishly, Troy dug a key out of his hip pocket. "I saw you get the key out of the gutter once. I-I took it." He stared down at the floor and squeezed his eyes shut, hunching his shoulders. "Sorry." He looked up at her with a tentative smile. "You staying, Jodi?"

"I hope so." Jodi gave him a final squeeze before she stepped away. "I really hope so." She sighed. "Come on. Let's get you back home."

They went outside and loaded Troy's 3-speed Schwinn into the back of Jodi's truck.

"There you go, Bessie," Troy said, giving the bike's handlebars a pat. "You sit tight."

Jodi smiled. Bessie was a girl's bike, a pawn shop cast-off Troy had been riding when she'd left for college. She wondered why Teague hadn't replaced it if he was as prosperous as he said.

They piled into the truck, then cruised down the driveway and turned right, passing Cissy's trailer.

"Turn left past the trailer," Troy said.

Jodi bounced the truck down a gravel-strewn road that hadn't been there six years earlier. The sound of pebbles pinging off the Ranger's undercarriage was the sound of home. Back in Pennsylvania where she'd gone to school, it seemed like the whole world had been paved.

The road curved and they spooked a herd of pronghorns that dashed away with a springy, bouncing lilt. She'd forgotten how big Wyoming's antelope were, how exotic. Natives laughed at how excited tourists got at the sight of a few 'lopes, but after six years away, Jodi could sense the thrill of it as strongly as any newcomer.

The Treadwell's land fanned out in front of her, stretching from the back of the trailer to a distant tree line. The ground was hard and dry, dotted with sagebrush and stones but rich enough to support a fair amount of grass. Her father had always said the Treadwells were wasting a fine piece of property. A seasonal stream wound through the acreage, disappearing in summer but rising in fall and spring when the mountain snowmelt fed the flats. A few trees grew on either side of the dry creek bed—cottonwoods, twisted and tortured by the land that nearly starved them, but still providing shade that would shelter a herd of cattle from the summer sun. Before, only Teague's swaybacked paint and a few motley Hereford crosses had enjoyed the cool haven. Now, a sizable herd of cattle dozed in the shade. They were black, with wide horns and slender, muscular bodies.

"What are those? Corrientes?"

Troy nodded. "We run about a hundred of 'em."

Jodi watched as a calf wandered over to its mother and nudged her side, looking to nurse. Corrientes were small Mexican cattle, bred for rodeo. They were quick, nimble, and athletic—perfect for roping and wrestling.

They passed the ramshackle old house generations of Treadwells had occupied before Teague's dad gave up on it and hauled in the trailer. The old place had tilted in the direction of the prevailing winds, and looked like a strong blast would knock it to pieces.

Next came the big Treadwell barn where Teague and Jodi had spent so many hours messing with horses, doing chores, and just talking. Back before she started on the queen circuit, Teague had always wanted to do something more than talk, but Jodi had been wary and he'd been respectful. Disappointed and a little sulky, but respectful.

She slowed down to scan the barn. It had been painted recently—a deep, traditional barn red with bright white trim. The roof was new too, and the broken windows she remembered had been replaced. It looked neat and efficient—not at all like the musty, drafty building where dust motes had danced in shafts of sunlight while she and Teague fought their way through puberty, circling each other like wary gunfighters.

As she and Troy passed the barn, a newer house came into view, set in the shelter of a small rise. It was big but homey looking, with cedar siding and a chalet roof jutting over a tall span of windows. A front porch stretched across the front, bordered by a rustic railing made of twisted lengths of pine.

The yard surrounding the house was neatly mown, and someone had planted several rows of evergreens on the windward side; the trees would create a windbreak in a few years if they survived the heavy snows and hungry antelope. Beyond was another pasture with dozens of horses grazing.

A beat-up Dodge pickup was parked in front of the two-car garage. The truck's body was mostly a dull green pocked with rust, but the driver's side door was white and the hood was primer gray. Jodi smiled. Between the new duds and the big house, she'd half-expected Teague to have a sports car, or at the very least a swanky new dually. But his truck was pure cowboy. There was hope for the man yet.

"That's home," Troy said, slanting his gaze her way.

"Nice," she said. It was nice, it really was, but it wasn't what she'd expected. It looked like an Easterner's version of a Western house. Rustic, rough-hewn, and a little phony.

"Yeah, but it's Teague's," Troy said, pouting a little. "I wanted to stay in the trailer, but Teague rented it out."

Oh, boy. Troy really was looking to break free. Knowing Teague, he'd never agree to let his brother move out. Troy had always needed Teague, and Teague needed to be needed. Jodi had always figured Troy was the only thing that kept him out of trouble.

"Cissy needs the trailer though, Troy," she said. "It's nice Teague rents it to her."

"I guess." Troy's lower lip jutted out in a pout.

"Anyway, you and Teague should stick together," she said. "Take care of each other."

"I guess," Troy said, heaving a heavy sigh. "But he's hard to take care of."

Chapter 6

As HER TRUCK CRUNCHED UP THE DRIVEWAY, JODI SAW Teague emerge from the front door of the house, snapping a cell phone shut. He stood on the porch, his arms crossed over his chest as he watched their arrival.

"Oh, boy," Troy said, staring down at his lap and shaking his head. "Oh, boy-oh-boy-oh-boy. He sure is mad."

Jodi flashed him a look, concerned. "Teague's not... *mean* to you, is he?"

She never would have thought such a thing possible until today. But the Teague she'd seen in the drugstore wasn't the Teague she remembered. Hopefully the inside hadn't changed as much as the outside, but you never knew. She'd been planning to drop Troy off and go, but maybe she'd better stick around and make sure everything was okay.

"No, but he'll be disappointed in me. Really, really disappointed." Troy sighed. "He counts on me for stuff, and then I mess up." He was breathing hard, as if he was trying not to cry. Jodi patted his shoulder.

"It'll be okay, Troy. And if Teague's a mean old bear, I'll set him straight. I'll tell him you were helping me clean house."

"You will?"

Jodi realized her mistake a moment too late. Teague might be a little miffed at his brother for neglecting his chores, but he'd be furious if Troy lied to him. And Jodi had just offered to help him do just that.

"We're not going to lie, Troy," she said. "But I'll tell him what a good job you did keeping my house clean while I was gone."

"No!" Troy clutched her arm. "Don't tell him! Don't! It's a secret!"

Jodi's eyes narrowed and she glanced up at Teague, who was still standing on the porch, his arms folded over his chest, a stern expression on his face. Teague wouldn't abuse Troy, would he? Sometimes caretakers got impatient with handicapped adults.

"I go there to be by myself," Troy whispered into his lap. "I like to pretend it's my house. That I don't have to live with my brother."

Jodi nodded. Maybe Troy was just feeling the need for more independence. She'd have to talk to Teague about how they could make him feel more self-sufficient.

"I won't tell him," she said. "But we won't lie either, okay?"

"Okay." Troy puffed out his chest. "I'll take it like a man. He'll yell at me, but I'll just shake it off." He shimmied all over like a wet dog. "Shake it off."

Smiling, Jodi climbed out of the car as Troy slouched to the tailgate to hoist his bike out. Ducking his head, he pushed it toward the shed.

"After you put that away I need to talk to you, buddy," Teague called from the porch. Jodi was relieved at his tone—calm, rational, in control. He turned to Jodi, his eyes assessing her with that arrogant top-to-bottom stare again as she stepped out of the truck cab. "Where'd you find him?"

"He came by the house," she said. "He was helping me."

Teague lifted a skeptical eyebrow. "How'd he know you were home?"

She shrugged, hoping he wouldn't pursue it any further.

He didn't. He was too busy watching her approach. She felt like he was eating up her body with those hard, hungry eyes, and her face heated with a blush. She was tempted to shake it off, like Troy had, but Teague would probably see that as a jiggle—and judging from the look in his eyes, he didn't need that kind of encouragement.

Chapter 7

"ROCKET'S RIGHT THROUGH HERE," TEAGUE SAID, leading Jodi into the barn. He knew he should be following up with Troy, helping his brother understand that he needed to keep his promises, especially when the animals were depending on him. But Troy had been with Jodi, so Teague kind of understood how he'd lost track of time.

Teague tended to forget stuff when she was around, too.

His dog Luna lifted her head as they entered the barn. The skinny black and white collie mix let out a shrill bark, then leapt to her feet and whirled in a joyful circle, graceful as a fox. Trotting over to them, all slender legs and dancing white paws, she shoved her nose hard into Jodi's hand, begging to be petted. Jodi knelt on the floor and obliged, burying her hands in the dog's shining coat.

"Who's this?" she asked, ruffling the thick fur over the dog's shoulders.

"That's Luna. She's supposed to be a cattle dog."

"Supposed to be?"

"Mostly she herds Troy." Teague rolled his eyes. Sometimes he felt like he was a cowboy at a crazy farm. "And me, sometimes. She's part border collie and all bossy."

Jodi shook the dog's proffered paw. "She's sweet."

"See if you still say that once you get to know her,"

Teague said, but he bent and stroked the dog's head too, his fingers brushing Jodi's for one warm half-second. "She pretty much figures humans were put on earth to serve her."

Jodi laughed and they strolled through the barn, the dog trotting comfortably behind, as if the three of them were a unit.

It was a shotgun barn with a wide alley stretching between broad sliding doorways front and back. Stalls lined the sides and sunlight beamed in through open stable doors of each compartment, striping the rough wooden floor with shafts of light. Bridles and halters dangled from pegs on the walls, and two well-used Western saddles were mounted on two-by-four racks that jutted from the wall by the back door.

He'd fixed the place up, but with Jodi here, it still felt the same. The scent of horses and hay, the calm in the air, the sunshine—it was where the two of them were meant to be.

"It's good to be here," she said.

He smiled. So she was feeling it too.

"It's good to have you back." The words came out low and husky, and he cleared his throat. It was good. Really good. In this moment, he and Jodi were comfortable again, best friends, with none of the tension between them that had grown up over the years as they floundered their separate ways toward adulthood—before they'd drowned the connection between them in hormones and adolescent drama.

"What brought you back?"

Me, something inside him pleaded. *Say it was me*. He muzzled his pathetic, needy inner voice and turned his attention to Jodi. There was no way she'd come back to reconnect with him. After the way he'd treated her, he was lucky she'd even talk to him.

"I came back for my mom." She didn't even have to think for an instant. "I need to make things right with her. I blamed her for everything when my dad died, and I've barely talked to her all these years."

He nodded. It had been the talk of Purvis, with half the town taking Jodi's side, the other half standing with her mother.

"I'm going to work with her at the boutique for a while. She's always wanted that. I'm hoping we can be close again."

"That's good," he said. "Family's important. When you've got a family that—you know."

She nodded. He didn't have to explain. She knew what his family had been like.

He led her out the barn's back door into the sunlight. The ground sloped down from the doorway and the world opened up in front of them, the land spreading out like a rural red carpet welcoming her home. The way the setting sun glinted gold on the grass seemed like the only gift he could offer her, and he felt something inside him give way, weakening his knees and tripping up his heartbeat to a speed that rivaled a Riverdance routine.

He glanced at Jodi to see if she felt it. Her eyes met his briefly, then slid quickly aside before he could read them. Breaking away, he lengthened his stride, putting more distance between them as he led her to the side of the barn where long narrow enclosures stretched from each stall door. A gigantic sorrel stallion with a broad back and heavy hooves stood impatiently at the gate of the first enclosure, swinging his big head to face them as they approached.

"This is Rocket," Teague said. Looking at the horse, he could feel his pulse slowing to normal, his world straightening on the axis Jodi had shoved sideways when she walked into the drugstore. Rocket was the core of his success, the heart of the ranch, and a bona fide masterpiece. God was serious about horses when he'd constructed that powerful combination of bone, muscle, and spirit.

Teague could tell Jodi couldn't take her eyes off the horse either. The animal was heavy like bucking horses always are, but perfectly proportioned and solidly built, with a strong arched neck and a broad, solid chest. At rodeos, the saddle broncs were always a little shaggy and disreputable looking, but now that he was retired, Rocket's coat shone like a new penny. He nickered as Teague approached and stretched out his muscled neck, lifting his upper lip over his teeth in an equine smile. Teague stroked his muzzle, grinning.

"No pride," he said. "Always looking for a handout."

As if to disprove the statement, Rocket lifted his front hooves and spun away from the fence, then trotted the length of the enclosure with his neck arched and his tail held high, kicking up his heels to prove his manhood.

"Looks pretty proud to me," Jodi said.

"Yeah, he's got an ego," Teague said. "But when it comes to food, he's shameless."

"Any of the cowboys figured that out yet?" Jodi asked.

"No. He doesn't work anymore. Unless you call

covering mares working. He does seem to take that duty pretty serious." He cocked his head and eyed the stallion, who stood blowing in the center of his pen. "Rocket's got a great work ethic when it comes to that stuff."

Jodi smacked him teasingly and he felt an electric rush shimmer up his arm. She smiled up at him, and for a minute he wondered if she'd let him kiss her. For a minute more, he was pretty sure she would—but then she turned her head aside as if nothing had happened.

"Who's that?" She pointed at an animal standing in a corral off to the side of the barn. Actually, it was more than an animal. Bruiser was a presence.

"That's Bruiser." Teague grinned. "Meanest bucking bull in three counties."

"I thought you just had broncs."

"Nope. Starting up with bulls, and that over there is step one."

"Yikes," she said. "Be careful."

"Oh, I am," he said. "He's a handful." He turned and gestured toward the pasture. "I'm going to run the mares in, since Troy didn't get it done. You said he was helping you?"

"Yeah," she said. "My house needed cleaning."

"He help much?"

"Oh, yeah," Jodi said. "He did a great job."

"Good." Teague kicked at the ground. "With me, he can't seem to stay focused for long. But he always wanted to please you."

It was true. Troy would do anything for Jodi. It had always been like that. With Teague, he was stubborn and resistant. With Jodi, he was an angel.

"I love him," Jodi said sincerely. "And I believe in him."

"So do I—most of the time. I guess it's the other times that are the problem." He hefted a bale of alfalfa from a stack by the side of the barn and lugged it to the pasture gate, where a half-dozen mares milled impatiently. "You girls hungry?" He fished his Leatherman out of his pocket and clipped the wire around the bale, then shook out all but two flakes on the ground by the fence. The other two he carried over to Rocket, who was bucking and crow-hopping along the fence like a teenager practicing for a hip-hop dance crew.

"Food, Rocky," Teague said. He shook out the flakes and the horse trotted over and grabbed a mouthful of hay, chomping greedily.

"You eat like a brontosaurus," Teague said fondly. "Try to have some manners."

They stood by the gate, watching the horse, avoiding each other's eyes.

"You want to see Vegas before you go?" Teague asked.

"You still have him?" Jodi squealed. She hopped up and down a couple times and clapped her hands, giving Teague a flashback to fifth grade. "Oh, I'm so glad! I was afraid to ask!"

"I shouldn't still have him," Teague grumbled. "I'm trying to run a business here, and all that horse does is eat and crap. But he's—well, you know. He's Vegas."

"You love him," Jodi said.

Teague grunted, then nodded reluctantly, looking away.

"Where is he?"

"On the other side. He doesn't like Rocket much."

"Jealous?" Jodi asked.

"No, just irritable, I think. He's gotten old."

"I guess. He'd be, what, twenty-five now?"

"Twenty-seven."

"He doing okay?"

"Yeah. Brace yourself, though. He's… changed. But he's doing all right."

They reached the other side of the barn, where all the stalls opened into one big paddock. Teague's old brown and white paint stood in one corner, staring off across the landscape, but he turned and ambled to the gate as they approached. The brown spots around his eyes had whitened with age.

"Vegas," Jodi whispered.

Vegas had been Teague's father's horse until his dad quit cowboying so he could get serious about drinking himself to death. The paint had become Teague's horse then, and he'd carried him and Jodi everywhere before her dad bought her a barrel horse. Seeing Jodi standing beside Vegas gave Teague a rush of nostalgia that almost hurt. He wished the two of them could mount up like they used to and take off at a gallop. Hell, he'd even let Jodi take the reins.

They used to fight about that every time they rode.

"He *has* changed," Jodi said.

She was right. The paint's flashy coat had lost his luster, and his withers and hip bones stood out. He just couldn't keep weight on anymore. The old horse walked slowly across the corral, his head hanging low, then butted his head against Teague's chest just like always.

"He's glad to see you," Jodi said.

"No. He's glad I'm here," Teague said. "But he can't see me. Not much, anyway."

Jodi looked closer at the horse. His brown eyes were cloudy, misted with cataracts. "He's blind?"

"Mostly." Teague ran his hand down the horse's long muzzle. "You'd never know it to watch him, though. Long as I keep his routine steady and don't move stuff around, he's fine. He misses riding out, though. He'll do it—he trusts me to guide him, and I think he can see shadows and stuff—but if I got distracted... well, he could hit a hole or something. I'd never forgive myself if anything happened to him."

Jodi tucked her hand up under the paint's mane and rubbed his neck. He turned and gave her the same treatment he'd given Teague, rubbing his forehead against her shoulder.

"He seems a little depressed. I think his days are kind of long," Teague said regretfully. It made his chest ache to see the way Vegas stood in the corner of the paddock day after day, gazing over the fence longingly at a world he could barely see. "And his goat died."

"His goat?"

"The other horses bully him, but he gets lonesome by himself, so I got him a goat. But it died."

"Poor Vegas." Jodi looked at the old horse thoughtfully. "He'll trust you, though? He'll let you lead him?"

Teague nodded.

"He'd be a great horse for kids," Jodi said. "Heck, he *was* a great horse for kids. For us. Remember?"

Teague remembered all right. Looking at her standing there beside Vegas, he could almost convince himself they were still the kids they used to be.

No such luck. They definitely weren't kids anymore.

Troy appeared at the barn door, his face creased with worry.

"Teague, you want me to feed the horses? I didn't mean to forget. I'm really, really sorry."

Teague shrugged. He'd meant to chastise Troy, but it wasn't really necessary. His brother did his best. He just forgot stuff sometimes.

"I did it, bro." He saw a look of dismay cross Troy's face and thought fast. "But if you clean up the workshop, that would help a lot."

"Okay." Troy ducked back into the barn. "I'll clean it really good. You'll see. I'm good at cleaning. Just ask Jodi." His voice faded away.

Jodi laughed. "You're going to have the cleanest workshop in three counties," she said.

"I know. And it doesn't even need cleaning. But if I don't give him something to do, he'll feel bad."

"You handle him really well," Jodi said.

Teague shrugged. "He's my brother." Compliments on his relationship with his brother always embarrassed him. He just did what he had to do.

He glanced around, searching for a way to change the subject. As he'd shown Jodi the horses and the barn, it seemed like she really was impressed with the changes he'd made. Maybe there really was hope for a resurrection of their friendship—or even something more. If there was, the house would clinch it.

"Want to see the house?" he asked. He took a step closer. "I could give you the tour."

Oh, man. For some reason, his voice had dropped into a lower register when he'd said that. It sounded like he was trying to seduce her or something. And he wasn't—not really. Jodi needed a lot more than he had to offer, especially if he was right about the reason she'd come home.

"You don't have to," he said. "I didn't mean…"

"No," Jodi interrupted. "I mean, yes. I want to."

Chapter 8

JODI FOLLOWED TEAGUE INTO THE HOUSE, IGNORING the warning bells clanging in the back of her mind. When he'd invited her inside, his voice had gone all soft and sexy and she felt something inside her warming and softening. And now they were headed inside, where he'd give her the tour, which would probably include the bedroom.

She'd fantasized about Teague for years, but now that she could conceivably live out those dreams, they seemed infinitely more dangerous.

The front door was solid oak, with an arched window of frosted glass inset in the top half. Like the rest of the structure, it was grandiose to the point of tackiness. But when Teague opened it, golden light spilled out onto the porch.

The place was beautiful, decorated in a cozy, homey way. Oak cabinets glowed with a subtle sheen, echoing the glint of copper cookware that hung from an iron rack over an island cook top. The brushed stainless appliances were surprisingly spotless, and a windowed alcove in the corner held an old oak table and four pressed-back chairs. Jodi would have figured it was all for show if it hadn't been for the clear signs of culinary ambition scattered around: a Mario Batali cookbook, spotted and stained, lying open to a recipe for short ribs; pots and pans, along with a copper colander and the work bowl from a Cuisinart drying upside down next to the sink; a glass pan of something baked, probably brownies, covered with aluminum foil on the countertop. A slow cooker bubbled in one corner of the counter, a rich, beefy scent wafting from under its glass lid.

"Nice," she said.

"Thanks."

He led her down a narrow hall, pausing so she could admire a bathroom fitted with a glass-fronted shower lined with river rock and double sinks set into a tiled counter. The first room past that was Troy's bedroom, heaped with a happy chaos of CDs, DVDs, and model cars.

Next was Teague's room. Jodi felt a warm awareness in the pit of her stomach as they stepped through the door. A rustic bed carved from raw pine was draped with a heavy tapestry comforter, woven in warm reds and golds. Matching nightstands flanked the bed, topped by graceful curving lamps made of antlers, and an enormous dresser crouched in one corner. Gleaming hardwood floors were decorated with strategically placed throw rungs whose rich colors matched the comforter, and the window was draped with lush velvet drapes. It looked like a suite at a swanky resort, not a rancher's bedroom.

"This is nice," Jodi said. Her voice came out husky and she cleared her throat and tried again, but Teague's eyes met hers and her mouth went suddenly dry. Her throat slammed shut and all she could do was look at him.

Who was this guy, anyway? He'd changed so much. The clothes were one thing, but it took a certain kind of person to create a nest this cozy. Only a person who cared about home and family could put together a home like this.

Only a person with a heart.

Maybe she'd stick around for a re-ride after all.

———

Teague wondered if Jodi could sense his nervousness. If she couldn't hear the thumping of his heart, she was bound to notice the catch in his breathing as he wondered if there could be a second chance for them after all. Maybe if he played his cards right he could erase all the ugliness of their last time together and start again.

She turned and he saw a flicker of—something— cross her face. Fear? No, she wasn't afraid of much of anything. Uncertainty, maybe. Whatever it was, she was remembering their last meeting.

He knew she'd never forget it. You couldn't erase something like that. Not the good part, and certainly not the bad.

He put a hand to his forehead and squeezed his temples, trying to wring out the memory of that crazy, desperate night. He hadn't meant to make love to her. He'd meant to avoid her. But she'd come to *him*. There she'd been, standing in his bedroom. His *bedroom*.

What was he supposed to do?

He remembered the scent of her, the taste, the softness of her skin. Their shared peak had been the one perfect moment of his life—the fulcrum where everything balanced, spun, and turned. It could dip, or it could rise. Afterward, he'd closed his eyes and tried to hold his breath so nothing would change.

But when she'd told him she was willing to change her

life for him, he'd realized what a disaster that would be. Jodi was headed for a golden future. Holding her here, locked in his sordid life, would be wrong on every level.

So he'd shut her down. Sent her away.

He'd done her a favor, really. There'd always been something between them—something they needed to finish. And they'd finished it, all right. Finished it for good, so she could get on with the life she deserved. He'd made it easy for her to leave town and never come back.

But she had come back.

He pushed his hair back from his forehead and tried for a smile, but it was shaky and tense. He could feel it, a cockeyed grin trembling on his face. He probably looked like an idiot, but at least Jodi didn't look scared anymore.

She stepped over to the dresser and picked up a bucking horse figurine, a cheap imitation bronze that didn't fit the rest of the room. "Didn't your dad give this to you?"

Teague looked away. "Maybe. I don't remember."

"I guess that's just as well." She set the sculpture down and leaned against the dresser. "I don't blame you for wanting to forget about him."

He hunched his shoulders and looked away. He'd put his childhood behind him. Long as he didn't think about it, he didn't need to drink to wipe out the memories, or punch something or someone just to release the anger that inevitably followed them. He'd managed to build a new, improved life—but ignoring your demons wasn't the same as conquering them for good.

"Teague?"

She had her hand on his arm and was looking up

into his face, her blue eyes wide. Shit. When had she gotten so close? He could smell her hair. She still used the same fruity shampoo she'd used as a girl. Without thinking, he put one finger under her chin and tilted her face up towards his.

Their eyes met, and there was no trace in hers of the fear he'd seen when they first walked into the room. All he saw was Jodi standing beside him, close enough to kiss.

Chapter 9

JODI HAD FELT SOMETHING PULLING HER TOWARD Teague from the moment she'd seen him at the Rexall, and now that they were alone the attraction intensified to the point where she wasn't sure she had a shred of free will left. One more second of silence, one more touch of his hand, and she'd drag him over to that bed and rip his clothes off.

The thought made her squirm inside, and something reckless swelled up in her heart. What the hell was wrong with acting on your impulses once in a while? She wasn't an eighteen-year-old anymore. More important, she wasn't a virgin. Teague had seen to that the last time they'd been together in his bedroom. She wondered if he knew he'd been her first.

But the main thing was, she was a woman now. She'd had casual relationships. She'd learned to separate sex from love and enjoy it for its own sake.

So what the hell? Why not?

She hiked up on her toes and touched her lips to his.

The minute she did it, she knew she'd made a mistake. There was no separating Teague Treadwell from anything. He was part of the fabric of her life, a piece of her: the first friend she'd had, the first boy she'd loved, the first man she'd slept with, and the first to break her heart.

And as much as she wanted to deny it, he had the power to do it all over again.

Teague cupped her head in his hands and answered her kiss with the urgency she'd dreamed of every night when she was lying alone in her dorm room, surrounded by girls who looked down on the country cowgirl from Wyoming. Once she'd started school her memory had wrapped their disastrous liaison in a golden glow, downplaying its hurtful ending and replaying one moment over and over: the moment she'd opened her eyes and caught him looking at her with helpless adoration, his eyes soft and shining with emotion. She'd always wanted Teague, but in that instant, despite his denial, she'd known he'd been hers all along. She'd treasured that thought and held the memory close all through school, using it to shut out what had happened afterwards and comfort herself when she felt alone, which was most of the time.

His breath brushed her cheek, warm and caressing. He smelled of mint and leather and clean laundry, laced with fresh-cut hay. She opened her eyes to meet his, and his gaze was as intimate as a touch. Her body warmed and softened and she knew there was no way she was leaving this room without making love to him.

He kissed her again and she closed her eyes and let go of all her inhibitions and her good sense, too, letting herself float in a sea of sensation while his hands brought her alive. He stroked her skin to a heated flush, making her nerves twitch with anticipation as he kissed his way down her neck and flicked his tongue at her throat, sending a tingle through her veins. His kiss grew harder, more insistent, probing and tasting as he unbuttoned her shirt with shaking hands and cupped her breasts through the thin fabric of her bra.

She opened her eyes and watched his face while he undressed her. He seemed unaware of her gaze, and the naked lust in his eyes heated her skin and filled her mind with an unbearable need to touch him, to hold him, to writhe against him until the two of them melted into one being. She was vaguely aware that there might be consequences to what they were doing, but the outside world seemed small and insignificant compared to the magnitude of what was happening in this room.

Teague was hers again. And she was his.

He was still dressed, right down to his boots, and she felt flagrant and shameless as she sprawled on the bed, letting him explore her naked body with his fingers. He traced the swell of her breasts, circled each swollen nipple, and traced a tingling line across her stomach and down her thighs, touching her everywhere but where she wanted him most. She let out a frustrated whimper but he didn't react, just continued his slow journey over her hills and valleys. She arched her back and he bent to follow his touch with his tongue, licking here, swirling there, spreading tender kisses all over. When she closed her eyes, his hands and tongue were suddenly everywhere at once, probing, stroking, driving her crazy. She let loose a moan and opened herself, whimpering as he did something complicated with his fingers and his tongue that sparked a faint tingle that grew to a full-body flush as she arched and cried out.

She opened her eyes, surprised to see they were still right where they'd started, on Teague's bed, in Teague's room. She'd felt like they'd ascended to heaven, floated up on a sweet pink cloud of sensation. But Teague was standing in the slanted light from the window, shucking his clothes aside like a rescuer stripping for a dive into deep water.

She bit her lower lip, tugging it between her teeth as he sat down beside her. She'd waited five long years for this, and whatever the consequences, she was helpless to stop herself. She stroked her hands over his chest, watching them trace a lazy path up over his shoulders, then down again, skimming over the dark nipples, sweeping over the flat, muscular plane of his stomach to cup his hips as she slid off the bed and knelt on the floor.

—◆◆◆—

Teague leaned back on his elbows and closed his eyes. He hadn't planned this, hadn't even expected it. It was probably a mistake, but the woman of his dreams was kneeling at his feet and licking her lips and he didn't care what happened later. He only cared what happened next.

He threw back his head and groaned as she ran the tip of her tongue up and around, and then everything got warm and wet and he couldn't tell what she was doing, only that it felt heavenly and he could barely hold on and keep control. He closed his eyes tight and literally saw fireworks, pinpoints of light exploding into a Technicolor sunrise in the dark sky of his consciousness.

He reached down and buried his fingers in her hair, letting himself luxuriate in the miracle of touching her for one more minute before he gently pulled away. Sitting up, he pulled her up onto his lap so she was facing him. She scooted up and pressed her body to his, and he looked into her eyes.

"Is this okay?" he asked.

She nodded, smiling.

"It won't hurt… anything?"

"It's fine, Teague," she whispered. "Just fine."

The last time they'd done this, they'd been kids, sneaking around. Now he could savor it, watch her face, lock his eyes on hers as she lowered herself onto him, gauge her expression as he eased inside her. She was tight and slick and hot, and the two of them closed their eyes and set to rocking with a gentle rhythm that sped up as he felt his thoughts fade.

He was hers. She was his. He clutched her hips and drove himself into her one last time as the tension that had built up over all those years left his body in one final, blinding rush.

***

Jodi lay sprawled on the bed, staring up at the ceiling, and told herself the God's honest truth for the first time since she'd arrived in Purvis.

This was what she'd come for.

This moment, and the all-out celebratory rhumba that had preceded it.

Teague might have thrown her out of bed five years ago, but he'd been more than willing to let her back in today. And judging from the look in his eyes when they made love, this meant something to him—as much as it had meant to her all those years ago.

She suddenly realized that all she had to do now was walk away the way he'd walked away from her, and the score would be even.

But this wasn't about revenge.

Much as she wanted to hide from the truth, she'd never lost her feelings for Teague. And what did that tell you? When you couldn't get a man out of your head even after he'd used you and tossed you away like a dirty Kleenex, you had a problem.

Especially if that man was Teague Treadwell. His brutal, abusive childhood had understandably left his heart wrapped in scar tissue. She wasn't sure he was even capable of loving anyone but Troy long-term, and if he was, he probably wasn't capable of admitting it to himself.

She couldn't believe she was risking a replay of the heartbreak he'd dished out last time they were together.

She turned over and looked at him. His eyes were closed, and he was smiling. It made her realize he'd never smiled back then. Being with him now felt different—safer. She could feel the solidity of him, the stability of his new life.

It was like being with another man—but he was still Teague. There was still a hot, hard danger at his core, and she realized that's what had been missing in the boys she'd bedded at school. They were safe. Superficial. What you saw was what you got. With Teague, there were depths inside she might never understand. Depths, and dangers.

Walking away was still the best plan.

She eased off the bed and gathered her clothes. Slipping into her jeans, she realized they'd forgotten about protection. Oh, well, she told herself, shoving her subconscious nervous Nellie to the back of her mind. It was only once. Once wouldn't matter.

Fully dressed, she sat down on the side of the bed and leaned over, letting her hair brush his bare chest as she kissed him gently on the lips. His eyes opened.

"I have to go," she said.

He sat up, rubbing his eyes. "Okay." He gave her a sideways look, as if he was trying to figure out how she felt about what had just happened. "You all right?"

"Sure. I'm fine." She turned away and stretched so he could see just how "fine" she was.

Besides, that way she wouldn't have to look him in the eye.

———

Teague watched Jodi stroll out of the room as if they'd just had lunch at Applebee's. She evidently didn't take things as seriously as she used to.

He wasn't surprised. They'd switched places in every other way. So now he was the one all caught up in emotion and she was the one who walked away.

Served him right.

At least they wouldn't have to have one of those after-sex conversations where they talked about their feelings. Good thing—because he had no idea what his feelings were.

Oh, he knew he loved her. There was no doubt about that. But he'd loved her all his life, and he didn't know if what had just happened between them signaled a change in their relationship.

After all, Jodi had grown up. She'd seen the world, and obviously she was a lot more experienced when it came to men. He wasn't certain, but he was pretty sure she'd been a virgin the last time they'd… gotten together.

Dang, he didn't even know what to call it. Had this been a casual encounter, a hookup? Or had it been a cataclysmic event that sealed them together forever?

It felt pretty cataclysmic to him, but judging from Jodi's casual good-bye, it hadn't meant that much to her.

So should he follow her?

He wanted to—right now. Hell, he wanted to tag along behind her and curl up on the foot of her bed like a stray dog. He wanted to sit, stay, speak, and roll over at her command.

But he had no idea what she wanted.

Chapter 10

THE BRAND BOUTIQUE: THE BEST OF THE WEST AND to Hell with the Rest.

The sign's sentiment might not be poetic, but it was sure as heck accurate. Jodi's mother loved Western clothes, Western men, and Western decor, but she hated everything else about Western life. Horses, dirt, hot summers, cold winters, cattle, rodeo—she hated it all. She'd especially hated the ranch—the center of Jodi's life, and her father's.

But you'd never know it to look at the Brand Boutique.

It was housed in a generic strip mall that crouched at the very end of Purvis's three-block-long city center. Tall brick storefronts housing the Rexall, the ancient movie theatre, the Okay Café, and an assortment of saloons and office buildings abruptly gave way to the low, blocky strip mall and a Conoco station that had better be any visitor's last stop before they launched themselves into the endless high plains beyond the city limits. The sign at the other end of the street read "Welcome to Purvis. Next Services 30 miles."

The outside of the boutique looked about as interesting as the dry cleaner and the dentist's office that shared the building, but once you stepped inside the door, a tinkle of bells signaled your entry into an alternate universe where all the men were cowboys and the women were buckaroo belles. Log walls lined the interior, and beamed ceilings held wagon-wheel chandeliers that lit rack after rack of Western shirts, rakish hats, and tight trousers. Everything was spangled, fringed, beaded, and bedazzled.

"Honey!" Jodi's mother slid off a high stool and jogged over to wrap her daughter in a rose-scented embrace. Jodi closed her eyes and breathed in the familiar perfume while her mother gave her three quick squeezes and stepped back, holding Jodi's shoulders and scanning her from head to toe.

"You look *fine*," she declared. Her dark hair, streaked with silver and cut in a springy pageboy, bounced as she nodded approval. "You don't look sick at all. Not a bit." She gave Jodi a firm shake and stepped away. "I know this is a small town, but that doesn't give Darla Black license to make stuff up. She just needs to dig deeper and find some *real* gossip."

"I knew it," Jodi groaned. "She's spreading it all over town that I've got cancer, isn't she?"

"Well, I have to admit, I thought something was wrong with you too when I got your e-mail, but I figured it was mental." Peggy Brand cocked her head and gave her daughter a bird-like, inquisitive once-over. "What's got into you? I'm thrilled to have you, but you never had a shred of interest in fashion. You really want to work here?"

"You said you needed help."

"And I do. Sales have gone through the roof." Her mother pointed toward the ceiling and made a noise like a rocket to illustrate her point. "I can't keep up." She swept her arm around the room to indicate the racks of clothes and accessories. "But this just isn't *you*."

"Well, ranching wasn't *you* either, but you put up with it for Dad's sake. And for mine."

Her mother stepped back, narrowing her eyes. "What are you talking about?"

"I got to thinking about things, that's all. And I realized I hadn't been fair to you."

"You were grieving too, honey, and you needed someone to blame."

"So I picked you? And that's okay? No." Jodi shook her head. "I was wrong."

It was true. When her father suffered a riding accident that left him paralyzed, it seemed to Jodi that her mother had been paralyzed too—at least where the ranch was concerned. She'd been suddenly incapable of lifting a finger to keep it running. At fourteen, Jodi had been mired in teen self-obsession. It hadn't occurred to her that the situation was as difficult for her mother as it was for her.

"I blamed you for everything, Mom." She pulled a beaded necklace from the clearance basket and threaded it between her fingers, her eyes pricking with hot tears.

"I know it was hard for you. You two were so close." Her mother pulled a pink T-shirt emblazoned with a rhinestone-studded bucking horse silhouette from a box beside the counter and folded it rapidly.

Jodi pulled a fringed Western shirt with pearlized snaps off a nearby rack and held it up to her body as if checking it for size. "I was such a little snit, though. All I could think of was that you'd sold the horses." She took a deep breath. It was still hard to talk about this stuff, even after five years. "I know you only did what you had to do."

"It was hard for everybody." Her mother set the shirt

on the counter and pulled out another. "But it's over and done."

"Not for me." Jodi slumped against the counter. "I can't sleep nights, thinking of how it must have been for you when I didn't answer your calls or return your e-mails. I want to make it up to you, and I thought if I helped out with the store..."

"Well, I'd like that, honey." Her mom set the second shirt on top of the first one and folded her hands. "But I thought you wanted to work with horses somehow, and if there's one thing I've learned in all this, it's that you should do the things you love. You can only go so long living your life for other people."

"I know. And I'm going to start a therapy riding clinic eventually, if I can raise the funds. It'll take it a while to get off the ground." Jodi rounded the counter and pulled a shirt from the box. Clumsily, she tried to emulate her mother's quick folding technique. "So I thought I'd at least help you set up a system to deal with the Internet orders. I took some computer classes in school."

"Well, that would sure help. And working together..." Her mom bit her lip and ducked her head as if the shirts suddenly required her full attention. "It would be nice."

Jodi smiled. Throughout her nearly six-year brat-fit, her mother had never complained, never stopped calling, never stopped trying. And now that they were reconciled, she'd never ask for anything—but it was obvious Jodi had hit on the one thing that would mean the most to her.

"I think it'll be nice, too, Mom."

"But take a week or so to settle in. Have you seen any of your old friends? I guess most of them have left."

"I saw Teague," Jodi said.

"Teague." Her mother pronounced the name the way most people would say *maggot infestation* or *uncontrolled vomiting*. "Of course he's still here."

Jodi swallowed back a snappy retort. Her mother had never liked the Treadwells. Keeping her distance from Teague's parents was understandable, but it wasn't Teague's fault his folks had been the town drunk and the village floozy.

"He looks like he's doing really well."

"You saw him already?"

"At the Rexall." Jodi got up and examined some belts on a nearby rack so her mother wouldn't see her face flushing. "I ran into him yesterday, right after I got to town." She unhooked a belt from a display rack. It looked like an obsessive/compulsive BeDazzler had attacked an innocent piece of leather with pink and blue rhinestones. "He was dressed really nice."

"You can dehorn the devil and dress him in feathers, but he's still no angel." Her mom pulled another shirt from the box. "That boy can't hide who he is. He can't even raise civilized livestock. Why anyone would raise bucking horses on purpose is beyond me."

"It's for the rodeo, Mom. And besides, it's not just Teague's clothes that have changed. He has a really nice house, too."

Her mother widened her eyes. "You went to his *house*?"

"Just—just to drop off Troy." Jodi turned her attention back to the belt, but her hands were shaking so much she dropped it. Bending to pick it up, she returned it to the rack. "Teague's an old friend, Mom. I was just visiting."

"Jodi, listen." Her mom put the shirt down and rested her elbows on the counter. "You know I love you, and I want what's best for you."

Jodi nodded reluctantly. In all her plans to reconcile with her mother, she'd conjured up memories of the fun things they'd done together over the years—shopping, baking cookies, even a birthday trip to Vegas when she'd turned sixteen. She'd conveniently forgotten the inevitable downside of their relationship—the lectures. They were picking up right where they'd left off.

It's only because she cares, she told herself.

"If you want to do one thing for me, stay away from Teague." Her mother held up a hand to stop Jodi's protests. "I know he can't help who his parents are, but you have to remember one thing: his father wasn't just a drunk, he was a wife-beater. And that kind of thing runs in families."

"Not all the time."

"Most of the time. Look at your friend Cissy."

"What does that have to do with Teague?" Jodi said. "And you would have loved it if I'd dated Cal."

"No, I wouldn't have. Did you know Cal's mother?"

Jodi thought back to high school football games. "I must have met her, but I don't really remember."

"That's because she was the mousiest, scaredest woman you ever wanted to meet. Cal takes after his dad. Ask Cissy. She'll tell you."

"But Teague wouldn't…"

"Did you ever think Cal would?"

Jodi reluctantly shook her head. "Not really. He always seemed so—together. So in control of everything." She thought a moment. "Cissy said things didn't go so well for him after high school. I guess when things got out of control…"

Her mother nodded. "And Teague always has been one to settle things with his fists. He's been in trouble over and over." She reached out and put a hand on Jodi's arm. "I know you've always liked him, honey. But use your head first and your heart second. Just *think*."

Jodi sighed. "I guess you have a point. But Mom, you worry too much."

"Oh, I know," her mother said. "Besides, he's found some greener pastures, anyway. Everyone says that Skelton girl's fallen for him."

"Really?" Jodi narrowed her eyes. Teague hadn't mentioned any Skelton girl. In fact, he'd said he didn't have a girlfriend. "The what girl?"

"Skelton. Her father's some financier or something from back East, bought up a bunch of land north of town." She patted Jodi's shoulder. "I hear they're a serious item, so I guess you're safe. I'm sorry, hon. I just worry. But I know you've got more sense than to fall for a Treadwell."

"Sure," Jodi muttered. "Right."

She regretted her tone when her mother turned quickly and gave her a questioning look.

"No, really, Mom. I'll stay away from him."

She was too late. Her mother reached across the counter and took both her hands.

"Promise me," she said, staring earnestly into Jodi's eyes. "Promise me you won't get involved with him."

Jodi started to protest, then slumped against the counter. She'd come back to Purvis to make things right with her mother. Ever since realizing how unfair

she'd been to the one person who loved her uncondi-
tionally, she felt uncomfortably off-balance. She had
to make it right.

And besides, her mother had a point. How much evidence did she need to see that Teague was trouble? His
father was an abuser, and he himself had a history of
solving his troubles by fighting, to the point where he'd
gone to prison for it. Well, to juvie, anyway. And when
she'd seen how nervous Troy was about returning home,
what had her first thought been?

That Teague might be abusing him.

Even she'd thought it was possible.

Then there was their own personal history. He'd
treated her like crap all those years ago. So what had
she done? She'd fooled herself into forgiving him, then
hopped back into bed with him the first chance she got.

At least she'd had the sense to walk away this time
without saying anything stupid. She'd evened the score.
They were one and one.

And that was where it needed to end.

"Okay, Mom," she said. She drew an enormous
imaginary "X" on her chest with one finger. "I promise.
Cross my heart."

An hour later, Jodi opened the door to the feed store,
savoring the familiar creak of the hinges and the homey
scent of grain, leather, and hay.

"Hey, Boss." She'd worked for Bucky Maines all
through high school, and she could never bring herself
to call him Bucky, or even Mr. Maines. He was Boss to
her, and always would be.

"Jodi!" Bucky rested his forearms on the top of the register and gave her a broad grin. "Pretty as ever."

"You're the first to say so. You should have heard Darla Black when she saw me. She thought I was sick or something." Jodi sighed. "Guess everybody expected me to stay a rodeo queen."

"Pshaw." Bucky flailed a hand in the air dismissively. "I never could understand why you wanted to cover yourself up with all that glitter and stuff. That's for ugly girls. You're pretty just the way you are."

"Well, thanks, Boss." Jodi was surprised to feel an ache tightening her throat. This was the welcome she'd wanted. She'd told herself Darla's words didn't hurt, but they did. Jodi might have grown up to be a swan, but she'd spent enough of her tweens as an awkward ugly duckling to be sensitive about her appearance.

"Darla just likes to gossip, though," Bucky said. "She don't mean any harm."

Jodi was surprised to see Bucky flush bright red before he turned to fool with some papers on the other side of the counter. He was a big man, with a walrus mustache and a cue-ball dome under his felt Resistol, and he'd been single as long as Jodi could remember. He'd always been fatherly at best with women—awkward at worst. But evidently, he was carrying a torch for Darla Black.

Lord, what a pair they'd make. The walrus and the widow.

When he turned back around, his face had dimmed down to pink. "Everybody's glad to see you, though. Never doubt that. The whole town's waiting to see what you make of yourself."

Jodi nodded. No doubt Bucky thought that was a compliment, but it just reminded her that the pressure was on. Everyone expected so much from her—the town sweetheart, the golden girl. Obviously, Cal had fallen short, so apparently they were waiting for her to step up and make her hometown proud. It was a silly, old-fashioned notion, but it had been burned into her heart since she was a kid.

"Whatcha need, kiddo? Grain? Supplements? You still got Eightball?"

"Yeah, he's on the way. I hired a transport company to haul him." Jodi leaned up against the counter. "He should be here in a couple days. I want to have everything ready so he knows this is home." Having her barrel horse here would help her feel at home too. Eightball had been the one constant in her life—the one element that had moved with her from home to school, and now he was coming home again.

She moved to the bulletin board by the front door. A stocky figure was fingering a handwritten notice that was pinned to the center of the board. "Job Wanted," it said. A series of tabs on the bottom let prospective employers tear off the applicant's phone number. Several slips were missing.

"Troy!" Jodi said, and the figure turned. "You're looking for a job?"

He grinned sheepishly, staring down at the scuffed toes of his boots. "Yeah. I need money. So I can get my own place."

Jodi wrapped her arm around his shoulders. "Troy, you can't move out. Teague needs you. How come you want to move?"

Troy shrugged and refused to meet her eyes. "Just wanna," he said.

"You want to be more independent?"

He looked uncertain, his eyes darting left and right before he shrugged again.

"Maybe a job's a good idea," she said. "Maybe it would be enough just to have your own money. You probably get tired of asking Teague when you want something, right?"

"Uh-huh. He's always saying I shouldn't buy stuff. Like candy. And music. I like AC/DC."

"Hmm." Jodi smothered a smile. It would drive Teague nuts if Troy blasted AC/DC all the time, and driving Teague nuts sounded like fun. It had been kind of fun, back there in his bedroom—although he'd driven her nuts right back. "Maybe you could work for me."

"I could?"

"Sure." Jodi nodded. "I need somebody to help at the ranch. I need to get the arena ready, and build a ramp for the riding therapy clinic I'm starting. Once we're up and running, you could lead the horses for the kids, and maybe help out in the stable some, too. And I need to string more fence."

Troy straightened and threw his shoulders back. "I'm good at stringing fence."

"I'll bet you are."

Troy nodded like a dashboard bobble-head on a dirt road. "Okay. When do I start? Tomorrow? Can I start tomorrow?"

"Why don't you come over for breakfast and we'll talk about it? Eight o'clock or so? We'll negotiate a salary and stuff."

"Yeah," he said, beaming. "Salary. I gotta go to Target. I gotta look at the AC/DC CDs." She watched him head out of the store, a new strut in his walk. With the modeling money she'd saved up and the money from leasing the ranch, she could afford an assistant.

Of course, having Troy work with her would inevitably lead to more encounters with Teague. But that was okay. She could handle it.

She was on the winning side in that relationship, and that's where she intended to stay.

Chapter 11

"Is that what you were looking for? An employee?"
Bucky asked as Troy headed out the door.

"Not really, but I figure it's better if Troy works for
me than somebody else. It'd be awfully easy to take
advantage of him."

"You got a point there."

"So what I'm really looking for is a couple more
horses. I need older ones. Calm and well trained. You
know of any?"

Bucky thought a moment. "Might," he said. "But
you always liked 'em feisty. You gone soft? Some old
cayuse is gonna bore you to tears."

"They're not for me," Jodi said. "I'm starting a business. A therapy riding clinic. I need horses I can trust
with handicapped kids. They need to be quiet, and super
bombproof. Old rodeo horses work great. They're used
to crowds yelling and parade music. That's good practice for dealing with my students."

"I think Caxton out at the Triple R just got a new
roping horse," Bucky said. "Maybe he's ready to retire
Triple Threat."

"Oh, he'd be perfect." Jodi remembered the chestnut
fondly. Bill Caxton had been a pretty good calf roper—
mostly thanks to Triple Threat. The horse would pull the
line taut and hold on like a pro no matter how much Bill
flailed around with the piggin' string.

"I'll call him, let him know you're looking. Couple other guys too. So what kind of therapy you doing? How do those kids even get on a horse?"

"I'm building a ramp. And most of the kids I work with have cognitive handicaps, not physical ones." Bucky looked confused, so she elaborated. "Kids with autism, Down syndrome, that kind of thing. Riding helps them focus, builds muscle, and makes them feel good about themselves. It's amazing what it does for them."

"I'd like to see that."

"Once we get going, you'll have to come watch." She hesitated. "I'm going to need a lot of supplies. Tack, and probably boots for the kids whose parents can't afford 'em. Maybe some youth saddles too. I'm going to talk to the Rotary, Kiwanis, Women's Club—all those groups that might be willing to give funding. But then I wondered…"

"You'll get a discount here at Bucky's." Her old boss nodded. "Course you will. And maybe I could be a sponsor or something."

The tin bells attached to the door tinkled and Jodi turned to see a tiny blonde Barbie-doll type entering the store. Flowing locks cascaded from under the brim of her perfectly shaped black cowboy hat, and she was wearing a black suede blazer with beading on the cuffs and lapels that matched the curlicues embroidered on her tight black jeans.

It looked like she'd bought out the entire stock of the Brand Boutique. The only non-Western element in her outfit was an oversized purse decorated with Louis Vuitton's initials repeated over and over in a dizzying pattern. Jodi thought at first that the purse had a furry pom-pom attached to the top, but then the pom-pom let out a sharp yip and grinned.

"Hush, Honeybucket," the blonde said, patting the pom-pom's head. She spoke a little too loudly, as if she was conscious of her audience, but her voice was high and childlike. "You be good now."

Honeybucket? Jodi smothered a laugh as she turned back to Bucky. "A sponsor? That would be… oh, never mind."

One look at the cowgirl fashion plate had Bucky blushing again, opening and closing his mouth like a grounded trout as he nodded maniacally. The woman—or girl; she was something in between—simpered and fluttered a finger wave his way, dipping her hips in something strangely like a curtsy.

"Hello, Bucky," she said in a breathy baby voice. She turned her blinking blue eyes on Jodi. For an instant her perfectly plucked brows arrowed down in a calculating squint, but she recovered fast. Turning her attention back to Bucky, she faked a strict schoolteacher scowl and wagged a finger. "You didn't forget our meeting, did you?"

"Forget?" Bucky shook his head in frantic denial. "Oh, no. I'd never forget. Not you. I mean the meeting. I'd never forget the meeting."

"Well, good." The girl sashayed past Jodi, stacked-heel boots clicking on the wooden floor. She set the doggie bag down and fished out a couple of well-worn catalogs.

"I brought those wholesale catalogs for you to look at. I can help you pick out some items that will help you cater to the needs of your new clientele."

The girl glanced toward Jodi, then slid her eyes

away as if what she saw embarrassed her. "As I said, it will be quite a *sophisticated* group." She trilled out a high-pitched giggle and did the little dipping motion again. It reminded Jodi of a prairie chicken doing its mating dance, and was evidently calculated to make your jeans tighten over your butt.

Not that the jeans needed any tightening.

The little dog stuck its head out of the bag again, looked both ways, and climbed out. Putting its pointy nose to the ground, it began investigating the myriad smells lingering on the floors and fixtures. As Jodi watched, it scampered down the feed aisle.

"Let me just help out Jodi, here, Miss Skelton, and then I'll be right…"

Jodi couldn't hear the rest of Bucky's sentence over the roaring in her ears.

Miss Skelton. *Miss Skelton.* So this… this *bimbo* was Teague's girlfriend. His *secret* girlfriend. The one he didn't tell her about before he lured her into bed. Jodi was struck with a sudden urge to slap her.

No, wait. Why would she be the one doing the slapping? She was the bimbo here, appearances to the contrary. From what her mom had said, Miss Skelton had a prior claim.

Maybe she ought to slap herself. Or better yet, Teague.

She cocked a hip and tossed her hair back, almost wishing she had her queen coif to add emphasis to the gesture. It wasn't that she was jealous; it was just that Teague deserved better. This girl was worse than the wanna-bes that plagued the rodeo queen circuit—pageant princesses who sat a horse like a straight chair and thought they were better than the cowgirl contestants just because they'd won a few rhinestone tiaras in state swimsuit competitions.

"Never mind, Boss." Jodi backed away. "I'll come back. I wanted to talk to you about that sponsorship, but I can see you're busy." She turned to the new arrival and offered her best queen smile. "It was *so* nice to meet you."

As she headed out the door, Honeybucket was just trotting in. He'd evidently managed to escape the feed store, and judging from the dirt caked in his long hair and the aroma wafting from it, he'd found himself something very special to roll in.

Jodi grinned. Those little pocket pets didn't get much of a chance to be real dogs. This one looked ecstatically pleased with himself as he trotted over to his mistress and pawed at her leg, leaving a wide brown streak on her fancy-pants jeans.

"Honeybucket—*oh!*" The girl skittered backward. "What have you *done*?"

Jodi grinned and headed for her pickup, wondering what business the Skelton girl had with Bucky. She seemed to be talking him into ordering new stock, for some "new clientele." What was that all about? There hadn't been anything new in Purvis since Cade Wilkins installed a new lift in his body shop in 1973.

She'd have to ask Darla. It was time to go back to the Rexall.

Jodi parallel parked her Ranger in front of the drugstore and yanked the parking brake into place. Frowning, she pulled down the sun visor and scanned her face in the mirror. In the unsympathetic light of day, she really did look washed out. Sighing, she dug a zippered pouch out of her purse and pulled out a compact and a tube of mascara. She was trying to break free of the image that convinced everyone she was a ditzy blonde whose only skill was riding a horse while carrying a flag, but this was an emergency. She'd never survive another twenty minutes fending off Darla's unsettling combination of curiosity and compassion. Not today.

Not after meeting Courtney Skelton.

Teague had always had his issues, but he'd never been a liar. Yet he'd told her—what was it he said?

No girlfriend. Don't let anybody tell you different.

It was her mother that told her about "the Skelton girl." And her mother definitely had an agenda. An anti-Teague agenda.

Maybe Jodi should give him a chance to explain. Maybe she should trust him more.

Yeah, right. She'd always been a fool about Teague, and it was getting worse.

She dabbed powder on her nose and glanced back in the mirror. She shouldn't be making excuses for any man. She deserved better. She might be pale, but her lips were full, her chin was strong, and her blue eyes fairly glowed once she'd stroked on a coat of mascara. Giving herself an encouraging nod, she rolled out of the truck and headed for the drugstore.

Darla was holding court behind the pharmacy counter when she entered, talking with another woman. The conversation broke off abruptly when Jodi walked in, and she felt a twinge of panic in the pit of her stomach. Were they talking about her? Had someone seen her with Teague? News could travel fast in a small town.

But no one could possibly know. No one had seen them. More likely Darla was spreading the news about her supposed illness. She was probably telling everyone Jodi Brand had come back to Purvis to die.

Well, that would sure help with the fund-raising for the clinic.

Jodi pretended to scan the shelves while she worked out a strategy. There was an art to small-town discourse she'd mastered in her youth and nearly lost in the real world. You couldn't just walk up to the counter and ask Darla to dispense gossip. You had to come at your question obliquely and make it seem as if the subject you were dying to dish on had come up naturally. Acknowledging that Darla was the gossip queen of Purvis was the surest way to shut her up.

Biting her lower lip, Jodi reached for a bottle of pills and pretended to scan the label while she thought out a winning approach. She was running two possible introductory sentences through her mind when a sudden silence jarred her into awareness. The two women at the counter were staring at her, their eyes wide. She jerked her attention back to the present and looked down at the bottle in her hand.

Prenatal vitamins.

Great. Now not only would everyone think she had cancer; they'd think she was about to give birth to an orphan. She shoved the bottle back on the shelf.

"Well," Darla said. "If it isn't our own little Queenie."

Perfect opening. "Oh, but you know, I'm not the rodeo queen anymore," Jodi said. "I just saw the new one over at Bucky's."

"The new one?"

"Blonde? Little tiny thing, dresses real, um, queen-like?"

"Oh, you must mean that Skelton girl," Darla's friend volunteered. It was Belle Arnold, who ran the Snag Bar with her husband. Belle looked soft and matronly, but she was tough enough to double as a bouncer when things got rough at the Snag. "That girl doesn't dress like a rodeo queen. She dresses like a boomtown hooker."

Jodi laughed. Belle was never one to mince words. "Well, kind of. She had on this crazy outfit. Fringe, embroidery—real flashy."

"Goes around looking like Yee-Haw Barbie," Belle muttered. "Hussy."

"Who is she?"

"Courtney Skelton," Darla said. "Her daddy's a millionaire—retired CEO of... something." She flushed. Darla never liked to admit there was something she didn't know about one of the locals. "They bought the Hunt acreage out west of town."

"Ray Hunt sold his ranch?" Jodi was shocked. The Hunts were the biggest landowners in Mead County—or at least, they used to be. If someone else owned that spread, things really had changed.

"Ray died, honey," Darla said. "Prudential had their signs hanging off his barbwire for two, three years before they could find a buyer. It was millions, you know." She licked her lips as if she could taste the money—or maybe it was just her reaction to the delicious morsels of gossip such a transaction inevitably served up.

"What about Virge?" Jodi had gone to school with Ray's son Virgil. He'd been head of the Future Farmers

of America and wore white shirts and bolo ties to school
from fourth grade on, looking like a miniature businessman and smelling like a sheep shack. Everyone had
always figured he'd be next to run the Hunt spread. "I
can't believe he would sell it."

"Virgil went off the road in his Ford and killed his-
self four years ago," Belle said. "You been gone a long
time, girl."

Jodi swallowed. Virgil Hunt hadn't been a friend of
hers by any stretch of the imagination, but it was still
a shock to hear he wasn't living out the future that had
seemed so assured. None of the kids in her graduating
class had ever doubted that Virgil would be a successful
rancher. Of course, they'd also believed that Cal's winning streak would continue off the football field, and
that Teague would continue on the road to hell, or at
least the path to jail. Everyone had their assigned roles
to play in this town, but with Virgil gone, Cal in jail, and
Teague on the street, it looked like Jodi was the only one
sticking to the plan.

"So this Skelton fellow bought the whole place."
Darla leaned her elbows on the counter. "He's got it sub-
divided into forty-acre lots. Ranchettes, they call them."

Things really had changed. The Hunt ranch was huge.
Forty-acre lots meant a whole lot of ranchettes—which
meant a whole lot of new folks coming to town. New
folks meant new businesses, new movers and shakers,
and new ideas. She'd probably arrived just in time to
watch her old-fashioned hometown burn itself out and
rise from the ashes like a phoenix, transformed into a
haven for Super Walmarts and fast-food joints. She
squelched a pang of sorrow. Progress was good. It was

about time Purvis slid into the twentieth century now that the rest of the world had hit the twenty-first.

"Skelton kept a big piece of the ranch for himself, though," Darla continued. "Supposedly he's building a polo facility, and the ranchettes are for polo people. He's got a bunch of his rich friends moving up from Florida."

"Polo?" Talk about transformation. Jodi didn't know much about polo, but she knew it meant big money. Huge money.

And money always changed things.

"So Courtney is this rich guy's daughter?"

Darla nodded.

"What's she like?"

"Just like you'd expect," Belle said. "Snooty. Spoiled. Treats everybody like some kind of servant."

"Almost everybody," Darla said. She had a smug smile on her face—an expression that usually presaged some juicy revelation. "There's at least one exception."

"Who's that?" Jodi had a feeling she knew the answer, but she needed confirmation.

"Teague Treadwell," Darla said. "She seems to like Teague just fine. And he seems to like her too."

Chapter 12

JODI COULD FEEL DARLA AND BELLE'S EYES ON HER. She'd better say something. She tried for a casual off-handed tone.

"So Teague likes that…" She struggled to think of a charitable description for Courtney Skelton. "…that… that…"

"That rich hooker bitch that's been throwing herself at him since she got here? You bet," Belle said. "He likes her just fine." She shook her head, scowling. "Men are fools."

Jodi had an urge to try and amp up the trash talk about the Skelton girl, but she smothered the impulse. She'd learned way back in her queen days that talking bad about people was a sure way to earn enemies, and you never knew how powerful those enemies might become. Courtney Skelton might be an easy target with her over-the-top cowgirl clothes, but she had money, and money was power. She had looks too, if she just toned down her outfits a little.

Jodi shook her head. "I can't see Teague falling for someone like that," she said. Matter of fact, she knew Teague wouldn't fall for someone like that. Hadn't he been her own best friend until she'd started dressing up and trying to better herself? He'd taken one look at her polished boots and high queen hair and accused her of trying to be somebody she wasn't. Why would he fool around with some rich girl? Teague liked his women real.

Or at least, that's what he'd said years ago. But who knew what Teague liked now? She thought of the new clothes, the big house, the gel spiking his stylishly cut hair. Maybe that was Courtney's doing. Maybe she'd given him a makeover.

She felt her heart drop into her stomach and gave herself a mental slap.

She needed to stop thinking about Teague Treadwell.

―⁂―

The next morning, Teague watched Troy strap on his helmet and throw one leg over his bike. His brother had bolted down his breakfast, and now he couldn't wait to get going.

"Let's go, Bessie," he said, setting his right foot on the pedal. Luna trotted out of the barn and circled the bike, letting out an excited whine.

"Where you headed?"

"Jodi's."

Teague nodded. Now that Jodi was home, Troy would probably want to be over there all the time. "Don't pester her, now."

"I'm not pestering." Troy drew himself up to his full five-foot-three and gave his brother a dignified scowl. "I work for her."

"You what?"

Troy nodded. "I work for her. We gotta fix up that ranch." He shook his head. "Needs a lotta work. A *lotta* work."

Teague smiled. "Well, good. I'm glad you're helping her. Maybe I'll come help out too."

Troy shook his head. "Sorry. I don't think she can hire more'n one of us."

Teague's head snapped up and his eyes narrowed. "She's paying you?"

Troy nodded. "Yup. Now I won't have to be askin' you for money all the time."

Teague tried to adjust the expression on his face to reflect approval, but he had a feeling it wasn't working. As long as Troy had to ask for money, Teague could keep tabs on what he was spending it on. Make sure it wasn't *Playboy* magazines or violent video games. Not that Troy had ever shown any inclination for either one—but you never knew. It was a rough world out there, and it was Teague's job to make sure Troy was protected from it.

"Well, I better talk to her. See what's going on."

"Nothing's going on," Troy said. "I got a job, that's all." He gave Teague a stubborn look, chin thrust out, shoulders set. "Why would you need to talk to her?"

"Okay," Teague said, backing off. He'd need to think about this. Figure out how to deal with it. "That's fine. That's okay, Troy."

"'Course it's okay," Troy said. "It's for Jodi." Setting one sneakered foot on the bike's upraised pedal, he hiked himself onto the Schwinn's padded seat and teetered off down the driveway with Luna loping behind him.

Teague set his fists on his hips and watched them go, the plump figure diminishing in the distance, moving farther and farther out of his reach. The bike hit a stone and Troy wobbled slightly; Teague took a step toward him, then sighed as his brother righted himself and picked up speed.

—∿∿—

"Hey, you're good at this." Jodi nodded approvingly as Troy stretched a length of wire tight and tweaked it with one finger to test the tension. "Nice work."

Troy grinned and pulled more wire from the spool. Beside him, Luna panted in the sun. "Told ya. Teague says I do it better than him."

"I think he's right. You okay if I go take care of Eightball while you check the line?"

"I'm sure." Troy furrowed his brow. "Long as you don't need help."

"Nope. I'm fine. But thanks." She gave him a brisk nod and swallowed the urge to heap him with praise. She really was impressed with how helpful he'd been, but she didn't want to patronize him. Troy was a grown man, and she'd do her best to treat him like any other worker. She'd just look out for him a little, that was all. Keep an eye on him.

She scuffed her boots in the dusty driveway as she headed for her horse trailer. Her father's land—her land now—was baked to a golden brown from the June sun, the grass brittle, the ground hard. It wasn't the Garden of Eden by any means, but it felt good under her feet.

The horse standing in the corral was familiar too. She'd had Eightball shipped from Pennsylvania so she could get home faster and get his quarters ready. She'd finished up last night, hammering the horse's brass name-plate over his door and refitting the tack and feed room with hooks for halters and bridles, racks for saddles, and a vermin-proof container for grain and supplements.

The horse nuzzled at her pockets, poking around for a treat as she clipped a lead to his halter and led him to the barn. Nickering, he tossed his head and pranced in place the way he had at the beginning of every barrel race, when he'd itched to explode out of the gate and pound his way around the cloverleaf.

"Glad to be home? Me too, buddy," Jodi said, giving him an affectionate pat. "But you're going to have to stop that dancing around. You're not a barrel horse anymore, okay? You're a therapy horse."

She led the horse into his stall, then headed for the trailer. It was a remnant of her queen winnings, a gift from one of her sponsors. It had space for two horses, along with a cubbyhole for tack and feed and small but comfy living quarters at the front she'd called home through many a rodeo. Everything was fitted out like a super-deluxe yacht on wheels with polished wood and brass hardware. She cared for it like it was a yacht too, keeping the two stalls sparkling clean, the wood polished, and the brass shining. She didn't use it much, since it was a bugger to tow with the Ranger, but the transport company she'd hired to haul Eightball had been happy to hook it to a diesel and haul it home.

She was clearing out the last of the dirty straw from the trailer when Teague's truck pulled into the drive. Looking up from her work, she watched him slide down from the cab and felt a flutter in her stomach. He wasn't dressed quite so much like a dude today. His jeans were a little faded, his shirtsleeves rolled up to expose tanned, muscular forearms. He was pure cowboy, and her heart did a happy little jitterbug at the sight while her body warmed and urged her closer.

She scanned him from hat to toes, looking for something to distract her from the way his shirt tapered from broad shoulders to slim hips, and decided his boots were a little too polished and his shirt was too crisply creased at the collar.

But finding flaws didn't do any good. Teague's style of dress might have changed, but his walk was still a loose-hipped swagger that made her heart dance in her chest. She remembered how he'd looked in the dim light of his bedroom, how his muscles had gleamed in the half-light from the window, and she had to take a deep breath to stop her hands from shaking. She felt suddenly self-conscious remembering the last time they'd been together, but she needn't have worried. Teague shoved his hands in his pockets and looked at the barn, the horizon, everything but her.

"Troy around?" he asked.

Evidently, it was business as usual for him. He was going to pretend their little roll in the hay hadn't happened.

Fine. She was fine with that. He'd hurt her once, but she wasn't going to let it happen again. This time, she'd known from the start that sex with Teague was just that: sex. Great sex, incredible sex, but nothing more. Not love. Not romance.

It was liberating, she told herself. She felt strong. Powerful. It was like being a man, taking what you wanted and refusing to let anyone put reins on your heart just because you'd shared your body.

Something in the back of her mind was nagging her, though, saying it hadn't been just her body she'd given. It had been something more—a meeting of souls as well as bodies. Hadn't Teague felt it?

Probably not. She was just being a girl. She'd been raised to think sex meant love, but it didn't have to. Sometimes sex was just sex.

She looked up and caught him eyeing her with a subtle sideways glance. There was a hint of yearning in his expression—just a hint, but unmistakable. Good. She was still ahead then.

"Troy's stringing fence." She stopped sweeping and leaned the broom up against the wall, then gestured toward her new employee, who was pounding another metal post into the ground halfway down the fence line.

"By himself?"

"Luna's with him. But yeah. He's good at it."

"I know. I taught him. But aren't you watching him?"

Shoot. She'd barely had time to appreciate Teague before he ticked her off. She grabbed a mop out of a bucket of soapy water and pulled the lever that wrung it out.

"It's electric fence, not barbed wire," she said. "And it's turned off. I gave him gloves too." She ran the mop across the floor of the trailer in short, angry swipes.

He stepped up into the small space, filling the doorway, stooping so his hat wouldn't brush the ceiling. Jodi could stand straight up in it and then some. She'd forgotten how tall he was.

"It's nice of you to give him a job," he said grudgingly. "I hope he's not too much trouble."

"I didn't hire him to be nice," Jodi said sharply. She dipped the mop into the water and wrung it out again, letting a few drops spatter onto Teague's polished boots. He stepped back and she mopped the place where he'd stood. "I needed somebody, and I trust Troy. Besides, he wanted a job. He's a grown man now, right?"

Teague nodded. "I know, I know. But you need to keep an eye on him. He could get hurt."

She concentrated on her job, refusing to look up at him. "Of course he could get hurt," she said. "So could I."

"You just need to look out for him. That's all I'm saying."

"I look out for him, Teague. I love your brother dang near as much as you do, you know."

"I know. He was always your favorite."

Jodi kept mopping, keeping her head down so Teague couldn't see her smother a smile. "You jealous or what?"

"No." Teague shifted his weight from one foot to the other and looked away. "I just think giving him a job is a bad idea."

Jodi shoved the mop back into the bucket, gave it a final rinse, then leaned it up against the wall beside the broom. "Why?"

"It just is."

She looked up at him, a challenge in her eyes. "Because he only works for you?"

"Because I'm the only one who really understands him."

Jodi grabbed the bucket and carried it to the door, tossing it out in a wide wet fan across the dry ground. "Teague, I understand him. I've spent the last four years getting a degree in special ed, remember? I'm dedicating my life to helping people like Troy." She hung the bucket on a hook, then turned. "What are you dedicating your life to?" She looked him up and down and quirked a faint smile. "Fashion?"

He frowned, hitching up his belt self-consciously. "I'm dedicating it to Troy. You know that."

"Yeah, and that's a lot easier to do if he never leaves the house, right?" She softened her tone. "I know it's hard, Teague. But he needs a life of his own. He needs validation, a purpose—just like anyone else."

"I give him a good life," Teague protested.

"Maybe he doesn't want you to give it to him," she said. "Maybe he wants to earn it."

"Maybe he… What was that?"

It was Troy. Jodi heard it too—a faint wail coming from across the pasture, followed by a barrage of sharp barks from Luna. She jumped off the trailer behind Teague and took off across the field, ducking through the fencing as he vaulted over.

On the far side of the field, Troy was crouched on the ground, his hands over his face.

Dang, Jodi thought. *Maybe Teague was right. Maybe I should have watched him closer.*

Chapter 13

TEAGUE SWORE TO HIMSELF AS HIS FOOT SLIPPED ON A cow patty and he almost went down. Scrambling for balance, he kept running, headed for the spot where his brother was kneeling in the grass beside the fence.

He'd known this was a bad idea. What if the wire had snapped and hit Troy in the eye? What if he'd cut himself? He slid to a stop and fell to his knees as he reached Troy, pulling his brother's hands gently away from his face.

"What happened, bud? You okay?"

"I—I'm fine." Troy looked up at him and Teague winced. A slash of red stood out on his right cheekbone, dangerously close to his eye. "I was picking up the roll and the end of the wire bounced up and bit me." Troy swiped a gloved hand across the cut and looked down at the blood staining the leather. "I need a Band-Aid."

"Let me see," Teague said. "You might need stitches."

Troy's eyes widened, then filled.

"Oh, for God's sake," Jodi said from behind them. "He doesn't need stitches. It's just a little cut. Come on, Troy. Let's get it cleaned up." She took Troy's hand and led him back toward the house. Luna trotted in anxious circles around them, her eyes never leaving Troy's face.

"But…" Teague had to practically jog to keep up with her.

"But nothing." Jodi turned and gave him a furious look. "It's nothing to *worry* about, okay? Right?"

"Oh. Right." Teague gave himself a mental slap. She *was* right. He was only making things worse. He always panicked when Troy got hurt, and then the kid got upset.

The man, not the kid, he reminded himself. He needed to stop thinking about Troy like he was a child. He was twenty-eight years old.

But truth be told, Teague didn't know how to deal with Troy except as a child. When he'd been a teenager, there'd been days he hated his brother—his *older* brother—for needing so much care and attention. He'd gotten frustrated, and on a few occasions, he'd said some things he wasn't proud of. It was only later, when he understood that Troy's mind had finished growing up while Teague's kept going, that he learned to love his brother without resenting him.

He thought of Troy as a child because Troy was a child in so many ways. A child in a man's body. But Troy was beginning to have a man's needs, too—the need to assert himself, to take care of himself, to feel independent and useful. No doubt he had other needs too, but so far those hadn't been a problem—because Teague kept Troy close. He watched him. He made sure he didn't get into trouble.

Now Jodi was threatening that setup by encouraging Troy to be more independent—and look where it had gotten them. His first day on the job, and already Troy was hurt.

"Let me see." Jodi settled Troy on a stool next to the sink and pressed a paper towel to the wound. "It's not deep or anything. Just a scratch."

"Just a scratch," Troy echoed. He rocked slightly on the stool, comforting himself.

Jodi headed for the bathroom for first aid supplies while Teague rested a hip against the counter, watching his brother and feeling helpless. Luna shoved her nose into his hand and let out a worried whine. Great. Even the dog knew he fretted too much over Troy.

"Does it hurt?" he finally asked.

"Nope. Not much."

"This might," Jodi said. She upended a plastic bottle of peroxide onto a clean paper towel and dabbed at the wound.

"It doesn't hurt," Troy said stoutly.

"Good." She patted the cut dry, then put a dab of antibiotic ointment on a Sesame Street Band-Aid and pressed it onto Troy's cheek. "You got Oscar the Grouch," she said.

"Cool." Troy giggled. "Like Teague. Teague's a grouch."

Jodi smiled. "Yeah, he kind of is, isn't he?" She punched Teague gently on the arm. "But it's just because he worries about you."

Troy rolled his eyes. "I know," he said. "I know. He worries too much."

A half-hour later, Teague watched Troy head back to his fence-stringing, his eyes protected by safety goggles, Luna trotting at his heels. He'd started to roll his sleeves up as he went back to work, probably in imitation of Teague, but Jodi had insisted he keep his arms covered too.

"Thanks," Teague said as his brother set off across the field, armed with his trusty pliers. "Sorry I freaked out."

"I'm sorry he got hurt," Jodi said. "It wasn't much, but it could have been worse. I'll be more careful. I guess it's a learning experience."

Teague nodded, but he couldn't quite rid himself of the nagging feeling that he didn't want his brother to be anybody's "learning experience"—not even Jodi's. He followed her into the trailer, where she picked up a frayed cloth and started polishing the brass rails of the ladder that led up to the top bunk.

Teague perched on the side of the lower bed's thin mattress, where he could keep an eye on Troy through the tiny sliding window. The trailer's sleeping area was small, and his knees doubled up in front of him like grasshopper legs. He stretched out instead, crossing his ankles in the doorway. "So what are your plans? You said you're starting a therapy clinic?"

"Uh-huh. It'll take a while to get it going, though. Mostly, I'm working for my mom." Jodi poured a dab of Brasso on the rag and rubbed it onto the brass trim on the top rung, then polished it off. "Until I get some funding together, the clinic'll have to wait." She backed away for a moment, assessing the shiny brass, then polished some more. The brass looked fine to him, but she'd always been obsessive about her trailer, keeping it clean as a house—maybe cleaner. The interior still looked brand new.

Jodi had won a lot of stuff in her rodeo queen competitions, but at least she didn't take it for granted, the way a rich girl would. He thought of Courtney Skelton. He'd seen her tooling around town in a sweet little

Beemer, but when he'd admired it, she said she was about to trade it in. She'd had it two years, so it was time for a new car, she said. When he'd peered inside, he'd seen fast food wrappers and junk littering the backseat.

He wondered what Courtney would think of Jodi's ten-year-old trailer. He sure couldn't see Courtney polishing brass.

He liked watching Jodi do it, though. She was stretched up onto her toes, reaching for the top rung. Since she was so busy polishing, he could look at her all he wanted—at her hips, round and firm under tight Wranglers, her breasts pressing against the stretched fabric of her T-shirt, the swath of flat belly the shirt exposed every time she reached her arms over her head.

Flat. Flat belly. She couldn't be pregnant—could she?

But he'd overheard Darla Black telling someone Jodi had checked out some prenatal vitamins at the Rexall. Maybe it was just too soon for her to show.

"Teague?" Jodi was cocking her head and smiling at him. "Earth to Teague."

"Sorry," he said. Dang. How long had he been sitting there staring at her? Gaping like an idiot, with his mouth hanging open, probably.

What the hell had they been talking about?

The riding clinic. Her new business.

"So," he said, forcing his mind back to the outside world. "You teach your patients to ride?"

"Not patients. Clients. They're not sick; they're challenged. And what I teach them depends on their needs. Sometimes they just do exercises on the horse. It helps them learn new skills, teaches them to focus, and gives them a feeling of empowerment," Jodi said.

"Yeah." Teague looked away as she moved down to the next rung of the ladder and her eyes met his. "I guess it would be nice for them to get the chance to go riding."

"It's not just a treat," Jodi said, giving the rung a vigorous rubdown. "It really is therapy. There are various exercises we do, depending on the client's needs. Some of them are physical, like riding with no hands. Others are more cognitive—like games where they guide their horse to a certain number hung on the corral fence."

"You're going to use Eightball for this?"

"I hope so." Jodi moved down another rung and repeated the polishing process. "I'm not sure he'll be calm enough. I'd really like to use Vegas."

"But he's blind."

"I know." Jodi draped the rags over the rung she was working on and sat down beside him, brushing his arm with one elbow. Teague felt an electric jolt bounce from his arm to his solar plexus and ricochet down to the danger zone.

"But we lead the horses when the kids ride them," Jodi continued. She seemed oblivious to the effect she had on him. Didn't she remember what had happened the other day? How could she be so casual about it?

"You know I'd take good care of Vegas," she said. "You said he was depressed. This would help."

"Maybe. But if he's in a strange place, he won't be able to find his way around."

"We'll get him accustomed to it. That would be a good job for Troy. He could lead him around—teach him where things are. It would give Troy a chance to be the teacher for a change."

"Yeah," Teague said. "That might be good."

"And having a job might liven Vegas up a little bit. Maybe he needs some change in his life."

"Maybe he does," Teague said. He was still struggling with the nearness of her, acutely conscious of the fact that they were sitting on a bed, that he could just reach out for her, push her back onto the mattress. He glanced sideways out the window so she couldn't see his eyes and read his thoughts.

Vegas wasn't the only one who needed some change in his life. Teague needed to find some outlet for these feelings—someone who didn't matter quite so much. Someone who could help him get over Jodi Brand and move on.

Trouble was, the only candidate applying for the job was Courtney Skelton, and he wasn't interested in what she had to offer. She was persistent, but it would never amount to anything. If Courtney's dad found out his daughter was hanging with a ragtag cowboy who raised bucking horses and was just as ornery as his livestock, he'd probably lock the girl up.

For once, Teague's bad reputation would do him good.

Jodi settled back on the bed, resting on her elbows.

"So," she said. "Can we do it?"

Wow. That was blunt. He knew she'd taken their earlier liaison pretty casually, but this definitely wasn't the Jodi he knew. He scanned her face to see if she meant what he thought she did, but his eyes skittered down to take a quick tour of her body from head to toe. He wanted to "do it," that was for sure. But he wanted "it" to mean something.

For him, this was anything but casual.

She laughed, nudging him with her elbow. "Bring Vegas over here, I mean."

"Oh." He tried not to sound disappointed. "Sure. I guess."

She shifted a little closer to him. 'What did you think I meant?" she asked teasingly.

"I thought…" He reached one hand up to stroke back a strand of hair that had swung down to dangle in her face. "I thought you meant… I don't know."

"I do." She reached up and readjusted the hair he'd moved. "It's not too hard to read your mind, Teague."

"No?" He reached up and stroked her hair again.

"No. You might have nicer clothes now, but you haven't changed much. But we can't… I'm not…"

Her voice trailed off as his hand drifted down and caressed the side of her neck, and suddenly he was bending over her, knotting his fingers in the hair at the nape of her neck, and kissing her like his life depended on it.

She parted her lips and pressed her breasts into his chest, flinging an arm around his neck and returning his kiss with a passion that was anything but casual. He felt himself growing hard against her as his kiss deepened and his hand wandered down to cup her breast. His thumb scraped over her nipple and he felt it peak under his touch, but he'd gone too far too fast. She jerked away from him and turned away.

"Teague, wait."

He could barely interpret the words. Wait? For what? Why?

He pulled her back against his chest.

"Jodi, let it happen," he murmured into her hair. "You know you want this too."

"I—I can't." She stiffened and shoved him away. "Dang it, I promised my mom."

She clapped one hand over her mouth as if she wished she hadn't spoken. The pounding of his heart slowed, burning-hot anger taking the place of passion.

"Your mom? What did you promise her?"

"That I wouldn't… you know."

"That you wouldn't get mixed up with that trailer trash Treadwell boy?"

"Teague, I'm trying to make things right between us—between me and her, I mean. I don't want to disappoint her."

"What about making things right between you and me?"

She looked away. "I don't know what right is when it comes to you and me, Teague. Hell, I've never known, and that's not entirely my fault." Her tone softened. "My mother's important to me, Teague. I won't feel whole 'til I fix it."

"And I won't feel whole 'til—never mind." He turned and pretended to be engrossed in the view from the window. "Forget it."

"Family comes first, okay? I can't sleep at night thinking about what I did to her. She lost her husband, and then she lost me too, right at the time she needed me most. I'm going to make it up to her, and I can't do that while I'm carrying on with you."

He leaned back on his elbows and tugged his hat down low to hide his eyes.

"Carrying on? Is that what that was?"

She shrugged.

He tilted his head up to peer up at her from under his hat brim. "Why does she hate me so much, anyway?"

Jodi flailed her hands helplessly. "She has her reasons, okay? It would worry her. And that's the last thing I want to do right now."

"Okay." He narrowed his eyes. "So tell me the reasons. Maybe I can do something to change her mind."

She wrung her hands and looked so distressed he knew this wasn't anything he could fix.

"It's not really about you. It's about your father. She—she thinks that kind of thing runs in families, like with Cal." She held up a hand to stop his response. "I know you're not like that, but you asked for her reason, and that's it. And given Cissy's situation, it's a hard one to argue with."

He stared down at the floor again, thinking. About the past, and how it haunted his present and shadowed his future.

"You know, you don't owe her anything," he said. "You did all that rodeo queen crap for her. You were the perfect daughter, and I know you hated that stuff." He raked his hands over his hair. "When are you going to start living your own life?"

She hunched her shoulders, refusing to meet his eyes. "Now," she said. "I'm living it now."

"No you're not. You're still trying to please everybody but yourself." In an exaggerated gesture, he raised an admonishing finger and lowered his brows. "You'd better settle down in the suburbs and have two-point-five kids, or everybody'll be disappointed. And don't do it with that Teague Treadwell. He's not *worthy*." He lurched to his feet. "To hell with it, anyway. I'm never getting married. Never having kids. That's for other people."

He spun and stalked past the two narrow stalls. "I guess your mom figured that out."

—⁓—

"Hey," said a voice from outside the trailer. "What're you guys doing?"

"Nothing." Teague slumped against the wall and ran a hand over his face as if he could erase his anger with one swipe. "Just talking."

Jodi sprang from the bed and picked up her polishing rag just as Troy passed through the stall area and stood in the doorway of the tiny bedroom. "I got all the way to the tree line," he said, waving his pliers like a warrior's sword. "I bet I can finish the job next time I come."

"Good," she said. "We'll finish it tomorrow. I'll help."

"Not tomorrow," Troy said. "I'm busy."

"Doing what?"

"I got another job," Troy said.

Jodi turned to look at him, startled. "Troy, are you quitting on me?"

"No. It's mostly going to be real early in the mornings, so I can still work for you after. But tomorrow I have training all day." He puffed out his chest. "I'll be making a lot of money."

"Who are you going to be working for?" Jodi was careful to keep the surprise out of her voice. Of course someone else had hired Troy. He was a good worker, and loyal. Or at least, he used to be loyal.

"Mr. Skelton," he said. "He called last night."

"What?" Teague looked shocked. "You're working for Skelton?"

Troy nodded so enthusiastically Jodi was afraid he'd

jar his brain loose. "He says I'm just the man he needs to take care of his horses. I won't be able to tell you much about it, though. Mr. Skelton said his operation is strictly confifluential."

"Yeah, I know. Everything that guy does is top secret." Teague turned to Jodi. "He keeps the horses locked up, trains in an indoor arena—it's crazy." He looked at Troy. "Did he tell you why it's confidential?"

"Because we can't let the competition see what we're doing." He winked, contorting one half of his face. "When we talk about secret stuff, Mr. Skelton winks. Like this." He winked again.

"What the hell." Teague's brows lowered, and his eyes took on the same hard, angry look he'd worn when she talked about her mother. Jodi remembered that expression from high school. *Teague against the world,* she thought. It was a non-stop battle.

"It's no big deal," she said. "He just doesn't want Troy to talk about how they train the horses." She shoved back the worries poking at the back of her brain. Skelton was apparently embroiled in some kind of cloak-and-dagger routine with his horses. It made her uncomfortable.

Teague stood and shoved his hands in his pockets, hunching his shoulders to keep his head from hitting the low ceiling.

"We'd better go, Troy," he said. "Start dinner."

She followed the two men down the steps and across the yard, Luna trotting in circles around them. Teague didn't look at Jodi or the dog until he'd hoisted Troy's bike into the bed of the pickup and opened the door to the truck cab.

"Well," he said. "See you."

He turned away and climbed into the truck, his Wranglers tightening over his trim behind, the muscles in his forearm flexing as he grabbed the steering wheel and climbed into the high seat. Jodi watched his profile as he started the engine. He looked more hurt than angry, and her heart went out to him. He got under her skin like no other man ever had. She'd never met a man who gave off sparks like Teague did—but she didn't need that distraction right now. Right now, she was going to mend what little family she had left.

"Come on, Luna." Teague leaned from the window and gestured toward the tailgate. "Hop up."

The dog stood by Jodi's side, staring at Teague like she'd never seen him before.

"She wants to stay with Jodi," Troy said. "She wants to visit longer."

Teague glared down at the dog.

"It's okay," Jodi said, bending down to stroke Luna's head. "Let her stay. I'll send her back with Troy tomorrow. Or you can pick her up later."

"You sure?" His eyes still had that hard, angry look. "I thought you promised your mother you'd stay away from me."

"I can *talk* to you."

"Well, hallelujah."

"Teague, we can be friends."

"You know, I don't really think so," he said. "I don't see how that could work."

He cranked the engine to life, hanging onto the key a little too long so the truck made an awful grating noise. Then he spun out, the pickup spitting gravel as it careened down the driveway.

Chapter 14

JODI SHOVED HER CHAIR BACK FROM THE TINY DESK IN her mother's cramped back room and clicked "shut down." As the computer screen went dark, she rubbed her knuckles in her bleary eyes. She'd rather shovel out twenty horse stalls than spend another minute crouched over the computer.

"The PayPal link works," she told her mother. "Now I just need to take some pictures of the merchandise and post them, and you'll be up and running."

"Wonderful. I'll model." Peggy Brand did a quick happy-dance in the doorway to the back room. She was wearing a vest dripping with beaded fringe, so her dance was accompanied by a click-clacking backbeat. "Then we'll just wait for the money to roll in."

"Right," Jodi said. Her mother had no idea how complicated Internet business could be. Neither had Jodi, until she started setting up the site. A well-thumbed copy of *Building a Web Site for Dummies* had given her the basics, but she had no idea if the thing was going to bring in any business.

She stood up and slipped into her denim jacket. Wyoming summer weather varied from ninety degrees down to forty. Today was a forty day.

"I'm off," she said. "Going to the Rotary lunch. I should be back by two or so."

"Who's taking you?"

Jodi rolled her eyes. She'd hoped to get through this without naming names. "Emmett Sage."

"Oh, honey, that's…"

"It's nothing." Jodi held up her palm in a traffic-cop gesture to stop her mother before the rhapsodizing got out of hand. "I went to him to get some release forms done up for the clinic, and he happened to mention that the speaker for today's lunch had backed out. It's a fund-raising opportunity, not a date."

"Well, at least you're not going with Teague."

Jodi laughed. "Teague in Rotary? Yeah, right."

"Oh, he's a member." Her mother's brows arrowed down in disapproval. "It's part of his plan to make himself over, I guess."

"Wow. You're kidding. Teague in Rotary?" Jodi cocked her head and stared at the ceiling, trying to picture Teague mingling with the pillars of Purvis. "I can't picture it."

"I know. Like I said…"

"Mom, stop." Jodi did the traffic cop thing again. "I promised not to see him, and I won't, but I'd appreciate it if you'd stop talking trash about him."

"Okay. Just remember what I told you. Like father, like son."

"Mom…"

Her mother made a zipping motion across her mouth and threw away an imaginary key.

"It's not like it's a big sacrifice anyway," Jodi said, tossing her hair as she headed for the door. "He's impossible to get along with."

—〰—

Teague hated Wednesday afternoons. The sheriff had insisted he needed to join Rotary if he was going to overcome his lousy reputation, but the weekly Wednesday lunch meetings made him remember why he'd been so ready to start trouble back when he spent his days stuck in school. There was still a part of him that wanted to raise hell when things got dull. Maybe if he stood up and shouted "fire" things would liven up a little.

He ran his index finger around the inside of his collar, tugging it away from his neck and stifling the urge to gag. The restaurant was way too warm. It didn't help any that Courtney had turned up. She'd commandeered a seat beside him, and kept rubbing up against him like a cat in heat. The girl was sex-crazed or something, and she was hardly subtle about it.

He wondered if she'd come with her father. He didn't see why she'd be a member herself; she didn't seem to do any kind of work besides dressing up and lugging that little dog around. Maybe she'd crashed the luncheon. He wouldn't be surprised. She'd been turning up everywhere he went for the past two weeks. He'd been nothing more than polite, but she took everything he said the wrong way. She seemed to think they were something more than friends.

He shifted away from her as Darla Black entered the room. The pharmacist stood in the doorway a beat too long once her eyes lit on him and Courtney. She watched them like the big bad wolf watching piglets at play, eating up the sight of them and no doubt planning to spew it onto the sidewalks of Purvis in a torrent of gossip and speculation.

Hell, the way Courtney was plastering herself to his side, he couldn't blame anybody for talking. All he could do was make it clear he was an unwilling participant. He picked up Courtney's hand and gently removed it from his thigh, but she flipped her hand over and intertwined her fingers with his, giving him a lash-fluttering smile. Now they were holding hands. How the hell had that happened? He shook himself loose, then saw her downcast face and gave her what he hoped was a brotherly pat on the leg.

He eyed the door, hoping somebody would come in and sit at his table. The sheriff's was already full, so he'd claimed an empty one rather than intrude on some other group. He wasn't exactly welcome here, despite the fact that he owned a successful business he'd started from scratch. For some reason, instead of seeing him as a self-made man to be admired, the people in Purvis seemed to see him as an upstart to be discouraged. Most people were barely civil, and a few were downright rude.

Okay, he'd been rude himself most of his life. Probably half the town had been on the receiving end of his teenaged acting-out. But he'd changed. Couldn't they see that? Reform school hadn't done the trick, but taking responsibility for his brother had made him a new man.

Darla sailed over to his table, her massive bosom thrusting through the crowd like the prow of a tall ship. Bucky Maines floundered in her wake, his face red from exertion—or from embarrassment; Teague couldn't tell which.

"May we join you, Mr. Treadwell?" Darla glanced back at Bucky, who flushed a little redder and pulled out the chair across from Courtney without waiting for Teague to answer. Darla lowered herself like a queen claiming her throne and folded her hands on the table. Leaning forward, she addressed Courtney.

"Hello, dear. I don't believe we've met."

"Oh!" Courtney offered a limp hand for shaking. "I'm Courtney Skelton. Of the Syracuse Skeltons. My father bought the Hunt ranch."

"Lovely to meet you." Darla licked her lips, no doubt anticipating the font of gossip she'd glean from this encounter. "I'm Darla Black. Of the Purvis Blacks. My family has been influential in this town for three generations."

Teague coughed, suppressing a guffaw. And he was Teague Treadwell, of the Purvis Treadwells. His family had been pestilential in this town for two generations.

He scanned the crowd again, seeking a rescuer. He didn't mind talking to Darla Black, but he'd never manage to keep a straight face if she and Courtney took to one-upping each other in some weird social status contest. Maybe Emmett Sage would show up. Emmett had been the Purvis High valedictorian well before Teague graduated, and went on to law school before coming back to take over his father's practice. Their social circles didn't exactly mesh, but they got along, which was more than Teague could say for just about anyone else in town.

Besides, Emmett was single and rich, so maybe Courtney would shift her attentions for a while and give Teague a break. Evidently, the place she came from was hard up for cowboys, and she thought Teague was some kind of shoot-em-up Western hero. She kept talking

about something she called "the cowboy code" and acting like he was some exotic species. He'd had about
enough of it.

Catching his eye, she flashed him a flirty smile. She
had on a neon green Western shirt with white nylon
fringe dangling off the yoke that shimmied every time
her boobs bounced—which was often. Her jeans were
white, and so tight he wondered how she could breathe.
She'd tried for an additional cowgirl touch by tying a
bandanna around her neck. It reminded him of the one
he put on Luna once in a while, except that instead of
old-fashioned paisley it was decorated with letters.
Some designer's initials, probably.

There were initials on her purse, too, and the dang
thing was enormous. He couldn't figure out why any
woman would need to carry around a suitcase full of
stuff everywhere she went.

"So tell me about those bucking horses you raise,"
she said. "How do you train them to buck?"

Teague stifled a snort that made him sound like one
of his own horses.

"Comes natural," he mumbled.

Courtney creased her forehead as if she'd been hit
with a sudden headache, but apparently, it was just a
thought. From his limited experience, he thought that
was probably a rare and possibly painful occasion
for her.

Actually, he was pretty sure her clinginess and dim-
witted comments were an act, but he couldn't figure out
why anyone would want to seem helpless and stupid.

"So you don't have to teach them how?" she asked in
her breathy, little-girl voice.

He was spared from answering by the appearance of Emmett Sage at the table. "Mind if we join you?"

Teague was nodding enthusiastic assent when he caught sight of Emmett's date.

Jodi Brand.

Perfect, he told himself bitterly. Emmett was just the guy for the town sweetheart. Smart, respectable, and a good guy to boot. He looked just right with Jodi, who was dressed in a crisp, clean chamois shirt that brought out the clear sky blue of her eyes and cowboy cut jeans that clung to her trim hips. There wasn't a shred of fringe to be seen, but she looked like the perfect cowgirl to Teague. Understated. Classy.

Real.

She looked comfortable, too—not nervous, like when she was with Teague. No doubt she knew that by going out with Emmett, she was playing her part, just like she was supposed to.

That was the difference between the two of them: She cared what other people thought, and Teague didn't. He'd done his best to break out of the mold they put him in, but he had no doubt Jodi would make every effort to fit into the cookie-cutter life everyone expected her to live.

And that was wrong. Just wrong. It was okay to try and please your parents, but some things were too important to leave up to other people. Nobody got to tell Teague who to love, and Jodi shouldn't let anybody tell her, either.

Well, she was obviously taking that promise to her mother seriously, but that didn't mean Teague had to abide by it. He hadn't made any promises to anyone, and he didn't see any reason why he shouldn't do his damndest to get Jodi to break hers.

———␣———

Jodi slid into the chair Emmett pulled out and glanced over at Teague. He was looking from her to Emmett, his eyes narrowed. She'd expected him to be upset when she turned up with Emmett, or even mad. Instead, he was smiling—but it was a predatory smile, the kind a coyote has when he notices the door to the chicken house is hanging open.

She didn't know what he was up to, and she didn't care. Courtney Skelton was snuggled up beside him like a kid with her favorite stuffed toy, flashing adoring glances his way every twenty seconds. He seemed to be ignoring her, but hey, he must have done something to get her stirred up. Jodi had seen him holding her hand when they walked in, but now he was acting like he barely knew her.

Teague really had changed. The old Teague would never have lied about having a girlfriend. She gave the girl a polite smile, and Courtney cleared her throat loudly, looking at Teague.

"Oh," he said. "Courtney, this is Jodi. Jodi, Courtney."

Jodi nodded. Courtney did the same, but her expression was enough to make icicles drip from the chandelier.

"There are other people at the table," she said.

"Oh. Sorry." Teague looked around wide-eyed, as if he'd just noticed everyone else, then introduced Darla and Bucky, and finally Emmett.

"Nice to meet you," Courtney said, addressing Emmett. She shifted in her chair so the fringe shimmied off her boobs. "Are you a cowboy too?"

"No." Emmett smiled, displaying his perfect teeth. "I'm a lawyer."

"Oh." Courtney looked down and fiddled with her fork. Jodi smothered a smile. Emmett probably wasn't used to girls being disappointed to hear about his lucrative profession.

"Well, I just think Teague's work is so interesting," Courtney said. "I've been asking him about how he trains his bucking horses, but he's too modest to tell me."

Jodi glanced at Teague. The girl was gazing up into his face like he'd just sprouted wings and a halo, but he was pretty much ignoring her. Jodi didn't blame him. The girl was hard to take seriously.

So why had he taken her to lunch? There was no way someone like Teague could have a real relationship with someone that shallow. And stupid. And fake.

Jodi wasn't jealous or anything. She had no right to be. But the girl was all wrong for Teague. Maybe he'd lied because he was ashamed of himself for dating her.

"Yeah, he works awfully hard on those horses," Bucky said. "Teaching them to buck is one thing, but teaching them to spin is really tough." He tapped his temple. "Gets you dizzy."

Darla started to say something, but Bucky gave her a nudge and she pursed her lips and clammed up. Hazing Easterners was a traditional cowboy sport, and he wasn't about to let her spoil the fun.

"Yeah, it gets tiring, running around and around like that," Jodi said. "And that's nothing compared to all the wrecks you have once the horse starts to get good. Teague must hit the dirt fifty times a day." She dropped her voice to a whisper. "He lands on his head a lot."

She was totally gunning for Teague, and he was looking right at her—but for some reason, he didn't react to her jibe. He just stared, to the point that Jodi looked down to make sure she still had her clothes on. When she looked back up, a slow smile was spreading over Teague's face and she wanted to slap him. He'd done that all through school—looked at her like her bra was showing or something, or tapped his mouth like she had something on her lip. Then he'd laugh when she reacted.

Some things never change. She resolved not to look at him anymore, in spite of the hot flush that told her his eyes were still smoking holes in her shirt.

"Oh, Teague, that's terrible," Courtney was saying.

"What?" He turned away from Jodi and blinked, obviously confused. "Sorry. I was thinking about—something else." He looked back at Jodi, the sneaky coyote smile returning.

"The way you risk your life every day training them to buck," Courtney said. "I knew it was more complicated than you said! I hate to think of you endangering yourself like that."

Judging from the way the girl's breasts were heaving, she actually enjoyed thinking of Teague risking his life. Obviously, the idea turned her on. Jodi figured she was probably the kind of girl who went to rodeos to see the wrecks.

On second thought, she'd probably never been to a rodeo.

"The horses buck on their own," Teague told Courtney. "It's, um, automatic."

Courtney gave Teague a gentle slap on the arm. "Oh,

you cowboys. So modest. I know it takes a lot of training
to make a good bucking horse."

Mercifully, the group's president was at the podium
banging a gavel, so the game was at a halt. The speaker
droned through the minutes from the last meeting, elicit-
ing a bored "aye" from the group when he asked for their
approval. Then everybody sang a couple songs. They
always sang. It was goofy, but it was a long-standing
Rotary tradition.

Today the songs were "Home on the Range" and
"Don't Fence Me In." As usual, Darla's dramatic so-
prano sailed above the crowd, giving the simple songs an
operatic boost. Teague moved his mouth along with the
words, but Jodi could tell he wasn't really singing. She
could hear Emmett's passable tenor beside her, and did
her best to keep her own voice on key. Courtney made
a game effort, but she didn't know the words and soon
fell silent.

Her purse was another story, though. As Darla's voice
rose into a high tremolo, the purse let out a single, soaring note, high-pitched as a police siren. Courtney gave
the bag a nudge with her foot and the noise stopped.

"Some ringtone," Teague whispered as the song ended.

"Oh, no, that's Honeybucket," Courtney said. She
opened the purse and tilted it forward, showing its contents
to her tablemates. Her tiny apricot-colored puffball of a
dog nestled inside. Courtney made a kissing noise and his
bright-eyed, smiling face thrust itself out of the purse.

"Honeybucket," Jodi said, trying not to laugh. "Such
a cute name."

"He's a teacup Pomeranian," Courtney said. "I take
him everywhere."

Jodi imagined Teague taking Luna with him to Rotary meetings. The collie would have all the members rounded up in a corner by now.

"What does it do?" Bucky asked dubiously, nodding toward the tiny dog. Ranchers expected a pet to have a purpose—like herding cows or keeping the rabbits down. But this little guy looked useless.

"He loves me." Courtney smiled and tucked the little dog's head back down into the purse. "Shh, baby. You're not supposed to be here," she whispered. She wagged a warning finger at the pup. "Don't you get us in trouble now!"

"And now our speaker for the day," the president intoned. "I'm sure you all remember Jodi Brand from her days as Miss Rodeo USA. She's starting a non-profit venture I think you'll all be interested in supporting. Jodi?"

She stood and brushed imaginary crumbs off her lap, then put on her best rodeo queen smile and headed for the front of the room.

Time to shine.

Chapter 15

TEAGUE WATCHED JODI GO, SMILING TO HIMSELF. Somehow, she'd gotten herself pushed to the front of the list of speakers waiting to pimp their causes to the Rotary crowd. Even after all these years, the girl had pull.

She stood and made her way through the crowd to the front of the room, smiling and nodding, patting old friends on the shoulder and squeezing proffered hands as she passed. Stepping up to the podium, she adjusted the microphone and smiled, scanning the crowd.

"Well, hello, Purvis!" she said. "I've missed you!"

The attendees burst into applause, accompanied by cowboy hoots and much foot-stomping. Obviously, Jodi was still their hometown sweetheart. After a few gracious nods that reminded Teague of her rodeo queen days, she began to outline the benefits of horseback riding for the handicapped. She was eloquent and impassioned, and by the time she finished, Teague was ready to bankroll the project all by himself if he had to. It sounded like a winner to him.

"So what I'm looking for is a small grant to buy feed and supplies. And if anybody's kids have outgrown their boots and saddles, we could sure use some child-sized tack. We're a registered non-profit, so you'd get a write-off for the donation." She scanned the room, obviously hoping for a response. "We need horses, too. Older ones with good manners. If you've got a retired roping horse on your hands, or an old barrel horse, it's a great way for them to be useful in their later years."

A man at the front table stood and Jodi nodded toward him.

"I wonder if you'd go talk to my daughter's Girl Scout troop," he said. "I think you'd be a great role model for them."

"Sure." Jodi smiled, and Teague couldn't blame her. Finally, she'd be a role model for what she was *doing*, instead of what she was wearing. Much as he'd teased her during her reign over the rodeo, he'd known she wasn't a superficial person. This had to feel good.

"I'd love to," she said. "We could even do a field trip to visit the horses and show them the exercises. What grade is Beth in now, Mr. Haines?"

Count on Jodi to know everybody's name. She'd always been like that.

"She's in sixth grade. But I wanted you to talk about being a rodeo queen. How to carry yourself, how important good grades are, all that."

Jodi's face fell, but she pasted the smile back on. "Sure, I could do that." Her voice was a little flat, but Teague doubted if anyone noticed.

"Next Friday? They meet after school."

Reluctantly, Jodi nodded. "Sure. I'll be there."

"And could you wear your uniform? You know, your queen clothes? I'm sure the girls would love that."

"Sure."

Another member stood up, and another. Jodi had trouble keeping up with all the requests for her rodeo queen expertise, but not another word was said about funding the clinic.

She headed back toward their table when the questions stopped, but one person after another demanded her attention. At the rate she was going, it would take her half an hour to get back to her seat.

Courtney nudged Teague's shoulder. "*She* was a rodeo queen?" She gave Jodi an assessing look. "She looks like a field hand."

"Jodi wasn't just any old rodeo queen," Teague said. "She was Miss Rodeo USA. She modeled for Wrangler, too." He couldn't believe he was spouting Jodi's pageant accomplishments like they were good things. He'd hated the whole rodeo queen thing. Jodi had always been from another class—another world, even—but her crown had really taken her away from him. Rodeo queens were all about old-fashioned Western values—home, family—all the things the Treadwells were hopelessly bad at.

"Well, she sure doesn't look like a rodeo queen now," Courtney sniffed. "And if she's a model, what's she doing *here*?"

"She just told you." Teague spoke sharply, and Courtney narrowed her eyes for half a second before she caught herself and pasted on a flirty smile

"Well, she said she needs older horses. Already trained ones. I guess she's not a real cowgirl. Not brave, like you." She squeezed his arm again. "Training those big, mean bucking broncos the way you do. I just can't get over that."

"Well, working with handicapped kids is a lot more of a contribution to society."

Courtney shrugged. "But you need funding for something like that, and it doesn't look like she's going to get anything out of this group." She looked up at the ceiling and tapped her chin with one manicured finger, pantomiming deep thought. "What she needs to do is a fund-raiser."

"Like a spaghetti dinner? Or a raffle?"

"Oh, no, nothing like that. I was thinking something bigger."

"Like what?"

"Like a polo benefit." She straightened in her seat, back on familiar ground. "My dad and his friends have all kinds of money, but they don't much like parting with it—unless it's something to do with polo."

"So you want us to put on some kind of polo party?"

It wasn't a bad idea. Jodi was only working at the boutique until she could get the clinic started, so the faster she got funding, the less time she'd be spending with her mother. Maybe then she'd forget about that stupid promise.

Especially if Teague did a lot of the fund-raising, and helped with the clinic, and generally made himself indispensable.

He felt a whoosh of excitement lift his heart. When he really set his mind to something, he always succeeded. That's how he'd worked his way out of the trailer. If he applied that same dogged determination to this project, he might not have to give up on Jodi after all.

He wouldn't push her. He wouldn't try to talk her into anything. He'd just be the best friend she'd ever had, and let nature take its course.

"We could put on a barbecue after a game," he said.

Courtney wrinkled her nose. "No, they wouldn't come to anything like that. I was thinking an actual polo match."

"That sounds like a big project," Bucky said.

"Oh, I've done it before, back in Syracuse," Courtney said. "I've always done a lot of work with non-profits."

"Well, I don't know much about polo," Teague said. "But if you could put it together, I'd be glad to print up flyers or something."

"I was thinking you could *play*," Courtney said. "You and some of your cowboy friends." She straightened and glanced around the table, pulling Emmett and Darla into the conversation. "Bucky's ordered all the equipment you'd need, and the clothes. And I've seen ranch horses on TV, cutting cattle. They're quick and nimble, just like polo ponies. A little bigger, but that might be a good thing, if you didn't mind fouling once in a while."

"Buck, you ordered those sissy clothes?" Teague had seen how polo players dressed, in tight pants and high boots. "You're not getting me to wear tights."

"They're breeches," Courtney said. "And they're not sissy."

"How 'bout we do something else horse related?" Emmett asked.

"Yeah, like a cutting competition, or a rodeo?" Teague scowled. "Something where we don't have to dress like… like girlie men."

She tilted her nose in the air. "Polo players are hardly girlie men. They're *very* masculine. And my father's friends would never come to a rodeo. That's way too blue-collar for them."

"We'd make fools of ourselves trying to play polo."

"No you wouldn't. It's like playing hockey on horseback. If you're good riders and your horses are well trained, you'll be fine. And just think." She scooted her chair closer to the table. "It would be the cowboys versus the aristocrats. Like a Johnson County War of Polo. That's how we'd promote it."

"That's brilliant," Emmett said, earning a glowing smile from Courtney.

"I agree." Darla's dark eyes were sparkling. She was probably thinking of all the gossip the matchup would lead to. If a bunch of rough-and-tumble cowboys got together with the *nouveau riche* newcomers, sparks were bound to fly.

"But your dad has professional players, right?" Teague asked. "They'd slaughter us."

"It doesn't matter who wins," Courtney said. "It's the entry fees that count. It would be such a novelty—all my dad's friends would come. And I'll bet everyone in town would come to cheer on the cowboy team. Don't you think?" She looked at Darla.

"I agree." The pharmacist smoothed down her skirt. "I'd be happy to publicize it amongst my circle. Which is substantial."

Teague grinned. She was still trying to one-up Courtney. Darla's contacts might not be as wealthy, but she knew everyone for miles around.

Courtney nodded. "Let's do it, then. Okay, Teague?"

He hesitated. Taking on this project meant he'd have to learn to play polo—and he'd need Courtney for that. The two of them would be thrown together even more, and he had no doubt she'd try to take advantage of the situation.

But it would be a giant step toward helping Jodi fund the clinic.

Courtney saw him dithering and went in for the kill. "The last benefit match made ten thousand dollars for the March of Dimes."

Teague widened his eyes. Ten thousand dollars. Hell, he'd play polo naked if it would get Jodi ten thousand dollars.

Where was Jodi, anyway? He craned his neck and looked around the room, finally spotting her standing at another table, no doubt talking to more old friends.

"Teague?" Courtney looked irritated, and he wondered if she thought this was an actual date. He hadn't invited her. He hadn't even asked her to sit with him. She'd just appropriated him all of a sudden.

But the polo match was a good idea. Or at least, the ten thousand dollars was.

"Let's do it," he said. "Where do we start?"

Honeybucket let out an excited yip, and Courtney fished him out of her purse and cradled him in her arms. "You'll need at least three other players, with horses," she said. "And supplies from Bucky's. They should be in within a few days, right, Bucky?"

Bucky nodded, and Teague almost laughed. Courtney had evidently been planning this for a while. He supposed it was a good way for her to get involved in the community. Unfortunately, he suspected it was also a way for her to get involved with him—but her plan was going to backfire, because in the end, it would set him up with Jodi.

"We must be going," Darla said, pushing her chair back. Bucky rose with her, taking her purse without being asked. Teague stifled a smile. Ol' Bucky was totally whipped. And pretty darn happy about it, judging from the look on his face as he watched Darla.

"Courtney, it's been a pleasure," Darla said. "You'll be in touch regarding our project?"

"Oh, yes," Courtney said. "Definitely."

Teague and Emmett stood until Darla and Bucky had left the table, then sat back down and turned to Courtney.

"So where do we start with this thing?" Emmett asked.

"Well, Teague should meet me at my house tomorrow morning."

Emmett sat back, looking disappointed.

"You want to come along?" Teague asked.

"Sure. I…"

"Can you ride?" Courtney asked. "You have to be a really good horseman to do this."

"Guess I'd be better on the organizational side," Emmett said.

"Well, if we need any legal forms, we'll let you know." Courtney turned to Teague. "So when you come tomorrow, don't knock. You don't want to wake my dad." She wriggled with excitement, setting the fringe on her shirt to swaying. "He doesn't like me to watch the practices, but Gustaldo doesn't mind. That's one of the players from Argentina. Gustaldo likes me. I'd like him too, except I met you." She gave his arm a squeeze.

"Gustaldo?"

"Oh, don't be jealous," she said. "He barely speaks English."

Teague hadn't been jealous—just curious—but it didn't seem polite to point that out.

"They start at six," Courtney continued. "I'll tell Gus to leave the arena unlocked. If we sit up in the stands and keep quiet, the guys won't tell Daddy." She tittered. "They like me too." She looked down at the dog in her arms. "They don't like Honeybucket, though. They say he riles up the horses. *Rata, rata*, they say. That means rat."

She held the dog up to her face and made a kissy face. "And Honeybucket's not a rat, is he? He's mama's little baby dog, that's what he is."

With its pointy nose and sharp little teeth, the dog really did bear a striking resemblance to a rat, but Teague thought it was better not to mention that.

"So will you come?" she asked, dropping her voice to a normal register.

"Okay." Actually, the whole thing sounded pretty interesting. He'd go watch, and see if it was something he and his friends could do without making absolute fools of themselves.

"You have to be careful, because it gets kind of rough sometimes," Courtney said. "You could get thrown. I'd hate for that to happen." She looked up at him and blinked her big blue eyes.

He laughed uneasily. "I've been thrown before. And I doubt polo's that dangerous."

"Oh, but it is. Sometimes the horses crash into each other. Once my father broke his leg. And one of our friends was actually killed. He fell off his horse and was trampled." She shuddered violently, making the fringe jiggle again. Teague was starting to think she'd give Darla a run for her money in the drama queen department.

"If I can stick a bronc, I imagine I could sit one of your polo ponies."

"Oh, do you ride in the rodeo?" Courtney practically squealed.

"I did—for a while. Still do, sometimes."

She shoved the little dog back in her bag and clapped her hands like a kid at the circus. "Oh, that's exciting."

Teague almost laughed. Everything seemed to get

this girl excited. The old Teague would have taken advantage of that—but he knew better now. Sex without strings attached didn't hold much meaning, and besides, he had a feeling Courtney would tie strings to everything, and she'd hang on like a rookie rider in a wild horse race.

Chapter 16

JODI EDGED SIDEWAYS THROUGH THE CROWDED TABLES, hoping her face wasn't sagging as badly as her spirits. The crowd had welcomed her so enthusiastically. They'd listened so raptly to her speech. She'd been sure they'd award her a grant on the spot, or at least move that it be considered—but her reputation had somehow outshone her accomplishments. Nobody cared that she'd been to college. Nobody cared that she was trying to help the handicapped. All they wanted was Miss Rodeo USA.

She stopped to greet the Rotary president, who smiled sympathetically.

"Sorry, hon," he said. "They didn't really listen, did they? Tell you what. We're having a board meeting on the twelfth. I'll see if you can't come talk to us then, okay? It might be a better setting."

Jodi nodded. "Sure. Thank you."

"And you might want to dress up next time," his wife said, smiling brightly. "You'll have much better luck with all these men looking like—well, you know, like you used to. I think you'll find it much easier to get what you want that way."

Jodi knew the woman was right, but heck, she could get what she wanted by sleeping with all of them too. That didn't mean she was willing to do it.

As the room began to clear, Courtney picked up her purse and let out a gasp.

"Honeybucket's gone!" She stood, clutching her purse to her chest, and glanced wildly around the room. "Oh, find him, please, Teague? He's so tiny! He could be hurt!"

Teague pushed back his chair. "I'll find him," he said. "He can't have gone far."

He made his way through the crowd, looking under tables and chairs and making occasional kissy noises. A few club members gave him sideways looks, but he was used to that.

He made a full circuit of the room without spotting the little puffball. Setting his hands on his hips, he surveyed the room and spotted the men's room door, propped wide open. Stepping inside, he spotted a familiar set of fluffy hindquarters through an open stall door. Honeybucket had hiked himself up on the rim of a toilet and was slurping water with his tiny pink tongue. As Teague watched, the pup tilted forward, kicked his little hind legs, and slid into the bowl. Letting out a panicked yap, he scrabbled at the slippery porcelain, his eyes bugging out with the effort.

"Damn." Gingerly, Teague picked the puppy up by the scruff of his neck and carried him to the sink. "Your mistress is not going to be pleased. Guess I'd better clean you up."

He turned on the faucet and went to work, using hand soap from the wall dispenser to scrub the critter's fine, fluffy coat. Wet, Honeybucket looked more like a squirrel than a dog. At least he was a good-natured little thing, still grinning despite the ordeal of a bath. If he'd just been normal-sized, Teague might have liked him.

He squeezed the water out of the matted fur as best he could, then rubbed Honeybucket down with a paper towel. The dog still looked like a drowned rat.

"Here, buddy." Teague punched the automatic hand dryer to life and held Honeybucket in the stream of warm air. "This'll get you dry."

Honeybucket squirmed and gave a sharp yip.

"What the hell?" The sheriff stepped inside and stared at Teague, who was turning the animal slowly in front of the dryer, working on the rotisserie principle. "What is that thing?"

"It's Courtney's dog," Teague muttered.

"The Skelton girl?"

Teague nodded.

The sheriff grinned. "Moving up in the world, aren't you?"

"Not really." Teague shifted the dog to dry its belly and frowned. "We're not dating or anything. I don't even know why she's here."

"I do." The sheriff waggled his eyebrows. "The girl's all over you, son."

"I know. I don't know how to get rid of her without being rude."

"Just stay away from her," the sheriff suggested. "It shouldn't be too hard. It's not like you run with the same crowd, or have the same interests."

"Right." Teague thought of the polo game and suppressed an urge to smack his forehead. Grimacing, he held out the dog. "Here," he said. "Hold this."

That stopped the conversation. The sheriff stared down at the animal in dismay while Teague washed and dried his hands, then grabbed the dog and gave the sheriff a nod. "Better get him back to his mistress," he said.

He dodged out of the men's room and made his way to Courtney, who was sitting at the table, tapping one impatient foot. Apparently she wasn't capable of looking for the dog herself. She probably had servants for that at home.

"Here you go," Teague said, handing Honeybucket over. The little guy wasn't quite dry, and his hair stuck out in rigid spikes that made him look like a punk rock Pomeranian.

"What did you *do* to him?" Courtney tried to finger-comb Honeybucket's hair, but she got caught in his mattered undercoat, which had congealed into a felted bodysuit beneath the spikes.

"Gave him a bath." Teague stifled a smile. "He fell in the toilet."

"Oh. Oh!" Courtney shoved Honeybucket back into his bag and waved her hands in the air. "Oh! You dirty thing!" She gave Teague a horrified glance, then ran off toward the ladies' room, still shrieking. "You dirty dog! You dirty, dirty dog!"

Teague watched her go, then realized the room had gone quiet. A low hum of whispering had replaced the din of conversation, and every eye that wasn't staring after Courtney was turned toward him.

Dang. If he had a reputation to ruin, that would have done it for sure. As it was, it just dug the hole he was in a little deeper.

Teague almost skipped the next morning's surreptitious

polo expedition. Things with Courtney were getting complicated.

But he'd heard about the Argentine players who sold their skills to rich polo sponsors in the States. They were supposed to be some of the best horsemen in the world. Maybe he'd learn something he could use.

And then there was that ten thousand dollars...

The sun was just starting to streak the eastern sky with pink and amber when he pulled up to the Skelton mini-manse. Two stories tall, with a long front porch and an assortment of dormers and turrets, it sported so much white-painted gingerbread that it looked like a mad Victorian architect's delirium dream. Courtney was waiting for him on the porch, dressed in her usual over-the-top Western regalia. It was quite a picture, the overdressed girl on the lace-bedecked porch. The kind of thing you'd see photographed in artsy black and white in a book called *The New West*, or something.

It would be a sad book—one of those that showed the real West eroding, getting hijacked by its own romantic image.

Courtney trotted out to the truck and climbed in. "Park the car behind the barn," she said. "That way Daddy won't see us."

"Why's this such a big secret?" Teague asked.

"Daddy's just weird," she said. "He doesn't like anyone to see the horses work. It's some kind of big secret." She tossed off an eye-roll that would have made a Valley Girl proud.

The two of them entered the arena through a side door Gustaldo had apparently left unlocked as promised. Climbing a set of metal bleachers, she led him to a seat high up in the corner, shadowed by the arena's tin roof. She slid close to him and put one hand on his thigh, then the other. With no dog to hang onto, she was free to paw him as much as she wanted. He tensed reflexively.

"Ooh, muscles," she said, kneading his leg.

He jerked it away.

"We'll have to be quiet once the trainers get here." She didn't seem to notice his discomfort. In fact, she scooted toward him again, edging over until her hip touched his, and blinked up into his face. He stared down at the empty arena. Courtney offered up an odd combination of innocence, helplessness, and brazen sexuality that made it stunningly clear she was his for the taking. Some men liked that kind of thing. Teague didn't. Not anymore.

"It's a good thing Daddy sleeps in, so you can see this." Courtney made a sour face. "He never gets up before noon. What a jerk."

It sounded like typical adolescent rebellion—the kind Courtney should have outgrown by now. Teague doubted her father was that bad. He'd never seen the guy drunk, stumbling down the street, or crouched over a beer at a bar in mid-afternoon. That was about all Teague knew to ask for in a father—sobriety.

"He's successful, though. And it seems like he's given you a good life."

Courtney huffed out a mirthless laugh. "Hardly. Unless you think it's good to have your mother kicked out of the house while your dad takes up with some floozy half his age."

Teague didn't have an answer for that one. His own parents had been as bad as parents could get, but Courtney's situation did sound kind of difficult.

"And he pretty much ignores me. He's too busy with his polo team." She rolled her eyes. "Mummy said he might as well flush his fortune down the toilet, and I think she's right. You wouldn't believe what he pays his players. All so he can show off to his rich friends." She slumped in her seat. "She says he's going through money like water, and he'll be broke in ten years if he keeps it up. Marissa—that's the floozy—actually encourages him." She thrust out her lower lip in a pout. "There won't be anything left for me when he dies. Not a dime."

Teague's stomach twisted with disgust. He'd had issues with his own dad—worse issues, he was sure, than Courtney had ever faced. But he'd never wished him dead. Not for real.

"Why do you live with your dad, then?" he asked. "Why not stay with your mom?"

"Well, *duh*," she said. "He's a *lot* richer. And anyway, she's busy looking for another husband." She gazed out the window. "But if Daddy's little slut has a baby, I bet he'll toss me out and she'll get everything. I found her birth control pills in her purse, and she hasn't been taking them." She laughed mirthlessly. "Mom said not to worry, though. She said the old man can't get it up anymore."

Teague was saved from responding by a beam of light slashing across the arena floor. The double doors at the end of the oval opened and two men in breeches and high boots strolled in, leading horses decked out with braided tails, red leg wraps, and tiny postage-stamp saddles. The men carried long, slender mallets, swinging them as they walked and chattering in what sounded like Spanish.

"That's Alejandro and Esteban," Courtney whispered. "Alejandro was on the team that won the world championship last year."

Teague eyed the horses critically. They were small, about fourteen hands, and wiry. They'd be nimble, no doubt, but they didn't have much muscle, and he wondered if they could put on much speed.

The trainers led their horses to the center of the ring and began swinging their mallets in circles around the animals' heads. Teague could hear the whir of air as the mallets spun and jabbed, almost touching the animals.

"That's to get them accustomed to the action," Courtney whispered. "They can't flinch when the rider takes a shot."

One of the horses twitched and took a half-step back. The trainer led it around in a circle, then squared it up and started up swinging the mallet again. The exercise went on for about twenty minutes, the trainers forcing the horses to move every time they flinched. Finally, once the animals had stood stoically for five minutes or so, the two men mounted.

The animals seemed well trained, but Teague wasn't impressed with their performance. One seemed stiff on the forehand, and the other stumbled on a lead change as his rider goaded him toward a small white ball in the center of the arena. Approaching the ball at a gallop, the rider gave his mallet a roundhouse swing and whacked the ball across the arena.

"See? You could do that," Courtney said.

Teague shrugged. Sure he could, but it didn't seem like something he'd want to pursue once the fund-raiser was over. At least cutting competitions had some application to the real world. Same with rodeo. Nobody broke horses by bucking them out anymore, but it was still a genuine ranch skill.

The two horsemen thundered after the ball. One swung for a hit, but despite the exercise with the mallet his horse shied at the last minute. The rider shouted an oath and yanked hard on one rein to spin the animal in place, swinging the mallet perilously close to the animal's head.

"Hey," Teague said. "That's kind of rough."

"You can't tolerate it when a horse shies," Courtney said. "Somebody could get hurt."

"We can only hope," Teague muttered.

"It's hard to tell from this how exciting it is when they're playing for real," Courtney said. She obviously hadn't heard him, which was just as well. "There are four players on a team, and the action's so fast, a horse can only handle it for seven minutes. That's how long a period is. It's called a 'chukkah.'"

"Interesting," Teague lied. He'd already seen enough. The riders were manhandling the horses, and for what? So they could play a game? It didn't make sense.

"So don't you think you could do that?" Courtney urged. Teague had a feeling she'd keep after him until he said yes. He felt like that horse, being pushed and spun, with the mallet swinging closer and closer.

"It's really the only way you'll get my dad's friends to help with funding," Courtney continued. "That rodeo queen act will never get a dime out of them." She tossed her head. "Too low class."

Teague grimaced. Being Miss Rodeo USA had lifted Jodi up into the highest echelon of Purvis's small-town society, far out of his reach. He'd spent years working his way up to her level, and now Courtney was calling it "low class."

What did that say about where he'd started? What did it say about who he was now?

What did it say about Courtney?

Suddenly the air in the arena seemed close and hot. He tugged at his collar and glanced right and left, wondering if there was a way to leave without being seen. He'd had enough of polo.

He'd had enough of Courtney.

"I don't mean *she's* low class," Courtney said, as if she'd sensed her mistake. "It's just that most of the people in my circle don't understand the cowboy code, you know?"

Teague didn't understand the cowboy code either. It was something you read about in books, or heard about in movies. Really, there was no cowboy code. He and his friends just tried to be decent human beings, that was all. They helped each other when they were down and razzed each other when they weren't. That was about it.

But Courtney apparently thought she knew all about cowboy morality.

"They don't understand what's *real*, you know?" she continued. "What really matters in life. Like being honest and forthright and a true buckaroo."

Had she really just said that? What was she raised on, Roy Rogers? Or was that from *Barney & Friends*?

"I just know you'll win the match if you try." She snuggled closer.

Teague looked down at the polo players, who were cantering figure eights in the arena, practicing lead changes. They rode well, he had to admit, but the horses seemed reluctant, as if they were being forced to perform. Their ears were pinned back, their eyes wild.

"Yeah, I think you're right," Teague said. "I think we'll win for sure."

"Well, come on then," she said, rising from her seat. "Come and meet my dad. You can issue the challenge right now."

Chapter 17

"I THOUGHT YOU DIDN'T WANT YOUR DAD TO KNOW I was here," Teague said as they climbed down the bleachers.

"Well, we won't tell him you watched a practice. But I want him to know you're here," Courtney said as they crossed the yard. "He needs to know I have my own life, my own friends. I do what I want."

Teague stopped dead. "Look, are you just hanging out with me to bug your dad? Because I'm not going to be a part of that."

"Oh, no." Courtney turned and plastered herself to his front, lacing her arms around his neck. "You know I love you, Teague. I mean, this is the real thing."

Teague gave her an incredulous look as she looked up at him with an expectant smile.

"Uh, Courtney," he said. "That's—I'm not looking for that, okay? I mean, we're just friends. Sorry."

He shoved his hands in his pockets and cursed himself. He knew he should stay away from this girl. He sure as hell didn't want to be loved by a woman he didn't even like. Besides, when girls loved you, they eventually wanted to marry you and have babies, and Teague's future plans definitely didn't include either activity. Especially not with Courtney.

"It's okay, Teague." Courtney slapped his arm playfully and he relaxed. She'd just been kidding. He should have realized.

"I know it's hard for real men like you to express yourselves," she continued.

"Uh, yeah."

Shoot. She was right, but not in the way she thought. What was hard to express was the fact that he was just here for the polo game, so Jodi could get her clinic started. How did you tell a woman you were only using her to get money for the girl you really cared about?

Hell, Shakespeare would have trouble coming up with a line for that one.

"Look, I should go," he began. "This isn't…"

"Oh, come on." She waved toward the house and dropped her voice into an urgent whisper. "I already told Daddy about this. If you don't talk to him, he'll think I screwed it up. Don't you dare make me look stupid." Grabbing his arm, she dragged him up the steps and through the front door, then motioned for him to wait while she headed down a hallway to the right.

Teague twisted his hat in his hands and tried not to look as nervous as he felt. The place was like a palace, with a soaring cathedral ceiling that swept up to a stained-glass skylight depicting knights on horseback on eight separate panes that radiated out from a sunburst in the center. A balcony edged by a carved wooden railing bordered the room on three sides. He wasn't a nervous guy, but this place was somehow intimidating. It made him feel totally out of his element. He wondered if that was deliberate.

After what felt like an hour but was probably only ten minutes, Courtney emerged from the hallway.

"Daddy will see you now," she said. She lowered her voice to a whisper. "Tell him about how it's for

charity. And don't tell him you're going to beat him."
She giggled. "Tell him it's an exhibition match."

Teague followed her down the hall and through a
massive oak doorway into a room lined with books.
Skelton was seated at a desk at the far end, backed by
a window that threw his features into shadow. He was
a slight man, made smaller by his massive leather desk
chair. As Teague entered, he leaned forward and folded
his hands on the table.

"Daddy, this is Teague Treadwell. Teague, this
is Daddy." She glanced from one to the other, then
turned toward the door. "I'll let you two talk." She
skipped out of the room. Evidently she didn't want
to spend any more time in her father's presence than
she had to.

"Mitch Skelton." The man rose and held out a hand.
Teague grasped it in his own and winced at the cold
clamminess of the man's limp handshake.

"Nice to meet you, sir. I don't know how much
Courtney's told you about our idea."

"A polo match, she said." Skelton dropped bone-
lessly back into his chair and crossed his ankle over one
knee. "A fund-raiser."

"Right." Teague shifted from one foot to the other.
Something about the man's air of confidence reminded
him of his high school principal. He felt like he'd been
called in for a scolding. "There's a—a woman in the
area who's starting a therapy riding clinic. Courtney
suggested that a benefit polo match pitting your riders
against some locals might draw attention."

"I suppose it would," Skelton said. "Courtney informs
me you would be competing yourself?"

"That was her suggestion. It would be the cowboys versus the seasoned players. I'm sure we'd make a poor showing, but it would bring out the town to watch."

"Hmf." Skelton looked down at his hands. "Well, I was never one to turn down a challenge. Though it would hardly be a challenge competing against *cowboys*." He looked Teague up and down as he pronounced the label. "You're hardly the kind of competitive player my men are accustomed to."

Teague felt anger rising in his chest. He swallowed it down and cleared his throat. "I think we'll surprise you, sir. Meanwhile, we'll need to establish a date—say a month or two from now? My team will need time to learn the game."

The tips of Skelton's lips turned up slightly in what apparently passed for a smile. "You'll need more time than that. But you choose the date." He leaned back in his chair. "As you can see, my time is my own. I spend a few hours a day studying the market, and the rest pursuing my passion for polo."

"Right. You're in investing?"

The man nodded. "After I retired from my firm, I began to dabble in the stock market. I've met with much success." He tilted his head back, looking down his nose at Teague. "Many of my friends have substantial sums to invest."

"Right." Teague had managed to resist clocking the guy, although he'd had to suppress a picture in his mind of Skelton pitching backward through the window, chair and all. "I have some substantial funds myself. Just sold a colt the other day for ten thousand. Cash."

He would have kicked himself if Skelton hadn't been

looking. It was low class to talk about money—but he couldn't let this pathetic little man think he was some field hand. He was a successful businessman—and he'd earned his money with hard work and smart choices, the same as anyone.

"Ten thousand?" Skelton steepled his fingers and raised his head, staring down his nose at Teague. "A substantial sum for you. Have you considered how you'll invest it?"

Teague tried not to take offense at Skelton's snobbishness. Judging from the elaborate house and pricey trappings, the guy was a brilliant investor. Sometimes smart people were kind of awkward socially. He'd give the guy a break.

He gave a lot of guys breaks these days. That's how he'd managed to stay out of trouble for so long. The old Teague would have decked this guy, or at least sworn and stormed out.

The new Teague kind of envied the old Teague sometimes.

"I haven't given much thought to investing," he said.

Skelton rose and came around the desk to sit casually on the corner, letting one leg dangle carelessly. "I could make some suggestions," he said.

"Sure," Teague said.

"Futures are the way to go these days," Skelton said. "Prices are set to rise across the board."

Teague laughed. "I have no idea how to go about doing that kind of thing," he said. "Generally I opt for something a lot simpler. A mutual fund is about as complex as my finances get."

"I could possibly assist you," Skelton said. "I

understand you've been seeing my daughter. That means it's in my best interest to help you move up in the world."

"Your daughter and I are just friends," Teague said. "I don't think you need to worry about my position in the world." He shoved his hands in his pockets and rocked back on his heels. "I'm about as far up as I want to go. Thanks, though."

"Hm." Skelton stared down at the rug for a moment. "Courtney told me otherwise."

"Well, she might be taking things a bit more seriously than she should," Teague said. "I'll make sure I tell her different."

"I can understand your concern over the difference in your backgrounds," Skelton said. "However, my daughter has always been drawn to the, shall we say, rustic type. And things can change. As I said, if you put the money in my hands we could possibly parlay that ten thousand into a substantial sum by year's end." He stretched his lips in what appeared to be his version of a smile and narrowed his eyes. Courtney didn't look much like her dad, but the expression reminded Teague of the scheming look he'd caught on Courtney's face a couple times when she didn't think he was looking. "If you'd let me advise you, we might be able to turn you into a fit match for my daughter. I know that would make both of you happy."

Teague felt his civilized persona shattering like glass, leaving Old Teague jutting his chin and clenching his fists.

"You don't know a thing about me," he said. "And besides, it's July. Anything that would parlay that money very far that fast would probably be a little on the sketchy side. So thank you, but I'll stick to my original plan and put it in the bank."

Skelton shrugged. "Suit yourself. But if you're not willing to better yourself, you might look for a match amongst your equals." He stood and whisked his hands together, as if dusting flour from his hands. "I'd appreciate it if you'd let my daughter down easy. She's—sensitive. Things could get—complicated."

"Sure," Teague said. "I'll be careful, all right. I can imagine her self-esteem is pretty weak, seeing as her father's willing to sell her off for ten thousand dollars."

He strode out of the room, not bothering to tread lightly. His boot heels struck the gleaming hardwood floors and rattled the crystal in a glass-fronted case in the hallway. Courtney came trotting down the hall.

"Did you tell him?"

"Sure did," Teague said. "I told him, all right."

—◦◦◦—

"Jodi, this is great." Cissy sat back in the diner's red vinyl booth and smiled down at a burger that was almost as big as her head, with a mound of fries beside it. "Thanks for buying. It'll be my turn next time—once I get my finances straightened out."

"I don't mind buying. I'm just happy to get our friendship back on track. We should make this a regular thing, okay?"

"Um, I can't really do that." Cissy munched contemplatively on a French fry. "Cal gets out Tuesday. I'll have to be careful for a while."

"Oh, Cissy." Jodi was tempted to tell her not to let

Cal limit her life, but who was she to tell anyone what to do? She'd never had to deal with anything like what Cissy had been through. "I wish I could help."

"You do, just by being here. And Teague, too. You know he helped me move out? Cal was out on bail, and I'd left without any of my things because he wouldn't let me in the house. Well, Teague said I ought to have my craft supplies and stuff, and he called Cal and told him we were coming to get it and he'd better clear out." Her eyes took on a faint teary sheen. "He helped me pack stuff up, and loaded it in his truck, and you know Cal never even showed his face? He's scared of Teague."

"He should be."

"Yeah, if there's one thing Teague won't put up with, it's a man abusing a woman. He really understands, because his dad—well, you know."

"Yeah, I do," Jodi said.

"I was scared to death Cal would show up. I didn't want Teague to get in trouble, and I wasn't sure what he'd do, you know?"

"I know."

"So are you two—you know." She waggled her eyebrows.

Jodi shook her head and pretended to concentrate on her food. "No." She tried to sound casual. "Nothing going on."

She didn't see any reason to tell Cissy something *had* gone on. It was over, after all. Over and done.

"That's too bad." Cissy bit into her burger and chewed thoughtfully, then wiped the corners of her mouth with a napkin. "I always thought you two would end up together."

"Don't tell my mom that. She's dead set against Teague."

"Well, you aren't going to let that stop you, are you? I mean, my parents were all for Cal, and look what happened. Only you know who's right for you. I should have listened to my heart, and you should listen to yours."

"Yeah, well, I'm not sure it's my heart that's telling me Teague's the one," Jodi said. "I think some other body parts are chiming in."

Cissy giggled. "I'll bet."

"And my mom has a point. Stuff like Cal did—like Teague's father did—it runs in families. Teague might be okay now, but he's pretty quick to use his fists. You never know what might happen if he got really mad or frustrated."

Cissy stared at her, open-mouthed. "Jodi, how can you believe that? Teague *hated* his father. He'd *never* hit a woman."

Jodi shrugged.

"That's just stupid. Don't let your mom tell you what to do."

"I have to." Jodi forked up a mouthful of salad greens and held them suspended over her plate. "I came here to make things right with my mom. I treated her like dirt, Cissy, and she's been so good about it."

"What did you do?"

"I blamed her when my dad died." Jodi set the forkful of food down uneaten. "I left for school right after, and I wouldn't take her calls or anything. I didn't speak to her for years."

Cissy shrugged. "So it took you some time to process your grief."

"*Years*, Cissy. And I was downright mean. I mean, she was grieving too, and instead of helping her cope, I disappeared. I wish I could change the way I acted, but I can't—so I'm doing everything I can to make it up to her now. If she doesn't want me to see Teague, that's a small sacrifice to make."

"Small sacrifice?" Cissy shook her head. "Have you *looked* at him lately?"

"I try not to." Jodi grinned. "Really, seriously, my priority is to straighten things out with my mom. And I think she has a point about Teague. I know he helped you, Cissy, but he was in jail himself, for God's sake."

"He was a kid. A kid who got in a few too many fights."

"A kid who's first impulse is to smack somebody when things don't go his way."

"Come on, Jodi, half the time it was because kids were giving Troy a hard time. Teague's first impulse is to protect the people he loves."

"I know." Jodi sighed and ate a shred of her salad, thinking. "I just need to take care of family first, you know? Maybe she'll change her mind about Teague someday."

"I hope so," Cissy said. "I love you both, and I'd love to see you together. I'm not trying to tell you what to do or anything."

"I know. It's okay." Jodi smiled. "Teague did a lot for you. I don't blame you for defending him." She munched another mouthful, then pointed her fork at Cissy while she swallowed. "So when does Cal get out?"

"Tuesday."

"And he doesn't know where you're staying?"

Cissy shook her head. "Nope. And if he finds out, I'll be okay. I've got Teague on speed-dial."

Chapter 18

FRIDAY DAWNED HOT AND HAZY, AND BY TWO O'CLOCK Jodi had had enough of the unaccustomed humidity. Pushing a lock of hair back under the bandanna covering her head she let out a long, slow breath. Her arm muscles ached, she was sweating like a three-hundred-pound Gator running back, and her clothes, skin, and even her hair were speckled with white paint. Luna lay beside her, panting, her black patches bearing white spatters as well.

"Quittin' time." Jodi set down the paint sprayer and waved for Troy to put down his brush. They'd spent the entire day constructing a wheelchair ramp and windbreak for the clinic and painting them white to match the house.

"But it's not done," Troy said.

"We'll finish tomorrow," Jodi said. "Nobody's going to see it between now and then."

"Okay. Can I go home now?" He set his brush on the lid of the paint can and bounced to his feet.

Jodi nodded, smiling. "Sure. You deserve a rest. Working all morning for Skelton, and then coming over here—you're a hard worker these days."

Troy scuffed one sneakered foot in the dust. "Yeah, but I might have to quit working for Mr. Skelton."

"Why?" Jodi tensed. "Doesn't he treat you right?"

"Oh, yeah. He doesn't even make me do that much. Mostly, I just clean stalls, and he pays me real good. But it's a conflagration of interests."

"A conflict?" Jodi suppressed a smile. "Conflict of interests?"

"Uh-huh. Because of the war."

"The war?"

"Yeah. The Johnson County War. It's the rich guys versus the cowboys, Teague says. And Mr. Skelton's a rich guy, and I guess I'm a cowboy, even though I am making a lot of money now."

"Troy, the Johnson County War was in 1892."

"No. It's in August," Troy said.

Jodi laughed. "What are you talking about?"

"The Johnson County War," Troy said. "Teague's in it, and so is Nate Shawcross and Trevor Baines."

Maybe her neighbors were planning an insurrection against the Skeltons. *Hmm,* she thought. *I might want to get in on that.*

"They're practicing right now," he said. "You want to come see?"

"No, that's okay." The last thing she needed was to see Teague. For some reason, the steamy weather made her thoughts turn in forbidden directions. "But I'll take you home. Let's just clean up our stuff."

"Okay. But maybe you could watch for just a minute."

She shrugged. "I don't need to watch Teague play cowboys and Indians, or whatever."

"It's not cowboys and Indians," Troy said. "It's cowboys and rich guys."

"Whatever. We need to get you home."

She didn't want to admit it, but she kind of wanted to know what Teague was up to. She was willing to bet it had something to do with Courtney Skelton.

—⁓—

Twenty minutes later she and Troy tooled into the turn-out in front of Teague's ranch house. Jodi could hear shouts and whoops coming from behind the barn. A sharp clicking sound punctuated the rumble of hooves.

"What are they doing back there?" she asked Troy.

"I told you. Practicing for the war." Troy tugged her arm. "Come see. Come on."

Whatever "the war" was, Troy was obviously excited about it. Jodi allowed herself to be led around the back of the barn to see Teague and two other riders galloping around the arena where he and Jodi had practiced team roping years ago. But there were no ropes today. Instead, the cowboys carried long mallets as they galloped in tight circles, leaning from their saddles to whack a small white ball around in the dirt.

"What the hell," Jodi said.

"It's to prove cowboys are better."

"Nobody needs to prove that," she said.

Teague caught sight of her and galloped over to the side of the arena. He was breathing hard, and his quarter horse was lathered with sweat.

"Whaddaya think?" He swung the mallet in a wide circle, making it whistle through the air. His quarter horse flicked an ear, but otherwise seemed unconcerned.

"You don't want to know," Jodi said.

Teague ignored her dry tone—or maybe he didn't even notice it.

"Know what we're doing?" he asked.

"Troy said something about a war between the cowboys and the rich guys. So you're learning polo?

That's nuts. Why don't you hold a roping contest? Or
bronc riding?" She grinned. "I'd like to put Courtney
on a bronc." Her grin widened. "Yeah, we could introduce Courtney to the joys of the rodeo. I'd enjoy
that." She paused. "What's going on between you and
her, anyway?"

He reached down to pat the horse's neck. "Nothing."

"Right."

"She's not for me, that's for sure." He swung a leg
over the horse's broad rump and slid to the ground.
Slinging the reins over the top rail of the fence, he
ducked through the bars and stood beside Jodi. "She and
her dad think everything we do is 'low class.' I figure
we'll show them what class is."

"And how do you plan to do that?"

"By kicking their asses at their own game." Teague
took off his hat and smacked it against his thigh, releasing a cloud of dust. "Players have to buy in, and we can
charge for admission and refreshments too. I'm going
to have it catered so they can nosh on their natural diet:
martinis and hors d'oeuvres."

Jodi snorted. "Have you lost your mind?"

"Nope."

"Don't you have anything better to do?"

"Nope."

Jodi glanced around Teague's ranch. Judging from
the neat, tidy appearance of the house and barn, he really didn't have anything pressing that needed doing.
She hiked herself up on the fence, keeping a healthy
distance away from him while they watched the two
cowboys whack the ball around. Even from two feet
away, she swore she could feel heat coming off him, or

pheromones or something. She scooched a little closer, then clenched her hands in her lap. *You promised*, she told herself. *You promised*. She concentrated on the polo players.

"Is that Nate Shawcross?"

Teague nodded.

"I can't believe you got him to do something fun."

"He's been different since he got married. Even talks once in a while now."

Jodi laughed. Shawcross was famous for his quiet, somber demeanor. She'd heard he married a wild child from New Jersey and started a riding camp for teens. It had been hard to picture Nate dealing with kids, let alone an Easterner, but love did funny things to people.

She looked over at Teague and felt a flutter in her chest. Funny things. Yeah.

Real funny. So funny they took up hobbies that were totally out of character.

"So this polo thing," she said. "Was it Courtney's idea?"

"She kind of suggested it."

"Great." Jodi rolled her eyes. "And I suppose she'll need to hang around here all the time, helping out."

Teague spread his hands, indicating the entire ranch. "You see her here anywhere?"

"Not yet."

"She's not coming. I didn't invite her. Besides, the polo game isn't about Courtney. It's about…"

"Never mind. It doesn't matter." At least, it shouldn't. What Teague did was his own business and none of hers. She hopped off the fence. "I've got to go. Stuff to do."

"You need help?" Teague asked.

"Nope. I'm good." She headed back to her truck,

slapping her dusty hands on the thighs of her jeans, then digging in her pocket for her keys.

"I thought I'd stop by—tomorrow, maybe?" Teague called to her. "Got a surprise for you."

"A surprise?" Dang. She was trying to stay away from him, but she loved surprises. And somewhere deep inside, the notion of a surprise from Teague lit her up like a spark hitting tinder.

"Nothing big," he said. "Well, actually, it is pretty big, but… Never mind. You'll like it."

The double entendre was apparently unconscious, but Jodi's mind jumped straight into the gutter and rolled around for a while. An image came to mind of Teague kicking off his boots and stretching out on her lace-bedecked canopy bed. She'd had the bed since junior high, and if dreams were dollars, he owned it.

Teague was looking down at her and smiling, and she realized she had a faraway look on her face and a smile on her lips that probably told him exactly what she was thinking. She gave herself a quick mental slap. No way was she signing up for another event in the mattress rodeo. Not with Teague. She'd won the last go-round, and she wanted to go out a champion.

Chapter 19

JODI WAS PUTTING EIGHTBALL OUT TO PASTURE THE next morning when Teague's truck pulled into the drive, hauling a battered one-horse trailer behind it.

Releasing her horse, she slipped out the gate and watched her neighbor stroll around the pickup to lift the trailer's metal latch. Vegas's spotted head hung over the door, his eyes cloudy but his expression placid. His ears were tilted forward, twitching one way, then another as he took in his new surroundings as best he could.

"Oh, Teague, you brought him." Jodi stroked the horse's nose and let him nuzzle her hand, mumbling it between his lips in search of a treat. "That's wonderful. I was just thinking I needed a new therapy horse. Eightball's just too antsy."

"Well, we'll see how it goes." Teague clipped a lead to Vegas's halter and dropped the trailer's ramp. Immediately a gray blur about the size of a large dog raced past them with a frantic jangling of bells, stopping dead in the center of the driveway to resolve itself into a black and white goat with long, spindly legs and a devilish smile on its face. A bell hung from a red leather collar around its neck.

"What the hell is that?" Jodi asked.

"A goat."

"No kidding. But I thought you said his goat died."

"Got another one."

The goat looked right, then left. It apparently decided the daylilies growing beside the house looked appetizing, because it rushed over and grabbed three mouthfuls of lily in quick succession, pulling them out by the bulbs.

"His name is Beelzy," Teague said.

"Beelzy?"

"Short for Beelzebub. He's the son of Satan."

Jodi watched the beast yank up another mouthful of flowers. "I believe you."

"No, really," Teague said. "His dad Satan was the one that died. I went back where I got him and they gave me Beelzy. They didn't even charge me for him."

Jodi laughed. "I think they should have paid you to take him."

Teague strode toward the goat, waving him away from the flowers. Beelzy turned, a wicked glint in his yellow eyes, and leapt up to spin in the air. He hit the ground with all four legs churning like a cartoon character and charged at Jodi, head lowered. She dodged away just in time and the goat hurtled past her, barreling into the corral gate with a painful clang.

Teague grabbed a leash from a hook by the trailer door and folded it in one hand. Dropping into a crouch, he stalked toward the goat as it munched on the tall grass near the gatepost.

"He wears the bell so that—*umph*!" He flung himself at the goat and it dodged away, leaving him to belly-flop onto the ground.

"So that Vegas knows where he is," he continued, scrambling to his feet.

Teague was evidently accustomed to belly flopping on the ground in pursuit of goats. As Jodi watched, he and the animal squared off. Teague crouched low like a wrestler looking for an opening as the goat ducked and dodged like a prizefighter. Finally Teague flung himself at it and hit the dirt again.

"Damn." He brushed off his shirt and pants, narrowing his eyes as Beelzy faced him and let out a vibrato-laced bleat. If goats could laugh, Jodi would have sworn that's what Beelzy was doing. The goat dodged left, and Teague followed suit. The goat dodged right.

"Help me out here." Teague feinted toward the goat again, and the animal bowed down on his front legs like a dog in play posture, skinny butt raised high.

Jodi looked from Teague to the goat and folded her arms across her chest.

"No," she said. "I'm not your goat girl."

"Come on." The goat made a dash toward Teague, then dodged sideways and hurtled forward. Teague grabbed for his tail as he rushed past, but he was too late.

"You guys are enjoying this," Jodi said. She was too, to tell the truth. She'd never seen this side of Teague before. "You're *playing*."

Even as a kid, Teague had never played. Everything he did had a purpose. He rode and roped to build rodeo skills so he could make money. He played baseball so he could make the team at school, though his notion of earning any kind of athletic scholarship died when he was cut for fighting two weeks after the season started.

But now he was playing. With a goat.

Beelzy bleated and scampered sideways, then rocketed past Teague and pranced in a wide circle around the house. As he came around the corner Jodi lunged for him, but he leapt out of her grip and spun her off balance. She hit the grass hard as Teague grabbed the goat and missed as well, thumping down beside her.

Well, sort of beside her. Mostly, he was on top of her. She opened her eyes to see his face inches away, his eyes wide with surprise. Every part of his body was rigid, pressing into her.

Every part.

"Either you really like goats or you're happy to see me."

She regretted the words the minute she said them. Now he'd get embarrassed and move, and the sweet, warm feeling that had blossomed between her legs and was slowly spreading through her whole body would go away.

And that would be good, she told herself sternly. *Step away from the cowboy.*

The cowboy closed his eyes, but he didn't move.

"You okay?"

"Yeah." He opened his eyes and looked down into hers. "How 'bout you?" His voice was low and he sounded a little breathless.

"I'm… yeah." She started to say something else, but suddenly his lips were on hers and danged if she could remember what she was going to say. She remembered the warm, liquid sensation of kissing Teague though— the sweet heat of his mouth, the taste of mint and the faint scent of sweat, sunshine, and sage that combined to make cowboy.

When they pulled apart, he closed his eyes and took a deep breath, then hiked himself up on his hands to rise, but the movement pressed his hips harder into hers. She squirmed against him, and he moved himself against her again, deliberately this time, watching her face.

Their afternoon in his bedroom came back to her with

such startling clarity that she felt like she'd gone back in time. Teague was kissing her again, his mouth hot on hers, his hands in her hair, and she couldn't help kissing him back, couldn't help moving beneath him. Closing her eyes, she tucked her hands under his shirt and ran them over his bare chest while the kiss deepened and their bodies rocked in rhythm.

Suddenly Teague stopped and pulled away. She opened her eyes to see him staring down at her, his eyes scanning her face.

"What exactly did you promise your mother?" he asked, his voice hoarse and breathless.

"I—I said I wouldn't get involved with you."

"Oh." He relaxed slightly. "That's okay, then. This isn't 'involved.' We're just playing."

She started to get up but he was immovable, his elbows on either side of her arms, his face inches away. Warmth was still flowing through her, slow as thick, hot honey in her veins. She struggled, not very convincingly, and the full length of a rock-hard erection pressed against her in exactly the place she wanted it. The honey flowed a little faster and she closed her eyes and threw her head back in full, delicious surrender.

He took full advantage of the opportunity, kissing her throat, rocking against her, bringing one hand up to caress her breast. She arched her back and pressed into his hand, gasping at his touch. She could feel herself peaking under his hand, her body begging for more.

The hand moved from her breast to the hot aching spot between her legs and she couldn't help pressing up against him to stop the need from overwhelming her. It felt so good she did it again, and again, and again… He was definitely winning the game this time. She felt like she was about to explode, like her body would shatter and fly off into orbit any minute.

"Teague," she gasped. "Teague. More."

His breathing was quick and harsh as he unsnapped her jeans. He watched her while he touched her, the heat of his fingers soothing the hot, needy heart of her. She tilted her face to the sun and closed her eyes while she pulsed against him, feeling the tension inside her rise and break so she cried out and clenched her thighs, gripping him as if she was urging on a fast horse while sweet, hot magic flooded her veins.

When the feeling eased, she sat up again, then closed her eyes and tipped her face to the sun.

"Damn," she said. "You won. You definitely won the game that time."

She started to rise but he gripped her arms, meeting her eyes with an honesty and intimacy she'd never seen from him.

"Is this really just a game to you?"

Was it? Of course it was. It had to be.

She was saved from answering by the goat, who chose that moment to gallop around the corner and slide to a stop, greeting them with a loud bleat.

"Son of a bitch," Teague muttered, rising on shaky legs and wincing as he made a quick adjustment to the fit of his jeans. "I'm going to kill that animal."

She stood and staggered a little, then caught her balance and set off after the prancing son of Satan. Darting toward the goat, she grabbed his collar.

"I got him."

She hung onto the bleating animal while Teague

picked up the leash where he'd dropped it on the grass and clipped it to the goat's collar. Beelzy allowed himself to be led across the grass, but once he reached the driveway he splayed all four legs in the dirt and refused to budge. Grimacing, Teague wrapped his arms around the animal's front and rear legs and lifted him to his chest. Jodi tried not to laugh as the goat let out a high, nasal protest.

"Put him in the corral," she said. "The pasture fence won't hold him."

Teague glanced over at the electric fence his brother had strung days before. "No, and it won't hold Vegas, either. If he gets shocked, he's liable to spin around and slam into it again. If something hurts him, he can't see what it is and he panics."

"Do you think he'll be okay in the corral?"

Teague scanned the metal panels lashed to wooden posts. "Probably. Those'll give if he hits them. And if you show him the boundaries, he'll remember where they are. He does really well, considering." He took a deep breath. "Jodi…"

"How much can he see?" She wasn't going to let him say a word about what had happened. Not a word.

"I'm not sure. He can see shadows out of his left eye, I think, but probably nothing out of his right. If something spooks him from the left, he'll dodge right no matter what's in the way—a fence, a wall, a human… he doesn't know it's there. You have to talk all the time to make sure he knows where you are." He looked troubled. "I'm worried one of your kids could get hurt. Your students, I mean. Or whatever."

"Clients." Jodi shrugged. "They'll understand better than anyone that Vegas needs special care."

Gathering the lead rope in one hand, Jodi led Vegas down the ramp. The old horse placed each hoof carefully, testing his footing before committing himself. Teague guarded the gate while she led the horse into the corral, waving Beelzy back when he bolted for the opening.

"I'll miss Vegas, but Beelzy? Not so much," Teague said. "It's almost worth giving up Vegas to get rid of him."

"Thanks." Jodi rolled her eyes. "Just what I've always wanted. A goat."

"Not just any goat. That's the son of Satan, there."

"I would have known even if you hadn't told me."

Jodi's legs still felt weak and shaky while she led Vegas around the perimeter of the corral, letting him nose the panels. She kept her eyes carefully averted from Teague while Beelzy frolicked around them, playing keep-away when Jodi tried to pet him, then trotting up behind her, head lowered. She dodged sideways and his effort to butt her turned into another headlong rush into the side of the corral. Vegas shied at the clang of the goat's horns against the metal.

"It's okay, buddy." Jodi stopped. She'd circled the corral twice. She turned to Teague, making her tone casual and offhanded. "You think that's enough?"

He folded his arms on the top rail and gave her a slow smile. "No. It definitely wasn't enough."

"I think it was too much." She unclipped the lead from Vegas's halter and stepped out of the corral to stand beside him, keeping a good foot of distance between them while they watched the horse settle in. The goat stood beside Vegas, still poised to run, and Jodi could swear he was smiling.

"Look at that goat," she said. "He's dreaming up more devilment."

"Me too." Teague moved behind her and held the rail on either side. His body aligned with hers and she could feel his arousal pressing into her back. He dropped his voice to a low rasp and spoke into her ear, ruffling the delicate curls that had escaped her ponytail. "We didn't finish our game."

"I—I can't." She checked her watch and straightened. "I have a client coming right now."

He released his grip and groaned. "Tell me you're kidding."

"No, really. Russell and his dad'll be here any minute."

He looked down and took a few deep, shaky breaths. When he looked up again, his gaze had cooled down from hot to warm.

"Okay," he said. "But you're not putting Vegas to work that fast, are you?"

Jodi shook her head. "Nope. Bill Caxton brought over Triple Threat for me to use."

"How'd you manage that? I must have tried a dozen times to get Bill to part with that horse."

"Feminine wiles. And the fact that Triple Threat has arthritis now didn't hurt." She waved a hand in invitation. "Come on. Let's go in the barn and wash up."

She led him into the barn and cranked on a faucet that arched over a battered tin laundry tub. Washing his hands, Teague shook his head.

"So you've got a blind horse, a lame horse, and a pain-in-the-ass goat. This isn't a clinic; it's a home for wayward critters."

Jodi shrugged. "They'll help the kids. It'll actually

be good for them to see that animals can overcome disabilities too."

Teague nodded and shook most of the water off his hands, then dried them on his jeans. "You mind if I stay and watch?"

"No, that's fine. Maybe you could even help." Working side by side with Teague would be great. Maybe they really could be friends. She just had to be careful he didn't fall on top of her again, that's all. She'd be fine as long as she didn't touch him.

She glanced over to where he was leaning against the wall, his hands in his pockets, his long, lean legs crossed at the ankles. He hadn't shaved, so stubble softened the angle of his jaw. His eyes were thoughtful, giving her an appraising look with a hint of a challenge in it.

Okay, maybe she shouldn't look at him either.

But she needed help, right? And she had a feeling Teague would be good with the kids.

"That would be great. Troy's over at Skelton's, working on some special project. Top secret, as usual." She rolled her eyes. "So I could use your help."

Teague hesitated. "I'm not really good with kids."

"You'll be fine." Jodi nodded sharply, her mind made up. "Go get Triple Threat, would you? Only we're calling him TT. I don't think parents will be too enthusiastic about their kids getting on a horse named something so—well—threatening."

He hesitated, looking faintly uncertain. The look reminded her of his teenaged self and she couldn't help smiling.

"All you have to do is lead the horse," she said. "And trust me, the kids are a lot easier to deal with than the goat."

Chapter 20

TEAGUE GRABBED A HALTER FROM A HOOK IN THE barn and headed for the pasture, still catching his breath. He didn't know how Jodi could recover so quickly from what had happened between them. Every time he touched her, he spun off into some alternate universe and had trouble returning to earth, but Jodi seemed to take their lovemaking right in stride. Didn't it mean anything to her? The old Jodi would have made the afternoon's activities into a long-running soap opera, but her new, citified self seemed to think nothing of it, standing up, brushing herself off, and getting right back to business.

Triple Threat was waiting at the fence, his ears pricked forward. The horse was gorgeous—a palomino with lots of flashy chrome—but he didn't hold his head quite as high as he used to, and Teague thought he looked tired and a little sad. Back in the day, The Threat, as Bill called him, had been one big ball of try. It was sad when animals got old.

He led the horse back to the barn and tossed a blanket and saddle on his back. Giving the cinch a firm final tug, he led him out into the sunlight. "Come on, old man," he said. "Let's go."

The Threat followed him obediently enough, and Teague was glad to see no trace of a limp. The lameness must not be too bad. Arthritis could render a horse too

lame for hard work like roping, with all its quick starts
and stops, but leave him perfectly fine for casual riding.

"There's your horse, Russell." Jodi was standing on
top of the ramp behind a wheelchair that held a little
boy who looked about eight, or maybe ten. He wore
thick, heavy-framed glasses and an English-style riding
helmet. A thick woven cotton belt was draped loosely
around his waist. "His name is TT."

"Hi, TT," the boy said. His voice was surprisingly
deep, and Teague suddenly realized the kid was a lot
older than eight. He was thirteen, maybe fourteen, but
his body was so wasted by some disease that he looked
like a child.

"Russell's dad will get him in the saddle, so you just
have to lead," Jodi said. "Russell, this is Teague. He's
going to help us today."

"Hello, Teague." The boy rocked slightly as he lifted
his right arm toward Teague. "Nice to meet you, sir."

Nervously, Teague led the horse over, threading him
between the ramp and a set of freestanding stairs, and
gave the boy's hand a hearty shake. The boy winced and
Teague softened his grip, worried he'd hurt him, but the
grin on the kid's face said otherwise. Teague breathed a
quiet sigh of relief. If Russell was anything like Troy, he
was probably tired of being treated like spun glass. Still,
the kid looked genuinely fragile. He'd better be careful.

"And this is Russell's dad Ben." Jodi nodded to-
ward a man who was standing on the steps. Teague led
Triple Threat into position, glancing nervously at Ben.
If Russell looked fragile, this guy looked indestructible.
He was huge—a gigantic hulk of a man, with tattoos
etched on biceps that bulged from a greasy-looking

black T-shirt decorated with skulls. He looked like a biker—a three-hundred-pound biker. Much of that weight appeared to be muscle, but his belly had escaped the rigors of the gym and hung over his belt, the shirt gaping upward to reveal a stretch of hairy pale flesh.

"Nice to meet you," Teague said, though he wasn't sure.

The biker dude grunted, then turned to his son. "Ready?" he said gruffly.

Russell nodded, but Teague saw a spark of fear in his eyes.

"You ever ride before?" Teague glanced over at Jodi, wondering if he'd stepped over the line. She gave him a faint smile and a nod.

"Oh, yeah." Russell faked a casual air that clashed with the treble note of tension in his voice. "I rode with Billy the Kid and the Wild Bunch back in the day." He cocked his head to one side and peered up at Triple Threat. "Think this nag's got any spunk?"

Teague laughed. "No, he's a pussycat. It'll be like riding your granny's striped tabby."

"You never met my granny, did you? Or her tabby." The boy grinned as his father laughed. Teague flushed as he thought of the kind of woman who might have given birth to Ben, Son of Meatloaf.

"Okay, Teague. Could you push TT back a little bit?" She watched him back the horse, nodding when they'd reached the position she wanted.

"Now hang onto him and don't let him move," Jodi said. She turned to Ben. "Don't worry, TT's steady, and Teague knows what he's doing."

"Yeah, you're a real cowboy, right?" Russell asked.

Teague nodded.

"Do you rodeo?"

"Not as much as I used to. But I raise bucking horses," Teague said. "And bulls."

"I met Ty Murray once," Russell said. "It was my Make-a-Wish. He was cool."

"I bet."

Ben bent to help his son out of the chair. Chattering had momentarily let the kid forget his fear, but now his face paled as he rose onto his spindly, unsteady legs.

"Ready?" Ben looked Russell in the face and the two shared a nod and a smile, Russell's tentative, his father's reassuring. Teague felt a sudden spasm of... something. Envy? That's what it felt like, but it couldn't be. He had Troy, after all. He knew what it was like to be responsible for someone. So why would he envy this guy?

Russell sucked in a frightened breath as Ben helped him onto the horse. TT stood patiently, enduring the complicated procedure of getting Russell mounted just as he'd held his ground in the rodeo arena, keeping the lariat taut while his rider trussed a bawling calf. Teague was concentrating on the horse, watching for any sign of movement, so he didn't look up at Russell until Jodi spoke again.

"Good job, Russ," she said. "You're riding."

"No, I'm just sitting here," Russell said, but the grin on the kid's face said sitting there was the best thing that had happened to him in a long time. He looked elated, victorious, and Teague felt something prick at the back of his eyes. Looking away from Jodi, he rubbed them, then quickly turned his attention back to the horse.

"Ready to get moving?"

Russell nodded. His father stood beside him, one

meaty hand on the small of the kid's narrow back, his eyes fixed on his son's face.

"Okay, to make the horse go, you click like this." Jodi clucked her tongue and Russell followed suit. Teague hadn't thought the kid's grin could get any wider, but when the horse stepped out, Russell's face looked like it might split in two.

TT paced slowly around the ring, his head bobbing with each step, his rider swaying with the motion. Jodi had moved to the off side of the horse. She gripped the front of the saddle with one hand and laid her arm on Russell's leg, her forearm parallel to his thigh. Ben was in the same position, except that he continued to support Russell's back.

"Can't he go faster?" Russell said breathlessly.

Teague looked back at the kid's hands, white-knuckled on the saddle horn. "Nope. He's got knee trouble. This is good exercise for him, but he can't go any faster. He'll have to work his way up gradually."

"Poor guy." Russell cautiously lifted one hand from the saddle horn and stroked the horse's neck. Jodi beamed at Teague and he felt a surge of pride. What she'd said about the kids seeing the animals overcome their handicaps made sense. Russell had stopped thinking about himself and focused on the horse, and he was relaxing bit by bit, sinking into the saddle and relaxing his grip on the horn.

"I think maybe he's limping a little," the boy said.

Teague turned and walked backward a few steps, eyeing the horse's feet. "He'll be okay," he said. "He won't ever get stronger if we don't challenge him a little."

"Man, I've heard *that* before," Russell said. "My physical therapist's even meaner than you." The kid stroked the horse's neck again, but as he bent forward, he started to fall onto the horse's neck. Overcompensating, he jerked backward. His father grabbed his belt and kept him in the saddle, but the kid's face turned white.

"You're okay," Jodi said soothingly.

"I know." Russell was steady again, but his face was pale and his hands gripped the horn again. "I'm fine."

After a series of slow circles and figure eights that gradually restored Russell's confidence, Teague pulled The Threat to a stop by the gate at a signal from Jodi.

"Thanks." She graced him with a smile that was equal parts gratitude, delight, and I-told-you-so. "Teague, could you help Ben get Russell down?"

Teague started to follow Ben to the gate, but Jodi stopped him.

"Ben'll get his chair," she said. "We dismount out here."

"Not at the ramp?" Teague asked.

Jodi shook her head. Teague looked up at the boy on the horse and his stomach clenched. There was no way he could refuse to help, but with his luck he'd drop the kid or something.

"Just swing his leg up and over, and then let him slide down to you," Jodi said.

Teague reached over and lifted the boy's leg while Ben rolled the chair to a stop and walked around the horse to play spotter on the other side. The kid was thin, but his limbs were practically dead weight, and Teague had to lift his leg over the cantle. He almost threw the kid forward, but Ben grabbed on and the two of them managed to get Russell seated sideways in the saddle.

"Now I'm riding like a girl," the kid said. "Get me off of here before the Wild Bunch catches me going sidesaddle."

Teague laughed and reached up. Russell slid into his arms, and Teague caught him easily and held him a moment before lowering him slowly to his feet. The kid clutched his arm, eyeing the wheelchair with a flash of dread in his eyes.

Teague lowered Russell into the chair. The kid sighed and settled in, his eyes glistening.

"Thanks," he said. "That was fun." He looked down at his hands. Obviously, the adventure was ending too soon.

"We'll be coming back next week," Ben said.

"Will you be here?" Russell looked up at Teague, his gaze hopeful.

"Sure," Teague said. "Hey, you want to meet my horse?" It was a spur of the moment thing. The kid probably spent every waking minute at home, staring at the walls, and Teague was danged if he'd send him back right away.

"Sure." The grin was back.

Teague shoved the chair across the yard without a backward glance at Jodi or Ben. He probably wasn't supposed to take over with the patients like this—the *clients*, he meant the *clients*—but Russell needed a little more time.

So did Teague.

"His name's Vegas." He paused by the corral. Vegas, turning at the sound of his name, walked over and thrust his head over the fence. Curious, he poked at Russell with his nose, breathing on him and snorting.

Russell laughed. "Don't let him eat me."

"He's just checking you out."

Smiling tentatively, Russell lifted one arm and stroked his hand down the horse's nose, looking at first one clouded eye, then the other.

"He's blind, isn't he?"

Teague nodded.

"That would suck. I'm glad I can see. I'd rather see than walk," Russell declared.

"Yeah." Teague's throat was suddenly tight, and he could barely get the words out. "Yeah, me too. If I had to choose."

———⁓⁓⁓———

Jodi watched Teague stride away, pushing Russell's chair over the rough ground. She'd known he'd do all right with the kids, but dang, he was doing great. Ben had told her Russell was fearful of strangers, but he and Teague had taken off like a couple of kids leaving the old folks behind on an outing. Teague hadn't asked or anything.

She glanced over at Ben. "Sorry."

"Hell, no." The big man grinned, but his eyes were glossy with tears. "Little buddy's having a blast. It's great. Who is that guy?"

"An old friend," Jodi said.

"Boyfriend?

"No," she said. It came out a little too loud. "Just a friend. We grew up together."

"Well, I hope he's here next week. Russell's got a thing about cowboys, and that guy looks like the real deal. You ought to do whatever you have to do to keep him around." Ben realized what he'd said and flushed. "I mean—I don't mean…"

"It's okay." Jodi looked away so he couldn't see her

face. She'd gotten a pretty good start on doing what she had to do to keep Teague around. Judging from the intensity of his gaze after their little frolic in the grass, the trouble might be getting him to go home—unless he'd come to his senses during the lesson.

But she'd promised, she reminded herself. And Teague couldn't be trusted. He'd given her that look before, all those years ago when she'd said good-bye—but it had disappeared from his face as suddenly and surely as if it had been erased. And even now, there was Courtney. Jodi couldn't quite figure out that situation.

Teague and Russell were still at the corral fence. Teague had yanked up some grass, and now Vegas was nibbling it from the boy's hand. The breeze carried their laughter down to Jodi and Ben.

"Whatever you have to do," Ben said. "I guess I did mean it."

Chapter 21

THE NEXT DAY'S POLO PRACTICE HAD BARELY BEGUN before Nate galloped up to Teague and pulled his horse to a sudden, skidding stop.

"Hey." He pointed off toward the east while his horse tossed her head and stamped one foot, mirroring his agitation. "You see that smoke?"

Teague and their other teammate, Trevor Baines, shaded their eyes with their hands and squinted at the horizon. A thin gray column rose in the air, then dissipated in a flat, diffuse gray cloud. As they watched, it thickened and turned dark.

"Isn't that about where the polo grounds are?" Nate asked.

Teague nodded. "Pretty close."

"It's that Skelton girl." Trevor grinned. "She's so damn hot she smokes."

Teague shot him a surprised glance. "Hey, I thought you had a girlfriend."

Trevor shrugged. "Just 'cause I'm on a diet doesn't mean I can't look at the menu. Besides, you can't have all the girls, Treadwell. Leave some for the rest of us."

"No problem." Teague grimaced. "You can have that one."

The three men turned as the faint whine of a siren rose in the distance.

"See? It's going to take the whole volunteer fire

department to put that girl out," Trevor said. He slid off his horse, grinning. "I've always meant to volunteer my-self. Think I'll head out there. See if she needs a good, ah, hosing down."

Teague frowned. "What about practice?"

"Later, I guess." Trevor patted his horse's flank. "Can you take care of old Riley, here?"

Teague nodded. Maybe Courtney would fall for Trevor. That would get her off his back. He was actu-ally surprised she hadn't shown up yet today, bringing some polo tip she'd supposedly forgotten or something.

The whir of an approaching engine joined the distant sirens, making Teague's horse snort and dance. He spun to see Courtney's silver Lexus SUV skidding to a stop at the fence.

Speak of the devil. Or the devil's daughter.

Nate laughed and flashed him a thumbs-up. Tight-ening his lips into a thin line, Teague shook his head.

"Here comes trouble," he said under his breath. Swinging a leg over his horse's rump, he slid to the ground and stepped out of the gate. "I'll just be a minute."

The car door swung open and Courtney spilled from the seat, almost falling in her haste to rush over to Teague and throw herself against him. She was dressed in her usual tight clothes, but her blonde hair was in total disarray, smooth on top and tangled halfway down with a crease showing where her hat had been. He'd never seen the girl look less than per-fect—in her way, of course. She wasn't perfect for him. Nowhere near.

Somehow, he was going to have to extricate himself from this relationship—or whatever it was. He didn't really understand how it had started. The girl was a little psycho.

"Oh, Teague." She was sobbing, her head against his chest. He looked down at her, his hands spread helplessly, then put his arms around her. He hated to do that, especially with Nate watching, but what the hell else did you do with a crying woman? The only other option he could think of was to run away, and much as he wanted to, that wouldn't be right. He patted her shoulder awkwardly.

"The stables are on fire," she blubbered into his shirt. "The horses—they're screaming—it's awful, and they don't know if they can save them."

"What?" Panic fluttered in Teague's chest like a trapped bird. Troy was over there today. He turned to Nate.

"I have to go. Skelton's barn's on fire and Troy's over there."

"Go." Nate made a shooing motion. "Go. I'll take care of the horses."

"Oh, thank you, Teague," Courtney said. "I knew you'd come. I knew you'd care."

"I'm not…" Teague urged her toward her vehicle. This was no time to explain his priorities. He needed to get to Troy. If Courtney wanted to think it was all about her, let her. He'd have a talk with her later.

It was past time for that.

"Come on," he said, opening the Lexus's passenger side door and shooing her into the seat. "I'll drive."

As the truck swept out onto the dirt road, Teague glanced over at the trembling, disheveled girl beside him. He'd never seen Courtney like this. A black smudge scarred her cheek, and her hair, so perfectly arranged most of the time, hung in lank tendrils around her face.

"Hurry," she said, wringing her hands in her lap. "Hurry!"

"I'm hurrying," he said. "Was Troy there? Did you see him?"

"My horse is in there," she wailed. She grabbed his arm, making him jerk the steering wheel to the right and almost putting them into the ditch. "Oh, hurry!"

Teague floored the accelerator and the truck bounced over a pothole, knocking Courtney sideways so she tilted into him. He couldn't find the complementary bump that would put her back to rights, so she leaned on his shoulder the rest of the way. He knew she wanted him to put his arm around her, but he needed both hands on the wheel on the rough country road and he didn't want to encourage her.

He glanced over and saw tears streaming down her cheeks. There was nothing worse than a woman crying in silence. When they sobbed and choked and blubbered, you could figure they were just doing it for attention. Silent crying was genuine grief.

He gave in and put his arm around her as the road smoothed out. The blubbering and choking started up as if he'd pressed an "on" button. Well, maybe that meant she felt a little better.

He turned and passed under the Skelton gate with its wrought iron arch. Silhouette ranch gates were common, but the scenes cut into the metal usually pictured horses and cattle, or elk and pine trees. Skelton's showed a threesome of polo players galloping from the right, while a single player on the left brandished his mallet in a decidedly unprofessional manner.

The smoke had been visible the whole way, ominous black clouds billowing into the sky, but now Teague could see its source. Flames, colored a surreal shade of orange that looked almost fluorescent against the blue sky, licked and flickered, blackening the barn as he watched. While he negotiated the potholes in the unpaved driveway, a beam fell and threw a shower of sparks into the sky. Courtney gasped and drew a little closer. He patted her shoulder.

"The horses," she whispered.

Teague pulled to a stop before he reached the turnout in front of the barn and scanned the landscape, searching for some sign of Troy. Any closer and he'd risk the showers of sparks the barn was spitting into the air. A fire truck from Chugwater, the nearest town large enough to have their own department, spouted water in a graceful arc that plunged into the center of the barn.

Teague stepped out of the truck and was greeted by acrid smoke that burned his lungs and an ominous silence. There was no whinnying, no neighing, no panicked thunder of hooves. Courtney stumbled behind him, hugging herself as if she could hold herself together through sheer effort.

"Troy?" he shouted. "Troy!"

The polo players turned as he approached, their heads moving in unison as if they were one big Argentine organism.

"You seen Troy?" Teague asked. "Troy Treadwell? He works here?"

"The simple one?"

Teague gritted his teeth. He hated it when people identified Troy by his disability.

"He's short. Stocky. Brown hair."

The players shook their heads in unison.

"He works in the mornings," one of them said. "Never in the afternoon."

"But he was here. He said he had something to do—a special project."

The polo player shrugged. "What would that be?"

"Who knows?" Teague almost growled with frustration. "Everything around here's a goddamn secret."

The players edged away, as if he was a rabid dog or something. He was probably about that dangerous. Ignoring Courtney, who was choking as if she could barely draw a breath, he headed for the barn.

"Stand back," hollered one of the firemen. "Beams are falling."

"My brother might be in there," Teague said. He slowed as another beam crashed and sent up sparks, but kept on toward the barn.

"Nothing in there but horses," the fireman said.

"You sure?" Teague paused and squinted toward the barn. It was hard to see past the smoke, but he could see something huddled in the doorway. Something green. It looked familiar. It was…

"*No*." He charged toward the barn, but a fireman grabbed his arm and spun him sideways. Teague stumbled to his knees and pointed. "That's his backpack. Right there in the doorway." Lurching to his feet, he tried to charge toward the burning barn again, but another fireman pitched in and held him back. Teague fought, but they were burly guys and held on tight.

"Mister. Come on. Calm down."

Teague slumped, panting. He'd have fallen to his knees again if the fire fighters hadn't kept hold of his arms.

"What did he look like?" one of them asked.

"Short. Stocky. Brown hair," Teague said. He twisted in their grip. "Let me go, dammit!"

"Somebody like that took off on a bike about the time we got here," another fireman said. "Green bike. Old-fashioned."

"That's him. He rode off?"

The fireman nodded and released Teague. As the adrenaline drained from his brain, he shook off their grip and dusted himself off. "It's okay then. Sorry." He bent over, resting his hands on his thighs while he caught his breath. "What about the horses?"

"Couldn't save 'em. Goddamn place was locked, can you believe it? By the time these guys showed up with the key, it was too late." He nodded toward the polo players, who were still watching the fire with Trevor.

"Shit." Teague glanced back at Courtney. "All the horses? None of 'em got out?"

The fireman nodded. Teague turned and walked back to Courtney, moving slowly to put off the inevitable. He reached her all too soon.

"Dutch?" she whispered.

Teague pressed his lips together and shook his head. "I'm sorry, honey," he said. "It was probably pretty painless. The smoke gets 'em before the flames do."

She fell against him, her sobs growing louder, and he cursed himself silently. Knowing the animals were dead before the fire reached them would have made him feel better, but Courtney was kind of fragile. She hadn't even come to terms with the horse being gone yet, and he'd gone and described how he'd died.

"I'm sorry," he said again. There was nothing like a woman's tears to make a man feel helpless. "But at least Troy's okay."

"Troy? Yeah, I saw him on his bike. He was leaving just when I took off to get you," Courtney said.

Teague cursed under his breath. It obviously hadn't occurred to Courtney to offer Troy a ride, or to tell Teague she'd seen him even after he'd asked. She was too concerned about her horse—about her own concerns. He'd been ready to run into the fire after Troy, and she'd known the whole time that he was okay.

He needed to tell her to leave him alone, but now was hardly the time. She'd be upset for days, maybe weeks. He groaned inwardly. How the hell was he ever going to cut loose? She was like a burr in wool chaps, digging in deeper and deeper the longer he let her hang on.

Chapter 22

TEAGUE WAS PRETTY SURE HE'D SET A LAND SPEED record on the way home, but they hadn't passed Troy.

"Are you sure you saw him leaving?" he asked Courtney for the third time. She sat beside him, shivering and sobbing, still so wrapped up in her own issues she couldn't understand his concern for Troy. He knew she was upset about the horses. He was too. But Troy was his brother, for God's sake.

He hadn't wanted to let her come along with him. But he couldn't leave her to watch the barn burn. That would just be cruel.

"You sure?" he asked again when she didn't answer.

"I'm sure." She pushed out her lower lip in a childish pout while they wheeled up the driveway.

The truck rocked and jerked as it hit the potholes at twice the normal speed. The minute they arrived at the ranch Teague jerked the door open and hit the ground running, ignoring the girl's exclamation of surprise and dismay. She could get out of the truck herself. He needed to find Troy.

He glanced toward the shed, but the space where Troy usually "stabled" Bessie the bicycle was empty. Teague swore softly, stifling the urge to run back to the truck and ask Courtney to confirm her Troy sighting one more time. The firemen had said Troy left the scene of the fire too. Courtney wasn't the only one who saw him going.

One thing was for sure—when this was over, Teague was buying his brother a new bicycle. Troy was ridiculously attached to Bessie, but the old bike wasn't exactly built for speed. Once Troy tried a newer racing bike, he'd probably like it.

And it would get him home faster.

Teague mounted the steps to the porch, figuring he'd watch the road from there. He'd give Troy ten more minutes to get home, and then he'd go look for him.

He'd pretty much forgotten about Courtney, and her voice from the porch swing in the corner startled him.

"Here comes somebody," she said.

Teague squinted down the driveway. Sure enough, something was kicking up a cloud of dust. As it approached, he realized it was Jodi's Ranger.

Well, at least he wouldn't be alone with Courtney.

As the pickup neared, Teague could see Jodi had someone with her. He grinned when he realized it was Troy. Jodi must have seen him and picked him up. He should have thought to call her.

Without thinking, Teague ran down the steps and yanked open the passenger door. As Troy stepped out, he grabbed his brother in a hard embrace and blinked back something that felt disturbingly like tears. He let go and turned away, swiping at his eyes so Jodi wouldn't see.

"Hey, buddy." He tried to sound casual. "I was worried about you." He turned back and realized Troy's eyes were swollen and red. "You okay?"

"The barn burned down," Troy said. "The horses got killed. They were locked inside. I could hear them. It was awful."

Teague nodded and slung an arm around his brother's shoulders. "I know. Sorry, bud. It's awful."

"I should have stayed to help, but I had to leave," Troy said. "I couldn't listen to it."

"You couldn't have helped." Teague went around to the back of the truck and lowered the tailgate. Lifting Bessie out, he handed her over to Troy. "You left your backpack, though. I think it probably burned up."

Troy shrugged. "There was nothing in it."

"I saw it in the barn. I thought—I thought you were in there."

"I was, earlier." Troy looked puzzled. "Mr. Skelton said he needed me to make sure the stalls were clean. I don't know why. The guys had already mucked them out."

Teague watched Troy wheel the bike over to the shed. He couldn't really figure out why Skelton had hired his brother, since he didn't seem to give him much to do. Maybe he figured hiring the handicapped made him look good, or he got a tax write-off or something. Teague didn't think for a moment the man had done it out of kindness.

Jodi rolled down her window as he approached the truck.

"Thanks for bringing him home." Teague shoved his hands in his pockets. "I was worried."

"He was upset about the fire and the horses. I saw him riding along and the bike was kind of weaving so I picked him up."

Teague felt another rush of anger at Courtney. She'd seen the same thing and driven right on by. Sure, she'd been upset herself, but still…

"Could you do me a favor?" He gestured toward the

porch. "Take Courtney home? She's upset and she keeps crying." He spread his hands helplessly. "Her horse was in the barn. I don't know what to say."

Jodi's eyes narrowed. "You don't want to comfort her?"

"Not really." He met her eyes. "Honestly, Jodi, there's nothing going on between us. I don't even like her." He hated to admit weakness, but he needed to make Jodi understand. "She's after me, and I can't seem to get away."

Jodi grinned. "You're scared, aren't you?"

"You bet," he said. "She's a very scary girl."

Monday morning, Jodi cursed herself for promising Courtney she could volunteer at the clinic. She hadn't known how else to shift the poor girl's attention from the death of her horse on the ride back to the Skelton estate. She couldn't imagine losing your horse in a fire like Courtney had, and she really did want to help—but why the hell had she scheduled the girl's orientation session for first thing Monday morning? This was no way to start the week.

And why the hell had Courtney brought her dog? She was clutching her mini-pom in the crook of her arm and stroking his head with one forefinger, totally distracted from all the things she needed to learn. The tiny pooch grinned up at Jodi, his little pink tongue flexed as he panted. It was driving Luna nuts.

Because Luna still hadn't gone home. She'd become Jodi's shadow, following her everywhere, sitting and staring at her as if she had an urgent message to relay if she could only talk. But with Honeybucket around, the border collie paced and whined, circling Courtney as if she wanted to separate her from the dog the way she'd cut a heifer from the herd when she worked with Teague.

"What's with your dog?" Courtney asked.

"I don't know. I think she wants to eat yours," Jodi said.

Courtney clutched Honeybucket a little tighter and looked up at Vegas, who had come over to the fence where they were standing.

"I think it's so sweet that Teague still takes care of this old horse," Courtney said, looking up at Vegas.

Jodi scowled. She'd just mucked out the animal's stall, led him around the arena a dozen times like she did three times a day to get him used to the space before she actually put kids on his back, and fed him his morning ration of hay, plus a hot mash she'd cooked up in the kitchen. But Teague was getting all the credit.

It wasn't worth arguing about, though.

"Yeah, that's Teague. Sweet," she said, struggling to keep the irony out of her voice. "Sweet" wasn't a word she'd ever heard used to describe her childhood friend before. She thought back to that afternoon in his bedroom. Teague wasn't sweet. He was more… *savory*.

"So as an equine therapist, what will my duties be?" Courtney asked, shifting the dog so it lay like a baby in her arms. "I just can't wait to get started working with those poor kids. I hope we can make them all better."

"Um, well, you won't really be a therapist," Jodi said. "That takes training and you have to be certified. And you might want to modify the way you think about the clients. They don't want to be pitied, and they don't need to be cured. They just want to be accepted for who they are."

"Oh." Courtney's voice was flat. "I thought I was going to be a therapist."

"Sorry. That takes time. What I need right now is another assistant. I've got Teague's brother Troy, but…"

"I'll be working with Teague's brother?" Courtney's eyes narrowed. "Well, I hope you're not going to have me cleaning stalls and stuff. I have a lot more to offer than that."

"So does Troy."

"Well, I wouldn't know. I just know that's all my dad has him do. He doesn't trust him with the horses or anything."

"I'd trust Troy with my life." Jodi paused by the barn door. "You know, he's the reason I got into this field. He's like my own brother, pretty much."

Troy looked up as they approached. He was dumping a pitchfork full of horse leavings into a wheelbarrow, whistling as he worked.

"Hey, Troy," Jodi said. "Here's Courtney. Remember I told you she'd be working with us?"

Troy looked up. "Yeah," he said, his tone flat.

Courtney trilled out a little laugh. "Well, this'll be so nice, honey." She touched Troy's arm with one hand, her perfectly manicured fingernails bright against the faded blue of his denim shirt. "Now you can be my friend, just like your big brother."

"He's my little brother." Troy squared his shoulders and turned back to his work. He had an unerring sense for condescension, and Courtney had spoken to him slowly, with exaggerated enunciation as if he was a child. "But I'm glad he's got a friend. Mostly, Teague's too grouchy to make friends."

"Well, I think your brother is very nice," Courtney pouted.

"Oh, he's nice," Troy said. "Just in a really grouchy way." He glanced down at Honeybucket. "Hey, what's that? Is that a puppy? Can I hold it?" He reached out for the dog, but Courtney drew back, covering the dog protectively with her free hand.

"No. He's delicate," she said. "You might hurt him."

Troy turned away, a flash of emotion crossing his face. Disappointment, Jodi thought, and hurt, mixed with a dash of anger. Courtney and Troy were definitely not getting off to a good start.

"Troy's my number one assistant," Jodi said, earning a smile. "He'll help you learn the ropes. You'll be cleaning out stalls once in a while, and raking the arena. But don't worry," she hastened to add as Courtney's smile faded. "You'll be participating in therapy sessions too. Leading the horses, helping the kids tack up—that kind of stuff."

"Here's how we clean the stalls," Troy said slowly, dumping a forkful of dirty straw into the wheelbarrow with an exaggerated motion. He held out the pitchfork toward Courtney. "Here. Now you try it."

"Um… in a minute." Courtney backed away. "Jodi, can I talk to you?"

"Sure." Jodi tried to suppress a smile. Well, that was easy. Courtney was going to quit before she even started.

Teague shut down the tractor and hopped off, mopping his brow with a bandanna. He was in the last phases of clearing extra acreage for pasture. It was past time for a break, and he just happened to be at the part of his property that bordered Jodi's. He glanced across the road. The Brand ranch house was surrounded by trees, a green oasis in the flat landscape, and it looked cool and inviting. He just bet she had a glass of iced tea in there somewhere. Shoving the bandanna in his back pocket, he hopped the fence and crossed the road, patting his thigh when Luna ran down the driveway and fell into step beside him.

"Hey, girl," he said. "Remember me?"

She whined and trotted toward Jodi's, then stopped, looking back as if urging him on.

"Coming," he said. "Hey, who's here?"

He didn't really need to ask the dog who owned the silver SUV parked in Jodi's driveway.

"Courtney," he said. "Shit."

He stopped, then trudged onward. He needed something wet and cool so bad, not even the prospect of dealing with Courtney could stop him. Besides, he wanted to know what she was doing at Jodi's. Hopefully she hadn't gone there looking for him.

But maybe this was an opportunity. Maybe if she saw how he felt about Jodi, she'd back off.

As he approached the house, the two girls walked out of the barn together, so deep in conversation they didn't even see him. Wonder of wonders, Courtney was wearing normal, everyday clothes—jeans and a T-shirt. The jeans were pretty much pasted onto her body, and the shirt was decorated with a rhinestone silhouette of a pair of crossed six-guns that glinted in the sun. It was an outfit that just might scare the horses into a stampede, but it was a step in the right direction.

He'd caught Jodi flashing a few hostile looks at Courtney during the Rotary luncheon, and he'd flattered himself that she was jealous—but judging from her body language now, when she didn't even know he was approaching, her feelings about Courtney didn't have a thing to do with him. He paused near the porch while they were still absorbed in conversation.

"I'm just a little concerned," Courtney said.

"About what?" Jodi sounded wary.

"Well, you told Troy he would be training me to do some of my tasks as a volunteer," Courtney said. "And I'm worried about how that's going to affect our relationship."

"What do you mean?' Jodi asked. "It'll be fine."

"But if he trains me, it might be hard for him to mind me later on."

"*Mind* you?"

"Well, yes, You know, accept my authority."

Oh, man. This was going to be good. Normally, Teague would have jumped in to defend his brother— but he had a feeling Jodi would do just fine on her own.

"Trust me, Troy doesn't accept anyone's authority." Teague could hear the smile in Jodi's voice. "Not even mine."

"Well, that might be something I could work on with him."

"Sure," Jodi said. "Maybe smack him around a little. Show him who's boss."

Teague had to stifle a snort at that one. Jodi was definitely taking care of business.

"Well, I didn't mean that. I meant…"

"Listen," Jodi said. "Let me explain this before you piss me off. Troy is my assistant. My number one. My right hand. When it comes to the kind of things you'll be doing as a volunteer, he's perfectly qualified to train you."

"I don't think you understand." Courtney's condescending tone made him bristle. He could just imagine how Troy felt. "I have a lot of experience with horses. My Hanoverian, Double Dutch, won the Fendi Cup at the Hampton Classic and was considered for the Olympic team." Her lower lip began to tremble. "He's gone now, but…"

Jodi tossed her hair. "Your horse won it? Where were you?"

"I was there," Courtney said. "I always oversaw Dutch's handlers. Like I said, I'm quite experienced."

"Well, Troy grew up ranching," Jodi said. "I'd say that makes you even at best. He did a lot more than watch somebody else ride his horse."

"Well," Courtney said. There was a long silence, but she broke it with an exasperated little huff. "But I don't want him touching Honeybucket. He's delicate."

"This isn't *Of Mice and Men*, and Troy's no Lenny," Jodi said. "He's perfectly capable of handling your… dog. And if the animal's that delicate, you shouldn't bring him here."

Teague couldn't help laughing, but he figured he'd better intervene before there was an all-out catfight and somebody got hurt. He knew Emmett had written up releases for the clinic, but he doubted Jodi was covered for murdering volunteers.

"Teague!" Courtney spotted him and posed against the railing. "I'm *so* glad you're here. I was just talking to Jodi about your brother Troy. I'm a little concerned she's not monitoring him closely enough."

Teague narrowed his eyes. Had Troy hurt himself again? When he'd overheard Courtney talking about his brother, it had gotten his back up—but maybe she'd had a reason to think Jodi wasn't giving Troy enough supervision.

"What happened?"

"Nothing, as far as I could see," Jodi said. "Why don't you explain your concerns to Teague while I get us some iced tea?"

She flashed a murderous look at Courtney, then tossed Teague the same baleful glare and stomped into the house, her jaw set. Teague made a mental note to watch his step. She was liable to get out her daddy's shotgun and shoot her new volunteer, and judging from her expression, anyone in a three-mile radius might end up as collateral damage.

—◦◦◦—

Jodi washed her hands, then slammed three glass tumblers down on the counter and clinked a handful of ice into each, almost enjoying the cruel bite of the cubes on her hands. She muttered a few curse words as she pulled a pitcher of iced tea and a lemon out of the refrigerator, then scanned the lit interior.

Man, she was hungry. She hadn't had breakfast, and it was practically lunchtime. But if she made herself lunch, she'd have to invite Courtney to eat, and Teague too. Glancing over her shoulder, she fished a piece of ham out of a deli bag, rolled it up, and ate it in three quick bites. That helped, but she needed something more.

Pickles. Belle Arnold had brought her a big jar of homemade baby dills as a housewarming present. Hauling it out of the fridge, she grabbed a fork and speared one, then stood at the counter, crunching it happily. Ham and pickles. That was a balanced meal, right? Protein and a vegetable.

The floor creaked behind her and she whirled to see Teague walking in the door. She quickly dropped the fork, pickle and all, in the sink and tried to look casual.

"So did you ease Courtney's worried mind?"

"Yeah. It was nothing," he said. "She just likes to stir up trouble."

"No kidding." She poured the tea, almost sloshing it over the edge of the glasses, then slapped the lemon onto the cutting board beside the stove and got a knife out of the drawer below. She turned to face Teague and he backed away, his hands palms out at chest level as if warding her off.

"Easy, there," he said. "Watch the knife."

"Sorry." She sighed and he lowered his hands as she turned and sliced the lemon into wedges. "I just hate to see you getting involved with somebody who doesn't understand Troy. I mean, you heard her. Talking about making him 'mind.'"

"I told you, I'm not involved with her."

Jodi tossed him a disbelieving glare.

"Why? You jealous?" He was giving her that sneaky grin again—the one that said he'd caught her looking at him, or thinking about him, or being jealous. But he was wrong this time. She gave the lemon a final whack and he flinched.

"There's no reason to even be civil to someone who talks about Troy like that."

Teague leaned against the counter. "I know how you feel. But you might as well get used to it, since half the population doesn't get who Troy is. You have to give people a chance to learn."

"It wasn't just that she didn't understand," Jodi said. "It was that she didn't want to. She was so upset at the notion she might have to take orders from him that she was about ready to quit. I wish she had."

"Yeah, I know. But it's our job to *help* people understand."

Jodi sighed. "Whatever." She arranged the wedges of lemon on a plate, then set the plate and the three glasses on a wooden tray with a burned-in design of a cowboy riding a bucking horse. Famous Wyoming brands rimmed the edge.

"So you don't want her around, but you're defending her?"

"I'm just trying to help with the Troy thing."

She snorted. It wasn't attractive, but then, she wasn't trying to attract Teague. She shouldn't even be talking to him.

"Hey." He stepped up behind her and put his hands on her shoulders. Evidently the snort had been more attractive than she thought. "I know how you feel." His arms swept around her in a hug that would have been brotherly if he hadn't put his lips so close to her ear. "You feel *good*." He drew out the last word and his breath fluttered the fine curls at the nape of her neck. She clenched her thighs as a spasm of lust made a line drive straight to her center.

"Teague." She spun around and shoved him away. "I'm busy."

"Hmm." He cocked his head and smiled. "So does that mean I should come back when you're not?"

"No." She lifted the tray, but her hands were shaking and the glasses slid toward the edge. "It means—*aack!*"

She barely righted the tray in time to keep the glasses from slipping off. Looking at Teague's expression made her want to set the whole deal on the counter and throw the glasses at him one by one. He was smiling, which was fine, except that the smile was a combination of smug satisfaction and good-natured mockery that made her want to belt him one, like she had when they were kids and he made fun of her for being a girl.

"Okay," he said, raising his hands in the air like a hold-up victim. "Sorry. But I didn't make any promise to your mother, and you can't blame me for trying. But Courtney and I are not a couple. I certainly haven't slept with her or anything."

She banged the tray down on the counter, making the ice jangle in the glasses, and spun to face him. "Well, if there's one thing I know about you, it's that sleeping with a woman doesn't mean you're serious about her."

The minute she said it, she regretted it. That was giving away way too much. He took a step toward her and she could feel her face heating in a blush.

"Jodi, what are you saying?"

He was standing way too close. She could smell fresh cut grass and sage, and the scent took her back to the days they'd spent in the summer sun with Vegas. Why did everything associated with Wyoming's outdoors make her think of Teague? She'd spent plenty of time riding horses and puttering around the barn without him. For some reason, he dominated her childhood memories just like he ruled her thoughts at night.

He reached up and shoved a lock of hair behind her ear and that spark of lust ricocheted from his touch and hit home base again. Dang. He knew that got to her. There was something so tender about that gesture—something caring and nurturing that was all the more touching when it came from someone who usually hid his tender side.

He wasn't hiding anything now. His eyes were serious, fixed on hers as if begging her to believe him.

"Sometimes you pretend you don't love somebody because you know you're not good for her," he said.

She looked down and away, avoiding his eyes, but he put one finger under her chin and tilted her face up to meet his eyes. "And then you try and try to become someone who *is* good for her. You do everything you can so that if you ever get another chance, you'll have something to offer."

She blinked. What was he saying?

His voice dropped into a whisper and he pulled her against him.

"Everything I did while you were gone—the business, the house... that was all for you."

She knew she should pull away, make a joke, something—but instead she rested her head against his chest and closed her eyes. His arms tightened and she could feel his chest rising and falling, his heart beating under her cheek.

She just wanted to stay there a while. Just wanted to take a break from resisting him for a minute. It was getting to be more and more of a struggle.

His chest rose again as he took in a deep breath. His arms tightened and suddenly, her heart thrummed with panic.

"Teague." She pulled away, avoiding his eyes. "I told you, my mother…"

He looked so hurt she could hardly stand it, but she'd promised, and he knew it. If he loved her, wouldn't he respect her decision?

"Stop, okay?" she said. "I told you, I made a promise. Can't you respect that and stop making this harder than it has to be?"

"No. I can't. I can't respect you letting other people tell you how to live your life."

"She's my *mother*, Teague. And she's all I have left. And you keep—*tempting* me."

"Sorry." He was smiling again. The expression definitely didn't match the words. "I don't mean to do it. It just happens."

"Oh, right. So that was an accident, back there at your house? And yesterday?"

"Pretty much. Yeah." He was staring down at the toe of his boot, his lips pressed together to hold back a smile. "Especially the part with the goat. That was an accident."

"Well, yeah. If we hadn't fallen…"

"But it wasn't all me. How am I supposed to behave myself when you… you know."

She cleared her throat. "Well, I'm sorry. I'll try not to slip up again."

He took a step closer. "I said it was an accident. I didn't say it was a mistake."

He was gazing at her so intently she felt totally exposed. Hell, she felt *naked* when he looked at her like that. She let out a frustrated little mew and spun back to the counter, pretending she needed to make crucial adjustments to the lemon slices.

Teague sighed. "Well, we'd better get out there. Miss Priss will be wondering what happened to us."

"Not that I care," Jodi said.

"Yeah, I kind of feel sorry for her," Teague said. "She's so… so different from everybody around here. Such an outsider." He looked away, as if something fascinating was taking place outside the window over the sink. "I know what that's like. I know she's annoying, but I think we should give her a chance."

Jodi thought back to high school—to the whispers in the hall as Teague passed; to the gossip about his father's drinking and his mother's affairs; to the hurt in his eyes when he'd overheard Jodi's mom calling him "that white trash boy." Teague had been an outsider, all right.

And she hadn't helped him the way he was helping Courtney. She'd been too worried about what other people would think. About how it might affect her chances at the rodeo crown.

Teague might be annoying as all get-out, but he was a better person than she'd ever be.

"Okay," she said. "I'll try to be nice. For you."

"For me?" He took a step closer. "So since you're in the mood and all, do you want to do a couple other things for me?"

She looked up, suddenly aware of his eyes probing hers with a new intensity. The look she'd backed away from before was hurt, and something like love—but this was pure, raw sex. She felt her body coming alive, the nerves dancing at the surface of her skin sending the signal from his touch to her breasts, to her heart, to the warmth between her legs. It shot through her body, knocking down all her sensible resolutions like a pinball hitting the bumpers, racking up a high score.

Teague licked his lips and leaned closer, letting his hand trace the side of her face. Lowering his face to hers, he touched her lips with his and the pinball zoomed straight down the middle, taking all her good sense with it.

She reached up, cupping her hand behind his neck, and pulled him close.

Their lips were almost touching when a noise made her turn toward the door.

―⁓―

Teague felt himself being drawn in by Jodi's eyes, her lips, the peaches-and-sunshine smell of her hair. The outside world faded away. She was magic for him, like a drug he couldn't do without. Her lips were inches from his, her eyes drifting closed, when a sudden sound made him look up.

Courtney stood in the doorway, and she looked like an outsider, all right. Honeybucket was still smiling, but judging from his doggie-mama's stiff posture and sour expression, she wasn't too happy to see Teague and Jodi headed for a clinch.

The girl's face was still puffy, probably from crying over her horse, and judging from the sheen in her eyes, seeing him and Jodi together was enough to make her start up again.

He'd hoped it would be enough to make her back off—but dang, the girl looked like her world had ended. She was going to cry, he was sure of it.

Not again. He just couldn't deal with more of Courtney's tears.

Without thinking it through, he stepped away from Jodi, blinked, and wiped one eye. "Thanks," he said. "I think you got it." He turned to Courtney. "Had something in my eye."

Courtney's expression didn't change. She obviously didn't buy his explanation. And Jodi looked furious.

He was just trying not to hurt anyone. And instead, he'd hurt everybody.

Story of his life.

Jodi grabbed the tray and stalked out the door, Courtney trailing behind. Teague was in no hurry to follow. He'd let them cool down a little.

Alone in the kitchen, he snuck a look at the pickle lying half-eaten in the sink. Weren't pickles one of those things women ate when they were pregnant? Sure they were. Pickles and ice cream. He'd heard about that.

Glancing toward the door, he cracked open Jodi's freezer. Holy crap. Ben and Jerry were apparently Jodi's two best friends. He counted four containers of ice cream, in flavors ranging from Cherry Garcia to Chubby Hubby.

Closing the freezer, he opened the fridge. Most of the top shelf was taken up by an enormous jar of disturbingly phallic pickles, each about six inches long, floating in briny soup. It looked like she must have eaten about half of them.

Shoot. He'd thought maybe he'd been wrong about Jodi being pregnant. He'd decided he'd jumped to that conclusion without sufficient evidence, and when Darla started spreading the same story, he'd told himself it was a vicious rumor—but evidently, it was true.

Chapter 23

JODI STALKED OUT ONTO THE PORCH, HER CHEEKS burning. Setting the tray on a white wicker table, she plopped down onto the porch swing so Courtney couldn't sit on it with Teague. No way was she going to watch Courtney cozying up to Teague like they were high school sweethearts.

Something in his eye. Yeah, right. If he wasn't interested in Courtney, why was he trying to hide the fact she'd almost caught them kissing? Because that's where they'd been headed. Jodi reached up and touched two fingers to her lips. They still felt hot with expectation, and she could swear they ached a little. She'd *needed* that kiss. It was hers, and he took it away.

Which was a good thing, she told herself. Her mother was right. Teague might dress different now, but he hadn't really changed. She'd been touched by his admission that he'd changed his life for her, but the next thing she knew, he was lying to Courtney. Was he playing her or what? He was still difficult, still dangerous and unpredictable.

Courtney eyed the two wicker chairs and the porch swing and finally sat down beside Jodi. *Great brains think alike*, Jodi told herself. Courtney was making sure Teague wouldn't share the swing with Jodi. Ironically, that left the two of them sitting hip to hip, like best friends.

She passed a glass to Courtney and took one for herself, glancing over at the door. Where the hell was Teague? Hiding? He had to know both women were pissed at him. Maybe he was afraid to come out of the kitchen.

Just when she'd given up on him, he appeared in the doorway. He saw the two of them sitting together and smiled at Jodi, probably thinking how nice it was that she and Courtney were getting to be such good friends.

Men were idiots.

"Tea?" she said.

"Thanks." His tone was hesitant and weirdly formal. "Don't mind if I do."

He rested one hip on the porch railing and gulped half his glass in one go while both women watched. There was something about a thirsty man tilting his head back and savoring a long, cold drink on a hot summer day that made Jodi warm inside in spite of her anger.

Teague took another glug from his glass, then shifted his weight against the railing and swirled the ice in his glass, his eyes darting from one girl to the other. Jodi flashed him a sarcastic smirk, and he seemed to take that as encouragement. Most men were a little lame when it came to reading social cues, but Jodi decided Teague was a total dimwit. Or maybe he only saw what he wanted to see.

"So," he said. "You want me to come help with Russell on Saturday?"

"No," she said.

"I thought you might want to introduce Vegas to the rest of the kids. You know, just to see how he responds. I could help with that too."

"Um," Jodi said. Dang it, bringing up Vegas wasn't fair. The old horse was the symbol of the bond between them—the last remnant of their childhood friendship. "Maybe."

"Oh, I could help too." Courtney was sitting up straight now, smiling at Teague. "That could be my first day. And you could tell me more about your brother."

Teague flashed Jodi a questioning glance and she responded by rolling her eyes. Why could men never see when women were after them? Courtney wasn't interested in Troy. She was only interested in Teague.

Teague, who'd jumped like he'd been hit with a cattle prod when Courtney caught them in the kitchen.

"Hey, Jodi, you want to go to the Snag tonight?"

"What?"

"The Snag. I wondered if you wanted to go."

Was he trying to make up for his mistake by asking her out in front of Courtney? It didn't matter. She obviously needed to stay away from him.

"Wasn't planning on it."

"I could go," Courtney said with a coy smile.

"Todd Dereemer's playing." Teague ignored Courtney as if she hadn't spoken. "Always draws a big crowd. It would give you a chance to see who's still around and maybe meet some new folks."

Jodi smiled in spite of herself. The Snag was Hank and Belle Arnold's bar, a wild place with a mechanical bull in one corner that had seen a lot of action. Hank Arnold was worried about liability, so he'd declared the bull off-limits years ago—but the crowd commandeered it on a regular basis, treating their friends to rides that increased in difficulty depending on the drunkenness of the volunteer operator. Maybe somebody would talk Courtney into a bull ride.

But she wasn't going anywhere with Teague. Not after that "something-in-my-eye" incident.

"No thanks," she said.

Courtney straightened in her seat, fidgeting like a little kid who wanted to go to the circus. "I'd like to go. I need to meet the natives." She trilled out a high-pitched giggle. "Get to know the local customs."

"Yeah. Jodi, you sure?" Teague asked. He looked a little desperate now that Courtney was angling for a date. "Don't you want to go?"

"No thanks." She flashed him an oh-so-sweet smile. "You two go ahead."

"Great." Courtney gave Teague a perky smile. "I'll meet you there."

Three hours later, Jodi sighed and stared out the window. No lights glimmered on the wide stretch of plains outside; all she could see was her own reflection, staring back at her like a ghost from the dark window. Teague had taken Luna home, and the place felt empty.

She wondered what he was doing. Probably sitting at the bar with Courtney, introducing her around, buying her drinks. Courtney would probably get drunk, and he'd have to take her home. She'd lure him inside, then into her bed.

Then she'd have him right where she wanted him.

Hopefully Teague would remember to use protection this time. Jodi put her hand on her stomach and closed her eyes. She didn't feel anything stirring inside her. Surely if anything had come of their carelessness she'd know it.

She was a little late, but that didn't mean anything. She was always irregular.

Shutting out the image of Teague and Courtney together, she tapped a bunch of papers on the tabletop to line up the edges. Grant applications were dull and time consuming. She almost regretted not accepting Teague's invitation. A drink would sure hit the spot about now.

Hell, what was she thinking? She'd didn't need Teague's invitation to go have a drink at her favorite watering hole. Shoving her chair back, she turned toward the window and considered her reflection. Her hair looked good, and in the dim light, the rest of her looked okay too. She'd just head over there and see who else was around.

A half hour later, she stepped into the bar. Purvis had undergone a few changes since she'd left town, but walking into the Snag was like stepping back in time. The same old black-and-white rodeo photos decorated the walls; the same scarred tables and rickety stools provided seating; and the same hideous painting of a plus-sized nude hung over the bar, an old bridle strategically draped over the naughty bits.

The crowd was mostly seated tonight, at the tables closest to the stage. Todd Dereemer was singing something slow and sweet, a love song. She was glad she was coming in on the end of that one. Todd was permanently love-struck, and she usually liked hearing his songs about his wife and kids—but tonight she wasn't in the mood.

He spotted her walking in and flashed her a grin, swinging into her favorite:

Rodeo Queen, Rodeo Queen
Cutest little girl that I ever did see.
Rodeo Queen, Rodeo Queen
My fantasies have a Western theme…

Jodi smiled, her mood brightening. She was definitely home now.

She scanned the room. A few men in Wranglers and
hats were playing pool on the far side of the room, and
another gaggle of cowboys was gathered near the dart-
board, though they seemed more interested in checking
out the female customers than playing. At a corner table,
a group of men were laughing raucously. She didn't recognize anyone except Teague and Courtney, who were
seated at a table watching the band. Courtney had one
hand on Teague's knee, which was jouncing nervously
in time to the music. He looked stiff and uncomfortable.

Good.

No, not good. Indifferent. That was how she should
feel. She didn't care. Didn't care one bit.

Jodi made her way up to the other end of the bar
and perched on a stool with a torn red vinyl seatback.
"Vodka tonic," she said to the bartender. She didn't
recognize the guy. Years before, she'd known everybody who set foot in the Snag. Now, it was just a bunch
of strangers.

"Comin' right up." The bartender, a thin man with
dark eyes and the nervous mannerisms of a scared rabbit, hustled over to the stainless steel counter and started
mixing her drink. She stared resolutely at the bottles
behind the bar for a while, but gradually, her gaze slid
sideways to see what Courtney and Teague were doing.

Courtney had taken her hand off Teague's leg, and he was leaning forward, watching the band as if his life depended on it.

The bartender shoved a tall glass across the bar. Jodi rummaged in her purse, but before she could find her wallet a large, masculine hand reached around her, thrusting out a five-dollar bill.

"I buy for the lady," a deep voice said.

Jodi turned and looked up to meet a perfect, gleaming smile, set in a tanned face topped by a mop of artfully tousled dark hair. She couldn't help staring. The guy was perfect—tall and muscular, with male-model cheekbones and dark, flashing eyes. Tight off-white pants clung to his form like Shakespearean tights and disappeared into black leather knee-high boots. A polo shirt, open at the neck, tightened over a healthy set of pecs.

He met Jodi's eyes and she realized her mouth was hanging open. This had to be one of Skelton's Argentine polo players. He was tanned and athletic-looking, and the beard shadow stubbling his square jaw indicated there was no shortage of testosterone coursing through that long, lean body. Jodi felt suddenly warm. She put her hand to her lips to make sure she wasn't drooling.

Nope. They'd gone dry.

Chapter 24

"Uh... thanks." Jodi stared in fascination at the man's face. She'd never seen anyone that good-looking outside of a magazine.

"You are most welcome." He sat down beside her, keeping one arm on the back of her stool. Leaning forward, he fixed his eyes on hers and upped the wattage of his perfect smile. He looked like an ad for men's cologne—the kind that makes ordinary mortal men believe that a dab of fragrance can earn them instant studhood—but he smelled like leather, fresh cut grass, and something else—something indefinable. Strength, maybe, or wind.

"I am Gustaldo," he said. "And you?"

"I am... I am Jodi," she said, suddenly embarrassed by her plain-Jane name. She should be called Esmeralda, or at least Tiffany or something. How could Gustaldo bestow his intoxicating attention on a mere Jodi?

"Joh-dee," he said.

Maybe her name wasn't so bad after all. The way he drew it out, it sounded like it tasted good.

He looked like *he* tasted good. The guy radiated heat—heat, testosterone, and sex.

She blushed, and he sat back a fraction of an inch, as if giving her room to breathe, but he was still smiling like he was contemplating some sweet dessert. His favorite sweet dessert. She felt her insides go all mushy and hot. Maybe his favorite dessert was Molten Lava Cake.

"Would you like to join me and my friends? We have a table," Gustaldo said.

Friends? He has friends? she thought. *There are more?*

She glanced over at the corner, where three more men were watching her. One of them raised his glass in a silent salute; and another gave Gustaldo a grinning thumbs-up. They were all stunningly good-looking, although none of them were quite as over-the-top hot as Gustaldo.

"Ah, no," Jodi said. "No, thank you. I'll just—my friends are over there." She gestured toward the table where Teague and Courtney had been a moment ago. Now there was only Courtney, but even hanging with Courtney would be safer than sitting at Gustaldo's table. His three friends were nearly as handsome as he was, and if they emanated the same heady essence of maleness she'd probably either pass out or rip her clothes off if she got within ten feet of them.

She glanced around, looking for Teague, and saw him coming up behind her.

"She's with me," he said, glowering at Gustaldo.

"Pardon me. But you are with Miss Skelton, no?" Gustaldo flashed his winning smile Teague's way, but Teague only scowled.

"You cannot have all the beautiful women," Gustaldo said. "You must choose, my friend." He let his hand drop from Jodi's seatback to hook around her waist. "I am hoping you will choose Miss Skelton."

Teague looked from Courtney to Jodi as if he couldn't make up his mind whom to choose—which made up Jodi's mind in an instant.

She chose Gustaldo, dammit. It served Teague right.

"It's okay, Teague." She flashed him a teasing grin. "I'm going to hang with Gustaldo and his friends for a while. Like you said, coming here's a great way to meet people."

"I didn't mean…"

"I'm fine, Teague." She turned away from him and smiled at Gustaldo, who shifted his hand slightly where it was gripping her waist. The movement sent a ripple of heat through her, along with a spasm of alarm. This guy's seduction skills were in the red zone, and he wasn't even trying. It was fun to make Teague jealous, but she was playing with fire.

Fire could be fun, though. Warm and bright. As long as you didn't let it get out of control…

"Come." Gustaldo stood, removing his hand from her waist and taking her hand. Leading her to the table, he was too busy grinning at his confederates to notice when she fell behind him a step and stuck her tongue out at Teague.

Teague watched Jodi go, his stomach roiling. What the hell was she doing, going off with the polo player? Courtney had told him about those guys. They were the hired guns of the polo world, expert players who farmed themselves out to the highest bidder. Courtney said they were a pretty wild bunch, raising hell and seducing trophy wives and heiresses everywhere they went. She'd even asked him to protect her from them.

He hadn't seen that she was in any danger. The guys had glanced at her once or twice, but they hadn't approached. He'd decided she was exaggerating and written them off as harmless, but now they had Jodi. Watching her go with her small hand in Gustaldo's muscular paw, he felt a sudden urge to go after her and drag her away.

He watched her sit down in a chair one of the other players drew up to the corner table. Her new friend sat beside her and all four men leaned toward her attentively as she spoke. She said something that made them laugh, and Gustaldo ran his hand up her back and patted her shoulder.

It didn't seem to bother her. She was laughing too, with her head back. Jodi had always been perfectly capable of holding her own with the guys. There was no reason for him to go over there and interrupt. Shoving his hands in his pockets, he moseyed back to Courtney and sat down again, folding his arms over his chest.

"There you are," she said. She patted his leg. He wished she'd stop touching him almost as much as he wished Gustaldo would stop touching Jodi.

He needed to do something about Courtney. He didn't even know how it had gotten started, really. One day he'd been nice to her, and the next she was acting like they were joined at the hip. He kept trying to get away, but he just seemed to get mired deeper in her swamp of convenient assumptions.

"Here I am," he muttered. He fixed his eyes on the band as if watching Todd belt out a Garth Brooks song was the most important thing in the world.

"Was that Jodi?"

He nodded and pulled his hat low over his eyes.

"I thought she wasn't coming."

Teague shifted his eyes her way and frowned. "Guess she changed her mind."

"Maybe she just wanted to go on her own. Looks like she's caught herself a polo player. She'd better look out. All those guys ever think about is sex."

"What makes you think that?" he asked.

"Oh, Daddy said so." She waved a hand toward Jodi and the men. "He says they're hot-blooded and not to be trusted."

Damn, Teague thought. He'd felt hot-blooded a few times with Jodi, and look what it had led to.

"And now, with the horses gone…" Courtney gave a small hiccup, but to Teague's relief there were no tears. "They don't have anything to do. I don't know why they're still here. They've got way too much time on their hands." She thrust out her lower lip. "I don't know what Jodi thinks is so interesting about them. They're hot, but they can barely speak English." She patted his leg. "You and I have such interesting conversations."

Teague grunted. In his opinion, this was about as interesting as any conversation he'd had with Courtney so far, mostly because they were talking about Jodi.

Although the next conversation would be even better. That would be the one where he told her to get lost.

"Listen, Courtney," he began. "We need to talk."

"I have to go to the little girls' room," she said—and she was gone.

He glanced back at the corner table. Jodi was telling some story to the polo players, waving her hands in the air to illustrate her point. The men looked enraptured. They were big, all of them, broad-shouldered and tall, with carelessly styled long hair that made them look even bigger. Jodi's pale, lithe figure looked miniaturized by comparison, like a tiny sparrow surrounded by eagles. Judging from the men's faces as they watched her, they were birds of prey, all right.

One of the players leaned back in his chair and waved broadly at Bruce, the bartender, who skittered over to the table in his smudged white apron. Moments later, the bartender hustled to the table with a full bottle of tequila, a plate of lemons, a salt shaker, and five shot glasses.

Five.

Teague watched as one of the men filled the glasses and shoved one toward Jodi. She shook her head, smiling.

Good. Smart girl. Teague smiled to himself.

"Teague?" Courtney was back.

He grunted.

"You want to dance?"

"No thanks."

"Oh. Okay." She started to sit down on the chair beside him, then slipped off and stumbled slightly before she managed to climb on board. That was weird. How many drinks had she had? She was doing rum and Cokes, and he could swear she'd only had two, but she was staggering like she'd downed a fifth of Captain Morgan.

He glanced over at Jodi again. She could take care of herself, he supposed. She'd made that clear when she stuck out her tongue at him. But she was naïve, and way too trusting—or at least, she had been when she'd left for back East. Maybe she'd hardened up out there, learned to be more careful.

Yeah, right. That was how she ended up naked in Teague's bed her first day in town.

The polo players had filled their shot glasses and were lifting them high in the air, obviously toasting their guest. They threw their heads back and downed the shots, then slammed their glasses down with a shout.

Courtney slid sideways on her chair and fell against him as Jodi's laughter rose above the crowd, sounding high and a little wild. One of the men was talking, gesticulating wildly, and Jodi was leaning against Gustaldo and laughing. She looked perfectly comfortable and at ease, and the rowdy polo team seemed delighted to have her with them.

Crap.

Courtney sat upright, then hopped off her chair. He looked down at her, surprised.

"You go on," she said. "I can tell you want to be with her." Her eyes glistened with tears. "I'll just go home." She lurched away from him and tried to grab her purse. She missed it on the first swipe, then finally managed to snag it. She slung it over her shoulder, blinking fast, and walked a crooked line down the aisle, bouncing off various obstacles as she stumbled through the tables and chairs.

Dang. She was wasted. How had that happened? The girl's tolerance for alcohol must be nonexistent. Teague sighed.

"Courtney," he said.

She turned sharply to face him and her purse swung in a wide arc, smacking a seated beer drinker in the face.

"Hey," the guy said.

Courtney staggered backward, looking surprised, and Teague took her arm, leading her back to her chair. She looked blearily at the chair, then up at Teague, obviously needing help to climb aboard.

"I don't think you should drive," he said. "Why don't you wait a while? Come on, I'll get you a plain Coke."

"Don't bother," Courtney said. Fishing her keys out of her purse, she dropped them on the floor. "Oops."

Teague bent swiftly and picked them up. "You're not driving, Courtney."

"Well, take me home, then." She struggled to stand. "I want to go."

He grabbed her around the waist before she could slide to the ground.

"Gotta go," she slurred.

He looked over at Jodi. She was getting up, leaving the corner table. He started to breathe a sigh of relief, but then her new friend stood too, and took her hand. Leading her to the dance floor, he spun her around like a ballerina and drew her close as the band started a slow song.

I don't know what I'd do
Baby if I lost you…

Teague felt all the air whoosh out of the room as Gustaldo took Jodi's hand and wrapped his other arm around her waist. As Teague watched, the polo player slipped his fingers into her the back pocket of her jeans. Teague's stomach clenched and he swallowed a bitter rush of stomach acid. Jodi had given the guy an inch, and Teague had no doubt Gustaldo would take a mile or more.

And if Teague took Courtney home, she'd be alone with the guy. What if he tried to take advantage of her or something? He parked Courtney in a chair before she could protest.

"Be right back." He strode over to the bar to grab a napkin. "Got a pen?" he asked the bartender.

Bruce unclipped a ballpoint from his shirt pocket and pivoted from the beer tap to slide it across the bar.

"Thanks." Teague jotted his cell number on the napkin and set off toward the dance floor. Edging around the perimeter, he waited for Jodi and Gustaldo to pass and shoved the napkin in her back pocket—the one not occupied by Gustaldo's hand. He felt Jodi stiffen at his touch.

"Cell number," he muttered. "Just in case you need me."

She flashed him a grimace and he backed away. Clearly, she didn't think she'd be needing him. But you never knew. If that guy got her alone...

Maybe she wanted to be alone with him. Probably the last thing she'd want to do was call Teague.

He didn't want to think about it.

He turned to see Courtney standing in the aisle, watching him with narrowed eyes. Earlier, she'd looked drunk, her mouth slack, her eyes half-closed. Now she looked pissed. But as he watched, her face relaxed into its drunken state.

"Come on," she said. "Gimme my keys." She hit a table with her hip, causing a drink to sway and slosh.

"Ow," she said, rubbing her hip. She turned to the customer whose drink she'd spilled. "Watch it." She stumbled backward and fell against Teague, and he reflexively put a steadying arm around her shoulders just as Jodi passed, clasped in Gustaldo's brawny arms. She stared at him and Courtney for a second, then closed her eyes and rested her head against the polo player's chest as he whirled her away.

"I think I'm going to throw up," Courtney said. "Maybe you're right. You should take me home."

Chapter 25

JODI TRIED TO IGNORE THE HEAT EMANATING FROM her dance partner's body. She tried to ignore the way his breath was warming her ear too, and the way his hand was massaging the small of her back, drifting lower and lower.

Had he just put his hand in her back pocket?

Yep.

She willed away a spasm of something that felt suspiciously like lust. What was it with these guys? They were pure sex on a stick, every one of them.

She winced. Sex and sticks were the last things she needed to be thinking about.

Gustaldo squeezed her hand and bent his head lower, letting his lips brush her hair. Holy crap. He was going to kiss her. She'd only had one drink—or was it two?— but she felt a sudden reckless urge to let him. In the back of her mind, she knew messing with Gustaldo was a bad idea. She turned her head away and pretended not to notice his obvious intentions.

As they passed the far side of the dance floor, she saw Teague watching her. She closed her eyes, only to feel his hand slip into her other pocket. What the hell? Was she wearing a "touch me" sign on the seat of her pants or what?

"Cell number," he said. "Just in case you need me."

Yeah, right. Who needed Teague? She had Gustaldo. He was more than enough.

Way more.

When the song ended, she pulled away and looked at her watch.

"Oh, wow," she said, faking surprise. "Look at the time. I need to get home."

"You have someone waiting?" Gustaldo said. He looked genuinely disappointed. She tried not to feel flattered.

"No, but I have to be up bright and early," she chirped.

"Ah." He took her hand. "I could help." He lowered his voice to a sexy whisper. "We could stay up all night and greet the dawn together," he said.

"Ah, no." Jodi wondered what kind of phrase book he'd used to learn English. The guy didn't seem to be able to say anything that wasn't seductive. Hustling over to the table, she slung her purse over her shoulder. "I don't—I can't. But it's been, um, great." She turned and graced the other three guys with her best rodeo queen smile. It had been great, actually. They'd been funny, entertaining, and most of all, attentive. Having that many stunningly attractive men hanging on her every word had been good for her.

For a while there, she hadn't even thought about Teague Treadwell. Of course, the fact that it took an entire polo team to distract her probably wasn't a good sign.

She fluttered a casual finger wave at the guys and headed for the door, only to stop short as Gustaldo took her hand.

"I will see you home," he said. "I must make sure you are safe."

"No. Gustaldo, no." She pulled her hand away. "I'm fine. Really."

His dark brows lowered over his eyes. "I insist."

"Gustaldo, this is America. You can't insist."

He looked pained, then sad, then angry.

"Never mind." He spun on his heel and walked away.

Jodi watched him go, biting her lower lip and wondering if she'd been rude. She just didn't want him to follow her home. She was pretty sure he'd try to follow her inside, and then God knew what would happen.

Well, not just God. She knew too.

She headed out the door and trotted to her truck. Turning the key in the lock, she climbed inside and started the engine. She was just pulling out of the parking lot when she glanced in her rearview mirror to see the polo team spilling out the front door. Throwing the truck into gear, she swept out of the parking lot. Fast.

Her headlights fanned through the darkness, lighting the pitted blacktop as she turned onto the county road. She could see lights on in a few houses along the way, but as the road eased out of town there was nothing but darkness. The wide open spaces that made her feel so free during the day made her feel a little exposed now. She glanced in her rearview mirror. Were those headlights behind her?

She tossed her hair, ignoring the queasiness in her stomach. *Don't be stupid,* she told herself. *They're not following you.* It was probably some other bar patron heading home.

Of course, hardly anybody lived out this way. Just her and Teague. Bill Caxton's ranch was about five miles down the road, but she hadn't seen him at the bar.

She glanced up again as she turned into the driveway. The lights were gone.

Good. Maybe she'd imagined them.

When she got inside, she puttered around in the kitchen for a while, cleaning up the day's dishes, then grabbed the paperback she was reading and headed for the bedroom. Slipping into an ancient, flimsy nightgown that had once been sexy and was now downright disreputable, she slid into bed and propped her head up on an extra pillow. That was the good thing about living alone. You could wear whatever you damn pleased to bed.

Sighing, she flipped open the book and let the world outside the bedroom fade away. No more Teague. No more Courtney. No more Gustaldo.

Her eyelids were starting to feel heavy when a slash of light crossed the far wall of the bedroom. The accompanying crunch of gravel and the unmistakable slam of a car door made her eyes pop open. Then there was another slam.

"Joh-*deeeeeee!*" sang a chorus of masculine voices. "Joh-*deeeee!*"

Gustaldo. And, by the sound of things, all his friends, too. It *had* been their headlights behind her earlier that night. They'd followed her to see where she lived, and now they were outside.

"Joh-*deeeee!*"

She flicked off the bedside light, then cursed herself. They'd see it go out and know exactly where she was.

Gravel crunched under heavy boots. The worn boards of the front porch creaked, then creaked again, and a heavy knock on the door resounded through the house.

"Joh-deeee!" The voice sounded playful. Amused. Drunk.

Had she locked the front door? She couldn't remember.

She held her breath as the knob rattled once, then twice. There was another knock on the door.

Good. She'd locked it.

That was about the only smart thing she'd done all night.

Someone said something in Spanish, and was answered with laughter and another barrage of *Español*. She heard her name mixed in with the foreign words and winced.

Damn. She didn't know these guys. They were probably harmless, but it was two o'clock in the morning, and they were undoubtedly drunk. Why had she gone and danced with Gustaldo? Why had she even sat with them?

Because of Teague. If he hadn't been there with Courtney, she wouldn't have given Gustaldo the time of day. It was all his fault.

Or was it? She remembered sticking her tongue out at him as she walked away with Gustaldo. She'd been petty and jealous and mean. Much as she'd like to blame Teague, it was her own stupidity that had gotten her into this.

"Joh-deee!" Gustaldo sounded impatient. "We have you a present!"

Oh, great. They'd brought her a gift. Like that would make her open the door.

She slid out of bed and stepped into her jeans. She wasn't going to let them in, but if they somehow got inside, she didn't want to greet them half-naked. She slipped on a T-shirt, then remembered Teague slipping the napkin into her pocket.

What the hell. Maybe she did need him.

Grabbing her cell phone off the nightstand, she hit the

"OK" button to light the number scrawled on the napkin, then poked the numbers into the phone, the digital "beep" of the keypad sounding like a trumpet blaring in the silence.

Teague shrugged Courtney off his shoulder for the third time as they rounded the bend and turned into the driveway of the Skelton mansion.

"Mmm," she said, snuggling closer as he stopped the truck. "Teague."

"What?"

She threw her arms around his neck and tugged him toward her until his face was all mashed up against hers.

"Oh, Teague." Her rum-scented breath was hot in his ear.

"Wait a minute." He wrenched himself away. "Let's get you inside." He'd be safe once he got her to the house. Let her father take care of her.

"Okay." She batted her lashes. "That would be better."

Teague slid out of the truck, then walked around to the other side and opened Courtney's door.

"I don't know if I can walk," she said, her lashes still fluttering. "I'm really drunk."

A warning light flashed in Teague's mind. Courtney's slurred speech had suddenly cleared right up. She didn't sound the least bit drunk now—but she wanted him to carry her?

"Give it a try," he said. "Walking will do you good."

She slid out of the truck and wavered on her high heels, falling against him. Instinctively, he backed away. She miraculously regained her footing.

"Come on," she said. "Help me inside."

She pitched sideways again, and this time he really had to catch her. Taking her elbow, he half-carried her toward the house. When they reached the porch steps, she seemed to lose what little strength she had. She tripped on the third step and almost took a header, so he scooped her up and carried her up to the door.

He hoped Mitch Skelton wouldn't wake up and come to see what was going on. The richest man in the county probably wouldn't be happy to see his daughter half-comatose in the arms of a man who wouldn't pay for the privilege. Shifting her in his arms, he carried her through the gingerbread archway and across the porch to the front door of her ridiculous wedding cake house.

"Hope your dad doesn't see us," he said.

She giggled and put her arms around his neck. "Oh, he's gone," she said.

The warning light was flashing again. "Gone?"

"He went to Arizona to look at some horses."

"Well, at least he won't see me bringing you home drunk."

She giggled again and gave him a squeeze. "Yeah, he'd have a fit. He thinks I ought to find some businessman or a lawyer or something. Not a guy like you."

"A guy like me?" Teague lowered his brows.

"Well, you know. You're kind of from the wrong side of the tracks."

"Right," he said. "And that upsets your dad."

"Yup," she said. "He's soooo pissed. I mean, you're like the town bad boy." She squirmed in her seat. "Everybody's scared of you, because you're so—so *disreputable*."

She said that last word like it meant something good.

She rested her head against his chest. "I heard you even went to jail."

"Not jail," he said, as if it mattered. How had she heard that little tidbit about his life? "I was in juvy. Reform school, back when I was sixteen."

"Oooh," she said. "You're a *felon*. What did you do?"

"Nothing." He felt his stomach twist with disgust—at himself and who he was, and at Courtney. The girl really was slumming—on purpose. She thought this was *West Side Story* or something.

Well, he was nobody's Romeo.

Except maybe Jodi's.

"You have a key?" he asked.

"In my purse. I left it in the truck."

Sighing, he settled her onto a white wicker chair beside the door.

He shifted from one foot to the other, staring down at her. He could just leave her here, he thought—just go. But it probably wasn't safe. Those Spanish guys probably lived on the grounds somewhere, and they'd be home soon. They didn't seem to be interested in Courtney, but you never knew.

They were sure as hell interested in Jodi.

Misinterpreting his look, Courtney simpered and adjusted herself into a languid pin-up pose. He turned away and trudged back to the truck and grabbed her purse off the front seat. Honeybucket poked his head out and blinked.

"Whoa. You've had quite a night, haven't you, Spike?" Teague wasn't about to call any animal Honeybucket. It was insulting. "You got the house key in there?"

He thrust his hand inside and felt around, shifting the little dog sideways as his fingers groped for the key.

"Ark!" said Honeybucket, then let out a disgruntled growl. Teague laughed.

"Come on, buddy." He lifted the dog out and placed him on the ground, then peered into the depths of the purse. The key gleamed at the bottom.

"All right." Teague headed back to the porch and climbed the steps. Shoving the key in the lock, he breathed a sigh of relief when the door opened.

"Come on." He urged Courtney off the chair and guided her inside. Stumbling, she made her way to a white upholstered sofa and grabbed his hand as she collapsed onto the cushions. Pulling free, he grabbed a throw from the back and spread it over her, being careful not to touch her. He stepped away quickly.

"Okay," he said. "Well, I'll see you."

She gave him the same squint-eyed stare he'd caught in the bar. She looked perfectly sober all of a sudden, and pissed as hell.

"You can't go," she said.

"I have to, Courtney. You need to sleep it off."

"I'm fine." She swung her feet to the floor and sat up. "See? Fine." She smoothed her face into a practiced smile and patted the cushion beside her. "Come on. Sit with me." She dropped her voice into a breathy growl. "I'll bet a big bad man like you can make me feel like a wild woman."

Dang. She wasn't drunk. Nobody recovered that fast. No, she'd been faking it, pretending to be helpless so he'd follow her into her parlor like a fly being coaxed into a spider's web. And now she was trying to seduce

him by letting him know just how low class and dangerous he was. That notion might turn her on, but it wasn't
doing a damn thing for him.

And he'd left Jodi at the mercy of the polo players to
look out for this woman. Clenching his fists at his sides,
he headed for the door.

"I'm leaving," he said.

"You can't." She was giving him the stink-eye again,
suddenly sober and no longer the least bit sexy.

"Watch me."

"Where's Honeybucket?"

"He's in the… shit," Teague said. "Hold on. I'll get
him."

He slouched back outside to get the dog. He'd set it
down in the drive and forgotten about it.

He scanned the driveway. There was his truck, and a
pot of flowers, and a rock.

No dog.

Scratching his head, Teague looked right, then left.

The damn dog was gone. Damn. Now he'd have to
hunt for it. He scanned the area, his hands on his hips.
Skelton had all kinds of shrubs and flowers planted
around the place. The dog could be anywhere.

A shrill ringing pierced the night, and he grabbed his
phone out of his pocket.

"Hello?"

"Teague."

"Jodi?"

"Those guys are here." She was speaking in a harsh
whisper.

"What?"

"They followed me home. They're at the door."

"They followed you—you're just now getting home?"

"*No, I've been home. I think they followed me, and then they went and had some more to drink, by the sound of it. They're knocking at the door.*"

"Shit."

"*Yeah.*" He heard her suck in a shaky breath. "*Can you come over?*"

"Yeah. I—I'll be right there." He glanced around the yard, praying the dog would magically turn up somehow. "I just have to…"

A sudden banging sounded through the phone.

"That's them," she said. "Hurry, Teague."

"Okay. I'll be right there…"

"Where are you? Are you home?"

"No, I'm at Courtney's. I…"

"Shoot. Forget it." She was talking in a normal tone now, too angry to whisper. "You'll never make it in time. Just—never mind."

He pulled the phone away from his ear and stared at it. She'd hung up.

Chapter 26

Jodi clicked off the phone and buried her head in her hands. Teague was at Courtney's. She wasn't surprised, and she wasn't angry. Well, not much, anyway.

But she was scared.

If Teague had been home, he could make it to her place in minutes, but Courtney's place was miles away.

A barrage of Spanish sounded from the porch, and then four male voices broke into song, harmonizing clumsily on something that sounded like a Spanish love song. Jodi felt tears stinging her eyes. What was she going to do?

The song trailed away into drunken laughter, and she held her breath. The men were talking again. If only she could understand what they were saying. She could make out her name, but nothing else. As she listened, the voices faded, along with the sound of boots crunching on gravel. She held her breath as one car door slammed, then another.

They were leaving. Thank God.

She felt a stab of guilt. They weren't bad guys. They were just out having a good time, and she'd kind of encouraged them to think of her as a friend. Maybe they really had brought her a present. Maybe they just didn't realize how late it was.

Maybe she should have let them in.

Yeah, right. She remembered the palpable aura of testosterone that had floated above their table. Letting them in the house would be asking for trouble. Hell, sitting at their table had been asking for trouble.

An engine cranked to life and she heaved a sigh of relief as a bar of light from their headlamps crossed her wall. The sound of truck tires on gravel receded into the distance and the night was silent again.

She slumped onto the side of the bed and stared at the wall. She needed to get a dog or something. The visit from Gustaldo and his merry men cast her country isolation in a pretty unattractive light.

She was helpless out here. And she hated feeling helpless. *Hated* it.

But wait a minute. She wasn't helpless.

She got up and slipped her feet into a pair of over-sized fluffy slippers. Traipsing out to the front hall, she opened the door to the coat closet and rummaged around behind the coats. Her father had a... *there* it was. She hefted a scarred old 12-gauge shotgun in her arms. *Now* she wasn't helpless. Let Gustaldo and his pals come back *now*.

She'd teach them to follow girls home.

Cradling the gun in her arms, she started back to the bedroom. She was exhausted. Setting it beside the bed, she slipped out of her jeans and threw her flimsy nightie back on. She just wanted to crawl back into bed and go to sleep. That was all she wanted. She just...

She stopped and cocked an ear. What was that? Was that...

That was tires on gravel.

They were coming back. A chill skittered up her spine, then down again. She gritted her teeth. She wasn't going to let them scare her. Grabbing the gun,

she returned to the hall and pressed her back against
the wall beside the front door. She broke the shotgun
over her thigh and peered into the barrels. No shells.
Dodging back to the closet, she rummaged around on a
high shelf until her hand closed over a small but heavy
cardboard box.

Kneeling beside the door, she winced at the loud *snap*
as she slipped a shell into each barrel, then clicked it
shut. If she remembered right, the roar of the first one
would be enough to set anybody running. It would also
be enough to punch a deep bruise into her shoulder with
the recoil, but she'd deal with that.

She waited, trying to breathe evenly as an engine
purred to a halt, then shut off abruptly.

A door slammed. Boots crunched gravel all the way
up to the front door.

She held her breath.

Someone stopped outside the door. A man, judging
from the heavy footfalls. She could hear him shifting
his weight, his boots scuffing on the worn boards of the
porch. There was no laughter now, no joking in Spanish.

Whoever it was had returned alone.

She squeezed her eyes shut. Why was he just standing there—whoever he was? Was he trying to find a way
to pick the lock? Was he looking for a rock? It would be
easy enough for him to break a window and get in that
way. She felt suddenly cold. Her palms were sweating
where she held the gun, but she was shivering.

Dammit. Whatever he was doing, she wasn't going
to stand here all night and tremble like a scared rabbit
while she waited for him to do it. He was bigger than
her, and stronger—but she had surprise on her side.

Grabbing the doorknob, she wrenched it open and swung the door wide, letting it bang against the wall, and lifted the shotgun to her shoulder.

——∿∿——

Teague stumbled backward as Jodi's door swung open. She stood in the doorway, dressed in a sheer, almost see-through nightie that would barely have reached her thighs under normal conditions. Since both arms were raised to her shoulders, one holding the fore end of a shotgun, the other poised on the trigger, the thing hovered within a hair's-breadth of uncovering her panties.

If she was wearing any.

She wasn't wearing a bra, that was clear. Very clear.

Man, with the gun in her hands and that see-through nightie skimming her breasts, the lace riding high on her thighs, she looked—well, he ought to be scared she'd shoot him, but he was getting too turned on to care.

He swallowed and backed away, lifting his own hands high.

"Don't shoot," he said. "It's me. Don't shoot." He took another step backward and felt the heel of his foot hit open air. The next thing he knew, he was pitching backward down the steps.

"Huh," he grunted as he hit the ground. He blinked, looking up at the stars. They were spinning slightly, leaving trails of light etched on the sky. *Pretty*, he thought.

Jodi's worried face slid into view.

"Teague?"

He squinted up at her. Her hair was tousled, and from his vantage point on the ground, he could almost see up her nightie.

He shifted sideways, hoping for a better angle. He was pretty sure she wasn't wearing any panties.

"Teague?" She knelt down beside him.

Rats.

"Uh." He'd meant to say *hi, I'm fine, don't worry about it,* but "Uh" was all that came out.

"You okay?"

"Uh."

"Here." She set down the shotgun and took his hand. "Can you sit up?"

He smiled. He was lying down, and she was holding his hand. He felt a little dizzy, and his head hurt, but he was happy. Really happy. He tugged on her hand, but she tugged back.

"Come on. Sit up." She reached behind his head to lift it from the ground, then sucked in a quick breath and pulled her hand away. She held it to his face so he could see blood tipping her fingers. "You're bleeding. Come on, get up."

"No," he said. "You lie down. It'll be easier that way." His voice sounded slurred, even to him. Had he had that much to drink?

"Come on." She was ignoring him, hauling on his hand. He couldn't help sitting up. She'd always been strong for her size.

"Hey," he said. "I was looking at the stars."

He wasn't looking at them now, though. He was looking at that nightie. The spinning had stopped, and he could see just fine.

Jodi clasped her arms over her chest.

"You fell," she said. "You all right?"

"Dunno."

The pain at the back of his head was fading. He was fine, but he wasn't about to tell her that. She looked so concerned, with her forehead wrinkled up and her eyes wide.

Of course, maybe she was just scared. He looked around at the dark outbuildings hulking around the house.

"Where'd they go?"

"The polo guys? They left."

"You shoot 'em?"

"No. They left a while ago." She tossed her hair. "No thanks to you. And then I thought you were them, coming back."

"Sorry."

She shrugged and led him up the steps and into the house. "Come on. Let me look at your head."

He let her lead him inside, enjoying the back view as she climbed the steps. The light from the front hall gleamed through her thin nightgown, and he could clearly see the outline of her body. The sheer fabric had thinned at the seat.

Dang, that's some outfit, he thought. *What's left of it.*

Chapter 27

JODI LED TEAGUE INTO THE KITCHEN. PULLING A CHAIR out from under the kitchen table, she let him sink into it and examined the back of his head. He'd hit the concrete walkway, and there was a good-sized gash under his hair. At least, she figured there must be a gash, because there was a lot of blood. His dark hair was clumped and matted around the wound.

"I'll need to clean this up," she said. "You're bleeding."

"That's okay." He turned. "We cowboys are tough. C'mere."

He caught her around the waist and pulled her into his lap, and she was suddenly conscious of the worn-out lingerie she'd worn to bed. She'd been worried about the polo players, and now here she was, practically naked in Teague's lap. Teague, who a half-hour earlier had probably been with Courtney.

She moved to stand, but his arms were tight around her.

"Let me up." She tried to turn, but the movement only made things worse as the hand that had been wrapped around her shoulders swept over one breast. She wrenched herself to her feet, feeling angry, aroused, and thoroughly confused. First there had been the polo players at the bar, good-natured and sexy; then Gustaldo, his body hard against hers on the dance floor. Then the fear, when they'd come to the house, and the anger when she realized where Teague was.

And now? She didn't know what she felt now.

She stalked over to the sink and snagged a few paper towels from a roll that hung under the cupboards. Moistening half of them under the tap, she carried them over to Teague and stood behind him, dabbing at his head wound with the wet towels, then wiping away the blood with the dry ones.

"It's not too bad," she said. "Head wounds bleed a lot. It's just a little cut."

"Good. I'm fine," Teague said. He grinned. "Come sit in my lap again."

She dabbed at the cut a little harder and he winced.

"Look, I had a few vodka tonics but I'm not that drunk. Besides, haven't you had enough for one night?" she asked.

"Enough what?"

"You know what." She pitched the towels in the wastebasket and stood in front of him, her hands on her hips. Then she remembered the nightgown and sat down at the table. Maybe she was tipsier than she'd realized.

"What are you so mad about? All I did was take Courtney home and drop her off. Oh, and I lost her dog."

"Honeybucket?"

"Yeah. I call him Spike, though. No respectable animal should be called Honeybucket." He put his hand up to touch the cut on his head. "Ow," he said, pulling his hand away.

"I'm not sure Mr. Bucket qualifies as a respectable animal." She took his hand. "You're still bleeding." She grabbed another paper towel and leaned over him, dabbing at the wound again. He reached up and ran his hand down her side from shoulder to hip.

"Don't do that." She smacked his hand. "Look, I appreciate you coming out, but I'm fine now. You should go." He blinked, and she heaved out an exasperated sigh. "You're okay to drive, right?"

He shrugged and shifted his gaze sideways. "Doesn't matter. I'm not going anywhere."

"Yeah you are. You're going home." She thrust a wad of paper towels into his hand and stepped away.

"I'm not leaving." He folded his arms over his chest and squared his jaw. "What if they come back?"

She gestured toward the gun. "I'll shoot them."

"No you won't," he said. "Not all four of them."

She set her hands on her hips and blew out an exasperated breath. "Look, I'm fine. I appreciate you playing knight in shining armor, but I can take care of myself now that I found the gun."

He frowned. "I'm not leaving."

"Well, you're not staying."

He stood up.

Good. He was leaving.

He walked over to the sofa. Holding a wad of paper towels to his head, he toed off his boots and laid down, shoving a throw pillow under his head. "You go on to bed. I'll be right here."

She looked down at him. "No."

He cracked one eye open. "Yes."

She sat down beside him. "No. Come on, Teague, you have to go."

—⁓—

Jodi tugged Teague's hand and he swung his legs to the floor and sat up so he was close enough to smell her hair, the same sweet peachy scent it had in high school. She must still be using the same shampoo. A couple days after their last good-bye, he'd gone through every bottle in the drugstore, trying to find what she'd used. He didn't find it, which was just as well. He didn't really want to smell like that himself. It was too girly. Fruity.

Sexy.

She shifted away and lifted one hand to nervously tuck her hair behind her ears.

"Your hands are shaking."

"No they're not." She held them out in front of her, and he had to smile. They were definitely shaking.

He took them in both of his and smiled. "Yeah, they are. It's okay, Jodi. Those guys are gone."

She nodded, but he could see her eyes glistening. Dang. She really had been scared. Impulsively, he pulled her close. Miraculously, she let him.

"You don't have to be scared," he said.

"It's just… I'm so alone out here."

"You don't have to be."

She pulled away and looked at him, her eyes probing his as if she was trying to read his mind. He hoped she could. He hoped she could see how much he wanted her, how much she meant to him. He met her gaze, trying his best to send a telepathic message straight to her heart. It had better work, because for some reason, he sure couldn't say it out loud.

But the telepathy must have worked. Slowly, the two of them drew together, and met in a kiss so tender Teague thought his heart would burst. He buried his fingers in Jodi's hair and tilted his head, trying to put everything he'd ever felt for her into the touch of his lips.

His hands moved down her body. He'd seen her breasts, the nipples dark under the sheer fabric of her nightgown, but he didn't touch them, just rubbed her back to soothe her. This wasn't about getting her into bed. It was about showing her how he felt.

Because the way he felt was surprising even him. When he'd seen her with Gustaldo, the truth had hit him hard. What he'd told her that afternoon on the porch had been true. Everything he'd done—building up the ranch, making deals, trying to work his way into respectable Purvis business circles—had been for her.

He'd known that all along. But now he realized that if he lost her, none of it would matter anymore. All his effort, all the times he'd swallowed his pride, all the hard work—it would have been pointless. He'd seen her dancing with Gustaldo and realized he couldn't lose her.

He loved her so much it hurt.

She whimpered, and he realized he was squeezing her to his chest. Now it was his hands that were shaking as he released her. She looked up at him, and her eyes were teary again.

"Oh, Teague," she said.

That was all she said, but the look in her eyes made him believe she might feel the same way. And when she stood up and headed for the bedroom, he followed her, hoping that was what she'd been trying to say.

———

Jodi wasn't sure what she was trying to say. Part of her was trying to lure Teague into the bedroom, but another part—the sensible part—was trying to run away.

The sensible part didn't have a chance.

The bedroom was dark except for a faint glow from the windows across the room. Teague's face was in shadow, but Jodi didn't need to see his expression to know something had changed. He wasn't playing anymore. This was serious.

He pulled her down onto the bed and took her tenderly in his arms. His kiss started out gentle and pleading as the one before, but when he upped the pressure she did too, and it turned into something hotter and hungrier. His hands moved to her breasts and she gasped as his rough palms grazed her skin and her nipples swelled and peaked.

Closing her eyes, she threw her head back, and Teague kissed her jawline and the soft skin just below it, then moved down her neck to the curve where it met her shoulder. His lips brushed her skin and heat and need flowed from his touch to every part of her body.

Easing her down onto the edge of the bed, he slid the gown's narrow straps off one shoulder, then the other. As the thin fabric fell away from her breasts and settled in her lap, she felt heat pool between her legs. His gaze moved from her breasts up to her face, and when their eyes met she felt the past drift away, and there was nothing but *now*.

Bending down, he flicked his tongue out to tease one pebbled nipple, then drew it into his mouth. If she hadn't lost all her inhibitions before, she lost them then. Falling backward onto the bed, she shimmied her hips to shed what was left of her gown and gave herself up to Teague's hands.

Once again, he was still fully clothed and she was naked, at his mercy, just like back in his bedroom. It should have bothered her. He was in control this way, and she was helpless. But there was something delicious and forbidden about giving herself up to Teague. She felt like a teenager again, like the good girl getting too close to the town bad boy.

Tonight, she was going to join him and be very, very bad.

He intertwined his fingers with hers and stretched her arms above her head, then let his fingers trail down across her palms to her wrists. Pausing to caress the soft, sensitive underside of her arms, he let his fingers trace every curve, traveling across her shoulder to circle her breast, spiraling slowly over her skin, the path narrowing until she shivered and arched her back. He bent and sucked one peaked nipple as he played with the other, and watching his tongue and fingers tease and tweak the swollen pink tips made her so soft and hot inside she felt like she'd melt. As if he'd read her mind, he moved his hand down and ran it from one hip to the other, making her nerve endings twitch and shimmer like summer lightning.

Moving lower, he dipped his hand under the lace of her panties and gently stroked her with a light, teasing touch as he ran his middle finger along the damp seam between her legs. She gasped and opened to him as he slid his finger inside and stroked it out. Rocking her hips, she closed her eyes and arched her back, leaving the dimly lit room behind to simply *feel*.

She forgot who she was. She forgot where they were. All she knew was the touch of his hands, the pleasure of his fingers touching her there, right *there*, right where she needed him. He kissed her again and upped the

tempo, and the kiss blended with all the rest of it in one
dizzying symphony of sensation as she pulsed her hips
in time with his thrusts.

She had just what she wanted, what she needed.
It was Teague. It had always been Teague, and no
promise she made could change that. Crying out, she
clutched at his shoulders and clung to him as the room
rocked and swayed and a wave of joy crested inside
her and broke.

Teague watched in wonder as Jodi closed her eyes and
gave herself up to the pleasure of his touch. She was
giving herself completely, holding absolutely nothing
back, and she looked more beautiful than he'd ever
seen her, her eyes closed in ecstasy, her blonde hair
tangled on the pillow, her back arched as she rode out
her orgasm.

A moment later she was looking up at him, blinking,
looking puzzled as if she couldn't quite remember where
she was. Her lips were pink and swollen from his kiss,
her eyes blurry with lust and love. It was the sweetest
thing he'd ever seen, and he had to kiss her again.

But everything had changed. She was fighting him,
pushing him away. He felt a hot bolt of panic shoot
through his heart. She'd remembered that damned
promise. He'd thought if he could just get her to himself,
just show her how he felt, she'd forget, and he'd have
a chance. But she was struggling against him, shoving
him backward.

He clutched at her for a moment, panicked, but then
her hands moved to his collar and he realized she was

undressing him, tugging off his shirt, pulling at his belt. He stood up and did it for her, shedding his clothes in record time so he could fall back down beside her and pull her close.

He rolled on top of her and paused, propping himself up on his elbows and settling his hips over hers, the head of his cock just touching her entrance. Their eyes met and she bit her lower lip, giving him a shy smile.

That was all the invitation he needed. He cut loose from everything that had ever held him back and thrust inside her, looking down in wonder at her face as she closed her eyes and tilted her head back. She moved gently beneath him like waves, like warm, buoyant waves lifting him and receding, lifting and receding, carrying him up and up and up, higher and higher.

He slowed his pace, biting the inside of his cheek to bring himself under control. He watched her face, taking his cues from the shades of emotion that flickered across her face.

Her hands clasped his arms and her grip tightened while she upped the tempo, her hips lifting off the bed to take all of him harder and faster. Pleasure built inside him with every thrust as he bent to kiss her with a claiming kiss, rough but tender, and he kept his lips pressed to hers until they both arched their backs and lost themselves in a swirling tide of passion and pleasure and all the love he'd been holding back seemed to rise in his heart and overflow.

Chapter 28

TEAGUE WOKE TO FIND HIMSELF STARING UP AT AN unfamiliar ceiling. It took him a minute to remember where he was.

Jodi's house.

Jodi's bed.

The night before swept over him in a rush of memory that made him hard all over again. He glanced over at the empty pillow beside him. Jodi was up already. He'd slept so soundly he hadn't heard her leave the bed.

He could hear her making coffee out in the kitchen. This felt so—domestic. Like they were married or something.

Maybe they should be. Between the prenatal vitamins and the pickles, he was pretty sure Jodi really was pregnant. He stepped into his jeans, a new kind of excitement fluttering in his chest. He loved her enough to take on anything. If he'd ever doubted it, the night before had proven it. He remembered how she'd looked, glowing like an angel against the sheets, her eyes half-closed, a sexy smile urging him on.

All of a sudden, he wanted that baby worse than he'd wanted anything in his life.

He'd never planned to have children. He'd always sworn the Treadwell genes needed to die out. But if it was someone else's child, it would still be half Jodi. Maybe it would be a girl, a little tomboy like she'd been when they were kids. He pictured a pint-sized blonde kid mounted on a pony, bent double over the animal's neck while its hooves ate up the countryside.

Something broke open in his chest and the coming day suddenly looked like the best one he'd ever seen. He'd seen a coffee commercial once where some guy got out of bed and spread his arms in joy. *Rise and embrace the day*, the announcer had said. At the time, Teague had laughed at it, but now he knew exactly how that guy felt.

Except it wasn't the day he wanted to embrace. He needed Jodi. He could see her at the kitchen counter pouring coffee, her back to him, wearing a soft pink robe. He wondered what the robe felt like—how it would slide over her skin if he came up behind her and wrapped his arms around her, slipped his hands inside the collar...

He was so eager to find out that he stepped out into the kitchen barefoot, still buttoning his shirt.

"Honey, I..."

He stopped. Courtney was seated at the kitchen table, a cup of coffee in her hand. She didn't look like she wanted to embrace the day. She looked like she wanted to smack somebody.

"Hi, Teague." There was none of her usual flirta-tiousness in her tone. "I figured I'd find you here."

Well, she'd figured right. Guilt pricked at the back of his mind, but there was no reason for him to feel bad. He'd never led the girl on. She'd tried to entrap him, really, and she'd failed.

Well, now she'd know it. The whole half-naked, barefoot thing made it pretty clear he'd just gotten out of bed. It probably wasn't the most graceful way to break up with a girl, but it should be damned effective.

He should have broken up with her the night before. Hell, he should have broken up with her the week before, or maybe the month before. Trouble was, he couldn't really pinpoint the exact moment she'd begun to see what they had as a relationship, rather than a friendship. The whole thing had snuck up on him somehow.

Jodi turned from the counter, where she was whisking eggs in a bowl. The sash of her robe was tied tightly around her waist, but one tug would pull it loose. He looked away. Certain parts of him tended to be feisty in the mornings, and it would be rude to fly the happy flag in front of Courtney.

"Want eggs?" Jodi asked.

As usual, Courtney assumed the question was meant for her.

"I'm not hungry." She flashed Teague an angry glare.

"You sure?" Jodi asked. "You're helping with the session this morning, right? You'll need your strength."

"I'll be fine," Courtney said.

"Okay." Jodi went back to her whisking. "Teague?"

Dang. So Courtney wasn't looking for him. She was volunteering—and that meant Jodi had things to do. Clients coming. The dreams that had been riding around on pink, puffy clouds that matched her bathrobe drifted away on a cooling breeze.

"Sure," he said. "I'm hungry."

"Well, I'm exhausted," Courtney said. "I was up, like, all night." She shifted in her chair to face Teague. "I spent the whole night looking for my *dog*."

Teague glanced at the purse she'd tossed on the

sofa. Judging from its limp appearance, there was no Pomeranian inside.

Shit.

"You find him?" he asked.

"Yes. *Finally*," she said. "He was in the barn. He rolled in something icky and his fur was all matted. I didn't even *recognize* him at first."

"Oh. Sorry," Teague said. "What did he get into?"

"What do you think?" Courtney shoved out her lower lip. "I tried to wash it out, but he's going to have to be clipped. I had to leave him home. He smells like—like poop."

"Oh. Sorry." Teague couldn't help smiling just a little. That poor little animal had probably had the time of its life. He wasn't sure it ever got to act like a real dog.

Courtney flashed him an angry look.

"It's not funny," she said.

"No," Teague said. "Not funny." He made a strangled noise, then looked over to see Jodi was fighting the same battle and both of them lost the fight simultaneously.

—∿∿—

Jodi felt bad for Courtney, but laughing released some of the tension that had been building inside her since she awoke to find Teague beside her and remembered the night before.

So much for keeping her promises. She wanted to blame the vodka tonics, but she knew she'd made a choice. She knew she should regret it too, but she felt unburdened somehow, light and carefree. It didn't make any sense, but then when had her relationship with Teague ever made sense?

The harsh jangle of the phone jolted her out of her reverie. She crossed the kitchen in two long strides to answer it.

"Hello?"

"Jodi, Cal's here."

"Cissy? Is that you?" She hardly recognized her friend's trembling voice.

"He's at the door. He keeps pounding at it and yelling and I'm—I'm scared."

"Does he know you're inside?"

"I think so. He went around and looked in windows. I hid, but he saw my car. Do you know where Teague is? I called his cell and he didn't answer."

Jodi glanced at the man who sat at her table barefoot, with tousled hair and a satisfied expression on his face that couldn't be ascribed to the coffee. She didn't blame Cissy for wanting his help, but throwing Teague into a situation like that was asking for trouble—and not just for Cal. Teague was liable to lose his temper, and it seemed like he'd only just started to escape his reputation as a hothead.

"Ciss, you should call the sheriff. That's what he's there for."

"But I don't want him to know. He's my boss, Jodi, and Cal's liable to say stuff…"

Jodi nodded. When Cal wasn't bashing Cissy physically, he was trashing her verbally.

"Nobody believes him, Ciss."

"Jodi, everybody believes him. He's the golden boy, remember? Ten touchdowns and you're a god in this town."

"Okay. You have a point."

Jodi glanced over at Teague. He was lounging in the

chair, sipping his coffee with a serene expression on his face despite Courtney's glowering stare. He'd changed a lot since she'd been gone. He could probably handle Cal without ending up in jail.

She ought to give the guy more credit.

Besides, if Teague could handle this, maybe she could convince her mother that he hadn't inherited his father's evil tendencies. What could be a bigger test than dealing with a replay of domestic violence at the childhood home that held so many bad memories for him?

If he passed it, she'd know he had his demons under control. If not… she didn't want to think about that.

Cissy's voice broke into her thoughts. "Cal's afraid of Teague, Jodi. He won't have to do anything, honest. If he just shows up, Cal'll leave."

Jodi sighed. She hoped that was true. "I'll send him. You sit tight, okay? He'll be right over."

She hung up the phone and looked up at Teague.

"Cal found Cissy," she said. "He's at the trailer, banging on the door."

"Damn. I thought we'd found one place he wouldn't look." He shoved the chair back and stood up. "Gotta go, okay? I'll call you later." He dodged into the bedroom and came out seconds later, boots on, hat in place.

Her heart fluttered in her chest. He hadn't even given it a second thought. A friend needed him, and he was there, no questions asked. Did he even realize what he was walking into? Cal's threats, the trailer—it was bound to bring back terrible memories.

"Be careful," she said. "This—this scares me. I'd go with you but…"

"You have your kids to take care of. I know. It's fine."

He leaned over and gave her a kiss. It was quick, with no real heat, but it still made her smile. It felt somehow domesticated, like a going-off-to-work kiss, and it warmed her up in a whole new way.

"I can deal with Cal," he said. "He won't ever bother her again."

"Geez, Teague, that's what I'm afraid of," she said, the warmth fading. "Don't kill him, okay?"

―――――

Jodi took a deep breath as she led TT out to the arena. A young couple and a single woman sat at a picnic table Jodi had set up and watched their kids get ready to ride. An older couple lounged in canvas folding chairs beside them and sipped sodas from a cooler. Meanwhile her students' brothers and sister were getting acquainted with Vegas over by the corral. Jodi wasn't sure she wanted that big an audience for a therapy session, but at least the kids had supportive families.

And maybe it would take her mind off of Teague. She knew he had a short fuse, and like everyone else in town, he loved Cissy. When she'd told him not to kill Cal, she hadn't been exaggerating the possibilities.

She shoved her worries out of her mind and focused on the kids. She had two little girls for the first session. Russell was coming later, and he'd be crushed if Teague wasn't there—but she'd deal with that issue when it came. Right now, the girls deserved all her attention. She hitched TT to the corral gate beside a small roan mare.

"This is Peach, and this is TT," she told the girls. Peach had belonged to Nate Shawcross's daughter before she outgrew her. She was perfect for the clinic—small and patient, and used to kids. The other horse was Triple Threat, once again working under the alias of TT.

"Tee-tee!" said Dorsey. Dorsey was eight years old and had autism. She also had a tousled blonde bob, wire-rimmed glasses over sparkling blue eyes, and the widest, sunniest smile Jodi had ever seen. It was impossible not to smile back.

"Tee-tee," repeated Constance, wrinkling her fore-head. She was six, with dark hair, a serious expression, and the manners of a tiny spinster aunt. Her parents said she'd been diagnosed with Asperger's.

Jodi diagnosed them both as adorable.

"Dorsey, Peach will be your horse today. Constance, you'll be riding TT."

"I want Tee-tee!" Dorsey said. The sunny smile faded, her brows lowered, and Jodi swore she heard distant thunder.

Jodi took her hand and led her over to Peach. "No, you're riding Peach," she said firmly. "Would you like to pet her?"

Dorsey cautiously stroked the horse's nose, and Peach blew out a gentle breath. The child put her hand in front of the horse's nostrils and turned it over to cup the warm air.

"Tickles," she said, the smile twitching back to life. She looked up at Jodi, delighted.

"I think she likes you." Jodi put an arm around the child's shoulders. "Do you want to help me put the saddle on her?"

Dorsey nodded enthusiastically and gave her a full-on grin that felt like a gift. "Okay," she said.

Crisis averted. Jodi turned to Courtney.

"Courtney, I need you to help Constance saddle her horse."

She wasn't about to say the magic word "Tee-tee" again. Dorsey was happy, and she wanted her to stay that way.

Courtney slid down from the top rail of the fence and headed for Constance. Jodi braced herself for a disaster as Courtney trotted across the arena. She'd probably treat the kid like she was stupid, and Constance was anything but stupid. She watched as the girl stopped and shook hands gravely with the child.

"Hi, Constance. I'm Courtney. Our names both begin with C, so I think we should be friends."

"Hello." Constance stared up at Courtney as if she was seeing a fairy princess. "You're beautiful."

Jodi had to admit the child was right. Courtney had curled and teased her hair queen-style, and blonde locks cascaded from her straw cowboy hat. She'd toned down her clothing, though. Her jeans were store-worn, not barn-worn, but her shirt didn't have one single rhinestone on it to distract the kids or the horses.

The jeans fit like the girl had been dipped in denim-colored latex, though. Jodi glanced over at Constance's dad. He was watching the seat of Courtney's jeans like he was Tim Gunn judging a new pocket design as the girl bent over to pick up Tee-tee's saddle blanket and aimed her tightly clad rump in his direction. Jodi wondered if Courtney was doing it on purpose, but she seemed genuinely absorbed in her task.

Jodi tossed her hair and went back to her work.

"First we put on the blanket," Courtney said to Constance. "Can you help me lift it up onto the horse's back?" She lifted one end while Constance helped hoist the other. Jodi felt the beginnings of a smile cross her face. Maybe Courtney wasn't as bad as she'd thought. The girl actually seemed to have a way with Constance.

And Dorsey had a way with Jodi. Once they'd saddled the horse, the little girl shoved one foot in the stirrup and clambered onto the horse's back. The minute she was mounted, she leaned forward and did her best to wrap her eight-year-old arms around Peach's neck and chest. Resting her head against the horse's sun-warmed pelt, she smiled wide and closed her eyes.

"I'm *happy*," she said.

Jodi smiled too. Dorsey spent every minute of the day struggling through a confusing cacophony of sound and sight that overwhelmed her senses. If she could recognize the magic of this moment, how could Jodi miss it? There was nothing better than spending this day in the warm Wyoming sunshine with kids and horses, doing good work.

Well, except for last night. That had been about as good as it got.

She caught herself glancing at the driveway for the umpteenth time. There was no way Teague could be back yet. It would take him a while to deal with Cissy's situation.

She just hoped he dealt with it in a way that wouldn't land him in jail.

She moved to the center of the ring while Courtney took TT's lead rope and Troy led Peach. Constance stared down at her hands, a worried expression on her face as she adjusted the reins over and over. She sat ramrod straight, her heels pressed down, her shoulders stiff. Dorsey, on the other hand, slumped in the saddle and tilted her face up toward the sun, an expression of total bliss lighting her face.

"Look at the clouds," she said, as if the whole world was a miracle. "Look at the blue, blue sky."

"It's a beautiful day, Dorsey," Jodi said.

Dorsey nodded so enthusiastically she almost fell off the horse.

"I'm *happy*," she said again.

Jodi had the horses circle the ring a few times to see how they adapted to their inexperienced riders. Once she figured everything was going smoothly, she put the kids through their paces, having them ride with hands on their helmets, with arms spread like airplane wings, with hands over their heads, and even backwards. The kids responded well, Dorsey giggling, Constance gravely executing each movement with perfect precision.

Next they played a game, matching numbered cards to painted sheets of cardboard Jodi had duct-taped to the fence.

"Number *two*!" Dorsey hollered, waving her card in the air. She swung around in the saddle and pointed dramatically at the matching sign. "*That* way!" She sounded like a tiny general commanding the troops.

Constance was more hesitant. "Four," she whispered. She scanned the fence, her forehead wrinkled with worry as if the fate of the nation rested on her success. Finally, she pointed toward the correct sign. "Over there?"

"Sure, honey." Courtney led the child to the fence, where she carefully leaned down from the horse to set the card in a hanging bucket.

"Did I do it right?"

"Perfect."

Jodi had to admit that Courtney was handling Constance just right, affirming her choices, helping her build confidence.

Next came basketball, where each mounted student threw Nerf balls through a hoop and cheered each other's successes. Dorsey's ball-throwing was a little wild, but her cheers could have urged the Cubs to a World Series victory.

Constance was more cautious. "Yay," she said every time she made a basket.

They finished with a ride to a mailbox perched on the rail near the gate. Each child rode up and leaned over to open the box and take a lollipop from inside.

"I got purple!" Dorsey waved her Dum Dum triumphantly. "That's *grape*!"

"Good!" Jodi said. "You guys did great! Now we're going to brush our horses and give them treats."

She grabbed two buckets containing brushes and hoof picks from the edge of the arena and turned to Troy. "Can you help Dorsey groom Eightball? Have her do it the way I showed you."

Troy nodded and turned to Dorsey. "Now look, you brush the horse like this. Can you brush his shoulder? Brush it ten times, okay? Let's count." He guided the child's hand as they counted each stroke. "Go with the hair. And be gentle," he said. His tone was professional, but knowing him so well, Jodi could hear the note of pride in his tone as he played the teacher role.

Courtney followed his lead, setting Constance to work on Triple Threat's shoulder.

"Brush it ten times," she said. Turning away, she

trotted back to the fence and pulled a compact out of her purse. Flipping it open, she scanned her face, frowned, and powdered her T-zone.

"Courtney! You can't leave her like that," Jodi shouted after her.

"I'll be right back. I just need to pretty up."

Jodi grimaced and walked over to help Constance, struggling to keep her mood in check. Constance didn't need to work with an agitated adult. It was Jodi's job to create an environment where these kids could learn, and that meant staying calm and serene.

"Look, Troy and Dorsey are brushing the horse's back now. Let's do that too. Ten strokes. Can you count with me?"

She set her hand over Constance's and guided her strokes, but she couldn't help watching Courtney out of the corner of her eye as she reapplied her lipstick and made a kissy face at the mirror. Dammit, if Courtney was going to help, she needed to stay focused. Jodi felt anger welling up in her chest like hot lava, threatening to spill over.

"Courtney!" she called sharply. "I need you over here!"

Courtney took her time putting the compact away, then trotted back to the arena like an obedient pony.

"When you're with a child, you're responsible for her," Jodi told her. "Don't ever leave one of the students like that again."

"Oh, pooh," Courtney said. "I was only gone for a minute."

"A lot can happen in a minute."

Constance looked from Jodi to Courtney, her forehead wrinkled with concern.

"Miss Jodi, are you mad?" she asked.

"No, she's not mad." Courtney smiled and turned back to Constance. "She's just having a bad day. Do you want to give the horse a treat, honey?"

Constance nodded and Courtney handed her a treat nugget from the bucket. The child immediately thrust it under the horse's muzzle, holding it between her thumb and forefinger.

"Not like that!" Courtney smacked the child's hand away. Jodi had been wondering if anything could shake the child's uncanny composure, and she had her answer now. Constance's face puckered up and tears stood in her eyes.

"You hold it like *this*." Courtney grabbed the child's hand and yanked the fingers straight. Setting the treat on the child's palm, she jerked the kid's hand toward the horse, her thumb holding the treat in place. Greedily, Triple Threat snatched it up, his teeth raking Courtney's thumb in the process.

"Damn it!" Courtney flicked her hand up and smacked the horse's muzzle. Triple Threat backed up, his eyes rolling to show the whites as he laid his ears back. "Don't you bite me, you big lug!" She smacked the horse's nose again. He lifted his front hooves slightly, almost rearing up, and spun away.

Jodi held her breath as the horse turned. One flick of his heels could put an end to her business forever— kick all her dreams to pieces. She didn't have to look across the arena to know the parents were watching the scene play out. She didn't have to look at their faces to know they were shocked at how poorly trained her assistant was.

"Courtney," she said, keeping her tone even. "Go sit on the fence."

"You can't let horses get away with sh—with stuff like that," Courtney said. "They have to be disciplined."

"Go sit on the fence," Jodi said. "Or better yet…" She lowered her voice. "Go the hell home and don't come back. You hit one of my horses again, or any other horse, and I'll hit you back."

"Are you threatening me? Because my father…"

"Go home, Courtney." Jodi ducked her head a moment. She needed to hang onto what little composure she had left. She swallowed, then plastered a perfect, gleaming rodeo queen smile on her face and stepped away from Courtney.

"Thank you for all your help, Courtney!" she said, loud enough for the parents to hear. "But I think you're getting tired. You go ahead home." She turned toward the kids. "Come on, Dorsey, Constance," she said. "Let's help Mr. Troy lead the horses back to the barn."

"Good-bye, Miss Courtney," Constance said.

"And good riddance," Jodi muttered as Courtney flounced out of the ring without a backward glance.

Chapter 29

TEAGUE PULLED UP TO THE TRAILER AND FROZE BEHIND the wheel.

Could he really go in there? The place was full of memories, none of them good. He hadn't been inside since the day he'd locked the door behind him and moved with Troy to the new house down the road. He'd been relieved and a little ashamed when Cissy volunteered to clean the place herself in return for the free rent he'd offered her. He'd said he could pay somebody but she'd declared the cleaning would do her good. It would keep her busy, keep her last encounter with Cal from running over and over in her mind like some kind of horror-show tape loop.

Teague knew all about tape loops. His cranked into motion the minute he stepped out of the truck. There were a few familiar sounds—the one loose shutter tapping the siding, the clicking of grasshoppers in the weeds gone wild that surrounded the place—that brought the past back in snippets of memory that built on each other like cancer cells invading his brain.

Buck up, he told himself. *Shake it off*.

This was no time to fall prey to memories. Cissy was in danger. Her asshole husband had figured out where she was staying, and having heard what she'd endured throughout their nearly five-year marriage, Teague had no doubt Cal had come to knock the crap out of her again. For old times' sake, apparently.

He'd endured too many of his father's rages and his mother's tears to let that happen to any woman.

He stepped out of the truck, letting the door hang open so the slam wouldn't alert Cal to the fact that he didn't have his helpless soon-to-be–ex-wife all to himself anymore.

When his boot struck the bottom step, the memories came in a rush. The sound of his father's voice, slurred and thick with booze. The panicked pleading of his mother. He took a quick step back. This was worse than he thought. It seemed so real—as if his parents were alive again. As if the fighting had never stopped. He paused with one hand on the railing, staring down at the ground and fortifying himself with a few deep breaths. When he lifted his head again, he realized he wasn't hearing ghosts. That was Cal's voice, and Cissy's.

Cal had gotten inside.

Adrenaline flooded his brain—adrenaline and a long-shuttered memory. He was twelve. He'd come home from school to find the door locked. Behind that door his mother was crying, his father was shouting, and then came the sickening thwap of fist on flesh. He'd been a skinny little kid, but adrenaline surged that time too, and convinced him he could go in there and make his father stop. He'd stormed up the steps and found the door locked. Then he'd run around the back and found that locked, too. He'd kicked and cursed and whaled on both doors until he was exhausted, partly in an effort to get in, partly as a release for his fury at his own helplessness, and partly to drown out the sound of his father shouting and his mother crying.

Well, he wasn't helpless now. There wasn't a door

that could keep him out. He'd get inside, and he'd stop it this time, no matter what it took.

He surged up the steps and slammed into the door with enough force to break the lock, and hurtled into the trailer, stumbling over his own feet and sprawling on the living room floor.

The door hadn't been locked. It hadn't even been latched. And he wasn't twelve, and that wasn't his father shouting.

Sobered by the impact, he rose to his knees and listened, struggling to sort out what was real and what was memory. That was Cal's voice, not his father's, and it was Cissy pleading with him. There was no sound of violence, only shouting.

He needed to get a grip on himself. That wasn't his father. This wasn't then—it was now. He took two deep breaths, shoved his memories back into the dark hole they'd come from, and set off down the hall.

Behind the closed bedroom door, he heard Cal's voice shouting.

"You bitch. You whore. I'll…"

Teague flung the door open, letting it smash against the wall to reveal Cal standing apelike in the center of the room, his arms bowed like King Kong, meaty fists clenched at his sides. Cissy cowered on the bed, her knees drawn up to her chin.

Cal turned around in what seemed like slow motion, raising his fists and setting his legs in a fighter's stance. Teague didn't bother to pose. He rushed into the room, head down, and tackled Cal, knocking him onto the bed while Cissy scrambled out of the way.

Grabbing the front of Cal's shirt, Teague hauled him

upright and waltzed him out of the room, shoving him backward down the hall, keeping him off-balance and stumbling. Shoving him through the living room, he barrelled through the open front door and the two of them tumbled down the steps.

They landed with Teague on top. Cal was bigger, but Teague had rage on his side. Looking down at his adversary's face, he hauled his fist back and then reminded himself: *This isn't my father*. Breathing hard, he scrambled to his feet and stood over Cal, looking down at the former football hero all curled up with his hands over his face, and resisted the urge to kick his unprotected ribs.

"Teague, man, I didn't touch her. We were just talking—honest, I didn't hit her or anything." Cal uncurled and crab-walked backwards through the weeds and junk that littered the lawn. "She's my wife, man, I got a right to talk to her…"

"You got a right to get in that car and drive away. And your wife—she got a right to file a protection order now, so if you come within thirty yards of her, she'll have you arrested. Again."

Cal backed into the side of his own car and sat on the ground like a giant baby on a blanket. "Aw, Teague, come on, you know how women are. I was just tryin' to talk some sense into her. I was just…"

"Cal." Teague held up a hand to stop the babbling. "You notice how I didn't kill you yet?"

Cal swallowed and nodded.

Teague rested one hip against the car and looked down at Cal. "You know, my dad used to hit my mom and yell at her, kind of like you were doing there. Right here, in this trailer."

Cal nodded.

"Thanks for the fucking flashback, Cal. You're lucky I didn't go all PTSD and kill your ass. You know that?"

Cal nodded again.

"Now go home. And don't cross my path. Not ever again. Because you just became a symbol of everything that fucked up my childhood, and if I see you again, I probably won't be able to control myself."

He looked down at his own fists, clenching and un-clenching, and realized he was back in his own body. Since he'd come through the door, he'd felt like he was watching what was happening from a distance, listen-ing to himself talk like an actor on a stage. Breathing slow and deep, he settled back into reality and took a step backward.

Watching him warily, Cal lumbered to his feet and opened the car door. Sliding behind the wheel, he started the engine and backed out onto the road. Teague watched him disappear in a cloud of dust, and hoped to God he was taking the memories with him.

Chapter 30

BACK HOME, THE RIVER ROCK SHOWER FELT LIKE A sanctuary as Teague washed off the dirt, the blood, and the memories he'd spilled in the struggle with Cal. He closed his eyes and let the water pelt his skin, cranking it as hot as he could stand it. Once he'd dried off and dressed, he strolled out to check on Rocket. He needed a few minutes with the big horse, a short conversation with the ultimate reality to ground himself.

"Rocky." He rested his arms on the top rail of the fence. The horse turned, eyed him a moment, then walked over for a visit, taking his sweet time getting there. "I did okay, Rocky. I didn't kill him. Guess we're both tamed now." The horse shoved his head over the top rail of the fence and Teague rested his forehead against his long muzzle. "Feels good, doesn't it?"

It did. It felt good knowing he could trust himself—that he could hold it together and act like a rational human, instead of attacking like an animal. Now if he could just convince the rest of the town he'd changed, he'd have peace. If he could convince Jodi's mother, he'd have everything.

Because changing wasn't enough. He didn't believe in living his life to earn anyone else's approval—that was Jodi's way. But he wouldn't be truly free of the Treadwell curse until he changed his reputation. If Courtney already knew how "disreputable" he was,

everyone in town must know—including the parents of
Jodi's clients. They wouldn't want to trust their children
to someone like that. Russell's father hadn't minded—
but then, Ben was pretty disreputable himself.

Russell. Shoot. He'd forgotten the kid had another
session today. He'd promised to be there.

He needed to get over to Jodi's.

He felt a little spasm of joy squeeze his heart at the
prospect. It wasn't all about Jodi this time; he was looking forward to seeing Russell too. The kid didn't know
or care about Teague's past. All he saw was a genuine
cowboy—someone to look up to. The admiration in his
eyes had done Teague more good than any of Courtney's
winks and nudges.

He squinted as a glint of light caught his eyes. Another
vehicle was turning into the drive—a big diesel pickup
with some kind of writing on the side.

Shit. It was probably the sheriff. Maybe he'd hurt
Cal worse than he'd thought. Or maybe the idiot had
gone and filed charges. They wouldn't stick, but everyone would think Teague had gone and lost it again,
solving his troubles with his fists just like his father,
and his victory over the ghosts of his past would gain
him nothing.

Except peace. He felt stronger inside—the kind of
strength he'd been looking for all his life. He used to
try to find it by fighting, but it never went clear to his
bones before. Now he felt like he could tackle anything
without losing control.

He stepped off the porch as the vehicle pulled to a
stop. That wasn't the sheriff's county crest on the side;
it was a prancing horse, framed by the words "Skelton

Polo Center." The driver's door opened and Courtney Skelton slid to the ground.

Shit.

Jodi was right. The girl was after him. That Sting song started running through his head. *Every move you make, every step you take, I'll be watching you.*

Yep. Courtney was a solid gold stalker.

"Hi, Teague!" She put a little skip in her step and her breasts bounced beneath her tight shirt.

"Hey," he said, pinning his gaze to her face. If she thought he was eying her boobs, she'd think she had a chance with him. Although judging from her behavior this morning, she'd been pretty mad about last night. He'd thought she was through with him.

She simpered and stepped in close so her breast brushed his arm. "So what are you doing this afternoon?"

So much for being through with him. She was back to her old ways.

Luckily, he had plans, so she couldn't hijack him and try to subject him to more of her jiggling and sex-starved sideways glances.

"I'm helping Jodi," he said. "Hey, I thought you were too."

"No, I'm done." Courtney tossed her hair and a fleeting hint of anger crossed her face. "She told me to go. Guess she doesn't really need any help."

"Yeah, she does," Teague said. "She's starting that business all by herself. It's a lot of work."

"Yeah, and then there's the baby," Courtney said.

Teague's heart sank into his stomach. "You know about that?" He shoved his hands in his pockets and looked off toward the horizon. He didn't want to talk about Jodi with Courtney. It seemed wrong somehow.

"I heard she was shopping for prenatal vitamins at the drugstore. And she sure looks pregnant."

"She does?" Teague didn't think Jodi looked pregnant. She looked the same as always. "No she doesn't. She's still—well, she's still just fine."

"You're a man. You wouldn't know." Courtney tossed her hair as if to demonstrate the superiority of women. "She's glowing."

"Glowing?" Teague remembered how Jodi had looked the night before. She'd been glowing, all right. He'd thought it was something he'd done, but maybe not.

Courtney's voice interrupted the memory. "So what are you going to do?"

"Whatever I can."

She barked out a laugh that sounded a like Honeybucket yipping. "Well, good luck. I doubt the Treadwell name is something she wants painted on her mailbox, though. Not if she's going to be trusted with other people's kids."

Courtney was only echoing his own thoughts, but her words sank into his gut like a dose of lead. Sometimes he managed to convince himself that he could overcome his past, but Courtney was right. In a town this small, the past was inescapable.

"I guess that's up to Jodi," he said.

Courtney thrust her lower lip out in a little-girl pout.

"Well, I guess I'll just go home then. Maybe I'll go see Gustaldo." She slanted a narrow-eyed glance his way, as if gauging his reaction.

"Whatever," he said.

"Aren't you going to tell me to be careful?" she

asked. "You were all concerned about Jodi and Gustaldo last night."

He shrugged. "I figure you can hold your own."

"Oh. I see," she said. She stuck out her chest and set her fists on her hips. "Just be careful over at Jodi's. You have a habit of leading girls on, making them think you care." She stalked toward her car, then turned as she opened the door. "Not that anyone expects anything of you. You're a Treadwell, after all." She tossed her hair and climbed into the car. "We all know what *that* means."

Chapter 31

RUSSELL WAS ALREADY MOUNTED BY THE TIME TEAGUE arrived, but they hadn't started the lesson. The kid's face brightened when he spotted Teague approaching the arena.

"Teague!" he said. "I thought you forgot!"

"No way, buddy," Teague said. He opened the gate and stepped into the arena, then stopped in his tracks and turned to Jodi. "You're using Vegas," he said.

She nodded. "Yup. I thought you'd want Russell to be the first one to ride him. They're doing great." She gave him a worried look. "Everything all right at Cissy's?"

"Everything's fine. I'll tell you later."

"Fine? Are you sure?" She looked worried, and a little wary, as if she was afraid of what he might have done. Dang. He'd always felt like Jodi was the one person who believed in him, but even she didn't think he could deal with a situation without hurting somebody.

"I'm sure." He stepped up and took the lead rope from Ben. "Cal won't be bothering Cissy again." Looking up at Russell perched atop his old horse's narrow back, he rubbed his eyes, telling himself it must be the dust from the arena's soft dirt footing that made them blur.

"Hey, Vegas," he said, patting the horse's neck. "Good boy."

"Hope you don't mind me riding your old horse," Russell said. "I bet you had all kinds of adventures on him, right?"

"Oh, yeah," Teague said. "I'll tell you about them later, okay? Right now I think we'd better get down to business."

"Okay," Russell said. "Maybe you could tell me sometime, though."

"Sure," Teague said. "Sure."

Jodi put them through their paces, repeating the lesson from the day before and adding a few more elements—Nerf basketball, and the game with the numbered cards. Russell didn't have any problems with the game itself, but it was clear to Teague that his muscles got fatigued after only a few rounds of the arena. Twice he started to slide sideways and his father had to grab the belt and pull him upright.

"That's okay," Jodi said. "You keep doing your exercises, and you'll get stronger."

"I've been doing them every day," Russell said. "Haven't I, Dad?"

Ben grunted in assent. "Yup."

"Keep it up, and we'll get you trotting," Jodi said.

"I know. That's what I think about when I do the exercises." Russell beamed down at Teague. "Jodi said once I'm strong enough, we can trot, and maybe even go on a real trail ride outside the arena."

"Great. Can I come?"

"Sure." Russell's expression grew serious. "I'd want you to, in case we ran into any snakes or anything."

"Or the Wild Bunch," Teague said. "I've heard they don't take kindly to their members defecting."

"That's right. They're gunnin' for me," Russell said. "But I'm ready for 'em. Nothing scares me."

Teague looked back at the slim boy perched high on the horse, his wasted legs shaking slightly with the effort of staying upright.

"I'd say that's true," Teague said.

An hour later, Jodi stacked a third scoop of Ben & Jerry's Dulce Delish onto a sugar cone and handed it to Teague.

"So tell me about Cal." She shook another cone out of the package and exchanged the Dulce Delish for a tub of Crème Brulée flavor. Scooping ice cream gave her an excuse to keep her back turned to Teague so he couldn't see how worried she was. Sure, he'd said everything went fine—but what exactly did it mean when he said Cal wouldn't be bothering Cissy again? Had he hurt him? And more important, how hard had it been for Teague himself, going back to that trailer? Dealing with Cal had to remind him of his father. He had to be hurting.

He was quiet so long she finally turned to face him. "Well? What happened?"

"He left."

Jodi topped off her cone and pulled out the chair across from him. "Well, no kidding." She gave her cone a lick. "I didn't think you left him there. What happened?"

Teague shrugged. "I told him Cissy was going to get a restraining order."

"That's it?"

Suddenly, his ice cream demanded all his attention. "This is good," he said.

"Teague?"

"What?" He shifted his gaze sideways, looking at the clock.

"Tell me what happened. Somehow, I doubt you walked in and reasoned with Cal and he walked away."

"Why do you doubt that?" He looked up from his cone, his eyes hard.

"Because…" She waved her cone helplessly. "Because I know you."

"Right. And so you figure I probably beat him up and left him for dead."

"No." She grimaced. "Well, it did seem like a possibility." She gave him a shaky smile. He didn't smile back.

"But you didn't," she continued. "But…" She leaned forward and ran her finger along a bruise just below the sleeve of his T-shirt.

"We fell down the steps."

"Right." She hesitated, frowning down at the bruise. His mother used to say she'd fallen down the steps when she'd ended up bruised and battered. She couldn't help wondering how many bruises Cal had.

Teague shoved his chair back from the table, slamming it into the wall, and pitched what was left of his cone in the garbage.

"I had to haul him out of there, okay?" He rested his fists on the table and loomed over her. "He was already inside when I got there. I dragged him out of the place and we stumbled on the steps. Then he got up and he drove away."

She brought a hand to her chest. "Okay. Thanks. I'm just—I'm worried about you. It must have been really hard, going back there and reliving all that."

His eyes were still cold and hard. "Well, I sure as hell don't want to relive it all now. Besides, it was fine."

"Teague, it couldn't have been fine. It had to be a real test."

"Is that what it was? A test?" He scowled. "Did I pass?"

"Teague, I didn't mean that. I just meant—it must have been hard. I thought you might want to talk about it."

For a moment, he dropped his guard and let the pain show in his eyes as he sank back into the chair. "Look, I'm sorry. I'm not a touchy-feely, talky person, okay? I'll deal with it."

"I just want to help, Teague."

"I know. Don't worry, though." The mask dropped back into place as he got back to his feet. "I need to get home. See what Troy's up to."

He swung out the door and she followed him to the porch, but he didn't say another word—just jogged out to the truck and took off like he couldn't get away from her fast enough.

Evidently he'd dealt with Cal just fine. But going back there, seeing and hearing so many things that must have reminded him of the bad old days, had shut something down in him—closed a door. And he wasn't about to let her in.

He'd only dropped his guard for an instant, letting her see the pain in his eyes, and in that moment, she'd seen a flash of the real Teague—wounded and damaged but always strong, even when it made the pain worse to keep it inside. She wanted to be there for him. She wanted to hold him all night, every night, and erase all the damage his parents had done.

But she'd made that promise…

A jaunty tune broke the day's hot sleepy silence and

she fished her phone out of her pocket. She normally didn't leave it on during sessions, but she'd been prepared for a call from Cissy, a call from Teague, or even a call from the sheriff while he was gone.

"Hello?"

"It's Cissy."

"Cissy." Jodi sank down on the porch swing. "Are you okay? Is everything all right?"

"I'm fine. Jodi, you should have seen Teague."

"What happened?"

"Well, Cal got inside right after I called you—I hadn't set the deadbolt, I'm an idiot—and Teague just walked in and dragged him out."

"Did he hit him?"

"No. He was so—so *controlled*. Like it was just business. He got Cal out of the trailer and next thing I knew that skunk of an ex-husband was driving away."

"That's great." Jodi looked up as Luna trotted up onto the porch and sat down, resting her chin on the swing beside Jodi's thigh. She must have come with Teague, and he'd been in such a hurry to go he'd left her behind. "So Teague didn't hit him? Didn't lose it?"

"No. Not a bit."

"Good. He was over here, and I asked, but he didn't seem to want to talk about it. I was afraid something happened."

"Nothing bad," Cissy assured her. "The sheriff himself couldn't have done better."

"Good. Thanks for letting me know."

"People ought to see now what a good man he is," Cissy said.

"Yeah," Jodi said. "You're right. If he can handle that situation, he can handle anything."

The two of them said their good-byes and Jodi clicked her phone shut. She breathed a sigh of relief and looked down at Luna.

"Maybe we need to spread the word, huh, girl?" She stroked the dog's head. "Maybe if people knew how well he handled that, they'd realize how much he's changed." She stood and the dog leapt to her feet, trotting anxiously to the edge of the porch and gazing back at Jodi. "I know, girl, you want to go home. But I have something to do first." She brushed the dust from the arena off her jeans. "I need to talk to my mom."

<center>~~~</center>

Jodi walked into the boutique to see her mother standing in front of the three-way mirror, bouncing and swaying in a red wool dress that appeared to be decorated with hundreds of shiny silver bells that jangled with every move. Lost in her own world, she didn't hear Jodi enter. She stamped her feet, spun in a circle, then stopped dead, arms outspread, when she caught sight of her daughter standing by the counter.

"Oh," she said. "Hello." She turned back to the mirror and rolled her shoulders, pretending to fuss with the fit of the dress.

"Mom, I saw you." Jodi laughed. "You were totally dancing. What the heck is that, anyway?"

"It's an authentic reproduction of a Native American jingle dress," her mother said. "The jingles are made from the tops of chewing tobacco cans, rolled to make bells. See?" She held out one of the bells for Jodi to look at. Sure enough, the word "Skoal" was embossed on the metal.

"Cool," Jodi said. "Looks expensive."

"It is," her mother said. Setting a hand on her hip and placing one foot in front of the other, she put the other hand behind her head and sucked in her cheeks, giving her best supermodel imitation. "How do I look?"

"Fabulous."

"I know." She sighed. "Guess I'd better take it off and put it on display." She waltzed behind the dressing room curtain, jingling all the way.

"What's going on?" she said from behind the curtain. Her arm thrust out of the dressing room with the dress hooked on one finger. Jodi grabbed the dress and glanced around for a hanger.

"Well, first, I'm sorry I couldn't work today. You been busy?"

"Nothing I couldn't handle. You?"

"Yeah. I had three clients. That's not many for a Saturday, but it's a start. I just wish my busiest day wasn't the same as yours."

"It's okay. I've done it on my own up to now. Guess I can manage." Her mother popped out of the dressing room, dressed in her version of normal: a fringed buckskin skirt that fell to mid-calf, a matching beaded vest, a red turtleneck, and soft deerskin boots fashioned cowboy-style but soft enough to bunch at the ankles.

"Is that all you came to tell me? You have that look."

"What look?" Jodi quickly rearranged her face into a placid smile.

"That look like you're going to tell me something I don't want to hear. Or maybe you're going to talk me into something I don't want to do."

Jodi sighed. "You're a mind reader."

"No, if I was a mind reader, we wouldn't need to have this conversation we're about to have. Which I assume would be a good thing."

"I guess." Jodi thought a moment. "Actually, it's good news."

"Oh." Her mother sat down in the chair outside the dressing room. "Well, go ahead then."

"Okay." Jodi sat down in the matching chair beside her and crossed her legs. "It's about Teague."

Her mother's facial expression dropped as if gravity had suddenly gone double strength, her dimpled smile transforming into a scowl.

"No, wait." Jodi held up one hand. "Hear me out. I know you don't like him, and I know you're worried about his father. I mean, about how he might take after his father."

"Pretty much everybody's worried about that," her mother said. "And there's no 'might' about it. His father was a batterer, and what do you know? Teague himself wound up in jail before he was even out of high school for a violent crime."

"Mom, the violent crime was that he beat up a guy who was tormenting his brother. His *disabled* brother."

"Beat him up? He almost killed the guy."

"I know. I know."

"And it wasn't the first time."

"I know." Jodi put her hands up, as if she could somehow smooth out the conversation. "But people grow and change, Mom. Let me tell you what happened today." She described the call from Cissy, and explained how Teague had gone over there and taken care of Cal without violence. "Mom, if he can face that situation, right there where it used to happen to him…"

"It's a good sign, honey," her mother said. "But just the fact that you're here tells me you think it's a real accomplishment for him. Honey, for most men, getting through the day without hitting somebody isn't a big deal."

"You're twisting this around." Jodi hopped to her feet and walked over to one of the circular racks of shirts and vests. Flicking the hangers left, then right, then left, she whisked the shirts back and forth to calm her agitation. "I know *you* think that's an accomplishment for him. I always knew he could do it."

Her mother shot her a penetrating stare. "Did you?"

Jodi remembered the dread that had sat in her stomach all afternoon like a cold, hard stone, and the overwhelming relief she'd felt when Teague told her he hadn't hurt Cal.

"I—I *hoped*," she said.

"Do you want to live your life that way?"

Jodi whisked the hangers back and forth a few more times until her mother stood up and put her hands over Jodi's.

"Stop," she said.

Jodi slumped her shoulders. "Sorry."

"Honey, if he means that much to you, there's not a thing I can do about it." Her mother squeezed her hands and shook them up and down while she tried to get her next words out. "If you love him, I can't stop you."

"But I promised," Jodi said.

"I don't have any right to make you keep that promise," her mother said. "Come here. Sit down." She led

Jodi to the chairs and they both sat, still holding hands. "My mother didn't like your father, you know."

Jodi nodded. Her grandma had died when she was little, but she remembered her as a loving but vaguely disapproving presence.

"She didn't like his cowboy ways," her mother continued. "She said I'd be unhappy living on a ranch, not having any neighbors, dealing with animals and weather all the time."

"But you…"

"She was right."

Jodi pulled her hands away and started to protest, but her mother held up a finger to stop her.

"I didn't like the ranch life. You know that. I'm not an animal person. I missed going to concerts and cocktail parties and wearing nice clothes—I missed so much. But I would have missed him more."

Jodi felt a faint glow of hope lighting her heart as she looked up at her mother's face.

"I loved your father. I would have been miserable without him. Being with him had its drawbacks…" she laughed shakily "…but it was worth it. Always, every day, it was worth it."

Jodi nodded, the glow growing brighter. Maybe her mother understood.

"You and Teague would have problems, you know. He has issues you can't possibly understand. You know that, right?"

Jodi nodded. "When I talked to him about today, I could tell he was holding a lot in. Keeping his feelings from me."

"There will always be a part of him you don't

understand, and if he's not willing to confide in you, that makes it even harder. You need to decide if you can accept that."

Jodi nodded again, then looked up with a hesitant smile. "Does this mean I don't have to keep my promise?"

Her mom smiled and shook her head. "Let's change the promise, okay? Promise me you'll think very, very hard before you pledge yourself to this man. Promise me to keep your eyes wide open, and listen to your head as well as your heart."

"I promise," Jodi said. "I really do promise to think it through."

Her mother sighed. "Being a cowboy is on a slightly different level than being—whatever Teague is. The child of an abuser. The man has deep-seated psychological issues."

Jodi shifted forward, ready to defend Teague, but her mother looked away and held up her hand to stop her.

"It's true, and you know it."

Reluctantly, Jodi nodded, but she couldn't help going for the last word. "Maybe he's learned from his experience, Mom. Maybe he's actually *less* likely to have that issue, because he's seen the effects."

"Maybe." Her mother sighed. "I sure hope so, because I don't think anything is going to keep you away from him."

⚬⚬⚬

Teague was out in back of the barn when Jodi arrived at the ranch. He was working with a black and white paint, apparently trying to get the horse accustomed to the motion of a polo mallet by waving it around his head. The horse had a shaggy, unkempt coat, stocky legs, and a coarse, bullet-shaped head. His tangled forelock dangled rakishly over one eye; he peered at his tormenter through the other and blew out a flaccid raspberry. Closing his white-lashed eyes, he cocked one hind leg and dozed off.

Teague turned to Jodi.

"Watch this."

He swung the mallet sideways, letting it skim the tips of the horse's ears. The horse sighed and shifted, cocking the other leg. "I'm thinking he'll make a great polo horse. Totally bombproof."

"Don't polo horses have to, like, run?" she asked.

"Yeah, that might be an issue with him. He's just not a high-energy kind of guy."

They both stood back and watched the horse snooze in the sun.

"Maybe he'd make a good therapy horse," she said.

"No way." Teague groaned. "If anyone finds out one of Rocket's colts is a kid's therapy horse, my reputation will be ruined."

"I'll change his name," she said. "Give him an alias. I'm thinking we'll call him Sleepy."

"That fits," Teague said. He leaned the mallet up against the fence and shoved his hands in his pockets, shaking his head.

"Hey," she said. "I've got news."

He arched an eyebrow and gave her a sideways look.

"I talked to my mom."

"Oh." He leaned up against the fence. "You tell her I passed the test?"

She looked away. "Sorry about that."

"It's okay. I can't blame you for thinking I'd go off. I'm just glad I passed."

"Me too. I don't think that's what did it, though."

"Did what?" A spark leapt in his heart, then died. It couldn't be what he was hoping. He couldn't be that lucky.

She spread her arms and grinned. "No more promise."

He was. He was that lucky. He felt weak and light-headed as he stared at the woman who could be his.

"You..."

"She realized it was wrong, and that..." Suddenly shy, Jodi stared down at her boot, scuffing it in the dirt. "That there was no stopping me anyway." She looked up at him through her lashes with a smile.

Teague grinned. "That's true. There is no stopping you when you want something."

She tilted her chin up and met his eyes full-on. "I want you."

"I sure won't stop that."

He stepped closer and looked down at her, his mouth working, and her eyes caught his with an unmistakable statement about just what he was to her. His whole body came alive with the awareness that she was finally his— but his lungs just died.

He couldn't breathe.

His arms swept around her, cupping her denim-clad bottom and tugging her toward him, and his tongue flicked out and touched hers, and it was like she lit a fire inside him. He was lost, gone, out of control; kissing her like he was starving and she was his last meal.

He buried one hand in the hair at the back of her neck and kissed her again, deeper, harder. He wasn't sure how it had happened, but she was backed up against the barn wall and his body was keeping her there, pressing into the warmth that radiated from her skin and the sun-warmed wood. He moved his hands down to savor the sweet shape of her, the tuck of her waist, the smooth swell of her hip, the heft of her breast… her breast… her breast… oh, God…

What was he doing?

Kissing Jodi, that's what. Kissing her long and hard, the way she needed to be kissed. Kissing her as if she was his. And she was kissing him back.

The way her lips caressed his, the way her hands fisted in her hair—there was more to this than wanting. In the back of his mind, he'd always believed she loved him. He'd figured maybe she kept her feelings hidden because she was ashamed to be seen with trailer trash, but when she'd told him what her mother had said, he'd understood why she didn't want to get involved with him. Sometimes he himself felt his father inside him, crouched like a demon in some dark part of his brain. He couldn't deny that it was a rational reason to stay away from him—but when had love ever been rational?

He moved his hands down her body, savoring the womanly curve of her hips, the way his hand swooped and smoothed when he caressed her. He'd been insulted when he realized she saw what had happened at the trailer as a test, but now he realized she'd been right. He'd faced his demon back there at the trailer, and he'd won. He'd proven he was more than his father's son.

She pulled away from him and a frustrated growl rose in his chest, but when she looked him in the eyes he felt a surge of love so strong it made him dizzy.

———∿∿∿———

Jodi knew she should stop. She'd promised her mother that she'd think this through, that she'd use her mind as well as her heart, but she couldn't let this moment pass. For the first time since that long-ago good-bye, there was a real possibility that she and Teague could be together for real. No hiding, no shying away. They didn't have to keep this a secret from the world.

Even though Teague still had his share of secrets. She remembered his guarded eyes when she asked him about Cal. He wasn't all hers. Not yet. There were parts of himself he kept hidden—but surely, now that they could really commit to each other, he'd come to trust her and confide in her.

She pulled away and held his face in her hands, looking into his eyes. There was love there, but mostly there was hunger. And lust.

Lots of lust. She felt an answering heat well up inside her and when he moved to kiss her again, she turned her head.

"Um, Teague?"

"Mmm?" He looked at her with dreamy, half-closed eyes.

"We're outside, you know. And where's Troy?"

"He's out." Teague glanced around, then smiled a slow, sheepish grin. "I'm glad you said something. Forgot where I was." He reached out and stroked her hair. "I think I forgot who I was too."

"Wouldn't the bedroom be more appropriate for… this?"

He nodded and slid one arm around her shoulders, then

bent down and hefted her in his arms. Carrying her down the hill to the house and kicking the front door open, he strode down the hall and swung her over the bed in a wide arc before lowering her gently onto the cushions.

There were a lot of cushions, heaped neatly against the headboard. Some of them had ruffled trim. Jodi shifted and sat up, looking around the room. Last time she'd been here, she hadn't really thought about the décor. This time, she was a little more conscious. More aware of her surroundings.

"What are you, some kind of metrosexual?"

He'd sat down on the edge of the bed to kick off his boots, but that made him pause. "What?"

"The decorating. You're like *Queer Eye for the Cowboy* or something."

"Hey."

She grinned. "Okay, I know you're definitely heterosexual. But really—what's with the decorating?" She sat up. "All of a sudden, you're like Martha Stewart or something. And it's not just the house. It's the cooking. I mean, Mario Batali? And your clothes." She looked him up and down. "You're like a cowboy fashion plate, Teague. What happened to the ripped jeans and T-shirts?"

Teague shrugged. "Hey, I got tired of Chef Boyardee, fiberboard furniture, and Walmart clothes. Thought it was time for a change."

"It's just that there's been a lot of change. It's like… I hardly know you anymore."

"You know me. You know me better than anyone." He eased closer and she felt a sudden tension, like a faint hum in her veins. "You knew me when."

She nodded. "Exactly. And I kind of miss 'when,'

you know? You've changed, Teague. What matters to you now—it's all this *stuff*."

"It's not the stuff." He stiffened and moved away slightly. "That's not what it's about."

"Then what's it about?"

"You." He bent his head and kissed her neck. She felt his fingers stealing into the hair at the back of her neck. He was going to kiss her, partly to make her stop asking questions. She pushed him out to arm's length and gave him her best schoolteacher glare.

"No, really. Teague. Tell me what brought this on."

"I told you," he said. "You." He scooted up beside her and took her hand. "When you left—I realized I'd missed my chance. I kept defending who I was, instead of trying to be somebody else."

"I don't want you to be anyone else." She waved her hand, indicating the nightstands with their antler lamps and the heavy draperies. "This is just stuff. Window dressing. Literally." She stepped closer and adjusted his collar. "You're still you."

"Yeah, well, don't tell anybody, okay?"

She grinned. "Okay. I won't tell them what you look like naked, either."

"Who says you're going to find out?"

"I do." She grabbed each side of the collar and pulled him in for a kiss. As their lips met, she yanked the shirt apart, unsnapping it all the way down to his belt. Tucking her hands under the fabric, she reached in to savor the warmth of his skin, the rippled muscles coursing his ribs, the faint dusting of hair that arrowed down to his belt buckle.

"Naked," she muttered against his lips. She swept

her palms over the swell of his chest, caressing his flat nipples as she moved down to kiss his neck, his throat, his collarbone, while her fingers fumbled with his belt buckle. She was taking her time, pausing to brush his fly teasingly with the flat of her palm, dancing her fingertips over the sensitive skin just above the waistband of his jeans. He closed his eyes and tilted his head back.

"There." She undid the buckle and unsnapped his jeans, then slipped the zipper down. He let out a sigh at the relief of release and she stroked him through the taut fabric of his shorts before she hooked them with her fingers and slid them down, along with his jeans.

"Here." She pushed him backward toward the bed. "Sit."

He sat, and she knelt between his legs, fondling him, taking her time, teasing him with light touches until he groaned and fell backward and she took him in her mouth.

Teague closed his eyes and gave in to the swirl of sensation that started at his groin and spread like licking, flickering flames through his veins. Jodi was taking her time, teasing him with her tongue, then letting him ease into her warmth just when he thought he'd die of wanting. He reached down and tugged at her shirt, bunching it above her breasts and holding them cupped in his hands, caressing the soft, giving flesh and kneading her taut nipples between his thumb and fingers while she lavished him with attention, first teasing, then giving in, then teasing again.

He was going to explode if she kept on like that.

Sitting up, he coaxed her up onto his lap. She straddled his hips, arching her back while he fondled her breasts and gave her nipples the same teasing treatment she'd lavished on him. She flexed her hips, grinding her still denim-clad seat into his thighs, and he made a sudden move that flipped her down onto the bed beside him and then over onto her back.

Now it was his turn to tease. He unsnapped her jeans and dipped his hand below the waistband, sliding his fingers under the elastic and skimming down her belly until he reached her hot, damp center.

"I always wanted to do this," he said.

She opened her eyes, and having her watching him, aware of him, made the scenario even hotter.

"Do what?" she asked.

"Make it with the rodeo queen." Fastening his lips on one peaked nipple, he teased it with his tongue while he slid his fingers against the satiny warmth between her legs. "The perfect, shiny, beautiful rodeo queen."

With a sweet, needy whimper, Jodi lifted her hips and pulled her jeans down to her knees, dragging her lace panties with them. Teague helped, tugging them off.

"Those tight queen jeans," he said. "And the panties. The special rodeo queen panties." He held up the thin scrap of lace. "I always wanted to see those."

She was naked now except for the T-shirt that was hiked up over her breasts.

"Could you wear the sash next time?" he asked. He pulled her wrists together over her head, holding them gently but firmly. "I could use it to tie you up."

Gently, watching her face, he caressed the warm, slick heart of her. She closed her eyes.

"You don't need to tie me up. I'll do anything." She opened them again and met his. "I'm yours."

Covering her body with his, he kissed her, upping the tempo of his stroking and deepening his thrusts until she let out a pleading whimper and arched her back. Gritting her teeth, she let out a guttural moan and tensed, her body trembling while he stroked her climax higher until she shuddered and shattered and rolled away.

Soothing her, kissing her quiet, he slid down to kneel between her knees. Pulling her thighs apart, he licked and probed with his tongue while his fingers went to work again. He found the swollen bud at her center and sucked it, flicking his tongue over it until she moaned and flung her hands over her head, giving herself up to another wave of pleasure he could see rippling through her just under the skin.

He took his time, moving slow, watching her reaction as he found the touches that made her tense and the ones that made her beg for more, tasting and licking and kissing until she buried her fingers in his hair and pulled him away.

"Now," she said, looking him in the eye. "Now." She closed her eyes and fell back and he moved up to slide inside her.

Now he was the one who was helpless. The minute her warmth enveloped him, he felt his consciousness recede and he was all animal, powerful and helpless all at once. The room went dark and hot and he pushed inside her and retreated, pushed and retreated, the rhythmic friction heating him until he reared back and pushed one last time, losing himself in a pleasure so intense he thought he'd die.

He relaxed, tucking his head in the crook of her neck and breathing in the peachy scent of her. She wrapped her arms around him and he felt totally overwhelmed with gratitude and love. Something stung the back of his eyelids as he pressed his body against hers and dropped into darkness.

Chapter 32

WEDNESDAY MORNING DAWNED HOT AND STILL. JODI had tied a bandanna over her hair, but she still felt like the sun was baking the top of her head to a crisp as she wheeled a barrow full of horse apples out to the manure pile behind the barn. Hopefully she'd have all her chores finished by noon. The day had all the marks of a scorcher, and she'd had a late night. She smiled, remembering Teague's touch and the feel of him inside her.

She was pushing the wheelbarrow back to the stalls when she heard tires crunching on the gravel drive. She straightened and stretched her back, squinting toward the approaching vehicle. It was the sheriff.

The sheriff? A stab of worry for Teague flashed through her mind, but she told herself it was a reflex born of long habit. She didn't have to worry about Teague anymore. He'd proven himself, and she believed in him.

She pushed back the strands of hair that had tumbled out from under the bandanna, then wondered if she'd left a streak of grime across her forehead.

Well, who cared? It wasn't like she was gunning for rodeo queen anymore.

Sheriff Marty Woodell stepped out of the SUV and hitched up his belt. "Troy around?"

"Nope. Not yet," Jodi said. "Why?"

"Had a few questions for him."

That was weird. Why would the sheriff need to talk to Troy?

"Anything I can help with?"

"Not really." Marty hitched up his belt again and looked away. He seemed nervous. "Well, maybe. He works here, right?"

"Uh-huh."

"He ever talk about that polo match his crazy brother was planning?"

"Yeah—some. Why?"

The sheriff shrugged, but he still wouldn't meet her eyes. "No reason. Just wondered what he had to say about it."

"He was excited," Jodi said. "He called it the War. The rich guys versus the cowboys, he said." She smiled. "He didn't know who he should cheer for, because he's making so much money now."

"Huh." The sheriff shifted his weight from one foot to the other. "So he wasn't rooting for his brother?"

"Oh, I don't know. Probably, in the end," Jodi said. "Mostly he was just excited there was something different going on, you know? And working for Skelton was a big deal to him. He was always talking about how everything with the horses was 'confifluential.'" She grinned. "That's confidential in Troy talk. Why? Is there some kind of problem?"

"No. It's—nothing, probably." He was trying to sound casual, but the way his eyes kept avoiding hers set off warning bells in Jodi's head.

"Is this about the fire?" she asked.

The sheriff shrugged. "I can't really go into it. But if Troy shows up, could you have him come see me?"

"Sure," Jodi said.

She was lying, and she felt totally justified. Something was going on, and she was going to find out what it was before she sent Troy anywhere. She'd talk to Teague too. Find out if he knew what this was all about.

Skelton's obsession with secrecy had unnerved her from the start. She'd had a feeling he was up to something, and that feeling was getting stronger by the minute.

She glanced at her watch. It was almost eight o'clock. Troy was due any minute, and she didn't want the sheriff here when he arrived.

"Well, I'd better get back to work," she said. She picked up the handles of the wheelbarrow and turned it toward the barn.

"Okay," the sheriff said. "Just be sure and tell him I need to see him. Maybe you could bring him over to the office."

"Sure," Jodi said. "Yeah."

She turned and headed for the barn before he could say anything more. When the sound of his engine trailed off into the distance, she breathed a sigh of relief. Of course, Troy was probably headed there on his bike by now, and the sheriff was bound to pass him. She frowned. Maybe she should have been more helpful. If the sheriff saw Troy now, he'd have a chance to question him by himself. If she'd helped find him, at least she'd be able to sit in on the questioning.

She stepped out of the barn and shaded her eyes with her hand. Something in the distance glinted in the sun. Troy? No, it was a car. A truck. She breathed a sigh of relief as it turned into her driveway. It was Teague. He must be giving Troy a ride over.

And he'd just missed the sheriff.

She folded her arms over her chest and leaned against the barn. She had to lean against something. Just thinking of Teague made her knees weak, and besides, he'd spent most of the night before wearing her out in the bedroom. She smiled and tilted her face to the sun.

She didn't know when she'd felt so complete. The only thing that would have made the night better was if she was still in his bed when she'd woken up this morning—but she had her own animals to tend, and then there was Troy.

She watched the truck pull to a stop and her heart did a little cha-cha in her chest. She'd planned to play it cool, but when he opened the truck door she ran to him like a kid whose daddy had just come home from the war. Throwing her arms around his neck, she whooped as he picked her up and spun her around.

"Goooooood morning!" he said, giving her a loud smack on the cheek and setting her down. Dang, she'd never seen Teague so happy. Maybe she was what he'd needed all along.

She gave herself a mental slap. She knew better. And she'd promised her mother she'd use her brain when it came to this relationship.

But Teague was looking at her like he was hungry, and not for eggs and bacon. It was hard to remember she even *had* a brain with all the other body parts that were clamoring for attention.

"Good morning." She rolled her shoulders to get her T-shirt to fall back into place and tried—and failed—to wipe the lovesick grin off her face.

"Morning, Jodi," Troy said. "Wow, you sure look nice today."

She looked down at her rumpled T-shirt and ratty jeans and laughed. "I do?"

"Yeah." Troy nodded. "You look happy."

That just made the lovesick grin widen while she nodded like a bobblehead.

"You want me to groom the horses?" Troy asked.

"Yeah. Thanks, bud. We're using TT and Peach again."

She and Teague watched Troy stride into the barn. "He's all business," she said. "I couldn't have hired anyone better."

"Yeah, and the job means a lot to him." Teague slung an arm over her shoulders. "You were right on that one. And he's done okay spending his money. Although if I hear 'Dirty Deeds Done Dirt Cheap' one more time…"

Jodi giggled.

"So," he said. "Want to go inside?" He smiled that bad boy smile and Jodi could feel her brain melting as her body heated up. He put his arms around her and pulled her close, sliding his hands into the back pockets of her jeans and tugging her hips into his as he bent and gave her a very thorough good-morning kiss.

"No," she said when she came up for air. "Can't. I need to talk to you."

"Bummer. What about?"

"Troy."

"Troy?"

"Yeah. Remember? Your brother." She laughed. "Did all the blood rush out of your brain, or what?"

He looked down, then gave her a sheepish grin. "Yeah, I guess."

"Well, get over it and pay attention. This is important."

"Okay," he said. "What about Troy?"

"The sheriff stopped by this morning, asking questions about him."

"The sheriff? Why?"

"I don't know. He was asking about the polo match. About whether Troy was excited about it, who he was rooting for, stuff like that. I think it was about the fire."

"The fire?" He looked puzzled.

"I think Woodell's thinking Troy was... involved."

"Like in arson?" Teague shook his head. "That's ridiculous."

"I know. But you said Troy was leaving when the fire department got there. Maybe someone saw him and thought he was fleeing the scene, or something."

"Maybe we should find out." He pushed himself up from the bench. "Want to go with me?"

"I can't go anywhere. I have clients."

"Oh," he said. "Yeah." He looked at the truck, then back at her.

"You go ahead, though," she said. "I think we'd better find out what's going on."

"We," he said, bending down to give her a gentle kiss. "I like that."

"Me too," she said. "But hey, when it comes to Troy, we've always been a team."

"And now we're a team in other things too."

"In everything." She nodded and gave his butt a playful slap. "So hurry back."

Chapter 33

"HEY." CISSY SET DOWN A ROMANCE NOVEL ON THE sheriff's reception desk and gave Teague a smile. "What brings my knight in shining armor into town?"

"Need to see the sheriff," Teague said gruffly. He was no knight. He'd just done what needed to be done. "Got some questions for him."

"What…"

Teague brushed past her before she could finish the sentence. His brain had kicked back into gear once Jodi had faded from sight in his rearview mirror, and the more he'd thought about what she'd told him, the more concerned he got. There was no good reason for the sheriff to be asking questions about Troy.

He shoved the door to Woodell's office open and strolled in like he owned the place.

"What's this about Troy?" he asked.

"Hello to you too," the sheriff said. He leaned back in his chair, spinning it to face Teague. "I just had a couple questions for him. Not for you, for him."

"You can ask me," Teague said. "You don't need Troy."

"I'm afraid I do."

Teague stepped up and set his fists on the desk, deliberately looming over the sheriff. "What's this about?"

Woodell held up his hands as if warding Teague off. "Take it easy, son. I have a job to do, that's all. There have been some serious accusations made, and it's my duty to check out the facts."

"What kind of accusations?" Teague gave the sheriff his best slit-eyed stare. He could out–Dirty Harry Clint Eastwood when he tried.

"You need to calm down, son."

"I'm calm," Teague said. "So spit it out."

The sheriff eyed him cautiously, like he was facing down a Doberman. "Now don't get riled up," he said. "You don't need any trouble."

"Damn straight," Teague said. He really should be more careful about how he talked to the sheriff, but whenever anything threatened Troy, he had trouble keeping himself calm. It had gotten him in trouble before. He took a deep breath. *Calm down,* he told himself. *Calm down.* "Look, why don't you tell me what you're accusing Troy of, and we'll make sure the trouble goes away?"

"I'm not accusing him."

"Then who is?"

The sheriff swallowed. Teague waited, tension knotting his gut.

"Your brother's been working for Mitch Skelton," the sheriff said.

"I know." Teague clenched and unclenched his fist, trying to ignore the sinking sensation in his chest. He'd known the job with Skelton was a bad idea. It just hadn't felt right—the secrecy, and the suddenness of it. There was no reason the guy needed Troy—no good reason.

"Okay. Don't get upset, now. We can talk this out." The sheriff took a deep breath. "According to Skelton, the fire that occurred the other day was arson, and it was your brother's doing."

"That's ridiculous. Why would Troy do a thing like that?"

"Apparently, you had some scheme to challenge Skelton to a polo match."

"It was for a fund-raiser," Teague said. "What does that have to do with anything?"

"Skelton believes your brother burned down the barn so that the horses would be killed and your team would win the match by default."

"You have got to be kidding," Teague said.

"I'm afraid not. So you see, I really do need to question your brother."

"No," Teague said. He could feel his muscles tensing, as if he was about to turn green and swell up like the Incredible Hulk.

"I'm afraid you don't have a say in this," the sheriff said. "Look, I don't think your brother would do that either. But it's my job to follow up on this kind of thing. Let me talk to Troy, and it'll all go away."

Teague shook his head. "This Skelton dude. What do we really know about him, anyway?"

The sheriff shrugged.

"So why take his word over Troy's?"

"Well, first of all, I don't have Troy's word yet. And besides, there's evidence."

Teague took a step back. "Evidence?"

The sheriff scooted his seat back a foot or so, as if trying to distance himself from Teague. "I shouldn't tell you this, but a tin of lighter fluid was found in your brother's backpack. The accelerant matched the chemical the fire marshal says was used to start the fire."

"Lighter fluid?" Teague almost laughed. "That's

ridiculous. Troy's not allowed to mess around with stuff like that. Somebody must have planted it. And what the hell were you doing searching his backpack? You have probable cause?"

The sheriff folded his arms over his chest. "I'm not at liberty to discuss the case."

"What?"

"We don't talk about ongoing investigations."

"So in other words, you did an illegal search and you don't want to admit it."

The sheriff fished a pair of mirrored sunglasses out of his shirt pocket and slid them over his eyes. "I'm not at liberty to discuss that. But I recommend that you find your brother and bring him down to the station at the first opportunity." He bent his head and began shuffling through papers, obviously dismissing them. "Otherwise, if Skelton presses charges, I may have to issue a warrant for his arrest."

—⁓—

The truck cab was hot and airless, setting Teague's anger to simmering like a pot on slow boil. He considered going home for a minute to calm down, but Jodi would calm him down better than being alone. Besides, he needed to talk to her. And to Troy.

She was over by the arena, talking to a woman in a red T-shirt, but when she saw him pull in she jogged over and met him at the truck.

"Am I interrupting?"

"We're in between sessions," she said. "Troy's saddling up Peach. What'd the sheriff say?"

"You were right," he said in a low growl. "Skelton's

accusing Troy of setting that fire." He kicked a pebble with the toe of his boot, sending it skittering across the driveway. "It's ridiculous. There's no way Troy would do anything like that. He's scared of fire, for God's sake. That's why he hightailed it out of there."

"You don't have to tell me," Jodi said. "I'm on your side, remember?"

"Sorry."

Troy led Peach out of the barn. Her coat was gleaming, and she was neatly saddled and ready to work.

"Could you tie her up, Troy, and come over here?" Jodi called.

Troy hitched Peach to the gatepost with a flourish and trudged over.

"Hey." Teague set one hand on his brother's shoulder and looked him in the eye. "Did you know the sheriff's looking for you?"

Troy looked away. "Oh."

Teague glanced at Jodi, lifting his eyebrows in surprise. Troy didn't seem at all surprised that the law was on his trail.

"Did you know he was looking for you?" she asked.

"Uh-huh." Troy ducked his head. "I was out by Mr. Skelton's barn the other day. I just went to get my backpack. Remember, I left it there? But he got real mad and said he was gonna call the sheriff." Troy sniffed. "He said to get off his land. I don't know why he doesn't like me anymore. He used to like me."

"What's going on with that guy?" Teague muttered. He looked at Troy a minute, chewing the inside of his cheek. "He still has your backpack, then?"

Troy hung his head. "Uh-huh. When the barn caught

fire and the trucks came, I left so fast I forgot it." His lower lip trembled. "And then when I went back for it, Mr. Skelton said he'd call the sheriff." He shrugged. "I don't know why he wanted it. There wasn't much in it."

In a flash, Teague remembered seeing the backpack in the barn's wide doorway during the fire. "Bastard put that stuff in it himself," he muttered, so low so only Jodi could hear. "He's setting Troy up. I'll bet he set the damn fire, too."

He turned abruptly and headed for his truck.

"Where are you going?" Jodi called after him.

"To Skelton's. I'm going to straighten this out."

"No." She ran up behind him and grabbed his arm. "Don't. You'll do something stupid."

"Thanks for having faith in me," Teague said. "I'll protect my brother, that's all."

He shook her off but she grabbed his arm again, her grip surprisingly strong.

"No. Stay here. We don't know for sure what happened, but maybe we can find out." She gestured toward the driveway, where the sun glinted off an approaching SUV. "Maybe Courtney knows something."

Teague groaned. Would the Skeltons just go away? He wished they'd never come to Purvis. He'd pay any amount of money to see them go.

The Lexus jerked to a halt and Courtney slid down from the driver's seat. She approached slowly, switching her hips to show off her tight pink jeans and sparkly tank top.

Cowgirl Barbie. Just what he needed.

"Teague, I found you," she said.

"Again," Teague muttered. "Girl's like a bloodhound

on my trail." He flashed Jodi a look he hoped she'd interpret as an apology and turned to Courtney.

"What's up?"

His tone was brisk, almost harsh. He felt mean treating the girl that way, but he wanted to make it clear to Jodi that he didn't care about Courtney. And if Courtney took offense, he didn't really care. He'd had enough of her scheming—and her father's.

"I need you to look at some papers." Courtney glanced over at Jodi, frowning. "In private."

"Anything you can say to me you can say to Jodi," Teague said. From the corner of his eye he saw Jodi's mouth quirk into a smile. For once, he'd said the right thing.

"It's okay," she said, waving them away. "You guys go ahead and talk or whatever."

Teague winced. He didn't want to "whatever" with Courtney. He didn't even want to talk to her.

Jodi walked away, her long hair swaying. Teague watched her a moment, admiring the cowgirl swagger in her walk. Her worn Wranglers did a fine job of showcasing her world-class derriere.

Shoot, the girl had him thinking in French. He was wrecked for sure.

Courtney cleared her throat and Teague turned back to her, scowling. Seeing the two women together made him realize all over again how different they were. Sure, they were both blonde and both attractive, and both of them were rocking the Western look. But where Jodi walked with confidence, Courtney was looking up at him like she couldn't make a move without his say-so. In fact, he realized, that was how she'd been holding him hostage all this time: She made him feel responsible for her. For some reason, she seemed to depend on him, and he felt bad letting her down.

But he'd never asked for her trust. He didn't owe her a thing.

"Okay," he said, keeping his voice flat and business-like. "What?"

"Well, I wanted Daddy to donate some money to the clinic since we couldn't do the polo game, but he said he doesn't have the money."

"Honey, I don't see how that concerns me."

"Honey" didn't mean anything in Teague's world. If anything, the tone he'd used made it an insult—the kind of endearment that might have been followed by Rhett Butler's "frankly, I don't give a damn." But Courtney obviously didn't take it in that context, judging from the smile that was lighting her face. Shoot. Every move he made, every word he said, plunged him deeper into trouble with this girl.

"Well, Daddy was out, meeting with the sheriff about the fire."

"I know," Teague said.

She didn't seem to notice his grim tone.

"So while he was gone, I started looking through his papers, trying to see if he's telling the truth, and I found something."

"Courtney, your dad's finances are none of my busi-ness. Besides, I'm sure his money matters are a whole lot more complicated than mine."

"These are just insurance papers. And there's a bill of sale for some horses. You know about that kind of thing, right?"

Without waiting for an answer, she leaned into the car and reached over to the passenger seat for some papers that were strewn around the cab. Her jeans tightened over her ass when she bent over, and Teague could have sworn she took a lot longer than she needed to gather up the pages, but no French came to mind. Just some very basic English.

"Here." She came over and stood beside him, too close, and held out a letter as he backed away. Reluctantly, he took it and looked it over. It was a bank statement, and if she didn't understand what it said, she was even dumber than she looked. It said her father was overdrawn to the tune of eight thousand dollars.

Teague shrugged and handed it back to her. "He's overdrawn. But don't worry, Courtney. He probably has money in another account to cover it."

Actually, he probably didn't. The way he'd lit up and gone after Teague's ten thousand dollars made Teague suspect the man had some kind of financial problem going on—and here was proof. But he didn't want to know.

He backed up a few steps toward the house. "But look, this is none of my business, even if I understood it."

She shook another sheet in his face. "Look at this one, though."

He thought about just turning away, walking off without a word. He'd had enough of the Skeltons, Courtney included. He didn't want to be involved with them at all—not in any way. But what could he do? Lock himself in the house and refuse to let her in?

Yeah, he could lock himself in with Jodi. He cast a longing look toward the house, then turned his attention back to the paper in his hand.

"See? This account's overdrawn too," she said. She whipped out another piece of paper. "And then there's this."

The paper she handed him next was the kind of paperwork Teague understood, and he couldn't resist taking a look at it. It was a bill of sale for ten horses—for a total of ten thousand dollars.

"Which horses are these? I thought he had some kind of expensive Argentinean breed."

"That's what I thought too. Criollos, he said. But I gathered up everything I could find about the horses, and he never paid more than fifteen hundred dollars for any of them, except Dutch." Her eyes started to mist over. "Dutch was expensive for real."

"So the horses aren't what he said." Teague wasn't terribly surprised. The two horses he'd seen in training had hardly impressed him.

"Uh-huh." She nodded vigorously. "He was lying. And all the paperwork was in the box beside the shredder. He was going to destroy it." She handed him the next paper with a flourish. "And he was going to send *this* to the insurance company."

She held out another sheet. It was a bill of sale for ten horses, valued at ten thousand dollars apiece.

"Well, then those are different horses."

"No, they're not. The descriptions match exactly. These are the thousand-dollar horses. Don't you see what this means?" She tapped the paper with a crimson-tipped nail. "He set that fire *on purpose*."

Teague snatched the paper and scanned it rapidly, swearing under his breath. He didn't want to get involved in this, but Courtney was right. These papers all but proved Skelton had set the fire himself—which meant they let his brother off the hook.

"He killed them, Teague. And he killed Dutchy. I loved that horse. I loved them all, and I heard them *dying*. He let them burn to death so he could cheat the insurance company and cover his debts."

"Whoa," said a voice behind them.

Jodi had evidently read his body language and come to his rescue just in time to hear Courtney's revelation.

"Okay, Courtney." Teague ran a hand through his hair as if he could stimulate thought that way. "You're right. Now what are you going to do?"

"I don't know." She shifted to include Jodi in the conversation. Evidently, she didn't care who heard the news. "If I turn him in, he won't get the money from the insurance company. He might even be arrested—and then what will happen to *me*?" She worked her mouth, struggling not to cry. "I don't want to be poor. I *can't* be poor." She looked down at the papers. "So I was thinking maybe I could use these as leverage."

Teague grimaced. "You mean blackmail?"

"No. Well, sort of. I could make sure he spends the money on good things." She glanced over at Jodi. "A donation to the clinic. Stuff like that."

"I don't want that money," Jodi said. "Not a dime of it. And Courtney, he's trying to say Troy set that fire."

"Well, we'll make him take that back. And you need the money."

"Not that bad. And neither do you. It's dirty money, Courtney."

Courtney's self-possession broke into a thousand pieces. Trembling, she clutched Teague's arm.

"Please, can we go inside? I need to talk to somebody. You're the only friend I have here. The only person I can trust."

"Damn straight," Jodi said. "'Cause you sure can't trust me."

Courtney whirled. "What do you mean?"

Jodi shrugged. "After what you just said, I've got an obligation to call the police—unless you're willing to do it yourself."

"No," Courtney said. "It would backfire. I don't want my father to go to jail. And maybe I'm wrong. Maybe…"

"Maybe your father will put Troy in jail. Courtney, we're giving this to the police."

"No. Please."

"Look, Courtney." Teague grabbed her shoulders and forced her to look him in the eye. "You heard those horses die. You'll never forget that, will you?"

Courtney's lower lip trembled and her eyes brimmed over.

"We can't let him get away with that."

"Or with what he's trying to do to Troy," Jodi said.

Courtney looked from Teague to Jodi and back again, anger and desperation flickering across her face as if she couldn't decide whether to attack Jodi or plead with Teague. She finally settled on the pleading. Flinging herself at Teague, she wrapped her arms around him and wept into his shirtfront. He stood stoically, his mouth set in a grim line. He knew she expected him to bring his arms up to hold her. He knew she expected him to comfort her, but he was done taking care of Courtney. She was selfish, she was manipulative, and she was nothing but trouble.

"You won't tell, will you, Teague?" Courtney sobbed. "I can't be poor. I just can't." She looked up at him, her face wet with tears and streaked with mascara. "You won't tell, will you? And you won't let Jodi tell either. I can trust you, right?" She twisted her fists in the fabric of his shirt. "*Right*?"

Chapter 34

"Wrong." Jodi set a hand on Courtney's shoulder, trying her best to radiate firmness and sympathy with her touch. It must have worked, because the girl gradually released her grip on Teague and slumped her shoulders in defeat.

"We'll help you, Courtney," Jodi said in what she hoped was a soothing tone. "Come on inside. Let's talk."

"They'll arrest my dad." Courtney choked back a sob. "I never should have told you. I'll have nothing. *Nothing*."

"You'll have us," Jodi said soothingly, patting her shoulder. "Me and Teague. We'll do everything we can to help you."

"I don't have Teague," Courtney said. "*You* have Teague. He doesn't care about me."

"Yes he does," Jodi said. "Teague's your friend."

She guided Courtney up the porch steps into the kitchen and led her to the table.

"Come on," she said. "Sit down, and we'll figure out all our options."

She took Courtney's elbow and pretty much forced her into a chair.

"There are a couple ways we could take care of this," she said. "We could call the police."

"No!" Courtney clutched at her arm. "Please, no. They'd arrest Daddy and take him to jail! I'd lose everything!"

"Not necessarily," Jodi said. "But I agree that might not be the best solution."

Courtney's face brightened and she sat up straight. "So you think it might be okay to kind of, like, hold these papers over his head? Make him do the right thing, or we'd turn him in?"

"No," Jodi said. "I don't think that would be right. Do you—really?"

Courtney looked down at her hands, twisting them in her lap while she bit her lower lip.

"No," she said. She sounded like a sulky child.

"The other thing we could do is make copies of these documents, and send them to the insurance company," Teague said. "We don't even have to say who's sending them. We could do it anonymously. That way Courtney's dad would never know it was her that turned him in."

"That's what I was thinking," Jodi said. "But what about Troy? It'll take the insurance company a while to react. Meanwhile, Troy's under suspicion."

"Troy?" Courtney looked from Jodi to Teague, and back again. "What about Troy?"

"I told you, your father accused him of setting the fire. I just got back from the sheriff's office."

"What?" Courtney shoved her chair back from the table and leapt to her feet. "That—that—that—oh, I don't know what to call him! How could he do that to someone like Troy?"

Teague shrugged and looked away. Courtney and her father obviously hadn't been close, but finding out what kind of man he really was had to be tough. It was as if he'd been raised thinking his father was a normal dad, and then found out about the drinking and the meanness all at once.

"I'll get him. I'll go to the police," Courtney said.

"We could maybe do that for you somehow," Jodi said. "I mean, he is your dad and all…"

"No." Courtney clenched her fists. "I want him to know it was me." She was shaking from head to foot. Jodi was worried she'd keel over from an overdose of raw emotion. "I want him to look me in the eye while I twist the knife in his no-good rotten gut. I want him to suffer like Dutch did." She stamped her foot and clenched her fists so hard they shook. "I want to burn him alive, the way he did my horse."

Jodi jerked backward, stunned by the intensity of Courtney's emotion. Maybe she'd feel the same way if she was in Courtney's situation. What if someone killed Eightball—killed him in the most horrible way imaginable? What if someone made her horse suffer like that?

She'd probably want him dead too. And she might even want to do the deed herself. But twist the knife? Burn him alive? That was heading into psycho territory.

Bursting into tears, Courtney collapsed into her chair and covered her face, her shoulders heaving. Jodi edged her chair closer and rubbed Courtney's back as the girl curled into her, sobbing like a two-year-old.

"But I'll be poor," Courtney sobbed. "I won't have any money, and I don't know how to… how to live like that. I'll have to get a…" she sucked in a deep breath, as if preparing to say the unspeakable, "a *job*."

"We could help you find something," Teague said. "Maybe you could… ummm…" He glanced over at Jodi, looking for help.

She already had that one figured out. "Court, my mom needs somebody to help in the boutique," Jodi said. "I was doing it, but the clinic's getting busier. You'd be perfect. I'll bet you'd be really good at selling clothes out front, and then my mom could concentrate on the Internet end of the business."

Courtney sat up, wiping her eyes, and gave Jodi a hopeful look that was almost a smile. "You think she'd hire me?"

"Oh, are you kidding?" Jodi gestured toward the girl's Cowgirl Barbie outfit. "Look at you. You look great in those clothes."

"I do? But I'm not a real rodeo queen like you," Courtney said, suddenly shy. "I don't really know much about this stuff." She fingered the fringe that dangled from the yoke of her shirt.

"You don't have to. You just have to make it look good." Jodi slung an arm around Courtney's shoulders. "We'll go talk to her tomorrow, okay? And meanwhile, you'll go show those papers to the sheriff."

Courtney nodded uncertainly, her eyes glistening. "Okay," she said. "All right."

Chapter 35

THE SPRING-LOADED BELL OVER THE DOOR TO THE Brand Boutique tinkled as Jodi and Courtney walked in. Peggy Brand looked up from the rack where she was rearranging elk-tooth earrings.

"Hi, honey," she said.

"Hi." Jodi felt a flash of guilt, remembering how much she still owed her mother.

She hadn't been spending much time at the boutique.

"Mom, I know I've been really busy lately, and I haven't been here when you needed me," she said.

"Oh, that's okay." Her mother waved a dismissive hand. "You need to stop this nonsense about making things up to me, hon. We're fine. I know you're busy with your clinic. And I suspect you're busy with some other things too." Her smile was a little tight, but considering she was referring to Teague, it was wonderful that she could smile at all.

"Well, okay. But I still owe you. So I brought Courtney over. She's interested in working here, and I think she'd be perfect."

Her mom looked up from the rack for the first time and gave Courtney a sunny smile. "Courtney." She turned to Jodi. "We've already met. Courtney is one of my best customers." She looked Courtney up and down and her smile widened. "And one of the best dressed."

"Why, thank you, Mrs. Brand," Courtney said in

her tiny, breathy voice. "That means so much, coming from you."

"But surely you're not looking for work." Jodi's mom eyed Courtney thoughtfully. "Unless—oh, I know. You're bored, aren't you, and need something to do?"

Courtney started to nod, then squared her shoulders and lifted her chin. "No, we've had a setback," she said. "I'm afraid I really do need the job."

Jodi smiled. Courtney had almost gone for the lie, but she'd found the strength to tell the truth. Considering the way the girl was raised, she'd somehow developed a pretty good backbone. Jodi felt proud of her.

"Well, when would you like to start?" Jodi's mother asked. "Can you come by in the morning? We can figure out salary and all the details before we open."

"Am I hired?"

"Oh my, yes. I think you'll be perfect."

Courtney gave a little hop of happiness. "Oh, thank you," she said. "A real job. I can't wait." She turned to Jodi, her expression suddenly serious. "I have to go now, though. I have something to do."

The sheriff, Jodi thought. *She's going to see the sheriff.*

"Do you want me to go along?"

"No." Courtney set her jaw. "I can do this on my own."

Jodi watched her walk out with her trademark hip-swinging walk. She turned to her mother.

"Well, there you go," she said. "She's perfect, isn't she?"

"She really is. Thank you, honey."

"This place really is 'her,' I guess." Jodi pulled a pair of earrings off the rack and fingered them thoughtfully. "I'm sorry I can't be like that, Mom. I wish I could help more. I really do."

Her mother cocked her head and gave her a sharp, birdlike glance. "Oh, I'm not sorry."

"No?"

"No." Her mother stepped closer and took the earrings out of her hand. Setting them on the counter, she pulled Jodi into a quick hug.

"I'm not sorry at all," she said, pushing her out to arm's length. "Jodi, you take after your dad, that's all. You love all the things he did. When he—you know…" She swallowed hard and Jodi realized she still couldn't say that her husband had died.

"You're all I have left of him," her mother said. "And I treasure that. It's why I missed you so much, when—you know."

"When I wouldn't talk to you. I'm so sorry, Mom. It wasn't right, that you lost us both at the same time."

Her mother shrugged. "I lost him long before he died. After the accident, he couldn't do any of the things he loved, and he just burrowed inside himself and stayed there. You know he did."

Jodi nodded. It was true. Her father had withdrawn from the world when he'd wound up in that wheelchair. Once in a while she'd been able to get a smile out of him, but it was only skin deep. He was like a hollow shell.

Jodi nodded, blinking back tears and staring down at the toes of her boots.

"You're a good daughter, Jodi. The best I could ask for."

Jodi nodded again, but she could hardly agree. She'd never put herself in her mother's shoes. Never made an effort to see the situation from any point of view but her own.

"I could be better," she said. "I'll try to be better."

"You're fine," her mother said. "How are things with Teague? Have you decided what to do?"

Decided? Jodi blanched. She hadn't actually made a conscious decision. She'd just charged full steam ahead into the relationship, following her heart and a few other bodily organs that were even less trustworthy.

Maybe she should be questioning things more. Thinking things through. After all, Teague lit her up like a tiki torch. How could she trust herself?

She'd slow down, she told herself. She'd slow down and think about what she was doing before it was too late.

Chapter 36

TEAGUE TURNED AWAY FROM HIS KITCHEN COUNTER and dove for the phone, reaching it an instant before Troy. They'd raced to answer the phone since high school, when Troy would tease Teague about the girls that called.

"'Lo?" Teague tucked the phone between his shoulder and his chin while he finished the sandwich he'd been making for Troy. Slicing it in quarters, he handed it to his brother and waved him away.

"Teague. 'Fraid I've got bad news."

"Sheriff?"

"I just got in, and it seems Mitch Skelton was down here this morning. He's decided to press charges against your brother."

"Shit."

"Look, I'm sorry," Woodell said. "From what they said, the guy was acting pretty weird. Kind of shaky and desperate, I guess. I'm sure this won't amount to anything, but he's a citizen of this county, and I've got a duty to pursue it."

"Right."

"You know where Troy is?" the sheriff asked.

"No. Sorry." He glanced over at the table where Troy was eating his sandwich and crossed his fingers.

"So he's not home?"

"Nope."

"I need some cooperation here, Teague," the sheriff said.

"What, so you can arrest my..." Teague glanced over at his brother and lowered his voice. "Look, you know he didn't do this. Matter of fact, Skelton's daughter has papers that prove the guy's planning to defraud his insurance company. She hasn't been there?"

"Haven't seen her."

"Damn." Teague took a deep breath. He could feel the rage spiraling inside him, building on itself. Why hadn't Courtney been to the sheriff yet? She'd been eager enough to go see about the job with Jodi's mother. Teague figured she'd have wrapped that up and made it to the sheriff's by now—but she hadn't followed through. He should have hung onto those papers, or made copies in case she changed her mind.

"Teague?"

"What?"

"I need to find your brother." Woodell sighed. "I'd like to take care of this myself, before one of the deputies takes it on. If you see him, can you bring him in?"

"Sure." Teague clicked the phone shut and strode over to the table. Grabbing his hat from the back of a chair, he shoved it on and headed for the door.

Troy watched, wide-eyed. "Where you going? Aren't you gonna eat your sandwich?"

"Later," Teague said. "I've got something to take care of first."

He'd take care of it, all right. He'd take care of Skelton. That's what he'd do.

Teague slid the truck to a halt in front of the massive

Skelton mansion, leaving muddy streaks on the pristine blacktopped driveway. Slamming the truck door behind him, he stalked up to the house, rang the bell, and waited for an answer.

He knew he should use his time on the doorstep to cool down, but he stoked his anger instead, picturing Troy's puzzlement over his knapsack, remembering how the man had angled to get Teague's money and practically offered Courtney for sale.

Staring at the door, he strained to hear if anyone was approaching. There were no footsteps, no sounds at all. He reached out and turned the knob.

The door swung open.

He stepped inside and scanned the vast interior. The place seemed to be empty, but maybe Skelton was in his study where they'd met before. Heading down the hall, Teague pushed the door open.

Bingo. The guy was sitting behind his desk, shuffling through some papers. When Teague entered, he looked up, lifting his hands to his chest like Peter Rabbit caught in Mr. McGregor's garden.

Striding over to the desk, Teague rested his fists on it so he could loom over Skelton in the most threatening manner possible. Skelton shuffled the papers in front of him, trying to hide them under some folders. Teague recognized them as the ones Courtney had shown him. The bill of sale and the insurance papers. He snatched up the bill of sale.

"Well, look at this," he said. "Thousand-dollar horses. I guess this is the one you should have shredded."

He folded the paper deliberately and shoved it in his back pocket. "I know what you're up to, Skelton.

You need to pick up that phone and call the sheriff." He pointed at a cordless handset that rested on one corner of the desk. "Tell him you've changed your mind about charging my brother with arson."

"Why would I do that?" Skelton said. He'd recovered himself somewhat, and managed to meet Teague's eyes, but his effort at an innocent stare wasn't convincing. "We both know your brother has problems."

"My brother has Down syndrome, buddy. *You* have problems."

"I certainly do. That fire killed my valuable horses. Now I know your brother probably didn't realize what he was doing…"

"Your horses weren't all that valuable, and my brother knows enough not to play with matches. He didn't start that fire, and you know it." He grabbed the phone and shoved it toward Skelton. "Call off the sheriff."

Skelton met his eyes with a challenging stare. "I have proof your brother set that fire. Back off, or I'll see to it he's sent away for a long time. People like him should be put away anyway, where the rest of us don't have deal with the pathetic consequences of inbreeding and substance abuse."

A black coil of rage spun in Teague's chest, whirling out of control. Stalking around the desk, he grabbed the front of Skelton's shirt, hauling him out of his chair. "You're the one who should be put away, Skelton. In Rawlins, at the state prison." He gave the man a shake. "And you'll go there, if I have anything to say about it."

"Get your hands off me," Skelton squeaked.

Teague hauled him up to face level, letting the man dangle with his feet barely touching the floor.

"You *bastard*." He shook him again. "What's your game, Skelton? You need money? Is that why you did it? You're not what you pretend to be, are you? You're a fake. A fraud."

Skelton squeaked, his head bobbling on his skinny neck.

"I—I don't know what you're talking about," he babbled. "Your brother—I was trying to help him. I gave him a job."

"You gave him a job knowing damn well what you were going to do," Teague said. "You wanted my ten thousand awfully bad, mister. And now your barn burns down, and you're falsifying insurance papers. You set that fire yourself."

Disgusted, he shoved Skelton away.

He'd figured the guy would land in the chair, but it skidded away on impact and Skelton pitched backward, his arms flailing as he slammed into the window behind the desk. The back of his head struck the glass with an audible *thunk* and a network of cracks spread out from the impact like a spider web.

Skelton fell to the floor along with a hundred shards of glass, a streak of blood trailing behind him. Teague backed away, all the way to the door and into the hallway. He leaned against the wall and struggled to collect himself, to ease the rage swirling inside him. His heart was ticking like an overheated engine.

He hadn't meant to hurt the guy. He'd grabbed him in a rage, and then all of a sudden, he hadn't been able to stand the man's presence, so he'd pushed him away. He turned and peered into the room.

Skelton hadn't moved.

Had he killed him?

He stepped into the room and a movement in the window caught his eye. A shadowy figure stood just beyond the glass. Its face was fragmented by the cracks, but for an instant Teague thought it was his father, glowering at him from the dark garden.

Then he realized it was his own reflection, wearing an expression so like his father's they could have been twins.

Chapter 37

TEAGUE PEERED OVER THE DESK. SKELTON'S CHEST rose with one breath, then another. Slowly, his eyes opened and he held up one shaking hand as if to ward Teague away.

Well, he wasn't dead.

In fact, he was struggling to his feet. His confused, loose-jointed movements reminded Teague of a horror-movie zombie.

"Give me the paper."

Teague fished the bill of sale out of his back pocket and unfolded it.

"This one? No."

"Give it to me."

Skelton extended a trembling hand, and Teague half-expected him to start asking for "*braaaaaaiiiins.*"

"No."

Skelton jerked open a desk drawer and whipped out a gun, some sort of revolver. Teague put his hands up.

"Whoa," he said, backing away. This was unexpected.

"Give me the paper," Skelton said.

Teague backed away, his hands in the air. He wasn't about to give up the paper. It exonerated his brother. Hopefully Courtney had a copy or something, but he didn't know for sure. He looked down at the paper in his hand, then back up at Skelton's face. He wouldn't shoot. Would he?

"Hold on." He started to unfold the paper and smooth it out, as if he was preparing to put in on the desk. Skelton's wrist relaxed, and the gun barrel's dark eye, which had been pointed directly at Teague's face, dropped.

Crumpling the paper in his hand, Teague dodged out the door and charged down the hallway. Behind him, the pistol fired and he glanced over his shoulder to see a black hole blossoming in the drywall across from the doorway.

"Shit." He took a turn at top speed, skidding on the slick marble floor of the foyer, and flew out the door as another shot broke the silence. He hadn't run away from many things in his lifetime, but Skelton was liable to kill somebody. The man wasn't just dishonest; he was crazy too.

Teague cursed himself as he climbed into his truck and cranked the engine. He'd managed to keep himself in check for years. For years, he'd swallowed his anger, harnessed the demon that was his father's only legacy. Even back at the trailer with Cal, he'd managed to control himself.

He'd fought it as hard as he could. But today, it had won.

That reflection in the window had shown him who he really was.

------***------

Teague stood in the center of his kitchen and turned around in a slow circle. Every counter gleamed, every appliance sparkled, and every dish was stacked neatly in its place—but he still felt like crap. He dragged himself into the bedroom and dropped down on the side of the bed, resting his elbows on his knees and putting his head

in his hands. At least he had some time to himself to figure things out. Troy had evidently gone out—probably
in search of more AC/DC. Teague had better get his
thinking done while he could.

The Persian-style throw rug at his feet didn't offer
any answers, but he lost himself in the ornate pattern and
the sound of the front door opening and closing didn't
register at first.

"Whatcha doing?" said a voice from the bedroom door.

He looked up to see Jodi leaning against the jamb.

"Nothing."

"Looks like moping to me."

"Some of that."

She sat down beside him, mirroring his pose. "What's
the matter?"

He stared down at the floor. "I damn near killed him."

He felt her tense as she turned to face him. "Who?"

"Skelton."

"Oh, no. Teague."

He sighed. "I got a call from the sheriff this morning.
The guy was going to press charges. Me being the great
negotiator I am, I thought I'd go talk him out of it."

"Uh-oh."

"Yeah. He said something about Troy—I don't even
remember what it was—and next thing I knew, he was
sliding down the window onto the floor." He spread his
hands, palms up, and looked down at them, mystified.
"I don't even know what happened."

"He's all right, though?"

"Damn straight. He got up and grabbed a gun. Shot
at me."

"You're kidding!"

"Nope. I hightailed it out of there, I can tell you."
He set his elbows on his thighs and dropped his head
into his hands. "Dang, Jodi, I don't blame him. I was
out of control."

She shrugged one shoulder. "Maybe he deserved it."

"No. Don't whitewash it, Jodi. I didn't have any
control over myself. Not a bit. I was—I could feel my
father in me." He edged away. "Jodi, I told you, I'm not
a touchy-feely, talk-it-out kind of guy. But I need to tell
you, this scares me. The thing with Cal? It wasn't as
easy as I made out."

She gave him a sad smile. "I kind of figured that."

"I had sort of a flashback. There was a moment
I couldn't figure out where I was. Who I was. I thought I
was twelve again, and he…" He looked down at the floor
and shook his head. "And then tonight, after I knocked
Skelton out, I thought I saw him in the window."

"Who? Your father?"

"Yeah, but it was me. It's just—for a minute there—I
looked just like him."

"You're nothing like him. You know that, right?"

"I think so." He sucked in a deep breath and took her
hand. "I hope so."

She nodded. "Teague, you're not. I'll tell you every
day until you believe it." She put her hands on his
shoulders and forced him to look at her. "You're nothing like him because you don't do it for yourself. Your
father did what he did to tame his own devils. That's
not you, Teague."

"It was tonight."

"No it wasn't." She scooted away and took his hands,
ducking her head to meet his eyes. "You hit him to

protect Troy. Fighting to protect the people you love is a *good* thing."

He shook his head. "How can hitting someone be a good thing?"

He could tell she was suppressing a smile. "Depends who you're hitting. You ever hit Troy?"

"No, but…"

"No buts. Troy's frustrating. He drives you nuts. And you're patient with him, all day every day. Teague, *I* would have hit Skelton if I'd thought it would make any difference."

"No, you wouldn't. It's not a natural reaction for most people like it is for me. Your mom was right, Jodi. It's *in* me, and there's not a damn thing I can do about it."

"Yes there is," she said. "You can fight it. And I'll help." She pulled him close. "That makes it two against one. We're bound to win."

―᷾ᚱ᷾―

Your mom was right. The words pricked at the back of Jodi's brain, reminding her that she was supposed to be thinking, not feeling. But with Teague's body pressed against hers, that was dang near impossible. She could feel tension tightening his muscles and his heart was thumping hard but slow. Something in her thrilled at the way he'd gone after Skelton to protect Troy. Maybe it was natural for a woman to be attracted to a man who would defend his family and damn the consequences.

And he'd finally confided in her. Finally told her how he felt—and that was what she'd been waiting for. Teague was so scarred by his father's issues that he couldn't see the impulse to protect his family as a strength. He was convinced it was a weakness.

He probably thought being a touchy-feely, talk-it-out kind of guy was a weakness, too, but she knew it took more strength to talk about his feelings than it had to slam Skelton into the window.

Passion and tenderness swirled and merged into a surge of love and she leaned in to brush her lips over his. The touch felt so warm and right that she repeated it, slower this time, savoring the sensation. He moved one hand to the back of her neck and slid his fingers up into her hair, drawing her closer while he deepened the kiss and slid his tongue between her lips.

The touch of his tongue was like an electric shock. Her whole body came alive and her chest seemed to swell with the effort to hold all the love she felt for him. She took his head in both hands and angled her own, trying to put every atom of love in her being into one kiss.

She'd never let go completely like this. When he'd confided in her, he'd broken down the last wall that stood between them and now they were truly one. As they rolled back onto the mattress, the kiss intensified and his hands moved down to her shoulders and then to her waist. He slid them back to cup her hips and pull her against him, and again his touch ignited her. She felt an urgency she couldn't control as she tore his shirt open, popping all the snaps in quick succession, and ran her hands over his skin.

"Jodi, wait."

She didn't want to wait, but when he quickly rose and closed the door, she realized it was a good thing one of them had a brain. Hers seemed to have vaporized the moment he'd kissed her.

Teague left a trail of cast-off clothing on his way back to the bed, and by the time he rejoined her he had nothing left on but a pair of boxer briefs that left almost nothing to the imagination. She pulled him toward her, running her hands down his back as he wrestled with her T-shirt, finally taking her hands and holding them above her head as he struggled with the shirt.

"Bossy," she said, giving him a flirty smile.

"I'm a take-charge kind of guy," he said.

He kissed her again, pushing her back down on the bed while his hands went to work unfastening, unzipping, and unbuttoning until she was naked except for a thin pair of white lace panties.

—✺—

Teague looked down at Jodi, lying on his bed naked with her blonde hair fanned out across the comforter and her hips spanned by the slightest scrap of lace. He couldn't believe his own luck. She knew him, inside and out, all his flaws and all his secrets, and it seemed like she loved him even more. He wasn't going to let her go this time. Not ever again.

He kissed the angle of her jaw, knowing the brush of his lips would make her quiver and moan, and then moved down her neck, running his lips over the pale perfection of it. Taking her hand, he drew her arm away from her body and kissed his way down her side while his other hand moved down to stroke her breast.

She sucked in a quick breath as his palm brushed her nipple, arching her back, and he shifted to swirl his tongue around it before taking it in his mouth and sucking gently while his fingers toyed with its twin. Her hands stroked his hair, then tugged him closer as she closed her eyes and threw her head back.

The unmistakable surrender in the gesture stirred something deep inside him and he upped the intensity, tormenting her sensitive nipples one after the other until the pale skin around them flushed and warmed. Moving his lips down her body, he kissed each delicate rib while he stroked one finger along the edge of her panties. She bit her lip and gasped, clutching at his hand.

He shoved the shred of lace aside as she opened her eyes and lifted her hips, offering herself and opening to him. She buried her fingers in his hair and pushed him lower.

"Who's bossy now?" he murmured.

"Me," she said, tugging him closer until he gave her what she wanted, slipping his tongue between the soft folds and licking the slick, hot heart of her. She closed her eyes and gave herself up to her need as he probed deeper, his tongue seeking and finding all her secrets.

How did he know what she wanted? It seemed like he knew her body better than she knew it herself. The boundaries between them blurred and disappeared as he used his fingers and his tongue to untether her from reality. She was weightless, boneless, and nothing existed but this moment as she arched and gasped and was carried away on an overwhelming wave of love.

The first thing she knew when she surfaced was his arms around her, his square, muscular chest supporting her head, and his breath rising and falling in rhythm with her own. Rolling to face him, she met his eyes and wondered how long she'd been lying there. His eyes fixed on her and focused; she'd interrupted a thousand-yard stare.

"What are you thinking about?"

"Everything." His lips tilted in self-mockery. "It's kind of a new experience." He brushed her lips with a quick kiss, as if he couldn't help himself, and held her a little tighter. "Mostly, I try not to think about things, but it's like talking about it opened a door."

"Is that a good thing?"

His gaze fixed on some distant point again. "I don't know. It's the door to a really messy closet. I'm just worried everything's going to fall out."

"I'll help you clean it up," she said. "Meanwhile, stop thinking for a while." She threw one leg over his hips, rolled him over, and hiked herself up to straddle him, her hands on his chest. "I'll help."

Teague looked up at her and realized not everything in that closet had been bad. He was freer to feel in every way, and it was as if his love for Jodi had doubled. He closed his eyes as she rocked herself against him, running her hands over his chest and setting every nerve in his body on high alert.

He held her hips and lifted her, and she reached down and held him as she lowered herself slowly, then tensed her thighs and rose again, lowered herself and rose, carrying them both away with a deliberate rhythm that let them savor every shred of sensation.

Setting her hands on the bed behind her, she leaned back and lifted her hips. He'd thought he couldn't get any more turned on, but he'd been wrong. Arching his back, he drove into her, watching his cock disappear inside her cleft. Groaning, he clenched his abs and sat up to reach around her and support her back. She lifted her hips and her breasts nearly brushed his face. He licked at her nipple as she pushed back, then slid home again, quickening her pace until she slammed down one last time and clenched around him, shivers rippling over her body. He held her tight and tensed, pulsing into her one more time as the sight, sense, and scent of her overwhelmed him.

Chapter 38

A BAR OF LIGHT SLIPPING THROUGH THE BLINDS WOKE Teague early. Stretching, he stepped over to the window, peering out to check the weather. "Shit," he said.

"Good morning," Jodi said. "Nice."

"Sorry. Do you have a session this morning or something?"

"No. All I have to do today is give that speech to the Girl Scouts this afternoon."

"Well, you've got a volunteer."

"Don't tell me."

"Okay, I won't. But she's almost to the door." He squinted. "Man, she looks like hell."

Jodi sighed and tossed off the covers. Slipping her toes into her slippers, she finger-combed her hair, then stood and shrugged into her robe.

"Coming," she called as a knock sounded on the door.

Teague hustled into his jeans. "I'll get it."

He ran for the door and swung it open to stare open-mouthed at Courtney. She was hardly rocking the Barbie vibe today. Her hair was disheveled, falling around her face in limp strands, and her eyes were bloodshot and red-rimmed. Her fringed shirt was half untucked, and her hands were shaking. She looked like a refugee who'd just spent a night running through the woods pursued by baying hounds.

"Teague?" She worked her mouth as if she could

barely manage to form words. "Teague, I need help. They won't let me in the house, and I want my music box. My daddy gave it to me, and…" She made a faint mewling noise and buried her face in her hands.

"Come on in." Jodi stepped up behind him and took the girl's elbow, urging her into the kitchen. "Come on. I'll make you coffee."

"I don't want coffee." Courtney plopped down into a chair and wiped her eyes with one hand. "I want my music box. It's mine, and they won't give it to me. I *need* it. I…"

"*Who* won't give it to you?" Teague asked.

"The police."

"The police?"

Courtney sniffed and nodded. "They won't let me in."

"The police are at your house?" Teague felt the world drop out from under his feet. Had Skelton been hurt worse than he thought? Or had the guy called the police himself? If he'd called the cops on Teague, why hadn't they shown up yet?

"Why are the police there?" Jodi looked almost as pale as Teague felt.

"It's my dad," Courtney said. "He's *dead*."

"*What?*" Teague, dizzy and sick, stumbled backward, pushing Courtney away. "It was an accident. I didn't mean…"

"He shot himself," Courtney blubbered. "It was terrible. I found him in his study. There was blood everywhere, and his face…"

"*What?*" Teague had seen the first shot hit the wall. Had Skelton turned the gun on himself next?

"His face…" Courtney flailed her arms helplessly.

"Breathe." Jodi put her arms around Courtney. "Take it easy. Did you tell the sheriff?"

"No," Courtney said, leaning into her. "But I screamed, and my stepmother came, and she called 911. But I need my music box, because I—I was working on something and I put it—well, and it's in my room." She stretched her mouth and let out a sob. "I wasn't done, but I went down there and he had the gun, and… and they won't give me my music box." She sucked in a long, shuddering breath. "They said I should wait, but I couldn't stay there. I couldn't stand to be in the house. I've been just driving around for like, an hour. I didn't know what to do. I don't want to go home where—where it happened."

The girl probably shouldn't have been driving. It was like she was delirious or something—and no wonder. Seeing your own father dead like that—well, it had to be trauma beyond anything Teague could imagine.

"Shhh." Jodi stroked Courtney's hair as if she was a child. "Shhh. We'll get your music box, okay? You need to calm down. Just calm down. I know it's hard."

"Thank you." Courtney shrugged her off and backed away, wiping her nose on the sleeve of her shirt. "I can't believe he's really dead. I didn't think—I didn't think it would be like this."

"It's not your fault," Jodi said. "Look, do you want me to take you home? Your stepmother…"

"No! I don't want to see her." Courtney clenched her fists. "I want my music box."

Jodi glanced over her shoulder, giving Teague a helpless look.

"I'll go get it," he said.

Jodi frowned. "Teague, you can't go back there."

He held a cautionary finger to his lips and nodded toward Courtney. "I think it's best if I do."

"Thank you." Courtney sniffed. "I just—can you believe he killed himself?"

Teague bit his lip and nodded. Of course he believed it. He just hoped everyone else did—because apparently he'd been the last person to see Skelton alive.

Chapter 39

THE SKELTON HOUSE SEEMED EERILY QUIET AS TEAGUE turned into the drive. Muddy tire tracks criss-crossing the blacktop were the only sign of what had happened. The blackened silhouette of the barn loomed beyond the house, the trees and fences around it strung with yellow crime-scene tape that fluttered in the faint breeze. There was no tape on the house's front door. Teague breathed a sigh of relief. Skelton's death must have been an obvious suicide.

He stepped up onto the porch, his boots resounding in the eerie silence. The place looked like a cross between Tara and Monticello, with a touch of Graceland tossed in via marble and gilt accents that glittered in the sun. The expensive shrubbery stood out green and lush against the sun-bleached backdrop of native sage that surrounded the sprinkler-fed lawn area.

Rapping on the door, he waited a moment, then walked over and peered through the lace-curtained window.

"Hello?"

Behind him, a bird piped out a hesitant trill, but there was no sound from the house.

"Mrs. Skelton?"

As he turned back toward the door, it swung open to reveal a dark-haired woman, Hispanic and slightly older than Courtney. She had the blowzy, boobalicious look of a stripper past her prime.

Skelton's wife, Teague guessed.

Her hair was tangled, and the generous coat of mascara that spidered her lashes was smudged into a bandit's mask around her eyes. She was wearing a thin cotton tank top that was almost as indecent as the nightgown Jodi had been wearing the night the polo players had come to call. It was sloppily tucked into a pair of tight pink sweatpants that revealed every cellulite dimple. Her unfettered breasts strained at the nearly transparent fabric of her top, and Teague kept his eyes fixed firmly on her face.

"Hello," he said. "I'm, ah, I'm Teague Treadwell. A friend of your daughter's. Stepdaughter's, I mean." He shuffled his feet and looked down at the ground so she wouldn't think he was looking at her breasts.

The woman shrugged, staring at him with cold eyes.

"I'm, ah, sorry for your loss," Teague said. "I came to get Courtney's music box. She's staying with my girlfriend, and she seems fixated on it for some reason."

"What, that ballerina thing? Why would she want that?" Her voice was harsh and grating, with definite cigarette and whiskey undertones and a faint Spanish accent.

"I don't know. I'm not sure she's being rational. But I'm trying to help."

"Well, aren't you the knight in shining armor." The woman's eyes were flat and hard as a snake's. Maybe she was in shock. He took a step back.

"Never mind. Don't worry about it. Sorry to bother you."

"No, I'll get it." She sighed and shrugged one shoulder in a motion that made a spaghetti strap slide off her shoulder, exposing a long swath of flesh and even more cleavage. She shoved it back into place. "Excuse me," she said. "I can't seem to grasp the fact that my husband…" She clenched one hand into a fist and brought it to her mouth. "I'm trying to grieve, but I… excuse me."

She turned and walked into the house before Teague could respond. He glanced nervously up toward the dome that enclosed the two-story cathedral ceiling of the entryway. A balcony with an ornate carved wood railing ran around three sides of the room, and he saw her hurry down the length of it. Several doors lined the wall opposite the railing; one of them opened as she passed and a head poked out.

A man's head. With tousled dark hair.

Teague froze. It was one of the Argentine horsemen— the one who'd been after Jodi. What was his name?

Gustaldo.

What the hell was he doing in the house?

The polo player muttered something in Spanish to Skelton's wife and she replied, then bustled past. As she departed, the man stepped out of the doorway and said something else to her.

He was shirtless, wearing only a pair of the tight breeches the polo players wore.

"Hey," Teague said without thinking.

The player whirled, fixed his gaze on Teague for half a second, then dodged back into the room and slammed the door.

Teague sucked in a quick breath. Skelton's wife sure had a strange way of grieving.

Maybe her husband hadn't taken his own life. Maybe he'd been murdered.

The wife looked like she might be from South America too, like the polo players. Maybe they'd cooked up some plot between them—she'd seduce the guy, marry him, and then the polo player would off him and they'd collect the inheritance. What other explanation could there be for his presence in the house?

Poor Courtney. No wonder she hated the woman. She probably knew something wasn't right.

The woman passed above him again, then trotted down the stairs, bare feet flashing quickly from under her robe.

"I can't find it," she said, spreading her hands. The gesture tightened the fabric over her breasts and Teague turned away.

"Uh, never mind." He stepped back and nearly stumbled over the doorsill. "I'll just—I'll just go."

Feeling his face heat with a blush, he hightailed it down the steps and headed for the truck.

The sheriff needed to know what was going on here. And once Teague told him that, he'd have to reveal his own part in Skelton's last hours. He couldn't just tell part of the story, and besides, he was a lousy liar.

He'd barely opened the truck door before a scraping noise and a shout from the house made him turn. Gustaldo was standing at an open window on the far side of the house, still shirtless. As Teague watched, he lofted something into the air. Instinctively, Teague ducked. The object hit the ground and flew apart as the polo player dodged back inside with what sounded like a Spanish curse and slammed the window.

Teague stepped out from behind the truck and surveyed the wreckage. A wooden panel. Another, and another. A porcelain ballerina, now headless. Several metal cylinders with spokes, and a delicate crank with a wooden handle. It was the music box. Or at least, it had been. The thing was just about destroyed. He cursed his irrational paranoia. What had he thought—that Gustaldo was throwing a bomb? He should have caught the damn thing. Courtney would be broken-hearted.

Making his way carefully over the gravel, he started picking up the pieces—the ballerina's head, another mechanical cylinder, a row of metal tongues that must have provided the tinkling soundtrack for the ballerina's dance. There were two crinkled sheets of paper, too, resting against the truck's front tire.

Gathering the pieces together, he laid them in the front seat of the truck and cranked the engine. He'd take it home and see if he could put it back together. It was the least he could do. Courtney had problems enough. He had to help somehow.

But first he needed to visit the sheriff. Someone needed to tell him about Gustaldo and Skelton's wife.

Chapter 40

THE DOOR TO THE OLD JAIL CREAKED OPEN AS TEAGUE stepped inside. Cissy looked up from the receptionist's desk as he entered.

"Sheriff here?"

"He's in the back." Cissy set a tattered paperback upside-down on the desk and leaned forward. "So what do you think of Skelton's suicide? You were dating that daughter of his for a while, right?"

Cissy was back to her old self, applying all the investigative savvy of a CSI tech to the ferreting out and confirmation of every shred of scandal that came her way.

"I heard she's kind of crazy," she continued. "That true?"

"No." Teague was in no mood to chat. "We never dated, either. That was a figment of her imagination."

"I wondered," Cissy said. "She isn't exactly your type."

"You got that right."

"The sheriff's in his office," she said. She straightened in her chair and smoothed her dark hair, pushing it behind her ears, then gestured vaguely toward the hallway. "You can go on in."

Teague strode down a paneled hallway lined with plaques from various service organizations. He rapped softly on a door that bore a faux brass plate with Woodell's name on it.

"Come in."

Teague stepped inside and found himself standing in front of the sheriff's desk. It was like a flashback to his adolescence. How many times had he stood in front of this desk, getting lambasted up one side and down the other for his latest escapade?

"What's up, Teague?" The sheriff tilted back in his chair so the harsh fluorescent light fell on his face, and Teague suddenly realized how much older the man had grown.

"I was over at the Skelton place. Miss Skelton asked me to pick up something her father had given her. A music box." Teague didn't know why he used the formal title for Courtney. Something about the sheriff made him go all stiff and officious, even after all these years. It was like hanging out with your old drill sergeant.

"You get it?"

Teague nodded.

"Don't know why she wanted it so bad," the sheriff said. "She was like a crazy woman, carrying on about it. Funny what folks fixate on when things go wrong."

"I got it from her stepmother," Teague said. "Skelton's wife. Widow. Whatever."

The sheriff nodded and cocked his head. "Okay. You came to tell me that?"

"No. I came to tell you a couple things. First of all, one of the polo players was in the house. Guy named Gustaldo, or something like that. There's something going on between him and the wife."

"Really." The sheriff tilted his hands forward and folded his arms on the desktop. "What kind of something?"

"She was wearing—well, she wasn't wearing much, and he was shirtless," Teague said. "I think I interrupted something."

"That's her brother," Woodell said. "He came in to calm her down."

"Oh. Well, maybe not, then." Teague paused. "You sure Skelton took his own life?"

"Pretty sure." The sheriff picked up a pencil and fiddled it between his fingers. "But there are some un-answered questions."

Teague sank into a side chair that faced the desk. "I might be able to answer some of those."

The sheriff gave him a hard-eyed stare. "Don't tell me you're involved in this somehow."

"I was there yesterday," Teague said. "I went to see him about Troy."

"Why?"

Teague shrugged. "I thought maybe I could talk him into dropping the charges."

"And how did you intend to do that?"

"I intended to use my elocutionary skills, but it didn't work out that way." Teague took a deep breath. "I didn't go there to hit him, I swear. I was just going to talk to him, but I—I lost control."

The sheriff eyed him sharply. "So you did hit him?"

"No, I threw him against the wall. Well, against the window, actually." He looked down at the toe of his shoes. "Couldn't seem to stop myself."

Woodell sighed. "You'd better tell me about it."

Teague relayed the whole encounter, from the time he entered the room to the gunshot. "I didn't stick around after that."

The sheriff narrowed his eyes. "You telling the truth, son?"

Teague raised a hand in the air. "I swear. He was fine when I left. Pretty upset, pretty angry, but fine. He must have realized I was going to turn him in. I guess he couldn't take the shame, so he turned the gun on himself."

Woodell narrowed his eyes and the room suddenly seemed hot and airless.

"I figured you'd probably find the head wound from when I—you know." He pantomimed shoving Skelton into the window. "I didn't want you to have to chase after some mystery."

"Head wound, hell. We could barely find the head."

"That bad?"

"That bad."

Teague jiggled his knee nervously, trying not to think about what that meant. Courtney had found her father, and it sounded like the scene was pretty bad. He'd better get that music box to her. It was the least he could do.

Although it might not be possible. He was probably under arrest.

Teague ran his fingers through his hair. He wished he had his hat. He needed it in his hands, something to fool with. You never realized how strong a nervous habit was until you couldn't do it. He stroked his fingers through his hair again.

"You got something more to say?" the sheriff finally asked.

Teague took a deep breath. "When I saw what I'd done—when I shoved him and he hit the window—I saw my reflection in the glass. Thought for a minute it was my dad standing out there, and when I realized it was me it scared the hell out of me. I looked so much like him, I…"

The sheriff waved a dismissive hand. "You're not your dad, Teague. Get that out of your head."

"I sure acted like him. Just picked the guy up and—you know." He pantomimed tossing Skelton into the window.

"What were you thinking?"

"I was thinking he was going to try and put Troy in jail, and then I couldn't stand looking at him anymore. I just shoved him away, but I was a little rougher than I meant to be."

"Hell, Teague, there wasn't anybody in town wouldn't have done the same thing or worse." He scooted forward and rested his forearms on the desk while he stared at Teague with his droopy basset hound eyes. "Cissy told me you put the fear of God into her ex the other day out there at the trailer," the sheriff said.

Teague nodded, but he wondered what that had to do with anything.

"She said you took care of it just right. Scared him, didn't go Treadwell or anything."

"Go Treadwell?"

The sheriff managed a grim smile. "It's the local expression for going postal. Used to be pretty accurate when your dad was alive."

"Still pretty accurate, apparently. I sure went Treadwell on Skelton."

"Not really. Your dad never needed a reason, and you had a good one. Plus, according to Cissy, you showed a lot of restraint with Cal."

"I tried."

"Couldn't have been easy." Woodell looked down

and shifted a pencil from one side of his desk to the other, as if the arrangement of his office supplies was the most important thing in the world. "Surprised you didn't have a flashback or something."

"I more or less did," Teague said.

"Son, when you saw your father in the window, he was outside looking in. Probably wishing he was half the man you are."

Teague's chest swelled and an ache filled his throat. "Thank you, sir. You had a lot to do with that."

The sheriff sat back and gave him a faint smile. "Get out of here. I'll talk to you later if I have any questions."

"I can go?"

"I don't see why not. I appreciate you coming to me with this." The sheriff waved him away. "I might have some questions for you later, so don't leave town."

"Thank you, sir."

Teague let himself out and stood a moment in the hallway, raking his fingers through his hair, then quickly wiping his eyes before he headed out to the lobby and the eagle-eyed Cissy. It was pathetic, but the sheriff's words had touched him deeply. The man had been more of a father to him than his own dad—not that that was saying much. He'd pretty much only been around when Teague had screwed up, but at least he'd tried to help.

And now he saw Teague as a good man, nothing like his father. It felt like those words were the last step in his long fight for redemption. He felt like a swimmer surfacing after a long dive, or an animal being released from a cramped and dirty cage.

He was finally free to live the life he'd always wanted.

Chapter 41

TEAGUE GATHERED THE PIECES OF COURTNEY'S MUSIC box from the front seat of the truck and carried them into the barn. He'd outfitted one small room toward the front as a workshop, with a rough wooden counter across one side and cabinets on the wall above it. Drawers, taken from various pieces of old and unwanted furniture, were tucked below and held an assortment of screwdrivers, hammers, and wrenches. Shovels, rakes, and pitchforks leaned in another corner, and a rusted but still service-able wheelbarrow was parked near the door.

Spreading the pieces on the counter, he shoved the parts to the wooden box away and sorted out the pieces of machinery that made the music—the metal cylinders with their strategically placed nubbins, the metal keys the nubbins plucked to make each note. He opened a drawer and rummaged around for some tiny screws and a set of tools that was made to repair glasses.

He found what he was looking for, then picked up the cylinder and examined it. It would help if he could figure out what song it was supposed to play. Probably some tinkly ballet thing. He picked up one of the crumpled pieces of paper and spread it flat. The handwriting looked fairly masculine. Maybe it was a note from Courtney's dad telling her why he'd given her the box. Maybe it said what tune it played, and why it meant so much to her.

I am so sorry for all the terrible things I have done, the note began. *I have wronged my daughter and there is no way to make it right.*

Whoa. The guy was being awfully dramatic. Yeah, he was a lousy dad—but terrible things?

And wasn't this a letter *to* his daughter? Why was he referring to her in the third person? Maybe there was more going on with Courtney than Teague realized. Maybe Skelton was some kind of abusive pedophile or something. He shuddered and looked down at the letter again.

It was wrong to drive her mother from my home and take up with that slut Marissa. Marissa is a greedy, skanky, money-grubbing whore.

Holy crap. That was a weird thing for a guy to say about his wife. Having met the greedy, skanky, money-grubbing whore in question, Teague was inclined to agree, but he wasn't married to the woman.

But evidently, the guy was really wrestling with his feelings. The writing was getting larger and rounder, and it looked like the pen was digging into the paper. There was even a tear where he'd crossed the "t" in "slut."

He kept reading.

Then I killed her horse. I set fire to the barn because I spent all my money on polo and on crap for Marissa and I didn't care that my daughter loved that horse like it was her own child and it was the only thing that made her life worth living. I killed Dutch and I should die for…

The letter degenerated into a series of illegible scrawls, which had been crossed out with large Xs that ripped through the paper.

Teague pushed it to the back of the table. No wonder Courtney was so screwed up. That letter was disturbing. And the language the guy used—"crap" and "skanky"— he sounded like a teenaged girl.

Teague picked up the other sheet of paper. This one had been crumpled even more, and he had trouble smoothing it out enough to read it. Finally, he managed to make out the first few lines.

They sounded very familiar.

I am so sorry for all the terrible things I have done. I have wronged my daughter and there is no way to make it right. It was wrong to drive her mother from my home and take up with that slut Marissa. Marissa is a greedy, skanky, money-grubbing whore. Then he killed my horse. He set fire to the barn because he spent all his money on polo…

This letter trailed off into scribbles and Xs even sooner. Teague looked at it again.

He set fire to the barn because he spent all his money on polo…

Not "I." "He."

Skelton didn't write this letter. Courtney did.

It read like a suicide note, but it hadn't been written by the dead man.

Skelton hadn't committed suicide. He'd been murdered.

Chapter 42

WHEN COURTNEY FINALLY RECOVERED ENOUGH TO leave, Jodi glanced at her watch. Teague was taking forever to get that damn music box.

Well, Jodi didn't have time to track him down. She barely had time to get ready for her speech. She hadn't wanted to put on her queen clothes with Courtney there, and she'd been starting to wonder if the girl would ever leave. Courtney had recovered almost as soon as Teague had left, and had spent the day following Jodi as she did her chores, chattering about all kinds of nonsense as if she'd completely forgotten that her father was dead. It was unnerving, but Jodi figured it was probably her way of coping with the trauma.

Sighing, she opened her closet and pulled out a plastic-draped hanger. Shifting the plastic aside, she laid the clothes out on the bed: the fitted shirt, decked out with pink fringe and a fancy beaded yoke. The jeans, a ridiculous shade of Pepto pink and tight, tight, tight. She hoped she could still slide into them. Then there was the sash, shiny satin embroidered with the title she'd chased all through high school and finally caught: Miss Rodeo USA.

Turning back to the closet, she stood on tiptoe and took her queen hat from the top shelf. It was pink felt, with a sparkling rhinestone tiara affixed to the front.

She skinned out of her jeans and T-shirt and turned to the mirror, sucking in her stomach and striking a pose in her skimpy, sexy black lace underwear. She'd thought of Teague when she'd picked it out that morning—Teague and his lust for the special rodeo queen underwear.

Well, she couldn't talk to the Girl Scouts in that. She picked up the jeans, wondering if they'd even fit. To her surprise, they slid over her hips as easily as ever, fitting like a second skin. She grinned. They'd pose a real challenge for Teague.

But the shirt wouldn't. She fastened the snaps, remembering how she'd yanked his open the night before. Tucking it in and slipping a concho-decorated belt through the loops on her jeans, she stepped over to the bed and picked up the sash.

She shivered, remembering what Teague had said about tying her up. She'd never wanted to give up control like that—but with Teague it might be, well, fun. She trusted him. For all his worries about turning into his father, he was the gentlest man she knew. But only she knew that side of him. To the rest of the world, he was dark and dangerous, a man to be reckoned with.

And she was the rodeo queen, a model of propriety and poise. She slipped the sash across one shoulder and draped it across her body, then tipped on the hat, tiara and all. Standing in front of the mirror, she struck a modeling pose and pasted on a smile.

Dressing like Queenie wasn't so bad. It was all the responsibility that went with it that gave her trouble. She'd thought success would set her free, but it had made her feel so beholden to the town that made her that she'd spent her life trying to live up to their expectations.

A half hour later, she stared out at the sea of girlish faces in front of her and lit into her speech as if someone had pushed her "talk" button. She'd given the rodeo queen role-model talk a hundred times, to thousands of little girls. She practically knew it by heart, and she'd read it over before she came, just to make sure. But watching the rapt expressions on those little faces was kind of unnerving.

She told them about poise. Confidence. Getting good grades. Listening to your parents, because they knew what was best for you. Being part of your community, and representing it with pride. Doing, saying, and *being* the right thing.

"You have to work really hard to become a rodeo queen. You have to study a lot, volunteer all you can, and make sure you always look your best. It's all part of being an exemplary citizen. Does anybody know what 'exemplary' means?"

A hand shot up in the air. It belonged to a little blonde with hair cascading down her back and a self-conscious smile—a tiny rodeo queen-in-the-making.

"Yes?" Jodi gave her a nod.

"You have to set an example."

"Right. You can't always do what you want to do, or say what you want to say. You have to think about how other people see you."

Her eyes lit on a freckled face in the first row—a little redhead whose tip-tilted nose and blue eyes reminded her of herself at that age. The kid squirmed in her chair, glancing out the window for the umpteenth time and earning a sharp look from the den mother.

Jodi paused, picturing little Red with her hair tamed into queen curls and her freckles hidden by makeup, and addressed the next part of her speech directly to her.

"But you still have to be yourself. A rodeo queen is an individual. She takes pride in her appearance, but she also takes pride in who she is." She looked around at the sea of little faces. "And she has a reason to be proud, because she's worked hard and made a lot of tough decisions. And once you make that goal, you know you can trust yourself."

That wasn't part of the speech, but it was truer than anything she'd planned to say. She stood up a little straighter.

"I know I can rely on myself to do the right thing, even when it's hard. I know I can accomplish anything I set my mind to. But most of all, I know I make good decisions. I've proved it, all my life."

The little girl in the front row was watching her, wide-eyed. Jodi smiled at her.

"Did you have a question?"

The little girl nodded and leaned forward. "So you don't have to listen to your *mom*?"

Jodi laughed. "Oh, yeah you do. You always listen." She sobered. "You always listen, but when you get older, you listen to yourself too. There are some things even your mother can't decide for you."

Teague stood in the middle of his workshop with the letter in his hand, wondering what he should do.

He'd take it to the sheriff, he decided. Woodell could take it from there. It wasn't Teague's job to deal with it.

He was heading out the door when he heard a car door slam.

"Teague?"

Damn. It was Courtney.

What the hell could he say? He folded the letters in quarters and shoved them in his back pocket. Maybe he could talk her into turning herself in. It wasn't like the girl would go to jail. She was clearly unbalanced. She needed help, and the court system would see that she got it.

Either that, or they'd lock her up and throw away the key. That wasn't the option Teague would choose, but it was better than leaving her loose.

He took a deep breath and stepped out of the barn. If he played this right, he could take care of this situation with the least amount of grief to all concerned—including Courtney. And if Marty Woodell was proud of him for now, imagine how he'd feel when Teague escorted Courtney to his office, handed her over, and closed the case. That would be one step toward paying the man back for all he'd helped Teague with over the years.

"Court," he said. "What's up?"

She was leaning against her SUV, her arms folded over her chest, a stormy expression on her face.

"I should ask you that," she said.

Teague shrugged and gave her his most charming grin. He'd just pretend everything was okay. "Not much."

"There's something up between you and Jodi."

"Well, yeah, there is." He walked over to her, his hands in his pockets. "Things with me and Jodi have kind of… changed."

"Really? What's changed? I know you've been sleeping together this whole time." She tossed her hair. "I know you got together the night you lost my dog."

"Yeah, where's Honeybucket?" he asked, jumping at the chance to change the subject.

Courtney scowled. "I took him to the shelter. He wasn't doing his job."

"His job?"

As far as Teague could tell, the dog's job had been to get hauled around like an animated stuffed toy and dragged out whenever Courtney wanted a little extra attention.

"He was supposed to love me," Courtney said. "But he took off every chance he got." She pouted. "He'd rather roll in shit than be with me, so I got rid of him. I'm going to get a new dog." She smiled down at the ground and swayed from side to side like a little girl savoring the anticipation of a birthday pony. "I'm getting a Chihuahua."

Teague couldn't hide his shock. "So you took Honeybucket to the pound?"

"That's what you do with dogs that don't behave," Courtney said.

Damn, the girl was cold. Teague couldn't believe he'd ever thought she was helpless.

He needed to be careful. How could he get her talking? She might have an ice cube for a heart, but he knew she was hurting inside too. If he could just get past all the layers of anger and vengefulness she'd piled up to defend herself, maybe he could find the scared little girl inside her and talk her into getting help.

"I'm so sorry about your—horse," he said. He'd almost said he was sorry about her dad, but that wouldn't have worked. She wasn't sorry about that; she'd killed him herself.

The letters felt huge in his back pocket. Hopefully she wouldn't go in the barn and see what was left of her music box spread out on the counter. That would really piss her off. And he was beginning to realize that Courtney was one woman you didn't want to cross.

"Thank you," she sniffed. "Dutchy was everything to me. And my father..." She closed her eyes and clenched her fists so hard her arms trembled. "My father killed him."

"I know." He reached over and patted her shoulder awkwardly. "You want to talk about it, Court?"

"No." She ducked her head and covered her face with her hands. "I don't want to talk about it. I don't want to think about it, even." She lifted her head and met his eyes. Her own were glossy with coming tears. "I just want to start all over. Okay?"

Teague nodded, humoring her. He could tell the tears were coming, and if there was some way to put a stopper in the weeping spell that was coming, he was going to find it.

"Okay." He wasn't sure how he was going to get her back to the subject of her father and get her to turn herself in, but he'd follow her lead. He'd read somewhere that deep inside, most murderers wanted to get caught. That's why they made dumb mistakes—like leaving those letters where someone could find them. Why hadn't she burned them, or thrown them away? It was a cry for help, that's what it was.

"Okay." She took a deep breath and made a visible effort to control herself, brushing her hair out of her face and setting her jaw. "So we'll start over. I'll forget about Dutch and my dad, and you forget about Jodi."

Teague blanched. She was nuts, no doubt about it. The poor girl was so fixated on her own problems she was grasping at straws, making the world over into the one she wanted.

When he didn't respond, a shaky smile tilted her lips. She took a step toward him. "Let's go in the house, Teague. You can make me forget everything." She gazed flirtatiously up at him through her lashes. "I can make *you* forget too."

This was going too far. She'd never get help if she didn't face reality. The first step toward getting help was admitting you had a problem, so he had to get Courtney to see the truth. Much as he wanted to avoid her tears, they were inevitable.

"No, Courtney." He set his hands on her shoulders. "You can't. I want to help you, I really do. But I…"

He couldn't say it. He should. He should tell her straight out that he loved Jodi and there was no chance of that changing—not now, not ever. But she'd cry for sure if he said that. Cry, or fly into a rage. And God knew what would happen if she got mad.

He patted her the way he might try to soothe a vicious dog. "But going in the house won't help." Man, that was the weirdest euphemism for sex ever. "We need to talk."

"Oh," she said in her little-girl voice. "Oh. Okay." She looked up at him, her lips pursed, her eyes wide as a china doll's. "But after we talk, can we do it? I want you, Teague." She reached out and stroked one finger down the buttons on his shirt. "I really, really want you."

"We'll see," he said.

That seemed to soothe her.

"You want to sit down?" Without waiting for an answer, he walked over to the bench that sat against the wall beside the barn door. She followed, and he made sure she sat down before he did. That way she couldn't plop herself in his lap, or cozy up too close.

He folded his hands in his lap. Courtney shimmied herself closer to him. So much for that strategy.

"What do you want to talk about?" she asked.

"I think we need to talk about your dad. Courtney, I know what really happened."

"No you don't," she said pertly.

"I think I do."

"He abused me." She used the same conversational tone she'd use to tell him her father had grounded her, or taken away her cell phone. Teague was pretty sure it was a lie, but who knew with this family? He'd humor her. See if he could steer the conversation to the point where she'd make a confession.

He wished Oprah was here. Or Barbara Walters.

No, not Barbara Walters. Then Courtney would cry for sure.

But Oprah would handle this just right. He wasn't much for TV, especially in the middle of the day, but a couple times when he'd been inside with a cold or something, he'd watched the way she handled people in her interviews. She'd get them talking, and then she'd ask questions that led them to reveal the truth about themselves. How did she do that? Teague wrinkled up his forehead, trying to remember.

"He abused me repeatedly," Courtney said in that same matter-of-fact tone.

Teague did his best to arrange his features in an Oprah-like expression of sympathy and understanding.

"How did that make you feel?" he asked.

"Mad," Courtney said. "Really mad. And—and violated. Dirty."

Teague nodded sagely. "I can understand how you would feel that way. What did you do then?"

"Nothing." Courtney swept her foot across the dry ground in front of the bench, leaving a streak in the dust. "I didn't do anything. I told my horse, though. I told Dutch."

"Sometimes it helps to talk to animals," Teague said. He really did understand that. He did it himself sometimes. Just the other day, he'd told Rocket he loved Jodi and wanted to marry her. He hadn't known it himself— not the marrying part, anyway—until he'd told the horse.

"But I can't talk to Dutchy anymore," Courtney said. The little-girl voice was back. "Dutchy is dead."

Oh, boy, Teague thought. *Here we go with the tears.*

Sure enough, the waterworks spurted into action. Courtney leaned her head on Teague's shoulder and soaked his shirt in two minutes flat. He put one arm around her and patted her shoulder. Damn. He never knew what to do when women cried.

"Dead," Courtney sobbed. "Oh, Teague, he's *dead.*"

"I know," he said, patting faster. "I know."

He was relieved when the sobs gave way to hiccups.

"I'm s-s-sorry," she said. She gulped and wiped her nose with a little snort.

"That's okay. It's okay to cry," Teague said. It wasn't okay, not in his world, but it seemed like the right thing to say. "You have to let it out."

"I know. And I did." Courtney lifted her tear-stained face from his shoulder. "I let it all out. So can we go in the house now?" She tried that seductive look again,

but with her eyes nearly swollen shut, it wasn't too effective. She looked like a pink baby mouse before its
eyes opened.

"No, Courtney." He tried for a stern, fatherly tone. "I
think there's some other stuff you have to let out."

She hunched her shoulders and stared down into
her lap.

"I don't want to talk about that other stuff."

"You'll feel better if you do," he said.

She bit her lip and he could feel her unbending, relaxing. It was going to work.

"You won't tell anyone?"

"Not unless you want me to."

"Okay." She straightened and took a deep breath,
folding her hands in her lap like a schoolgirl who was
about to recite the state capitals. "My daddy didn't really
kill himself."

"I know," Teague murmured in what he hoped was
an encouraging tone.

"My stepmother killed him."

Teague sighed. Turning sideways on the bench, he
reached into his back pocket and pulled out the letters.

"Courtney, I went and got your music box for you."

"Oh, thank you. I…" She saw the letter and her eyes
widened. "No!"

"Yes. I know what happened."

Courtney grabbed the top letter and glanced at it.

"Oh look," she said in an unconvincing monotone.
Good thing the girl wasn't headed for Hollywood. She
was a lousy actress. "It's a suicide note. Daddy must
have left it for me." She crumpled it in her fist and
grabbed for the other one.

"No, Courtney," Teague said. "You wrote these. You were going to leave them with the body, weren't you? But you couldn't do it."

She grabbed again for the other letter, her fingers spread like claws, but he crumpled it in his fist and hid it behind his back. Throwing herself at him, she pummeled him with her fists, then raked her nails down his face.

"*Give it to me! Give it to me!*"

He dropped the letter to the ground and grabbed her arms before she could dive for it. She'd dropped the first one while she fought him, and both papers blew up against the barn on the faint breeze and fluttered in the grass.

"*No!*" Courtney shrieked. She twisted in his grip but he held on and waited her out, keeping his calm as best he could and trying to control her with a firm grip and steady gaze. That's what worked on bulls—but bulls, even at their worst, were more rational than this crazy woman.

He held on while she writhed and shrieked some more. He half-expected her to turn into a snake, like some witch in a fairy tale, but she finally gave up and slumped in his hands, almost falling to the ground. Teague waltzed her over to the bench in a stumbling, clumsy two-step and sat her down.

Courtney put her head down and cried in earnest now, huge, racking sobs shaking her delicate frame. She was a monster—but she'd been de-fanged. She didn't make any effort to hit him again, or claw at him. Teague looked away so he wouldn't be tempted to comfort her.

"I'm sorry," she wept. "I'm sorry, Teague. But he

deserved it. He killed my horse. He ditched my mom. He didn't care about me. Not one bit." The sobbing choked out whatever else she'd been about to say.

Finally, she seemed to get control of herself. She sat up.

"What'll I do, Teague?" She sniffed and wiped her nose with a faint snort. "What'll I do?"

"I think you should turn yourself in," Teague said as gently as he could. "Did your dad have a lawyer? We should probably have him meet us there."

She glanced at him, her swollen eyes narrowed to slits, and for a minute he thought he caught a glimpse of the old scheming Courtney in her gaze. It was like she was gauging him, assessing him... but no. The look was gone in an instant, and weeping Courtney was back.

He must have imagined it.

Chapter 43

COURTNEY SNIFFLED AND LOOKED UP AT TEAGUE through red-rimmed eyes. "Okay," she said. "My dad's lawyer is Steve Reynolds." She sniffed again. "He was always nice to me."

"You know his number?"

She nodded. "It's in my phone." She looked at Teague expectantly. "My phone's in my purse, in the car."

Teague set his hands on his knees and hoisted himself to his feet. He felt exhausted—wrung out. He wondered how Oprah managed to do this stuff day after day. Of course, most of her guests weren't psychotic.

He walked over to the car and opened the door. The purse was on the floor on the passenger's side. He leaned over to get it, stretching to grab the strap. The damn thing tipped when he hauled on it and dumped its contents on the floor. Grabbing the cell phone, he turned back to Courtney.

"I've got it. Now—hey!"

She was gone.

"Courtney!"

Dang. He was an idiot. He hadn't imagined that scheming, assessing look. She'd been trying to figure out how to get away from him. Obviously, it hadn't been too difficult a problem. He was an idiot.

"Courtney!"

He glanced around the yard. Where could she have

gone? His eyes lit on the grass beside the barn and he realized the letters were gone. She probably figured she'd destroy the evidence and run.

Well, she couldn't run far—not with him standing by her car. But how had she disappeared so fast? He looked right, then left.

There was only one way she could have disappeared that fast. She must have run into the barn.

He paused. She probably planned to head for the back door, then go out and run around the side to get back to her vehicle while he chased her through the barn. If he waited, he could head her off.

He folded his arms and leaned against the Lexus. He'd wait her out. She'd have to come out eventually. And while he waited, he'd call the sheriff.

He should have done that in the first place. He'd wanted to present Woodell with a done deal, the case wrapped up and solved, a contrite criminal on his arm.

He'd overestimated himself. A blonde bimbo heiress had outsmarted him.

Damn. It was like having Paris Hilton beat you at chess.

Just as he flipped the phone open a high-pitched scream sounded from the barn. It wasn't Courtney. It wasn't human.

It was a horse.

The scream tore the air again, and he dropped the phone and ran for the barn. What the hell was she doing?

Just as he dashed for the barn door, there was a low bellow. He didn't have time to react before an enormous black-and-white blur shot out of the barn door and knocked him over. He hit the ground hard and started to struggle to his feet, but Bruiser hooked him with one black horn and tossed him in the air. He felt himself flying, helpless as a ragdoll, and then he hit the ground hard and the air whooshed out of his lungs as something heavy hit his chest.

The last thing he saw was the barn, tilted sideways and wreathed in stars, and the bull's huge hoof suspended in the air above his head.

Jodi headed for Teague's as soon as she finished thanking the den mother. She wondered if he'd had any luck finding Courtney's music box. If he had, he'd have returned by now—unless Courtney intercepted him along the way.

It was a five-minute drive to Teague's place, but it seemed like eternity to Jodi as she eased the truck along the pitted dirt path. Teague really needed to get his ranch road graded. She was concentrating so hard on protecting her truck's suspension she almost didn't see Rocket in the road, trotting straight down the middle as if he was headed somewhere important. Thinking fast, she jerked the emergency brake so the truck skidded sideways, blocking the road and frightening the horse enough to make him skid to a stop and turn around to gallop back toward the ranch.

What the hell was he doing loose? She backed the truck up and eased back onto the road, following the galloping horse. Teague would never, ever let Rocket run loose, she was sure. Something was wrong.

As she rounded the curve, the first thing she saw was Courtney's SUV parked beside the pasture fence.

Dang. It figured. Would the girl ever give up? Jodi felt sorry for her with all that had happened, but didn't she have someone else to run to besides Teague? Why couldn't she go for Gustaldo or one of the other polo players?

As the ranch house and barn came into view, she jammed on the brakes and blinked at the scene before her. Courtney was the least of her problems. Rocket had reached the barnyard and stopped short, tossing his head in the air. He seemed almost as shocked as she was to see the enormous bulk of Bruiser standing dead-center in front of the barn, his head lowered, one paw scraping the ground like a cartoon bull about to charge. His furious gaze was fixed on something that was lying on the ground in front of him.

Teague.

Without thinking, Jodi leapt out of the truck and ran to the man collapsed in the middle of the driveway. She was halfway there when the bull bellowed and charged. Letting out a shout, she waved her hands and ran past him, away from Teague. She'd seen the bullfighters at rodeos save cowboys a hundred times. She knew how they did it.

They did it by turning the bull's attention to themselves, and then getting in the barrel before they could get gored.

But there was no barrel at Teague's.

Glancing around as she ran, she spotted the paddock gate. She also spotted a momentarily confused Bruiser, mere feet away, looking from her to Teague and back again. Putting on a burst of speed, she shouted at the bull and clambered up the metal rungs of the gate moments before the animal's horns hit the steel with a resounding *clang* that bounced him backward, stunned. The vibration ran through her body like a stun gun shock. She and Bruiser stared at each other for a dumbstruck, electrified moment before either of them could figure out what to do. She shook her head and her mind cleared.

Trouble was, it stayed clear. There wasn't a thought in her head. She had no idea where to run, what to do, how to react.

Bruiser swung his great head from side to side and lowed like he was complaining about the headache he'd no doubt earned from his collision with the gate. The bull seemed to be looking for a new target to vent his rage on. For a minute, he fixed his gaze on Rocket, and Jodi felt sick. She couldn't let the bull hurt the horse. Teague's livelihood depended on both animals.

The bull paced toward the horse slowly, stiff-legged as a stalking cat. While his attention was otherwise occupied, Jodi climbed down from the gate and ran over to Teague. She didn't want anything to happen to the horse, but Teague had to be her first priority.

"*Teague*," she hissed. "*Teague!*"

He didn't react. Her stomach churning, she pressed her fingers to his neck.

He was alive, anyway. But who knew what injuries he'd suffered? She didn't want to move him. If he had a head or spinal injury…

A muffled sob escaped her.

Big mistake.

The bull turned his huge head to look at her. Moving in what seemed like slow motion, he shifted his feet until he was facing her, his head lowered. She stared back at him, shocked motionless. What could she do?

Maybe if she talked to him. She knew it was stupid, but it was all she could think of.

"Bruiser," she said softly. "Hey."

Maybe he was tamer than he looked. Maybe he'd just hurt Teague because he'd been upset. People fed him and cared for him, right? Maybe she could soothe him somehow and get him to follow her into the barn.

Stepping away from Teague, she waved one hand cautiously. "Bruiser. Bruiser, baby," she said in a soothing, singsong tone.

Bruiser was evidently not musically inclined.

He charged.

She was vaguely aware of Rocket blasting back down the driveway while she ran for the gate and climbed on top. This was the worst kind of *déjà vu*—the nightmare kind. Once again, the bull's head hit the gate. At least this time she was ready for him, balancing on her hands and feet instead of sitting on the top rail, and the vibration wasn't nearly so bad.

Bruiser tossed his head and lowed again. His tiny eyes looked more confused than angry now. This was taking a lot longer than the eight-second rides he was used to.

Taking advantage of the momentary lull in the action, Jodi reached down and fumbled with the chain that held the gate closed, wincing as it clanged against the metal. She finally undid the clip and pulled it loose. Freed from the chain, the gate swung slowly inward, Jodi clinging to it like a monkey on a wire.

Lowing again, the bull dipped his head and charged. He wasn't quite as fast as he'd been before, and his aim was off. Bellowing, he dashed past her and slammed into the fence on the far side of the paddock.

Chapter 44

JODI DIDN'T WASTE ANY TIME. LEAPING FROM THE gate, she dragged it behind her as she ran out of the enclosure. Her hands shook as she refastened the chain. Would it hold the bull?

Not if he really wanted out. She'd have to hope that he wouldn't try to bulldoze his way out of the paddock. Maybe he'd assume the fence was as sturdy as the one in his pen. Bulls weren't the sharpest tools in the shed, after all. They were too amped up on testosterone to be much smarter than your average Saturday night drunk.

He turned from the fence and watched her through his mean little eyes. Letting out a low moan, he dropped his head and took a bite of the coarse grass beside the fence. It must have hit the spot, because he turned away from her and made it a meal.

She ran to Teague and knelt beside him. His eyes were closed, and when she tried his pulse again, it seemed weaker and slower than before. He needed an ambulance. She glanced up and looked around. Rocket was nowhere to be seen, so the coast was clear. She'd get her phone out of her car and…

No. Wait. There was a phone lying just a foot away from Teague's outstretched hand. It was a pink Blackberry decorated into further pinkness with press-on rhinestones.

Dang. That had to be Courtney's.

Where the hell was Courtney, anyway? She glanced around, then picked up the phone. She didn't give a darn whose phone it was. They all dialed 911 the same.

Cissy answered in her best professional dispatcher voice. It was a good thing somebody was calm and collected, because Jodi hadn't realized how rattled she was until she tried to talk.

"Teague," she said breathlessly. "He—the bull—I got him in the paddock, but he's—please."

"Honey, slow down. Is this Jodi?"

"Yeah. He's…"

"Where are you?"

"I'm at the Treadwell Ranch. The bull got out, and Teague—shit!" She dropped the phone and dove to cover Teague with her body as best she could while Rocket thundered toward her at a speed that explained his name. Somehow, he passed over them, or went around them—Jodi wasn't sure which, since her eyes were closed tight and the thundering of hooves was rivaled only by the pounding of her heart.

When she opened her eyes, she was surprised to find she was still in one piece, unhurt. But a few feet away, the pink phone lay crushed in the dirt.

Hopefully Cissy had gotten the message that something was wrong at Teague's. She was a smart girl. She'd figure it out.

Jodi glanced around. Teague was still unconscious. There was nothing she could do until the ambulance came, if it came at all. But Rocket was standing near the barn, breathing hard, the whites of his eyes showing his panic.

Jodi stood up slowly, keeping her eyes fixed on the

barn, the ground—anything but the horse. Lacing her hands behind her back, she approached him at a slow, dirge-like pace. He had a halter on. If she could just get a hold on it…

Yeah, right. If she got a hand on that halter, Rocket was liable to toss his head and pull her off the ground. He was a massive animal, and dang near as ornery as the bull. But it was her only chance. Bruiser obviously believed the fence would hold. Maybe Rocket would figure anyone who grabbed that halter was the boss of him.

"Easy, boy," she said. "Easy." She sidled up to the horse, careful not to meet his eyes, and brought her hand up to grasp the cheek strap. Without putting any pressure on it, she simply stood there for a full minute, breathing slowly, trying to communicate peace and goodwill to the nervous animal. When his eye rolled back to a normal position, hiding the white again, she gave the halter a gentle tug and led him forward.

For a half-second, he set his feet and resisted, but then he seemed to change his mind. Placid as a pony, he strode into the barn at her side.

His stall gate stood open under the plate bearing his name. Jodi led him inside and stroked his neck, readying herself to turn and go, but he shied and took a step back, obviously agitated.

Jodi followed his gaze. There was something in the straw, hunched in the corner.

A person.

She squinted in the barn's dim light and made out a hank of blonde hair and an arm decked in fringe.

"Courtney?"

The girl looked up at her and blinked. Her eyes were bleary and swollen almost shut, and a dark smudge stretched from the corner of her mouth up to her forehead.

"You," the girl said, struggling to her feet. Her voice rose to a shriek. "*You*. You ruined *everything*."

—◆◆◆—

Teague opened his eyes and blinked. There was the barn again, tilted sideways. His eyes felt gritty, and no wonder. He was lying in the dirt, his leg twisted beneath him.

He sat up, gritting his teeth against a pain that zapped from his foot all the way up his leg, and glanced around. Courtney's phone lay a few feet away, crushed in the dirt. Everything else looked okay. The barn was quiet, and Bruiser was standing quietly in the—paddock?

What the hell was the bull doing in the horse paddock?

He'd been in his pen. He was always in his pen, unless he was on his way to a rodeo. Handling Bruiser was almost impossible. He was a great bucking bull, but hardly a house pet. How had anyone gotten him into the paddock? Courtney couldn't control a teacup Pomeranian. No way could she herd a two-thousand-pound bull.

Teague rose to his hands and knees, then tried to stand, but the pain shot through his leg again. With the pain came a dim memory of the bull standing in the barn entry, head lowered, pawing the ground.

Bruiser must have knocked him down. He remembered the animal's horns lifting him in the air, tossing him to the ground.

But the bull was in the paddock now, and Teague was alive. Neither scenario made any sense.

And there was Courtney's phone, lying crushed in the dust. Where was Courtney?

A high-pitched shriek of rage rose from the barn.

There she was!

He remembered the horse's scream earlier. Courtney had done something to the animal, and God knew what she was doing now. He had to get to the barn. He had to stop her.

He set his hands on the ground and rose up onto one knee, keeping the hurt leg off the ground as best he could. Wobbling, he pushed himself up to a standing position. A wave of nausea and dizziness almost overwhelmed him, but he stood still and waited 'til it cleared before trying to take a step. Gingerly, he placed his injured foot on the ground and shifted his weight onto it.

This time, the nausea and dizziness were too powerful to resist. The barn faded from view as he hit the ground.

Chapter 45

"YOU RUINED *EVERYTHING*," COURTNEY REPEATED. She struggled to her feet.

Jodi couldn't believe what she was seeing. Courtney was always perfectly coiffed, with queen-quality makeup and hair and her clothes neatly pressed. Now she was filthy. It looked like she'd taken a page from Honeybucket's playbook and rolled in something nasty. Her face was smeared with something that looked suspiciously like horse crap, and her clothes were filthy.

"Courtney, what happened?"

Seeing Jodi and Teague together this afternoon must have pushed the girl over the edge. It had to hurt, seeing the man you loved—or at least the man you'd made up your mind you wanted—with another woman. Jodi reached out to pat Courtney's shoulder, wanting to comfort her, wanting to help.

Courtney slapped her hand away. Letting out a shriek that sounded like a combination between a cat in heat, a bellowing bull, and a screaming stallion, she grabbed Jodi's hair, jerked her out of the stall, and slammed her against the barn wall.

Jodi wasn't hurt; just shocked. She froze against the wall for what felt like a full minute. Courtney stood in front of her, swaying from side to side, her arms held loose like a MMA fighter searching for a hold. Finally, she rushed at Jodi, but Jodi was ready and grabbed her wrists.

"Courtney, stop," she said. "Calm down. Beating the crap out of me isn't going to change anything."

Courtney didn't reply; she just struggled to free herself. Her eyes were wild, her face pale, with two streaks of red standing out on her cheekbones. She looked deranged.

She *was* deranged, apparently.

Jodi glanced around the barn. The ambulance would be here any minute. If she could just hang onto Courtney until it came, they could probably give the girl a shot that would calm her down.

Too bad Teague didn't keep a tranquilizer gun around anywhere. It would have come in handy for the bull, and nailing Courtney in the butt with a large-animal dart would feel pretty good about now.

She scanned the barn, her eyes lighting on the box stall at the front that Teague had turned into a workshop. Putting Courtney into a room filled with hammers, saws, and shovels probably wasn't a great idea, but if Jodi could get the door shut and locked, she'd be safe.

She tugged on Courtney's wrists, dragging her down the alleyway. Courtney fought for a minute, then went limp. Pulling her dead weight was almost worse than fighting her, but at least she was little. Jodi hauled back and dragged Courtney's limp body in a slow circle, speeding up as she built up centrifugal force and finally letting go of the girl's wrists and flinging her through the door into the workshop.

As she skidded over the concrete floor, Courtney scrambled to her feet, but Jodi kicked her away and slammed the door. Grabbing the rusted padlock hanging from a hinged hasp, she flipped the hasp into place and threaded the lock through the hole.

She didn't need to lock it. There was no way Courtney could get at it from inside. Jodi leaned against the door and blew a strand of hair out of her face as the sound of a distant siren pierced the air.

Chapter 46

Teague was vaguely aware of the sounds around him—the siren blaring, then suddenly cutting off as tires skidded to a stop; the low hum of voices; the sound of hoarse, steady wailing coming from the barn. It sounded like someone was skinning one of the barn cats.

The darkness that enveloped him suddenly slit open and a face entered his field of view. A bright light flashed in his eye.

"He's responsive," a woman's voice said.

The slit closed and another one opened. Light again.

"Mr. Treadwell?"

Teague blinked and opened his eyes. Some lady was kneeling beside him. She looked worried. He struggled to sit up and tell her everything was okay, but as it turned out, everything hurt. His back. His leg. His arm and shoulder. His eyes, when the light hit them.

"Don't try to move, sir. We need to check you out first."

Well, he was used to getting checked out by the ladies, but this was a little different. He tried to sit up again, and this time he succeeded.

"Please, sir, don't try to move."

Since when had he done what he was told? Obviously, this lady didn't know Teague Treadwell. He looked around. The bull was still in the paddock. Courtney's SUV was parked in the drive, along with Jodi's little Ranger.

"Jodi?"

He looked left, then right. It took the world a while to catch up with the turn of his head and he had to lie down again. Turning his head, he saw Jodi standing in the dark barn doorway. But it wasn't the Jodi he'd seen yesterday. Somehow, he'd gone back in time. She was wearing that damn sparkly hat, along with a pink embroidered jacket and jeans to match.

Hell, she was a rodeo queen again.

He was thinking she'd gotten over that phase. She looked good, though.

She approached him, smiling, and knelt by his side. He struggled up to a sitting position again.

"Please, sir. You need to stay still."

Teague waved the EMT away. "I'm fine. Really. It's just my leg."

"And your arm," Jodi said. "And your back, and maybe your head. You really ought to do what she says."

He shrugged. It hurt. Jodi looked concerned.

"You okay, pardner?"

"Yeah. Foot hurts, though. And they ruined my boot." He looked ruefully down at his foot. The EMT had cut his boot off, and his ankle was swollen to twice its normal size. "What happened?"

"I have no idea." She laughed. "When I got here, Rocket was running around loose, Bruiser was working you over in the driveway, and your girlfriend Courtney was hiding in the barn, covered with horseshit. I was thinking maybe you could tell me what happened."

"So where's Courtney now?" Teague asked.

Jodi blanched. "Oh, shit. I forgot."

The sheriff narrowed his eyes. "You know where she is?"

"Well, yeah. I locked her in the barn. She's in the workshop."

"She's what?"

"She was hiding in Rocket's stall when I brought him in. She attacked me, so I shoved her in the workshop and locked the door." She turned to the sheriff. "Turns out she's even crazier than I thought."

Teague nodded. "I found a suicide note she'd tried to write for her dad. It was pretty clear what had happened."

The sheriff frowned. "When was this? First I've heard of it."

"Well, it was right before she set the bull on me," Teague said. "Sorry I didn't call."

"I guess unconsciousness is an okay excuse," the sheriff said. "You got a key to that workshop?"

"You won't need it," Jodi said. "I didn't fasten the lock."

The sheriff looked down at Teague.

"You okay?"

"I'm fine. Just a little banged up. I've had worse rodeos," Teague said. "And Queenie here showed up and saved my life."

"So did Courtney sic the bull on you, or what?" Jodi asked.

"I guess so," Teague said. "One minute I was standing at the barn door, the next minute I was on my ass with two thousand pounds of raw hamburger on the hoof standing over me. The minute after that, I was flying. That's about all I remember."

He squinted up at her. "How'd he end up in the paddock?"

She grinned. "Well, I had to put him somewhere."

"You did it? How the hell…"

She grinned and tilted her hat to a more rakish angle. "I told him I'd make him wear the pink hat," she said.

He reached up and coiled one spiral curl around his finger. "You really are the queen."

"Of the rodeo?" She grimaced.

"Of the Treadwell ranch," he said. "And the Brand ranch. And pretty much the whole town."

"Thanks. I guess." She looked down at her tight pink jeans. Damp circles of dirt marred the knees, and they were streaked with dirt—or maybe something worse. "I don't really want to be the queen anymore," she said. "I was hoping this would be the last time I'd have to wear these clothes."

Teague smiled and brushed her hair back over her shoulder. "It doesn't matter what you're wearing," he said. "You're the real deal." He grinned. "And I'll help you out of those later, if you want."

"Teague, you're injured," she said. "You have to be careful."

"It's not that bad," he said. "Nothing could be that bad."

"Mr. Treadwell?" It was the paramedic. Teague lifted his eyebrows in inquiry.

"We need to take you to the clinic. Get you checked out."

Teague started to shake his head, but Jodi was already tugging him to his feet.

"He's right," she said. "You're pretty banged up. I know you hate doctors, but you need to go."

"Okay." Teague gave her a lopsided grin. "The queen has spoken."

Chapter 47

TEAGUE SHIFTED IN THE PLASTIC CHAIR.

"You okay? I can't believe they're making us wait this long." She looked up at the receptionist. "How much longer?"

"Could be a while," the woman said. "A half hour, maybe."

Jodi groaned.

"It's okay," Teague said. "Gives us time to talk."

"About what?"

"The baby."

"The baby?" Jodi winced. Shoot. The rumor had apparently moved fast.

He nodded, his jaw set in an expression she recognized. It was vintage Teague—a stubborn, mulish expression that told her he'd made up his mind about something and he wasn't about to be dissuaded.

"I wanted to tell you it doesn't matter. We're a team, Jodi. We're a team when it comes to Troy, and we'll be a team for the baby too. I don't know if you can get over all the things that happened between us. I don't know if you want what I'm offering. It's—it's not much. But we belong together—you, me, and the baby. And Troy." He sucked in a long, shuddering breath. "I was worried I'd just make things worse. I was afraid you wouldn't want it to have the Treadwell name, because—well, because." He made a vague gesture. "But between the two of us, we can make damn sure nobody hurts him. Or her. Or, um, whatever." He flushed and sat back, exhausted.

Jodi stifled a smile. "The Treadwell name?" she asked.

Teague stared out the window as if a flock of purple aliens had just landed on the lawn outside the emergency room doors.

"Teague, is that some kind of proposal?"

He still wouldn't look at her, but he swallowed hard and nodded. "Look, I know I'm not the best man in the world. I'm like a scratch-and-dent special, you know? Damaged goods. But I'd—I'd do anything for you. And I thought maybe that counted for something."

"You want to *marry* me?"

"A kid should have a father."

She shook her head. "Teague, there is no kid."

"But you said—you…"

"I'm not pregnant."

He stared at her. "You're not?"

"No. What made you think that?"

"I don't know. You said something about having kids soon, and then Darla said you bought prenatal vitamins. And you had pickles and ice cream."

She laughed. "I didn't buy prenatal vitamins. I picked them up by accident, and Darla blows everything out of proportion." She shook her head. "The truth is, nobody around here can believe I just wanted to come home. They all think I have some dark inner secret."

"So there's no baby."

"No. I still don't understand what made you think that."

"I asked if you had kids, and I figured you probably did, because it had been four years and why would you be single? Why wouldn't you have moved on? And you

JOANNE KENNEDY

said 'not yet,' or something like that, and it sounded like you meant you were going to."

She shook her head. "No. I never moved on." Now it was her turn to play with the place mat.

"Then why did you come back?"

She shrugged. "The ranch, partly. And partly—I don't know." She sighed and looked up at him. "Like I said, I never moved on."

———

Teague scanned Jodi's face, wondering if he could have heard her right. If she was saying what he thought she was saying.

All those years he'd spent trying to be worthy of her—had she been thinking of him too?

She met his eyes and he knew he was right. And he knew the two of them belonged together. They always had. And somehow, while he'd been building himself up, Jodi had been returning to her roots—and now they were meeting in the middle, a perfect match.

He scanned her eyes again, just to make sure he was right.

He was.

Chapter 48

JODI STEPPED OUT OF HER PICKUP TO SEE TEAGUE tinkering with the mower. His foot was still swathed in a white hospital boot, but he was getting around all right. Luna lay in the sun a few feet away.

"She's finally relaxed," Teague said, nodding toward the dog as Jodi approached. "She knew we belonged together all the time."

"Yeah. Animals know," Jodi said. "Oh, and speaking of animals, I got you a present."

She trotted back to the truck and pulled her purse off the front seat. As she carried it back to Teague, a fluffy head poked out of the top.

"Honeybucket?"

Jodi hoisted the tiny pooch out of the bag and set him on the ground. The little dog ran around in a circle once, twice, three times, then headed straight for the barn.

"I think we're going to have to keep him clipped," Jodi said.

"I think we're going to have to give him a new name," Teague said. He turned toward the barn and whistled. "Spike! Come on, Spike!"

The dog let out a high-pitched bark and ran over to sit at Teague's feet.

"I'm not sure what he's going to do around here," Teague said. "A ranch dog should have a job."

"I know. Courtney said his job was to love her, but

she didn't think he performed up to standard," Jodi said, rolling her eyes.

"Bet she wishes she had him back."

"I know." Courtney had been convicted of the murder of her father and was adjusting to life at the woman's prison in Rawlins. "I feel bad for her. I'm not sure she knew what she was doing. She needs help."

"She knew. Sometimes I'd catch her with this look on her face, like she was plotting something. Trust me, she knew."

"Well, I guess Spike could love the baby."

"The baby?" Teague creased his forehead. "But you said there was no baby."

"There is now," Jodi said, patting her stomach. "That's where I went before I picked up your new pet. The doctor's office." She watched the truth dawn on him, bit by bit, and was relieved to see a smile tilt his lips slightly, then grow into a full-on grin.

"Mine?" he asked.

"Of course." She punched his arm. "Remember that first time at your house?"

"Do I." He grinned. "Best night of my life. Up to that point." He slung an arm around her shoulder. "There have been a bunch of good ones since."

"Well, we kind of forgot to be careful."

"Hey, I forgot my name that day, so I guess it's understandable." He pulled her close, then held her out at arm's length, scanning her face. "You think it'll be okay?"

"Doctor says it's healthy."

"No, I mean… it's a Treadwell. I always said I wouldn't…"

"And I always said you should." She met his eyes, trying to burn her words into his brain. "Teague, look how you turned out. You grew up in that miserable trailer, with parents who did nothing but fight and drink—and yet you're successful, good, and kind." She gestured toward his house. "This baby's going to grow up here. A little Teague, or a little Jodi. He's going to have the best start a baby could have. He'll be amazing."

Teague nodded, then cocked his head. "He?"

"I don't know yet, but I have a feeling. He'll have everything you didn't, Teague. Everything we can give him. He'll turn out fine."

"I guess you're right. He'll be fine, because he'll have the most important thing of all."

"What's that?"

He pulled her close. "Two parents who love each other."

"You're right." She raised her face to his. "They love each other like crazy."

THE END

Acknowledgments

Thank you to all the usual suspects: my parents, Don and Betty Smyth; my family, Scrape McCauley, Brian Davis, Scott McCauley, and Alycia Fleury; and my friends at B&N Cheyenne.

Thanks are also due to the parents, therapists, kids, and horses who taught me about therapeutic riding, including Anita, Kelly, and Kati at Cheyenne Therapeutic Riding Center and the amazing Helen Sinclair, who gives so much time, love, and dedication to children with autism.

Autism affects one out of every 150 children today, and families struggling with this challenge deserve all the help and support you can give them. If there's a therapeutic riding center in your area, please consider giving a donation or scholarship and help a child enjoy the tremendous benefits of Equine Assisted Therapy.

If you're interested in learning more about therapeutic riding, the following organizations are a great place to start:

Cheyenne Therapeutic Equestrian Center (http://www.ctecriding.org/home)

The North American Riding for the Handicapped Association (http://www.narha.org)

About the Author

After dabbling in horse training, chicken farming, and organic gardening, **Joanne Kennedy** ran away to Wyoming twenty years ago and was surprised to discover that cowboys still walk the streets of Cheyenne. Her fascination with her adopted state's unique blend of past and present led her to write contemporary Western romances with traditional ranch settings.

A member of Romance Writers of America and Rocky Mountain Fiction Writers, she is the author of *Cowboy Trouble* and *One Fine Cowboy*. Her next contemporary Western romance, *Tall, Dark and Cowboy*, will be released in November 2011. Joanne loves to hear from readers and can be contacted through her website, www.joannekennedybooks.com.

For more from Joanne Kennedy,
read on for an excerpt from

Tall,
Dark AND
COWBOY

Coming in November 2011
from Sourcebooks Casablanca

A WOMAN APPROACHED THE MUSTANG, TEETERING ON HEELS that rivaled Lacey's own for sheer impracticality. They were espadrilles, probably a Walmart Special, as were the woman's hotpants-style short-shorts. Judging from the way they hugged the woman's tiny heiny, the fabric had to be some kind of cheap Lycra blend.

Quit being a snob, Lacey told herself, cranking down her window. *Without Trent's money, you can't afford anything better. You've got hand-crank windows, for God's sake.*

She looked down at her sporty Steve Maddens, scuffed almost beyond recognition. She wasn't sorry to leave her old life behind, but she was going to miss high-end footwear. She already missed automatic windows.

"You gonna trade this in?" The woman snapped her gum and patted the side of the Mustang.

Lacey tightened her lips and shook her head. "Not today."

She wished she could trade it in, because the car was clearly going to die on her. It looked like death, with paint chipping from the hood and a jagged crack that had spread from a rock chip on the windshield, but its appearance wouldn't matter if the alternator hadn't failed in Missouri and the starter in Kansas. The Mustang wasn't just a gas guzzler; it was a cash guzzler, too. Thanks to the repair bills and the Tennessee Attorney

General, who'd frozen her assets along with Trent's, she barely had enough cash left to pay for a few nights in a motel.

She really *was* depending on Chase Caldwell. His devotion had never wavered, surviving from sixth grade all through high school. The kid had been like a Golden Retriever—sweet, faithful, and eager to please.

"I'm here to see Chase."

The woman shot her a hostile stare, then snapped her gum again and nodded toward the trailer. "He's in there." She spun on one heel and sashayed off across the lot with her Lycra-clad butt twitching.

"Be right back," Lacey told the plug-ugly little dog in the back seat. Sinclair's brown eyes regarded her with an accusatory, bitter gaze, as if it was her fault someone had dumped him at a gas station in the middle of nowhere. His sparse, spiky hair and bushy eyebrows gave him the air of an angry and slightly mad senior citizen. But she was glad she'd picked up the little dog. He made her laugh, and laughing made her feel like something inside her had given way and released the real Lacey from the stiff little Stepford wife she'd become.

She mounted the worn wooden steps that led up to the door of the aluminum-clad trailer that served as the car lot's office. Pausing at the top of the steps, she glanced back at the crumbling brick buildings lining the street. Ancient glass shop windows reflected wavering funhouse renditions of their neighbors across the street, so only the signs jutting out over Grady's pitted sidewalk offered clues to their contents. *Pookie's Candles and More*, read a fading oval. *Dollar Mart,* said a cracked

white plastic sign in bold red letters. The only place that
looked reasonably prosperous was the Quick Lube next
door and the café across the street.

She took one last look at the Mustang to make sure
the windows were cracked open so Sinclair wouldn't get
heat stroke, then opened the door to the trailer, digging
her best cheerleader smile out from under all the bag-
gage she'd accumulated in eight years as a trophy wife.

She aimed the smile at the man behind the counter
and faltered, one foot twisting slightly on its high heel.

This couldn't be Chase Caldwell. It must be his
partner or something. The Chase she remembered had
big brown eyes and a love-struck, goofy grin. Two-time
president of Future Farmers of America, a budding Mr.
Greenjeans in button-down shirts and string ties. This
guy had a simmering, sexy, scorch-your-clothes off
stare that made her feel suddenly naked.

She glanced down to make sure she hadn't forgotten
to put her pants on that morning. Nope. She was still
wearing her white capris—her favorite pair, tight enough
to showcase her gym-toned derriere but still classy. She
adjusted the collar of her silk T-shirt, wishing she'd chosen something that showed a little less cleavage.

His eyes dipped to the cleavage in question and the
smile widened. Lacey cleared her throat, feeling her lips
tremble along with her knees, and glanced down again
to make sure her nipples didn't show through the shirt.

Because her nipples were definitely happy to see this
guy.

Who was definitely not Chase Caldwell.

Because this was no farmer. This was a cowboy—
tan and muscular, with sinewy arms exposed by the

carelessly rolled-up sleeves of a snap-button shirt and slim-hipped Wranglers suggestively worn white at the thighs and fly. Lacey had never felt the effects of air-borne testosterone before, but this guy made her wobble like a Weeble.

His gaze traveled from her cleavage over to one happy nipple, then the other, lingering a moment before it drifted downward on a long, leisurely journey that took in her hips, her thighs, and the tips of her French-manicured toes. His gaze would have been insulting if it hadn't been so appreciative—and so very much appreciated on her end, too. Overheated and exhausted from the long road trip, Lacey couldn't help doing a self-congratulatory mental fist pump at the guy's obvious interest.

She let him finish the once-over and met his eyes just in time to see his appreciative assessment harden into shock, then pass through something that looked almost like fear before it froze into a cold, hard glare.

"Lacey Bradford," he said. "Holy…" He pressed his lips tightly, suppressing a curse.

Lacey squeaked. She couldn't help it—it was that much of a jolt to hear Chase's husky Southern drawl coming from this paragon of masculinity. She knew boys matured later than girls, but he hadn't just improved with age; he'd transformed. It was like watching Clark Kent step out of a phone booth in a cape and tights.

"Chase," she said. "Um, hi."

"What the hell are you doing in Wyoming?" he asked.

It was a question that should have been accompanied by a smile, or at least a curious tilt of the head. Instead, Chase scowled when he said it.

Scowls always made Lacey babble. She could feel the urge coming on and was helpless to stop it.

"I need—I need help. Things went—well, *wrong* in Bum's Rest. Very wrong."

"Join the crowd," Chase said dryly.

"I got a divorce," Lacey continued. The words were spilling out and she had the sudden sensation of tumbling down a steep hill, limbs flailing, completely out of control. "Trent was…" She sucked in a deep breath. Trent had told her not to tell anyone anything, but it was all going to come out eventually anyway. Besides, Trent wasn't the boss of her. Not anymore. "He was a liar and a cheat. I couldn't stay married to him once I knew what he'd done, and now everybody hates me and nobody can find him and they're after me."

"They?"

"My ex-husband's business associates."

"What, you've got a bunch of vicious real estate agents on your tail?" Chase's lip quirked up on one side in the first indication Lacey had seen that he might have a sense of humor.

"No. I've got Wade Simpson on my tail."

That got his attention.

"Wade Simpson? The guy who…"

"The guy who cornered me at that party and practically raped me. The guy you rescued me from."

"That was a long time ago."

"It was." She nodded.

"I was a different person then."

She scanned him from his broad shoulders down to the big square belt buckle that guarded his fly. "Yeah. You sure were."

Had she just licked her lips? She couldn't believe she'd licked her lips. She was normally more dignified than that. More subtle.

But the blatant come-on didn't seem to have any effect. He was still eyeing her with undisguised disdain. "So you've been living on dirty money all this time?"

She set her fists on her hips and glared at him. In response, he gave her another once-over, and this time it was downright insulting. When had that sweet boy who'd followed her around like a lost puppy all through school become this bitter, caustic man?

"I've been trying to find a job. Nobody would hire me. Besides, I didn't know."

"You should have."

He was right. Lacey sucked in a deep breath and blew it out, wishing her guilt would go with it. She wasn't responsible for what her husband had done. She hadn't had any idea how he managed to buy so much land cheap from the government. But it was hard to admit that she hadn't known she was living on ill-gotten gains for the past eight years. She might not be evil like Trent, but she'd been stupid. Stupid and naïve.

"It was complicated. Trent was bribing people. Getting them to condemn land, so he could buy it cheap. There's a law in Texas—it's called Eminent Domain— where the state can take people's land if they want to build a highway or something."

"I know."

She resisted the urge to scowl back at Chase. He wasn't just mean and sarcastic; he was a know-it-all, too. "But then the highway project would get canceled, and Trent would buy the land cheap from the state, and…"

Chase's brown Golden Retriever eyes looked more like a Rottweiler's now. A mean Rottweiler. She half-expected a growl to rise from his throat.

This was not going well.

"He was a crook," she admitted.

"I know," Chase said again. "So that makes you Mrs. Crook, right?"

"Not anymore." She splayed her hands. "Look, I made a mistake. I never loved him. He wasn't—wasn't what I thought he was."

"I could have told you that."

"Well, you should have."

"How could I? You kept the whole thing a secret."

He was right. Her relationship with Trent had been hushed up practically until the day they married. She'd been seventeen when they met, and the twelve-year age difference between them had been more than a challenge; it had been a legal obstacle. Trent could have gone to jail for their relationship. The day they could go public as a couple was only a week before her wedding.

Her eighteenth birthday.

"Look, I married way too young. I married the wrong guy. He turned out to be a crook. But lots of girls make bad decisions. It's not like I did drugs or anything."

She bit her lip. Chase had probably never made a bad decision in his life. He'd pursued his chosen future so single-mindedly that he probably didn't have a clue what it was like to be young and foolish.

"No, but you drank."

"Just that one night."

He would have to bring that up. It had been a week before her wedding, and she'd realized at some point during a graduation celebration that this might be her last carefree high school party. She'd had a few too many drinks—way too many, really—and ended up alone and unprotected in an empty bedroom with a drunk and determined Wade Simpson. Chase, straight-arrow Chase, had hauled Simpson off her and taken her home. It was a good thing, too. She'd been so loopy on sloe gin fizzes she couldn't even remember the drive, or how she'd gotten in the house.

She'd relied on him then, and she'd thought she could rely on him now. She just had to make him understand the danger she was in.

"Once Trent testifies, a lot of important people will go to jail," she said.

"Good."

"So they're desperate. And dangerous. Wade came to my house. He—he threatened me."

"What did he say?"

"It's not what he said. It's how he said it."

One Fine
COWBOY

By Joanne Kennedy

The last thing she expects is a lesson in romance…

Graduate student Charlie Banks came to a Wyoming ranch for a seminar on horse communication, but when she meets ruggedly handsome "Horse Whisperer" Nate Shawcross, she starts to fantasize about another connection entirely…

Nate needs to stay focused if he's going to save his ranch from foreclosure, but he can't help being distracted by sexy and brainy Charlie. Could it be that after all this time Nate has finally found the one woman who can tame his wild heart?

Praise for *Cowboy Trouble*:

"A fresh take on the traditional contemporary Western… There's plenty of wacky humor and audacious wit in this mystery-laced escapade." —*Library Journal*

"Contemporary Western fans will enjoy this one!" —*Romantic Times*

"A fun and delicious romantic romp… If you love cowboys, you won't want to miss this one! Romance, mystery, and spurs! Yum!" —*Wendy's Minding Spot*

978-1-4022-3670-9 • $6.99 U.S./$8.99 CAN/£4.99 UK

COWBOY Trouble

BY JOANNE KENNEDY

All she wanted was a simple country life,
and then he walked in…

Fleeing her latest love life disaster, big city journalist Libby Brown's transition to rural living isn't going exactly as planned. Her childhood dream has always been to own a farm—but without the constant help of her charming, sexy neighbor, she'd never make it through her first Wyoming season. But handsome rancher Luke Rawlins yearns to do more than help Libby around her ranch. He's ready for love, and he wants to go the distance…

Then the two get embroiled in their tiny town's one and only crime story, and Libby discovers that their sizzling hot attraction is going to complicate her life in every way possible…

"I'm expecting great things from Joanne Kennedy! Bring on the hunky cowboys." —Linda Lael Miller, *New York Times* bestselling author of *The Bridegroom*

"Everything about Kennedy's charming debut novel hits the right marks…you'll be hooked." —*BookLoons*

978-1-4022-3668-6 • $7.99 US / $9.99 CAN / £4.99 UK

Lucky IN LOVE

BY CAROLYN BROWN

BEAU HASN'T GOT A LICK OF SENSE WHEN IT COMES TO WOMEN

Everything hunky rancher "Lucky" Beau Luckadeau touches turns to gold—except relationships. Spitfire Milli Torres can mend a fence, pull a calf, or shoot a rattlesnake between the eyes. When Milli shows up to help out at the Lazy Z ranch, she's horrified to find that Beau's her nearest neighbor—the very man she'd hoped never to lay eyes on again. If Beau ever figures out what really happened on that steamy Louisiana night when they first met, there'll be the devil to pay…

Praise for Carolyn Brown:

"Engaging characters, humorous situations, and a bumpy romance…Carolyn Brown will keep you reading until the very last page." —Romantic Times

"Carolyn Brown's rollicking sense of humor asserts itself on every page." —Scribes World

978-1-4022-2435-5 • $7.99 U.S. / $9.99 CAN

ONE *Lucky* COWBOY

By Carolyn Brown

No big blond cowboy is going to intimidate this spitfire!

If Slade Luckadeau thinks he can run Jane Day off his ranch, he's got cow chips for brains. She's winning every argument, and he's running out of fights to pick. But when trouble with a capital "T" threatens Jane *and* the Double L Ranch, suddenly it's Slade's heart that's in the most danger of all.

Praise for *Lucky in Love*:

"I enjoyed this book so much that I plan to rope myself some more of Carolyn Brown and her books. Lucky in Love *is a must read!"* —Cheryl's Book Nook

"This is one of those rare books where every person in it comes alive... as they share wit, wisdom, and love."
—The Romance Studio

978-1-4022-2437-9• $7.99 U.S. / $9.99 CAN

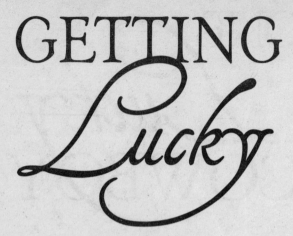

GETTING *Lucky*

BY CAROLYN BROWN

Griffin Luckadeau is one stubborn cowboy...

And Julie Donovan is one hotheaded schoolteacher who doesn't let anybody push her around. When Griffin thinks his new neighbor is scheming to steal his ranch out from under him, he's more than willing to cross horns. Their look-alike daughters may be best friends, but until these two Texas hotheads admit it's fate that brought them together, running from the inevitable is only going to bring them a double dose of miserable...

Praise for Carolyn Brown:

"A delight to read." —Booklist

"Engaging characters, humorous situations, and a bumpy romance... Carolyn Brown will keep you reading until the very last page." —Romantic Times

"Carolyn Brown's rollicking sense of humor asserts itself on every page." —Scribes World

978-1-4022-2436-2• $7.99 U.S. / $9.99 CAN / 4.99 UK